Pisistratus Caxton

My Novel; or, Varieties in English Life by Pisistratus Caxton

Vol. II

Pisistratus Caxton

My Novel; or, Varieties in English Life by Pisistratus Caxton
Vol. II

ISBN/EAN: 9783337001926

Printed in Europe, USA, Canada, Australia, Japan

Cover: Foto ©Andreas Hilbeck / pixelio.de

More available books at **www.hansebooks.com**

"My Novel"

OR

VARIETIES IN ENGLISH LIFE

BY
PISISTRATUS CAXTON

[17.]

" Neque enim notare singulos mens est mihi,
Verum ipsam vitam et mores hominum ostendere."
PHÆRUS

VOL. II

LONDON
GEORGE ROUTLEDGE AND SONS
BROADWAY, LUDGATE HILL
GLASGOW AND NEW YORK
—
1888

THE POCKET VOLUME EDITION

OF

LORD LYTTON'S NOVELS

ISSUED IN MONTHLY VOLUMES

Styles of Binding.

A Paper Cover, Cut Edges.
B   ,,   ,,   Uncut Edges.
C Cloth Cover, Cut Edges.
D   ,,   ,,   Uncut Edges.
E Half-bound Gilt Tops. Cut Edges.
F   ,,   ,,   ,,   Uncut Edges.

MY NOVEL.

BOOK SIXTH.

(CONTINUED.)

CHAPTER VI.

LEONARD opened his door and stole towards that of the room adjoining; for his first natural impulse had been to enter and console. But when his touch was on the handle, he drew back. Child though the mourner was, her sorrows were rendered yet more sacred from intrusion by her sex. Something, he knew not what, in his young ignorance, withheld him from the threshold. To have crossed it then would have seemed to him profanation. So he returned, and for hours yet he occasionally heard the sobs, till they died away, and childhood wept itself to sleep.

But the next morning, when he heard his neighbour astir, he knocked gently at her door: there was no answer. He entered softly, and saw her seated very listlessly in the centre of the room—as if it had no familiar nook or corner as the rooms of home have—her hands drooping on her lap, and her eyes gazing desolately on the floor. Then he approached and spoke to her.

Helen was very subdued, and very silent. Her tears seemed dried up; and it was long before she gave sign or token that she heeded him. At length, however, he gradually succeeded in rousing her interest; and the first symptom of his success was in the quiver of her lip, and the overflow of her downcast eyes.

By little and little he wormed himself into her confidence; and she told him, in broken whispers, her simple story. But what moved him the most was, that, beyond her sense of loneliness, she did not seem to feel her own unprotected state. She mourned the object she had nursed, and heeded, and cherished; for she had been rather the protectress than the protected to the helpless dead. He could not gain from her any more satisfactory information than the landlady had already imparted, as to her friends and prospects ; but she permitted him passively to look among the effects her father had left—save only that, if his hand touched something that seemed to her associations especially holy, she waved him back, or drew it quickly away. There were many bills receipted in the name of Captain Digby—old yellow faded music-scores for the flute—extracts of Parts from Prompt Books—gay parts of lively comedies, in which heroes have so noble a contempt for money—fit heroes for a Sheridan and a Farquhar ;—close by these were several pawnbroker's tickets ; and, not arrayed smoothly, but crumpled up, as if with an indignant nervous clutch of the helpless hands, some two or three letters. He asked Helen's permission to glance at these, for they might afford a clue to friends. Helen gave the permission by a silent bend of the head. The letters, however, were but short and freezing answers from what appeared to be distant connections or former friends, or persons to whom the deceased had applied for some situation. They were all very disheartening in their tone. Leonard next endeavoured to refresh Helen's memory as to the name of the nobleman which had been last on her father's lips : but there he failed wholly. For it may be remembered that Lord L'Estrange, when he pressed his loan on Mr. Digby, and subsequently told that gentleman to address to him at Mr. Egerton's, had, from a natural delicacy, sent the child on, that she might not witness the charity bestowed on the father ; and Helen said truly, that Mr. Digby had sunk latterly into an habitual silence on all his affairs. She might have heard her father mention the name, but she had not treasured it up ; all she could say was, that she should know the stranger again if she met him, and his dog too. Seeing that the child had grown calm, Leonard was then going to leave the room, in order to confer with the hostess ; when she rose suddenly, though noiselessly, and put her little hand in his, as if to detain him. She did not say a word—the action said all—said, " Do not desert me." And Leonard's heart rushed to his lips, and he answered to the action, as he bent down and kissed her cheek, " Orphan, will you go with me ? We have one Father yet to both of us, and He will guide us on earth. I am fatherless, like you." She raised her eyes to his—looked at him long—and then leant her head confidingly on his strong young shoulder.

CHAPTER VII.

AT noon that same day, the young man and the child were on their road to London. The host had at first a little demurred at trusting Helen to so young a companion; but Leonard, in his happy ignorance, had talked so sanguinely of finding out this lord, or some adequate protectors for the child; and in so grand a strain, though with all sincerity—had spoken of his own great prospects in the metropolis (he did not say what they were!)—that had he been the craftiest impostor he could not more have taken in the rustic host. And while the landlady still cherished the illusive fancy, that all gentlefolks must know each other in London, as they did in a county, the landlord believed, at least, that a young man so respectably dressed, although but a foot-traveller—who talked in so confident a tone, and who was so willing to undertake what might be rather a burthensome charge, unless he saw how to rid himself of it—would be sure to have friends, older and wiser than himself, who would judge what could best be done for the orphan.

And what was the host to do with her? Better this volunteered escort, at least, than vaguely passing her on from parish to parish, and leaving her friendless at last in the streets of London. Helen, too, smiled for the first time on being asked her wishes, and again put her hand in Leonard's. In short, so it was settled.

The little girl made up a bundle of the things she most prized or needed. Leonard did not feel the additional load, as he slung it to his knapsack; the rest of the luggage was to be sent to London as soon as Leonard wrote, (which he promised to do soon,) and gave an address.

Helen paid her last visit to the churchyard; and she joined her companion as he stood on the road, without the solemn precincts. And now they had gone on some hours; and when he asked if she were tired, she still answered "No." But Leonard was merciful, and made their day's journey short; and it took them some days to reach London. By the long lonely way they grew so intimate, at the end of the second day, they called each other brother and sister; and Leonard, to his delight, found that as her grief, with the bodily movement and the change of scene, subsided from its first intenseness and its insensibility to other impressions, she developed a quickness of comprehension far beyond her years. Poor child! *that* had been forced upon her by Necessity. And she understood him in his

spiritual consolations—half poetical, half religious ; and she listened
to his own tale, and the story of his self-education and solitary
struggles—those, too, she understood.   But when he burst out with
his enthusiasm, his glorious hopes, his confidence in the fate before
them, then she would shake her head very quietly and very sadly.
Did she comprehend *them?*   Alas ! perhaps too well.   She knew
more as to real life than he did.   Leonard was at first their joint
treasurer ; but before the second day was over, Helen seemed to
discover that he was too lavish ! and she told him so, with a prudent
grave look, putting her hand on his arm as he was about to enter an
inn to dine ; and the gravity would have been comic, but that the
eyes through their moisture were so meek and grateful.   She felt he
was about to incur that ruinous extravagance on her account.   Somehow or other, the purse found its way into her keeping, and then
she looked proud and in her natural element.

Ah ! what happy meals under her care were provided ; so much
more enjoyable than in dull, sanded inn parlours, swarming with
flies, and reeking with stale tobacco.   She would leave him at the
entrance of a village, bound forward, and cater, and return with a
little basket and a pretty blue jug—which she had bought on the
road—the last filled with new milk ; the first with new bread, and
some special dainty in radishes or water-cresses.   And she had
such a talent for finding out the prettiest spot whereon to halt and
dine : sometimes in the heart of a wood—so still, it was like a forest
in fairy tales, the hare stealing through the alleys, or the squirrel
peeping at them from the boughs ; sometimes by a little brawling
stream, with the fishes seen under the clear wave, and shooting
round the crumbs thrown to them.   They made an Arcadia of the
dull road up to their dread Thermopylæ—the war against the million
that waited them on the other side of their pass through Tempé.

"Shall we be as happy when we are *great?*" said Leonard, in
his grand simplicity.

Helen sighed, and the wise little head was shaken.

CHAPTER VIII.

AT last they came within easy reach of London ; but Leonard
had resolved not to enter the metropolis fatigued and
exhausted, as a wanderer needing refuge, but fresh and
elate, as a conqueror coming in triumph to take possession
of the capital.   Therefore they halted early in the evening of the

day preceding this imperial entry, about six miles from the metropolis, in the neighbourhood of Ealing, (for by that route lay their way). They were not tired on arriving at their inn. The weather was singularly lovely, with that combination of softness and brilliancy which is only known to the rare true summer days of England ; all below so green, above so blue—days of which we have about six in the year, and recall vaguely when we read of Robin Hood and Maid Marian, of Damsel and Knight in Spenser's golden Summer Song—or of Jacques, dropped under the oak tree, watching the deer amidst the dells of Ardennes. So, after a little pause at their inn, they strolled forth, not for travel but pleasure, towards the cool of sunset, passing by the grounds that once belonged to the Duke of Kent, and catching a glimpse of the shrubs and lawns of that beautiful domain through the lodge-gates ; then they crossed into some fields, and came to a little rivulet called the Brent. Helen had been more sad that day than on any during their journey. Perhaps because, on approaching London, the memory of her father became more vivid ; perhaps from her precocious knowledge of life, and her foreboding of what was to befall them, children that they both were. But Leonard was selfish that day ; he could not be influenced by his companion's sorrow ; he was so full of his own sense of being, and he already caught from the atmosphere the fever that belongs to anxious capitals.

"Sit here, sister," said he imperiously, throwing himself under the shade of a pollard tree that overhung the winding brook, "sit here and talk."

He flung off his hat, tossed back his rich curls, and sprinkled his brow from the stream that eddied round the roots of the tree that bulged out, bald and gnarled from the bank, and delved into the waves below. Helen quietly obeyed him, and nestled close to his side.

"And so this London is really very vast ?—VERY ?" he repeated inquisitively.

"Very," answered Helen, as, abstractedly, she plucked the cow-slips near her, and let them fall into the running waters. "See how the flowers are carried down the stream ! They are lost now. London is to us what the river is to the flowers—very vast—very strong ;" and she added, after a pause, "very cruel !"

"Cruel ! Ah, it *has* been so to you ; but *now !*—now I will take care of you !" he smiled triumphantly ; and his smile was beautiful both in its pride and its kindness. It is astonishing how Leonard had altered since he had left his uncle's. He was both younger and older ; for the sense of genius, when it snaps its shackles, makes us

A 2

both older and wiser as to the world it soars to—younger and blinder as to the world it springs from.

"And it is not a very handsome city either, you say?"

"Very ugly, indeed," said Helen, with some fervour; "at least all I have seen of it."

"But there must be parts that are prettier than others? You say there are parks: why should not we lodge near them, and look upon the green trees?"

"That would be nice," said Helen, almost joyously: "but—" and here the head was shaken—"there are no lodgings for us except in courts and alleys."

"Why?"

"Why?" echoed Helen, with a smile, and she held up the purse.

"Pooh! always that horrid purse; as if, too, we were not going to fill it. Did not I tell you the story of Fortunio? Well, at all events, we will go first to the neighbourhood where you last lived, and learn there all we can; and then the day after to-morrow, I will see this Dr. Morgan, and find out the Lord."

The tears started to Helen's soft eyes. "You want to get rid of me soon, brother."

"I! Ah, I feel so happy to have you with me, it seems to me as if I had pined for you all my life, and you had come at last; for I never had brother, nor sister, nor any one to love, that was not older than myself, except—"

"Except the young lady you told me of," said Helen, turning away her face; for children are very jealous.

"Yes, I loved her, love her still. But that was different," said Leonard. "I could never have talked to her as to you: to you I open my whole heart; you are my little Muse, Helen: I confess to you my wild whims and fancies as frankly as if I were writing poetry." As he said this, a step was heard, and a shadow fell over the stream. A belated angler appeared on the margin, drawing his line impatiently across the water, as if to worry some dozing fish into a bite before it finally settled itself for the night. Absorbed in his occupation, the angler did not observe the young persons on the sward under the tree, and he halted there, close upon them.

"Curse that perch!" said he aloud.

"Take care, sir," cried Leonard; for the man, in stepping back, nearly trod upon Helen.

The angler turned. "What's the matter? Hist! you have frightened my perch. Keep still, can't you?"

Helen drew herself out of the way, and Leonard remained

motionless. He remembered Jackeymo, and felt a sympathy for the angler.

"It is the most extraordinary perch, that!" muttered the stranger, soliloquizing. "It has the devil's own luck. It must have been born with a silver spoon in its mouth, that damned perch! I shall never catch it—never! Ha!—no—only a weed. I give it up." With this, he indignantly jerked his rod from the water and began to disjoint it. While leisurely engaged in this occupation, he turned to Leonard.

"Humph! are you intimately acquainted with this stream, sir?"

"No," answered Leonard. "I never saw it before."

ANGLER (solemnly).—"Then, young man, take my advice, and do not give way to its fascinations. Sir, I am a martyr to this stream; it has been the Delilah of my existence."

LEONARD (interested, the last sentence seemed to him poetical).— "The Delilah! Sir, the Delilah!"

ANGLER.—"The Delilah. Young man, listen, and be warned by example. When I was about your age, I first came to this stream to fish. Sir, on that fatal day, about 3 P.M., I hooked up a fish—such a big one, it must have weighed a pound and a half. Sir, it was that length;" and the angler put finger to wrist. "And just when I had got it nearly ashore, by the very place where you are sitting, on that shelving bank, young man, the line broke, and the perch twisted himself among those roots, and—cacodæmon that he was—ran off, hook and all. Well, that fish haunted me; never before had I seen such a fish. Minnows I had caught in the Thames and elsewhere, also gudgeons, and occasionally a dace. But a fish like that—a PERCH—all his fins up, like the sails of a man-of-war —a monster perch—a whale of a perch!—No, never till then had I known what leviathans lie hid within the deeps. I could not sleep till I had returned; and again, sir,—I caught that perch. And this time I pulled him fairly out of the water. He escaped; and how did he escape? Sir, he left his eye behind him on the hook. Years, long years, have passed since then; but never shall I forget the agony of that moment."

LEONARD.—"To the perch, sir?"

ANGLER.—"Perch! agony to him! He enjoyed it:—agony to me. I gazed on that eye, and the eye looked as sly and as wicked as if it was laughing in my face. Well, sir, I had heard that there is no better bait for a perch than a perch's eye. I adjusted that eye on the hook, and dropped in the line gently. The water was un-usually clear; in two minutes I saw that perch return. He ap-proached the hook; he recognized his eye—frisked his tail—made a plunge—and, as I live, carried off the eye, safe and sound ; and I saw him digesting it by the side of that water-lily.   The mocking fiend ! Seven times since that day, in the course of a varied and eventful life, have I caught that perch, and seven times has that perch escaped."

LEONARD (astonished).—"It can't be the same perch ; perches are very tender fish—a hook inside of it, and an eye hooked out of it—no perch could withstand such havoc in its constitution."

ANGLER (with an appearance of awe).—"It does seem supernatural.   But it *is* that perch ; for harkye, sir, there is ONLY ONE perch in the whole brook !   All the years I have fished here, I have never caught another perch ; and this solitary inmate of the watery element I know by sight better than I knew my own lost father. For each time that I have raised it out of the water, its profile has been turned to me, and I have seen with a shudder, that it has had only—One Eye !   It is a most mysterious and a most diabolical phenomenon, that perch !   It has been the ruin of my prospects in life.   I was offered a situation in Jamaica : I could not go with that perch left here in triumph.   I might afterwards have had an appointment in India, but I could not put the ocean between myself and that perch : thus have I frittered away my existence in the fatal metropolis of my native land.   And once a week from February to December, I come hither—Good Heavens ! if I should catch the perch at last, the occupation of my existence will be gone."

Leonard gazed curiously at the angler, as the last thus mournfully concluded.   The ornate turn of his periods did not suit with his costume.   He looked woefully threadbare and shabby—a genteel sort of shabbiness too—shabbiness in black.   There was humour in the corners of his lip ; and his hands, though they did not seem very clean—indeed his occupation was not friendly to such niceties— were those of a man who had not known manual labour.   His face was pale and puffed, but the tip of the nose was red.   He did not seem as if the watery element was as familiar to himself as to his Delilah—the perch.

"Such is Life !" recommenced the angler, in a moralizing tone, as he slid his rod into its canvas case.   "If a man knew what it was to fish all one's life in a stream that has only one perch :—to catch that one perch nine times in all, and nine times to see it fall back into the water, plump ;—if a man knew what it was—why, then "—Here the angler looked over his shoulder full at Leonard— "why, then, young sir, he would know what human life is to vain ambition.   Good evening."

Away he went treading over the daisies and king cups.   Helen's eyes followed him wistfully.

"What a strange person!" said Leonard, laughing.

"I think he is a very wise one," murmured Helen; and she came close up to Leonard, and took his hand in both hers, as if she felt already that he was in need of the Comforter—the line broken, and the perch lost!

CHAPTER IX.

AT noon the next day, London stole upon them through a gloomy, thick, oppressive atmosphere; for where is it that we can say London *bursts* on the sight? It stole on them through one of the fairest and most gracious avenues of approach—by the stately gardens of Kensington—along the side of Hyde Park, and so on towards Cumberland Gate.

Leonard was not the least struck. And yet, with a very little money, and a very little taste, it would be easy to render this entrance to London as grand and as imposing as that to Paris from the *Champs Elysées*. As they came near the Edgeware Road, Helen took her new brother by the hand and guided him. For she knew all that neighbourhood, and she was acquainted with a lodging near that occupied by her father, (to *that* lodging itself she could not have gone for the world,) where they might be housed cheaply.

But just then the sky, so dull and overcast since morning, seemed one mass of black cloud. There suddenly came on a violent storm of rain. The boy and girl took refuge in a covered mews, in a street running out of the Edgeware Road. This shelter soon became crowded; the two young pilgrims crept close to the wall, apart from the rest—Leonard's arm round Helen's waist, sheltering her from the rain that the strong wind contending with it beat in through the passage. Presently a young gentleman of better mien and dress than the other refugees, entered, not hastily, but rather with a slow and proud step, as if, though he deigned to take shelter, he scorned to run to it. He glanced somewhat haughtily at the assembled group—passed on through the midst of it—came near Leonard— took off his hat, and shook the rain from its brim. His head thus uncovered, left all his features exposed; and the village youth recognized, at the first glance, his old victorious assailant on the green at Hazeldean.

Yet Randal Leslie was altered. His dark cheek was as thin as in boyhood, and even yet more wasted by intense study and night vigils; but the expression of his face was at once more refined and manly, and there was a steady concentrated light in his eye, like

that of one who has been in the habit of bringing all his thoughts
to one point. He looked older than he was. He was dressed
simply in black, a colour which became him; and altogether his
aspect and figure were not showy indeed, but distinguished. He
looked to the common eye, a gentleman; and to the more observant,
a scholar.

Helter-skelter!—pell-mell! the group in the passage—now
pressed each on each—now scattered on all sides—making way—
rushing down the mews—against the walls—as a fiery horse darted
under shelter. The rider, a young man, with a very handsome
face, and dressed with that peculiar care which we commonly call
dandyism, cried out, good-humouredly, "Don't be afraid; the
horse shan't hurt any of you—a thousand pardons—so ho! so ho!"
He patted the horse, and it stood as still as a statue filling up the
centre of the passage. The groups resettled—Randal approached
the rider.

"Frank Hazeldean!"

"Ah—is it indeed Randal Leslie!"

Frank was off his horse in a moment, and the bridle was consigned
to the care of a slim 'prentice-boy holding a bundle.

"My dear fellow, how glad I am to see you. How lucky it was
that I should turn in here. Not like me either, for I don't much
care for a ducking. Staying in town, Randal?"

"Yes; at your uncle's, Mr. Egerton. I have left Oxford."

"For good?"   ‑

"For good."

"But you have not taken your degree, I think? We Etonians
all considered you booked for a double first. Oh! we have been
so proud of your fame—you carried off all the prizes."

"Not all; but some, certainly. Mr. Egerton offered me my
choice—to stay for my degree, or to enter at once into the Foreign
Office. I preferred the end to the means. For, after all, what
good are academical honours but as the entrance to life? To enter
now, is to save a step in a long way, Frank."

"Ah! you were always ambitious, and you will make a great
figure, I am sure."

"Perhaps so—if I work for it. Knowledge is power."

Leonard started.

"And you!" resumed Randal, looking with some curious attention at his old school-fellow. "You never came to Oxford. I did
hear you were going into the army."

"I am in the Guards," said Frank, trying hard not to look too
conceited as he made that acknowledgment. "The Governor

pished a little, and would rather I had come to live with him in the old Hall, and take to farming.   Time enough for that—eh?   By Jove, Randal, how pleasant a thing is life in London!   Do you go to Almack's to-night?"

"No; Wednesday is a holiday in the House!   There is a great Parliamentary dinner at Mr. Egerton's.   He is in the Cabinet now, you know; but you don't see much of your uncle, I think."

"Our sets are different," said the young gentleman, in a tone of voice worthy of Brummell.   "All those Parliamentary fellows are devilish dull.   The rain's over.   I don't know whether the Governor would like me to call at Grosvenor Square; but pray come and see me.   Here's my card to remind you; you must dine at our mess.   Such capital fellows!   What day will you fix?"

"I will call and let you know.   Don't you find it rather expensive in the Guards?   I remember that you thought the Governor, as you call him, used to chafe a little when you wrote for more pocket-money; and the only time I ever saw you with tears in your eyes, was when Mr. Hazeldean, in sending you five pounds, re-minded you that his estates were not entailed—were at his own disposal, and they should never go to an extravagant spendthrift. It was not a pleasant threat that, Frank."

"Oh!" cried the young man, colouring deeply.   "It was not the threat that pained me; it was that my father could think so meanly of me as to fancy that—Well—well, but those were school-boy days.   And my father was always more generous than I deserved. We must see a great deal of each other, Randal.   How good-natured you were at Eton, making my longs and shorts for me; I shall never forget it.   Do call soon."

Frank swung himself into his saddle, and rewarded the slim youth with half-a-crown—a largess four times more ample than his father would have deemed sufficient.   A jerk of the reins and a touch of the heel—off bounded the fiery horse and the gay young rider. Randal mused; and as the rain had now ceased, the passengers under shelter dispersed and went their way.   Only Randal, Leonard, and Helen remained behind.   Then, as Randal, still musing, lifted his eyes, they fell full upon Leonard's face.   He started, passed his hand quickly over his brow—looked again, hard and piercingly; and the change in his pale cheek to a shade still paler—a quick compression and nervous gnawing of his lip—showed that he too recognized an old foe.   Then his glance ran over Leonard's dress, which was somewhat dust-stained, but far above the class amongst which the peasant was born.   Randal raised his brows in surprise, and with a smile slightly supercilious—the smile stung Leonard;

and with a slow step Randal left the passage, and took his way towards Grosvenor Square. The Entrance of Ambition was clear to *him*.

Then the little girl once more took Leonard by the hand, and led him through rows of humble, obscure, dreary streets. It seemed almost like an allegory personified, as the sad, silent child led on the penniless and low-born adventurer of genius by the squalid shops, and through the winding lanes, which grew meaner and meaner till both their forms vanished from the view.

CHAPTER X.

"BUT do come ; change your dress, return and dine with me ; you will have just time, Harley. You will meet the most eminent men of our party ; surely they are worth your study, philosopher that you affect to be."

Thus said Audley Egerton to Lord L'Estrange, with whom he had been riding (after the toils of his office). The two gentlemen were in Audley's library. Mr. Egerton, as usual, buttoned up, seated in his chair, in the erect posture of a man who scorns "inglorious ease." Harley, as usual, thrown at length on the sofa, his long hair in careless curls, his neckcloth loose, his habiliments flowing *simplex munditiis*, indeed—his grace all his own ; seemingly negligent, never slovenly ; at ease everywhere and with every one, even with Mr. Audley Egerton, who chilled or awed the ease out of most people.

"Nay, my dear Audley, forgive me. But your eminent men are all men of one idea, and that not a diverting one—politics ! politics ! politics ! The storm in the saucer."

"But what is your life, Harley ?—the saucer without the storm ?"

"Do you know, that's very well said, Audley ? I did not think you had so much liveliness of repartee. Life—life ! it is insipid, it is shallow. No launching Argosies in the saucer, Audley. I have the oddest fancy—"

"*That* of course," said Audley, dryly ; "you never have any other. What is the new one ?"

Harley (with great gravity).—"Do you believe in Mesmerism ?"

Audley.—"Certainly not."

Harley.—"If it were in the power of an animal magnetiser to get me out of my own skin into somebody else's ! *That's* my fancy ! I am so tired of myself—so tired ! I have run through all my ideas—know every one of them by heart. When some pretentious impostor of an idea perks itself up and says, ' Look at me—I'm a new acquaintance,' I just give it a nod, and say, ' Not at all—you have only got a new coat on ; you are the same old wretch that has bored me these last twenty years ; get away.' But if one could be in a new skin ! if I could be for half-an-hour your tall porter, or one of your eminent matter-of-fact men, I should then really travel into a new world.[1] Every man's brain must be a world in itself, eh? If I could but make a parochial settlement even in yours, Audley—run over all your thoughts and sensations. Upon my life, I'll go and talk to that French mesmeriser about it."

AUDLEY (who does not seem to like the notion of having his thoughts and sensations rummaged, even by his friend, and even in fancy).—" Pooh, pooh, pooh ! Do talk like a man of sense."

HARLEY.—" Man of sense ! Where shall I find a model? I don't know a man of sense !—never met such a creature. Don't believe it ever existed. At one time I thought Socrates must have been a man of sense ; a delusion ; he would stand gazing into the air, and talking to his Genius from sunrise to sunset. Is that like a man of sense ? Poor Audley ; how puzzled he looks ! Well, I'll try and talk sense to oblige you. And first (here Harley raised himself on his elbow)—first, is it true, as I have heard vaguely, that you are paying court to the sister of that infamous Italian traitor ? "

" Madame di Negra ? No : I am not paying *court* to her," answered Audley, with a cold smile. " But she is very handsome ; she is very clever ; she is useful to me—I need not say how or why ; that belongs to my *metier* as a politician. But I think, if you will take my advice, or get your friend to take it, I could obtain from her brother, through my influence with her, some liberal concessions to your exile. She is very anxious to know where he is."

" You have not told her ? "

" No ; I promised you I would keep that secret,"

" Be sure you do ; it is only for some mischief, some snare, that she could desire such information. Concessions ! pooh ! This is no question of concessions, but of rights."

" I think you should leave your friend to judge of that."

" Well, I will write to him. Meanwhile, beware of this woman.

---

[1] If, at the date in which Lord L'Estrange held this conversation with Mr. Egerton, Alfred de Musset had written his comedies, we should suspect that his lordship had plagiarized from one of them the whimsical idea that he here vents upon Audley. In repeating it, the author at least cannot escape from the charge of obligation to a writer whose humour is sufficiently opulent to justify the loan.

I have heard much of her abroad, and she has the character of her brother for duplicity and—"

"Beauty," interrupted Audley, turning the conversation with practised adroitness. "I am told that the Count is one of the handsomest men in Europe, much handsomer than his sister, still, though nearly twice her age. Tut—tut—Harley; fear not for me. I am proof against all feminine attractions. This heart is dead."

"Nay, nay; it is not for you to speak thus—leave that to me. But even *I* will not say it. The heart never dies. And you; what have you lost?—a wife; true: an excellent noble-hearted woman. But was it love that you felt for her? Enviable man, have you ever loved?"

"Perhaps not, Harley," said Audley, with a sombre aspect, and indejected accents; "very few men ever have loved, at least as you mean by the word. But there are other passions than love that kill the heart, and reduce us to mechanism."

While Egerton spoke, Harley turned aside, and his breast heaved. There was a short silence; Audley was the first to break it.

"Speaking of my lost wife, I am sorry that you do not approve what I have done for her young kinsman, Randal Leslie."

HARLEY (recovering himself with an effort).—"Is it true kindness to bid him exchange manly independence for the protection of an official patron?"

AUDLEY.—"I did not bid him. I gave him his choice. At his age, I should have chosen as he has done."

HARLEY.—"I trust not; I think better of you. But answer me one question frankly, and then I will ask another. Do you mean to make this young man your heir?"

AUDLEY (with a slight embarrassment).—"Heir, pooh! I am young still. I may live as long as he—time enough to think of that."

HARLEY.—"Then now to my second question. Have you told this youth plainly that he may look to you for influence, but not for wealth?"

AUDLEY (firmly).—"I think I have; but I shall repeat it more emphatically."

HARLEY.—"Then I am satisfied as to your conduct, but not as to his. For he has too acute an intellect not to know what it is to forfeit independence; and, depend on it, he has made his calculations, and would throw you into the bargain in any balance that he could strike in his favour. You go by your experience in judging men; I by my instincts. Nature warns us as it does the inferior animals—only we are too conceited, we bipeds, to heed her. My instincts of soldier and gentleman recoil from that old young man. He has the soul of the Jesuit. I see it in his eye—I hear it in the tread of his foot; *volto sciolto* he has not; *i pensieri stretti* he has. Hist! I hear now his step in the hall. I should know it from a thousand. That's his very touch on the handle of the door."

Randal Leslie entered. Harley—who, despite his disregard for forms, and his dislike to Randal, was too high-bred not to be polite to his junior in age or inferior in rank—rose and bowed. But his bright piercing eyes did not soften as they caught and bore down the deeper and more latent fire in Randal's. Harley did not resume his seat, but moved to the mantelpiece, and leant against it.

RANDAL.—"I have fulfilled your commissions, Mr. Egerton. I went first to Maida Hill, and saw Mr. Burley. I gave him the cheque, but he said, 'it was too much, and he should return half to the banker;' he will write the article as you suggested. I then—"

AUDLEY.—"Enough, Randal! we will not fatigue Lord L'Estrange with these little details of a life that displeases him—the life political."

HARLEY.—"But *these* details do not displease me; they reconcile me to my own life. Go on, pray, Mr. Leslie."

Randal had too much tact to need the cautioning glance of Mr. Egerton. He did not continue, but said, with a soft voice, "Do you think, Lord L'Estrange, that the contemplation of the mode of life pursued by others *can* reconcile a man to his own, if he had before thought it needed a reconciler?" Harley looked pleased, for the question was ironical; and, if there was a thing in the world he abhorred, it was flattery.

"Recollect your Lucretius, Mr. Leslie, the *Sauve mare*, &c., 'pleasant from the cliff to see the mariners tossed on the ocean.' Faith, I think that sight reconciles one to the cliff—though, before, one might have been teased by the splash from the spray, and deafened by the scream of the sea-gulls. But I leave you, Audley. Strange that I have heard no more of my soldier. Remember I have your promise when I come to claim it. Good-bye, Mr. Leslie, I hope that Burley's article will be worth the—cheque."

Lord L'Estrange mounted his horse, which was still at the door, and rode through the Park. But he was no longer now unknown by sight. Bows and nods saluted him on every side.

"Alas, I am found out, then," said he to himself. "That terrible Duchess of Knaresborough, too—I must fly my country." He pushed his horse into a canter, and was soon out of the Park. As he dismounted at his father's sequestered house, you would have hardly supposed him the same whimsical, fantastic, but deep and subtle humorist that delighted in perplexing the material Audley. For his expressive face was unutterably serious. But the moment he came into the presence of his parents, the countenance was again lighted and cheerful. It brightened the whole room like sunshine.

CHAPTER XI.

"MR. LESLIE," said Egerton, when Harley had left the library, "you did not act with your usual discretion in touching upon matters connected with politics in the presence of a third party."

"I feel that already, sir; my excuse is, that I held Lord L'Estrange to be your most intimate friend."

"A public man, Mr. Leslie, would ill serve his country if he were not especially reserved towards his private friends—when they do not belong to his party."

"But, pardon me my ignorance. Lord Lansmere is so well known to be one of your supporters, that I fancied his son must share his sentiments, and be in your confidence."

Egerton's brows slightly contracted, and gave a stern expression to a countenance always firm and decided. He however answered in a mild tone.

"At the entrance into political life, Mr. Leslie, there is nothing in which a young man of your talents should be more on his guard than thinking for himself; he will nearly always think wrong. And I believe that is one reason why young men of talent disappoint their friends, and remain so long out of office."

A haughty flush passed over Randal's brow, and faded away quickly; he bowed in silence.

Egerton resumed, as if in explanation, and even in kindly apology—

"Look at Lord L'Estrange himself. What young man could come into life with brighter auspices? Rank, wealth, high animal spirits, (a great advantage those same spirits, Mr. Leslie,) courage, self-possession, scholarship as brilliant perhaps as your own; and now see how his life is wasted! Why? He always thought fit to think for himself. He could never be broken in to harness, and never will be. The State coach, Mr. Leslie, requires that all the horses should pull together."

"With submission, sir," answered Randal, "I should think that there were other reasons why Lord L'Estrange, whatever be his talents—and of these you must be indeed an adequate judge—would never do anything in public life."

"Ay, and what?" said Egerton, quickly.

"First," said Randal, shrewdly, "private life has done too much for him. What could public life give to one who needs nothing? Born at the top of the social ladder, why should he put himself voluntarily at the last step, for the sake of climbing up again? And secondly, Lord L'Estrange seems to me a man in whose organization *sentiment* usurps too large a share for practical existence."

"You have a keen eye," said Audley, with some admiration; "keen for one so young. Poor Harley!"

Mr. Egerton's last words were said to himself. He resumed, quickly—

"There is something on my mind, my young friend. Let us be frank with each other. I placed before you fairly the advantages and disadvantages of the choice I gave you. To take your degree with such honours as no doubt you would have won, to obtain your fellowship, to go to the bar, with those credentials in favour of your talents :—this was one career. To come at once into public life, to profit by my experience, avail yourself of my interest, to take the chances of rise or fall with a party: this was another. You chose the last. But, in so doing, there was a consideration which might weigh with you; and on which, in stating your reasons for your option, you were silent."

"What is that, sir?"

"You might have counted on my fortune, should the chances of party fail you :—speak—and without shame if so; it would be natural in a young man, who comes from the elder branch of the house whose heiress was my wife."

"You wound me, Mr. Egerton," said Randal, turning away.

Mr. Egerton's cold glance followed Randal's movement; the face was hid from the glance, and the statesman's eye rested on the figure, which is often as self-betraying as the countenance itself. Randal baffled Mr. Egerton's penetration—the young man's emotion might be honest pride, and pained and generous feeling; or it might be something else. Egerton continued, slowly—

"Once for all, then, distinctly and emphatically, I say—never count upon that; count upon all else that I can do for you, and forgive me, when I advise harshly or censure coldly; ascribe this to my interest in your career. Moreover, before decision becomes irrevocable, I wish you to know practically all that is disagreeable or even humiliating in the first subordinate steps of him who, without wealth or station, would rise in public life. I will not consider your choice settled, till the end of a year at least—your name will be kept on the college books till then ; if, on experience you should prefer to return to Oxford, and pursue the slower but surer path to independence and distinction, you can.   And now give me your hand, Mr. Leslie, in sign that you forgive my bluntness ;—it is time to dress."

Randal, with his face still averted, extended his hand.   Mr. Egerton held it a moment, then dropping it, left the room.   Randal turned as the door closed.   And there was in his dark face a power of sinister passion, that justified all Harley's warnings.   His lips moved, but not audibly ; then, as if struck by a sudden thought, he followed Egerton into the Hall.

"Sir," said he, "I forgot to say, that on returning from Maida Hill, I took shelter from the rain under a covered passage, and there I met, unexpectedly, with your nephew, Frank Hazeldean."

"Ah!" said Egerton, indifferently, "a fine young man ; in the Guards.   It is a pity that my brother has such antiquated political notions ; he should put his son into parliament, and under my guidance ; I could push him.   Well, and what said Frank ?"

"He invited me to call on him.   I remember that you once rather cautioned me against too intimate an acquaintance with those who have not got their fortune to make."

"Because they are idle, and idleness is contagious.   Right— better not to be intimate with a young Guardsman."

"Then you would not have me call on him, sir ?   We were rather friends at Eton ; and if I wholly reject his overtures, might he not think that you—"

"I !" interrupted Egerton.   "Ah, true ; my brother might think I bore him a grudge ; absurd.   Call then, and ask the young man here.   Yet still, I do not advise intimacy."

Egerton turned into his dressing-room.   "Sir," said his valet, who was in waiting, "Mr. Levy is here—he says, by appointment ; and Mr. Grinders is also just come from the country."

"Tell Mr. Grinders to come in first," said Egerton, seating himself.   "You need not wait ; I can dress without you.   Tell Mr. Levy I will see him in five minutes."

Mr. Grinders was steward to Audley Egerton.

Mr. Levy was a handsome man, who wore a camellia in his buttonhole—drove, in his cabriolet, a high-stepping horse that had cost £200 ; was well known to young men of fashion, and considered by their fathers a very dangerous acquaintance.

CHAPTER XII.

AS the company assembled in the drawing-rooms, Mr. Egerton introduced Randal Leslie to his eminent friends in a way that greatly contrasted the distant and admonitory manner which he had exhibited to him in private. The presentation was made with that cordiality, and that gracious respect by which those who are in station command notice for those who have their station yet to win.

"My dear Lord, let me introduce to you a kinsman of my late wife's (in a whisper)—the heir to the elder branch of her family. Stanmore, this is Mr. Leslie, of whom I spoke to you. You, who were so distinguished at Oxford, will not like him the worse for the prizes he gained there. Duke, let me present to you Mr. Leslie. The Duchess is angry with me for deserting her balls; I shall hope to make my peace, by providing myself with a younger and livelier substitute. Ah, Mr. Howard, here is a young gentleman just fresh from Oxford, who will tell us all about the new sect springing up there. He has not wasted his time on billiards and horses."

Leslie was received with all that charming courtesy which is the *To Kalon* of an aristocracy.

After dinner, conversation settled on politics. Randal listened with attention, and in silence, till Egerton drew him gently out; just enough, and no more—just enough to make his intelligence evident, and without subjecting him to the charge of laying down the law. Egerton knew how to draw out young men—a difficult art. It was one reason why he was so peculiarly popular with the more rising members of his party.

The party broke up early.

"We are in time for Almack's," said Egerton, glancing at the clock, "and I have a voucher for you ; come."

Randal followed his patron into the carriage. By the way, Egerton thus addressed him :—

"I shall introduce you to the principal leaders of society ; know them and study them : I do not advise you to attempt to do more —that is, to attempt to become the fashion. It is a very expensive ambition : some men it helps, most men it ruins. On the whole, you have better cards in your hands. Dance or not as it pleases you—don't flirt. If you flirt people will inquire into your fortune —an inquiry that will do you little good ; and flirting entangles a young man into marrying. That would never do. Here we are."

In two minutes more they were in the great ball-room, and
Randal's eyes were dazzled with the lights, the diamonds, the blaze
of beauty.   Audley presented him in quick succession to some
dozen ladies, and then disappeared amidst the crowd.   Randal was
not at a loss: he was without shyness; or if he had that disabling
infirmity, he concealed it.   He answered the languid questions put
to him, with a certain spirit that kept up talk, and left a favourable
impression of his agreeable qualities.   But the lady with whom he
got on the best, was one who had no daughters out, a handsome
and witty woman of the world—Lady Frederick Coniers.

"It is your first ball at Almack's then, Mr. Leslie?"

"My first."

"And you have not secured a partner?   Shall I find you one?
What do you think of that pretty girl in pink?"

"I see her—but I cannot *think* of her."

"You are rather, perhaps, like a diplomatist in a new court, and
your first object is to know who is who."

"I confess that on beginning to study the history of my own
day I should like to distinguish the portraits that illustrate the
memoir."

"Give me your arm, then, and we will come into the next room.
We shall see the different *notabilités* enter one by one, and observe
without being observed.   This is the least I can do for a friend of
Mr. Egerton's."

"Mr. Egerton, then," said Randal—(as they threaded their way
through the space without the rope that protected the dancers)—
"Mr. Egerton has had the good fortune to win your esteem, even
for his friends, however obscure?"

"Why, to say truth, I think no one whom Mr. Egerton calls his
friend need long remain obscure, if he has the ambition to be otherwise.   For Mr. Egerton holds it a maxim never to forget a friend,
nor a service."

"Ah, indeed!" said Randal, surprised.

"And, therefore," continued Lady Frederick, "as he passes
through life, friends gather round him.   He will rise even higher
yet.   Gratitude, Mr. Leslie, is a very good policy."

"Hem," muttered Mr. Leslie.

They had now gained the room where tea and bread and butter
were the homely refreshments to the *habitués* of what at that day
was the most exclusive assembly in London.   They ensconced
themselves in a corner by a window, and Lady Frederick performed
her task of cicerone with lively ease, accompanying each notice of
the various persons who passed panoramically before them with

sketch and anecdote, sometimes good-natured, generally satirical, always graphic and amusing.

By and by, Frank Hazeldean, having on his arm a young lady of haughty air and with high though delicate features, came to the tea-table.

"The last new Guardsman," said Lady Frederick ; "very handsome, and not yet quite spoiled. But he has got into a dangerous set."

RANDAL.—"The young lady with him is handsome enough to be dangerous."

LADY FREDERICK (laughing).—"No danger for him there,—as yet at least. Lady Mary (the Duke of Knaresborough's daughter) is only in her second year. The first year, nothing under an earl ; the second nothing under a baron. It will be full four years before she comes down to a commoner. Mr. Hazeldean's danger is of another kind. He lives much with men who are not exactly *mauvais ton*, but certainly not of the best taste. Yet he is very young ; he may extricate himself—leaving half his fortune behind him. What, he nods to you ! You know him ?"

"Very well ; he is nephew to Mr. Egerton."

"Indeed ! I did not know that. Hazeldean is a new name in London. I heard his father was a plain country gentleman, of good fortune, but not that he was related to Mr. Egerton."

"Half-brother."

"Will Mr. Egerton pay the young gentleman's debts ? He has no sons himself."

RANDAL.—"Mr. Egerton's fortune comes from his wife, from my family—from a Leslie, not from a Hazeldean."

Lady Frederick turned sharply, looked at Randal's countenance with more attention than she had yet vouchsafed to it, and tried to talk of the Leslies. Randal was very short there.

An hour afterwards, Randal, who had not danced, was still in the refreshment-room, but Lady Frederick had long quitted him. He was talking with some old Etonians who had recognized him, when there entered a lady of very remarkable appearance, and a murmur passed through the room as she appeared.

She might be three or four and twenty. She was dressed in black velvet, which contrasted with the alabaster whiteness of her throat and the clear paleness of her complexion, while it set off the diamonds with which she was profusely covered. Her hair was of the deepest jet, and worn simply braided. Her eyes, too, were dark and brilliant, her features regular and striking ; but their expression, when in repose, was not prepossessing to such as love

modesty and softness in the looks of woman.   But when she spoke
and smiled, there was so much spirit and vivacity in the countenance,
so much fascination in the smile, that all which might before have
marred the effect of her beauty, strangely and suddenly disappeared.

"Who is that very handsome woman?" asked Randal.

"An Italian—a Marchesa something," said one of the Etonians.

"Di Negra," suggested another, who had been abroad: "she is
a widow; her husband was of the great Genoese family of Negra—
a younger branch of it."

Several men now gathered thickly around the fair Italian.   A
few ladies of the highest rank spoke to her, but with a more distant
courtesy than ladies of high rank usually show to foreigners of such
quality as Madame di Negra.   Ladies of a rank less elevated seemed
rather shy of her;—that might be from jealousy.   As Randal
gazed at the Marchesa with more admiration than any woman,
perhaps, had before excited in him, he heard a voice near him say—

"Oh, Madame di Negra is resolved to settle amongst us and
marry an Englishman."

"If she can find one sufficiently courageous," returned a female
voice.

"Well, she's trying hard for Egerton, and he has courage enough
for anything."

The female voice replied, with a laugh, "Mr. Egerton knows the
world too well, and has resisted too many temptations to be—"

"Hush!—there he is."

Egerton came into the room with his usual firm step and erect
mien.   Randal observed that a quick glance was exchanged between
him and the Marchesa; but the Minister passed her by with a bow.

Still Randal watched, and, ten minutes afterwards, Egerton and
the Marchesa were seated apart in the very same convenient nook
that Randal and Lady Frederick had occupied an hour or so before.

"Is this the reason why Mr. Egerton so insultingly warns me
against counting on his fortune?" muttered Randal.   "Does he
mean to marry again?"

Unjust suspicion!—for, at that moment, these were the words
that Audley Egerton was dropping forth from his lips of bronze—

"Nay, dear madam, do not ascribe to my frank admiration
more gallantry than it merits.   Your conversation charms me, your
beauty delights me; your society is as a holiday that I look forward
to in the fatigues of my life.   But I have done with love, and I
shall never marry again."

"You almost pique me into trying to win, in order to reject
you," said the Italian, with a flash from her bright eyes.

"I defy even you," answered Audley, with his cold hard smile. "But to return to the point : You have more influence, at least, over this subtle ambassador ; and the secret we speak of I rely on you to obtain me. Ah, Madam, let us rest friends. You see I have conquered the unjust prejudices against you ; you are received and *fêtée* everywhere, as becomes your birth and your attractions. Rely on me ever, as I on you. But I shall excite too much envy if I stay here longer, and am vain enough to think that I may injure you if I provoke the gossip of the ill-natured. As the avowed friend, I can serve you—as the supposed lover, No—" Audley rose as he said this, and, standing by the chair, added carelessly, "Apropos, the sum you do me the honour to borrow will be paid to your bankers to-morrow."

"A thousand thanks !—my brother will hasten to repay you."

Audley bowed. "Your brother, I hope, will repay me in person, not before. When does he come ? "

"Oh, he has again postponed his visit *to* London ; he is so much needed in Vienna. But while we are talking of him, allow me to ask if your friend, Lord L'Estrange, is indeed still so bitter against that poor brother of mine?"

' Still the same."

"It is shameful !" cried the Italian with warmth ; "what has my brother ever done to him that he should actually intrigue against the Count in his own court ? "

"Intrigue ! I think you wrong Lord L'Estrange, he but represented what he believed to be the truth, in defence of a ruined exile."

"And you will not tell me where that exile is, or if his daughter still lives ?"

"My dear Marchesa, I have called you friend, therefore I will not aid L'Estrange to injure you or yours. But I call L'Estrange a friend also ; and I cannot violate the trust that——" Audley stopped short, and bit his lip. "You understand me," he resumed, with a more genial smile than usual ; and he took his leave.

The Italian's brows met as her eye followed him ; then, as she too rose, that eye encountered Randal's.

"That young man has the eye of an Italian," said the Marchesa to herself, as she passed by him into the ball-room.

CHAPTER XIII.

LEONARD and Helen settled themselves in two little chambers in a small lane. The neighbourhood was dull enough—the accommodation humble ; but their landlady had a smile. That was the reason, perhaps, why Helen chose the lodgings : a smile is not always found on the face of a landlady when the lodger is poor. And out of their windows they caught sight of a green tree, an elm, that grew up fair and tall in a carpenter's yard at the rear. That tree was like another smile to the place. They saw the birds come and go to its shelter ; and they even heard, when a breeze arose, the pleasant murmur of its boughs.

Leonard went the same evening to Captain Digby's old lodgings, but he could learn there no intelligence of friends or protectors for Helen. The people were rude and surly, and said that the Captain still owed them £1 17s. The claim, however, seemed very dis- putable, and was stoutly denied by Helen. The next morning Leonard set off in search of Dr. Morgan. He thought his best plan was to inquire the address of the Doctor at the nearest chemist's, and the chemist civilly looked into the *Court Guide*, and referred him to a house in Bulstrode Street, Manchester Square. To this street Leonard contrived to find his way, much marvelling at the meanness of London : Screwstown seemed to him the handsomer town of the two.

A shabby man-servant opened the door, and Leonard remarked that the narrow passage was choked with boxes, trunks, and various articles of furniture. He was shown into a small room containing a very large round table, whereon were sundry works on homœo- opathy, Parry's *Cymbrian Plutarch*, Davies' *Celtic Researches*, and a Sunday newspaper. An engraved portrait of the illustrious Hahnemann occupied the place of honour over the chimney-piece. In a few minutes the door to an inner room opened, and Dr. Morgan appeared, and said, politely, "Come in, sir."

The Doctor seated himself at a desk, looked hastily at Leonard, and then at a great chronometer lying on the table. "My time's short, sir—going abroad : and now that I am going, patients flock to me. Too late. London will repent its apathy. Let it !"

The Doctor paused majestically, and not remarking on Leonard's face the consternation he had anticipated, he repeated peevishly— "I am going abroad, sir, but I will make a synopsis of your case, and leave it to my successor. Hum! Hair chestnut; eyes—what colour? Look this way—blue, dark blue. Hem! Constitution nervous. What are the symptoms?"

"Sir," began Leonard, "a little girl——"

DR. MORGAN (impatiently).—"Little girl! Never mind the history of your sufferings; stick to the symptoms—stick to the symptoms."

LEONARD.—"You mistake me, Doctor; I have nothing the matter with me. A little girl——"

DR. MORGAN.—"Girl again! I understand! it is she who is ill. Shall I go to her? She must describe her own symptoms—I can't judge from your talk. You'll be telling me she has consumption, or dyspepsia, or some such disease that don't exist: mere allopathic inventions—symptoms, sir, symptoms."

LEONARD (forcing his way).—"You attended her poor father, Captain Digby, when he was taken ill in the coach with you. He is dead, and his child is an orphan."

DR. MORGAN (fumbling in his medical pocket-book).—"Orphan! nothing for orphans, especially if inconsolable, like *aconite* and *chamomilla*." [1]

With some difficulty Leonard succeeded in bringing Helen to the recollection of the homœopathist, stating how he came in charge of her, and why he sought Dr. Morgan.

The Doctor was much moved.

"But, really," said he, after a pause, "I don't see how I can help the poor child. I know nothing of her relations. This Lord Les—whatever his name is—I know of no lords in London. I knew lords, and physicked them too, when I was a blundering allopathist. There was the Earl of Lansmere—has had many a blue pill from me, sinner that I was. His son was wiser; never would take physic. Very clever boy was Lord L'Estrange—"

"Lord L'Estrange!—that name begins with Les—"

"Stuff! He's always abroad—shows his sense. I'm going abroad too. No development for science in this horrid city—full of prejudices, sir, and given up to the most barbarous allopathical and phlebotomical propensities. I'm going to the land of Hahnemann, sir,—sold my good-will, lease, and furniture, and have bought in on the Rhine. Natural life there, sir—homœopathy needs nature: dine at one o'clock, get up at four—tea little known, and science appreciated. But I forget. Cott! what can I do for the orphan?"

---

[1] It may be necessary to observe, that homœopathy professes to deal with our moral affections as well as with our physical maladies, and has a globule for every sorrow.

"Well, sir," said Leonard, rising, "Heaven will give me strength to support her."

The Doctor looked at the young man attentively. "And yet," said he, in a gentler voice, "you, young man, are, by your account, a perfect stranger to her, or were so when you undertook to bring her to London. You have a good heart—always keep it. Very healthy thing, sir, a good heart—that is, when not carried to excess. But you have friends of your own in town?"

LEONARD.—"Not yet, sir; I hope to make them."

DOCTOR.—"Pless me, you do? How?—I can't make any."

Leonard coloured and hung his head. He longed to say "Authors find friends in their readers—I am going to be an author." But he felt that the reply would savour of presumption, and held his tongue.

The Doctor continued to examine him, and with friendly interest. "You say you walked up to London—was that from choice or economy?"

LEONARD.—"Both, sir."

DOCTOR.—"Sit down again, and let us talk. I can give you a quarter of an hour, and I'll see if I *can* help either of you, provided you tell me all the symptoms—I mean all the particulars."

Then, with that peculiar adroitness which belongs to experience in the medical profession, Dr. Morgan, who was really an acute and able man, proceeded to put his questions, and soon extracted from Leonard the boy's history and hopes. But when the Doctor, in admiration at a simplicity which contrasted so evident an intelligence, finally asked him his name and connections, and Leonard told them, the homœopathist actually started. "Leonard Fairfield, grandson of my old friend, John Avenel of Lansmere! I must shake you by the hand. Brought up by Mrs. Fairfield!—Ah, now I look, strong family likeness—very strong!"

The tears stood in the Doctor's eyes. "Poor Nora!" said he.

"Nora! Did you know my aunt?"

"Your aunt! Ah!—ah! yes—yes! Poor Nora!—she died almost in these arms—so young, so beautiful. I remember it as if yesterday."

The Doctor brushed his hand across his eyes, and swallowed a globule; and, before the boy knew what he was about, had in his benevolence thrust another between Leonard's quivering lips.

A knock was heard at the door.

"Ha! that's my great patient," cried the Doctor, recovering his self-possession—"must see him. A chronic case—excellent patient

—tic, sir, tic. Puzzling, and interesting. If I could take that tic with me, I should ask nothing more from Heaven. Call again on Monday; I may have something to tell you then as to yourself. The little girl can't stay with you—wrong and nonsensical. I will see after her. Leave me your address—write it here. I think I know a lady who will take charge of her. Good-bye. Monday next, ten o'clock."

With this, the Doctor thrust out Leonard, and ushered in his grand patient, whom he was very anxious to take with him to the banks of the Rhine.

Leonard had now only to discover the nobleman whose name had been so vaguely uttered by poor Captain Digby. He had again recourse to the *Court Guide;* and finding the address of two or three lords the first syllable of whose titles seemed similar to that repeated to him, and all living pretty near to each other, in the regions of May Fair, he ascertained his way to that quarter, and, exercising his mother-wit, inquired at the neighbouring shops as to the personal appearance of these noblemen. Out of consideration for his rusticity, he got very civil and clear answers; but none of the lords in question corresponded with the description given by Helen. One was old, another was exceedingly corpulent, a third was bedridden—none of them was known to keep a great dog. It . is needless to say that the name of L'Estrange (no habitant of London) was not in the *Court Guide.* And Dr. Morgan's assertion that that person was always abroad unluckily dismissed from Leonard's mind the name the homœopathist had so casually mentioned. But Helen was not disappointed when her young protector returned late in the day, and told her of his ill success. Poor child! she was so pleased in her heart not to be separated from her new brother; and Leonard was touched to see how she had contrived, in his absence, to give a certain comfort and cheerful grace to the bare room devoted to himself. She had arranged his few books and papers so neatly, near the window, in sight of the one green elm. She had coaxed the smiling landlady out of one or two extra articles of furniture, especially a walnut-tree bureau, and some odds and ends of ribbon—with which last she had looped up the curtains. Even the old rush-bottom chairs had a strange air of elegance, from the mode in which they were placed. The fairies had given sweet Helen the art that adorns a home, and brings out a smile from the dingiest corner of hut and attic.

Leonard wondered and praised. He kissed his blushing minis- trant gratefully, and they sate down in joy to their abstemious meal; when suddenly his face was overclouded—there shot through him the remembrance of Dr. Morgan's words—"The little girl can't stay with you—wrong and nonsensical. I think I know a lady who will take charge of her."

"Ah," cried Leonard, sorrowfully, "how could I forget?" And he told Helen what grieved him. Helen at first exclaimed "that she would not go." Leonard, rejoiced, then began to talk as usual of his great prospects ; and, hastily finishing his meal, as if there were no time to lose, sate down at once to his papers. Then Helen contemplated him sadly, as he bent over his delighted work. And when, lifting his radiant eyes from his manuscripts, he exclaimed, "No, no, you shall *not* go. *This* must succeed—and we shall live together in some pretty cottage, where we can see more than one tree,"—*then* Helen sighed, and did not answer this time, "No, I will not go."

Shortly after she stole from the room, and into her own ; and there, kneeling down, she prayed, and her prayer was somewhat this—"Guard me against my own selfish heart ; may I never be a burden to him who has shielded me."

Perhaps as the Creator looks down on this world, whose wondrous beauty beams on us more and more, in proportion as our science would take it from poetry into law—perhaps He beholds nothing so beautiful as the pure heart of a simple loving child.

CHAPTER XIV.

LEONARD went out the next day with his precious manuscripts. He had read sufficient of modern literature to know the names of the principal London publishers ; and to these he took his way with a bold step, though a beating heart.

That day he was out longer than the last ; and when he returned, and came into the little room, Helen uttered a cry, for she scarcely recognized him. There was on his face so deep, so silent, and so concentrated a despondency. He sate down listlessly, and did not kiss her this time, as she stole towards him. He felt so humbled. He was a king deposed. *He* take charge of another life ! He !

She coaxed him at last into communicating his day's chronicle. The reader beforehand knows too well what it must be, to need detailed repetition. Most of the publishers had absolutely refused to look at his manuscripts ; one or two had good-naturedly glanced over and returned them at once, with a civil word or two of flat rejection. One publisher alone—himself a man of letters, and who in youth had gone through the same bitter process of disillusion that now awaited the village genius—volunteered some kindly though stern explanation and counsel to the unhappy boy. This gentleman read a portion of Leonard's principal poem with attention, and even with frank admiration. He could appreciate the rare promise that it manifested. He sympathized with the boy's history, and even with his hopes; and then he said, in bidding him farewell—

"If I publish this poem for you, speaking as a trader, I shall be a considerable loser. Did I publish all I admire, out of sympathy with the author, I should be a ruined man. But suppose that, impressed as I really am with the evidence of no common poetic gifts in this manuscript, I publish it, not as a trader, but a lover of literature, I shall in reality, I fear, render you a great dis-service, and perhaps unfit your whole life for the exertions on which you must rely for independence."

"How, sir?" cried Leonard—"Not that I would ask you to injure yourself for me," he added, with proud tears in his eyes.

"How, my young friend? I will explain. There is enough talent in these verses to induce very flattering reviews in some of the literary journals. You will read these, find yourself proclaimed a poet, will cry 'I am on the road to fame.' You will come to me, 'And my poem, how does it sell?' I shall point to some groaning shelf, and say, 'Not twenty copies!' The journals may praise, but the public will not buy it. 'But you will have got a name,' you say. Yes, a name as a poet just sufficiently known to make every man in practical business disinclined to give fair trial to your talents in a single department of positive life;—none like to employ poets; —a name that will not put a penny in your purse—worse still, that will operate as a barrier against every escape into the ways whereby men get to fortune. But, having once tasted praise, you will continue to sigh for it: you will perhaps never again get a publisher to bring forth a poem, but you will hanker round the purlieus of the Muses, scribble for periodicals—fall at last into a bookseller's drudge. Profits will be so precarious and uncertain, that to avoid debt may be impossible; then, you who now seem so ingenuous and so proud, will sink deeper still into the literary mendicant—begging, borrowing—"

"Never—never—never!" cried Leonard, veiling his face with his hands.

"Such would have been my career," continued the publisher. "But I, luckily, had a rich relative, a trader, whose calling I despised as a boy, who kindly forgave my folly, bound me as an apprentice, and here I am; and now I can afford to write books as well as sell them.

"Young man, you must have respectable relations—go by their advice and counsel; cling fast to some positive calling. Be anything in this city rather than poet by profession."

"And how, sir, have there ever been poets? Had *they* other callings?"

"Read their biography, and then—envy them!"

Leonard was silent a moment; but, lifting his head, answered loud and quickly,—"I *have* read their biography. True, their lot was poverty—perhaps hunger. Sir, I—envy them!"

"Poverty and hunger are small evils," answered the bookseller, with a grave kind smile. "There are worse,—debt and degradation, and—despair."

"No, sir, no—you exaggerate; these last are not the lot of all poets."

"Right, for most of our greatest poets had some private means of their own. And for others—why, all who have put into a lottery have not drawn blanks. But who could advise another man to set his whole hope of fortune on the chance of a prize in a lottery? And such a lottery!" groaned the publisher, glancing towards sheets and reams of dead authors, lying, like lead, upon his shelves.

Leonard clutched his manuscripts to his heart, and hurried away.

"Yes," he muttered, as Helen clung to him, and tried to console—"yes, you were right: London is very vast, very strong, and very cruel;" and his head sank lower and lower yet upon his bosom.

The door was flung widely open, and in, unannounced, walked Dr. Morgan.

The child turned to him, and at the sight of his face she remembered her father; and the tears that, for Leonard's sake, she had been trying to suppress, found way.

The good doctor soon gained all the confidence of these two young hearts. And after listening to Leonard's story of his paradise lost in a day, he patted him on the shoulder and said, "Well, you will call on me on Monday, and we will see. Meanwhile, borrow these of me;"—and he tried to slip three sovereigns into the boy's hand. Leonard was indignant. The bookseller's warning flashed on him. Mendicancy! Oh no, he had not yet come to that? He was almost rude and savage in his rejection; and the Doctor did not like him the less for it.

"You are an obstinate mule," said the homœopathist, reluctantly putting up his sovereigns. "Will you work at something practical and prosy, and let the poetry rest awhile?"

"Yes," said Leonard, doggedly. "I will work."

"Very well, then. I know an honest bookseller, and he shall

give you some employment; and meanwhile, at all events, you will be among books, and that will be some comfort."

Leonard's eyes brightened—"A great comfort, sir." He pressed the hand he had before put aside to his grateful heart.

"But," resumed the Doctor seriously, "you really feel a strong predisposition to make verses?"

"I did, sir."

"Very bad symptom indeed, and must be stopped before a relapse! Here, I have cured three prophets and ten poets with this novel specific."

While thus speaking, he had got out his book and a globule. "*Agaricus muscarius* dissolved in a tumbler of distilled water—teaspoonful whenever the fit comes on. Sir, it would have cured Milton himself."

"And now for you, my child," turning to Helen—"I have found a lady who will be very kind to you. Not a menial situation. She wants some one to read to her, and tend on her—she is old, and has no children. She wants a companion, and prefers a girl of your age to one older. Will this suit you?"

Leonard walked away.

Helen got close to the Doctor's ear, and whispered, "No, I cannot leave *him* now—he is so sad."

"Cott!" grunted the Doctor, "you two must have been reading *Paul and Virginia*. If I could but stay in England, I would try what *ignatia* would do in this case—interesting experiment! Listen to me—little girl; and go out of the room, you, sir."

Leonard, averting his face, obeyed. Helen made an involuntary step after him—the Doctor detained and drew her on his knee.

"What's your Christian name?—I forget."

"Helen."

"Helen, listen. In a year or two you will be a young woman, and it would be very wrong then to live alone with that young man. Meanwhile, you have no right to cripple all his energies. He must not have you leaning on his right arm—you would weigh it down. I am going away, and when I am gone there will be no one to help you, if you reject the friend I offer you. Do as I tell you, for a little girl so peculiarly susceptible (a thorough *pulsatilla* constitution) cannot be obstinate and egotistical."

"Let me see him cared for and happy, sir," said she firmly, "and I will go where you wish."

"He shall be so; and to-morrow, while he is out, I will come and fetch you. Nothing so painful as leave-taking—shakes the nervous system, and is a mere waste of the animal economy."

Helen sobbed aloud; then, writhing from the Doctor, she exclaimed, "But he may know where I am? We may see each other sometimes? Ah, sir, it was at my father's grave that we first met, and I think Heaven sent him to me. Do not part us for ever."

"I should have a heart of stone if I did," cried the Doctor, vehemently; "and Miss Starke shall let him come and visit you once a-week. I'll give her something to make her. She is naturally indifferent to others. I will alter her whole constitution, and melt her into sympathy—with *rhododendron* and *arsenic!*"

CHAPTER XV.

BEFORE he went, the Doctor wrote a line to "Mr. Prickett, Bookseller, Holborn," and told Leonard to take it the next morning, as addressed. "I will call on Prickett myself to-night, and prepare him for your visit. But I hope and trust you will only have to stay there a few days."

He then turned the conversation, to communicate his plans for Helen. Miss Starke lived at Highgate—a worthy woman, stiff and prim, as old maids sometimes are. But just the place for a little girl like Helen, and Leonard should certainly be allowed to call and see her.

Leonard listened and made no opposition;—now that his day-dream was dispelled, he had no right to pretend to be Helen's protector. He could have prayed her to share his wealth and his fame; his penury and his drudgery—no.

It was a very sorrowful evening—that between the adventurer and the child. They sate up late, till their candle had burned down to the socket; neither did they talk much; but his hand clasped hers all the time, and her head pillowed itself on his shoulder. I fear, when they parted it was not for sleep.

And when Leonard went forth the next morning, Helen stood at the street door watching him depart—slowly, slowly. No doubt, in that humble lane there were many sad hearts; but no heart so heavy as that of the still quiet child, when the form she had watched was to be seen no more, and, still standing on the desolate threshold, she gazed into space—and all was vacant.

CHAPTER XVI.

MR. PRICKETT was a believer in homœopathy, and declared, to the indignation of all the apothecaries round Holborn, that he had been cured of a chronic rheumatism by Dr. Morgan. The good Doctor had, as he promised, seen Mr. Prickett when he left Leonard, and asked him as a favour to find some light occupation for the boy, that would serve as an excuse for a modest weekly salary. "It will not be for long," said the Doctor; "his relations are respectable and well off: I will write to his grandparents, and in a few days I hope to relieve you of the charge. Of course, if you don't want him, I will repay what he costs meanwhile."

Mr. Prickett, thus prepared for Leonard, received him very graciously, and, after a few questions, said Leonard was just the person he wanted to assist him in cataloguing his books, and offered him most handsomely £1 a week for the task.

Plunged at once into a world of books vaster than he had ever before won admission to, that old divine dream of knowledge, out of which poetry had sprung, returned to the village student at the very sight of the venerable volumes. The collection of Mr. Prickett was however, in reality, by no means large; but it comprised not only the ordinary standard works, but several curious and rare ones. And Leonard paused in making the catalogue, and took many a hasty snatch of the contents of each tome, as it passed through his hands. The bookseller, who was an enthusiast for old books, was pleased to see a kindred feeling (which his shop-boy had never exhibited) in his new assistant; and he talked about rare editions and scarce copies, and initiated Leonard into many of the mysteries of the bibliographist.

Nothing could be more dark and dingy than the shop. There was a booth outside, containing cheap books and odd volumes, round which there was always an attentive group; within, a gas-lamp burned night and day.

But time passed quickly to Leonard. He missed not the green fields, he forgot his disappointments, he ceased to remember even Helen. O strange passion of knowledge! nothing like thee for strength and devotion.

Mr. Prickett was a bachelor, and asked Leonard to dine with him on a cold shoulder of mutton. During dinner, the shop-boy kept the shop, and Mr. Prickett was really pleasant, as well as loquacious.   He took a liking to Leonard—and Leonard told him his adventures with the publishers, at which Mr. Prickett rubbed his hands and laughed, as at a capital joke.   "Oh, give up poetry, and stick to a shop," cried he; "and, to cure you for ever of the mad whim to be author, I'll just lend you the *Life and Works of Chatterton.*   You may take it home with you and read before you go to bed.   You'll come back quite a new man to-morrow."

Not till night, when the shop was closed, did Leonard return to his lodging.   And when he entered the room, he was struck to the soul by the silence, by the void.   Helen was gone !

There was a rose-tree in its pot on the table at which he wrote, and by it a scrap of paper, on which was written—

"Dear, dear Brother Leonard, God bless you.   I will let you know when we can meet again.   Take care of this rose, Brother, and don't forget poor   HELEN."

Over the word "forget" there was a big round blistered spot that nearly effaced the word.

Leonard leant his face on his hands, and for the first time in his life he felt what solitude really is.   He could not stay long in the room.   He walked out again, and wandered objectless to and fro the streets.   He passed that stiller and humbler neighbourhood, he mixed with the throng that swarmed in the more populous thorough-fares.   Hundreds and thousands passed him by, and still—still such solitude.

He came back, lighted his candle, and resolutely drew forth the "Chatterton" which the bookseller had lent him.   It was an old edition, in one thick volume.   It had evidently belonged to some contemporary of the poet's—apparently an inhabitant of Bristol—some one who had gathered up many anecdotes respecting Chatterton's habits, and who appeared even to have seen him, nay, been in his company; for the book was interleaved, and the leaves covered with notes and remarks, in a stiff clear hand—all evincing personal knowledge of the mournful immortal dead.   At first, Leonard read with an effort; then the strange and fierce spell of that dread life seized upon him—seized with pain, and gloom, and terror—this boy dying by his own hand, about the age Leonard had attained himself.   This wondrous boy, of a genius beyond all comparison—the greatest that ever yet was developed and extin-guished at the age of eighteen—self-taught—self-struggling—self-immolated.   Nothing in literature like that life and that death !

With intense interest Leonard perused the tale of the brilliant imposture which had been so harshly and so absurdly construed into the crime of a forgery, and which was (if not wholly innocent) so akin to the literary devices always in other cases viewed with indulgence, and exhibiting, in this, intellectual qualities in themselves so amazing—such patience, such forethought, such labour, such courage, such ingenuity—the qualities that, well directed, make men great, not only in books, but action. And, turning from the history of the imposture to the poems themselves, the young reader bent before their beauty, literally awed and breathless. How this strange Bristol boy tamed and mastered his rude and motley materials into a music that comprehended every tune and key, from the simplest to the sublimest? He turned back to the biography—he read on—he saw the proud, daring, mournful spirit, alone in the Great City like himself. He followed its dismal career, he saw it falling with bruised and soiled wings into the mire. He turned again to the later works, wrung forth as tasks for bread,— the satires without moral grandeur, the politics without honest faith. He shuddered and sickened as he read. True, even here his poet mind appreciated (what perhaps only poets can)—the divine fire that burned fitfully through that meaner and more sordid fuel—he still traced in those crude, hasty, bitter offerings to dire Necessity, the hand of the young giant who had built up the stately verse of Rowley. But, alas! how different from that "mighty line." How all serenity and joy had fled from these later exercises of art degraded into journey-work. Then rapidly came on the catastrophe—the closed doors—the poison—the suicide—the manuscripts torn by the hands of despairing wrath, and strewed round the corpse upon the funeral floors. It was terrible! The spectre of the Titan boy, (as described in the notes written on the margin,) with his haughty brow, his cynic smile, his lustrous eyes, haunted all the night the baffled and solitary child of song.

CHAPTER XVII.

IT will often happen that what ought to turn the human mind from some peculiar tendency produces the opposite effect. One would think that the perusal in the newspaper of some crime and capital punishment would warn away all who had ever meditated the crime, or dreaded the chance of detection. Yet it is well known to us that many a criminal is made by pondering over the fate of some predecessor in guilt. There is a fascination in the Dark and Forbidden, which, strange to say, is only lost in fiction. No man is more inclined to murder his nephews, or stifle his wife, after reading "Richard the Third" or "Othello." It is the *reality* that is necessary to constitute the danger of contagion. Now, it was this reality in the fate, and life, and crowning suicide of Chatterton, that forced itself upon Leonard's thoughts, and sate there like a visible evil thing, gathering evil like cloud around it. There was much in the dead poet's character, his trials and his doom, that stood out to Leonard like a bold and colossal shadow of himself and his fate. Alas! the bookseller, in one respect, had said truly. Leonard came back to him next day a new man; and it seemed even to himself as if he had lost a good angel in losing Helen. "Oh that she had been by my side," thought he. "Oh that I could have felt the touch of her confiding hand—that, looking up from the scathed and dreary ruin of this life, that had sublimely lifted itself from the plain, and sought to tower aloft from a deluge, her mild look had spoken to me of innocent, humble, unaspiring, childhood! Ah! If indeed I were still necessary to her—still the sole guardian and protector —then could I say to myself, 'Thou must not despair and die! Thou hast her to live and to strive for.' But no, no! Only this vast and terrible London—the solitude of the dreary garret, and those lustrous eyes, glaring alike through the throng and through the solitude."

CHAPTER XVIII.

N the following Monday, Dr. Morgan's shabby man-servant opened the door to a young man in whom he did not at first remember a former visitor. A few days before, embrowned with healthful travel—serene light in his eye, simple trust in his careless lip—Leonard Fairfield had stood at that threshold. Now again he stood there, pale and haggard, with a cheek already hollowed into those deep anxious lines that speak of working thoughts and sleepless nights; and a settled sullen gloom resting heavily on his whole aspect.

"I call by appointment," said the boy, testily, as the servant stood irresolute. The man gave way. "Master is just gone out to a patient: please to wait, sir;" and he showed him into the little parlour. In a few moments, two other patients were admitted. These were women, and they began talking very loud. They disturbed Leonard's unsocial thoughts. He saw that the door into the Doctor's receiving-room was half open, and, ignorant of the etiquette which holds such *penetralia* as sacred, he walked in to escape from the gossips. He threw himself into the Doctor's own well-worn chair, and muttered to himself, "Why did he tell me to come? What new can he think of for me? And if a favour, should I take it? He has given me the means of bread by work: that is all I have a right to ask from him, from any man—all I should accept."

While thus soliloquizing, his eye fell on a letter lying open on the table. He started. He recognized the hand-writing—the same as that of the letter which had enclosed £50 to his mother —the letter of his grandparents. He saw his own name: he saw something more—words that made his heart stand still, and his blood seem like ice in his veins. As he thus stood aghast, a hand was laid on the letter, and a voice, in an angry growl, muttered, "How dare you come into my room, and pe reading my letters? Er—r—r!"

Leonard placed his own hand on the Doctor's firmly, and said, in a fierce tone, "This letter relates to me—belongs to me—crushes me. I have seen enough to know that. I demand to read all—learn all."

The Doctor looked round, and seeing the door into the waiting-room still open, kicked it to with his foot, and then said, under his breath, "What have you read? Tell me the truth."

"Two lines only, and I am called—I am called—" Leonard's frame shook from head to foot, and the veins on his forehead swelled like cords. He could not complete the sentence. It seemed as if an ocean was rolling up through his brain, and roaring in his ears. The Doctor saw, at a glance, that there was physical danger in his state, and hastily and soothingly answered,—"Sit down, sit down —calm yourself—you shall know all—read all—drink this water;" and he poured into a tumbler of the pure liquid a drop or two from a tiny phial.

Leonard obeyed mechanically, for he was no longer able to stand. He closed his eyes, and for a minute or two life seemed to pass from him; then he recovered, and saw the good Doctor's gaze fixed on him with great compassion. He silently stretched forth his hand towards the letter. "Wait a few moments," said the physician, judiciously, "and hear me meanwhile. It is very unfortunate you should have seen a letter never meant for your eye, and containing allusions to a secret you were never to have known. But, if I tell you more, will you promise me, on your word of honour, that you will hold the confidence sacred from Mrs. Fairfield, the Avenels— from all? I myself am pledged to conceal a secret, which I can only share with you on the same condition."

"There is nothing," announced Leonard, indistinctly, and with a bitter smile on his lip,—"nothing, it seems, that I should be proud to boast of. Yes, I promise—the letter, the letter!"

The Doctor placed it in Leonard's right hand, and quietly slipped to the wrist of the left his forefinger and thumb, as physicians are said to do when a victim is stretched on the rack. "Pulse decreasing," he muttered; "wonderful thing, *Aconite!*" Meanwhile Leonard read as follows, faults in spelling and all:—

"DR. MORGAN,

"Sir,—I received your favur duly, and am glad to hear that the pore boy is safe and Well. But he has been behaving ill, and ungrateful to my good son Richard, who is a credit to the whole Famuly, and has made himself a Gentleman, and Was very kind and good to the boy, not knowing who and What he is—God forbid! I don't want never to see him again—the boy. Pore John was ill and Restless for days afterwards. John is a pore cretur now, and has had paralyticks. And he Talked of nothing but Nora—the boy's eyes were so like his Mother's. I cannot, cannot see the Child of Shame. He can't cum here—for our Lord's sake, sir, don't ask it—he can't, so Respectable as we've always been!—and such disgrace! Base born—base born. Keep him where he is, bind him prentis, I'll pay anything for That. You says, sir, he's clever, and quick at learning; so did Parson Dale, and wanted him to go to Collidge and make a Figur—then all would cum out. It would be my death, sir; I could not sleep in my grave, sir. Nora, that we were all so proud of. Sinful creturs that we are! Nora's good name that we've saved now, gone, gone. And Richard, who is so grand, and who was so fond of pore, pore Nora! He would not hold up his Head again. Don't let him make a Figur in the world—let him be a tradesman, as we were afore him—any trade he takes to—and not cross us no more while he lives. Then I shall pray for him, and wish him happy. And have not we had enuff of bringing up children to be above their birth? Nora, that I used to say was like the first lady o' the land —oh, but we were rightly punished! So now, sir, I leave all to you, and will Pay all you want for the boy. And be sure that the secret's kept. For we have never heard from the father, and, at leest, no one knows that Nora has a living son but I and my daughter Jane, and Parson Dale and you—and you Two are good Gentlemen—and Jane will keep her word, and I am old, and shall be in my grave Soon, but I hope it wont be while pore John needs me. What could he do without me? And if *that* got wind, it would kill me straight, sir.   Pore John is a helpless cretur, God bless him.   So no more from your servant in all dooty.

"M. AVENEL."

Leonard laid down this letter very calmly, and, except by a slight heaving at his breast, and a deathlike whiteness of his lips, the emotions he felt were undetected.   And it is a proof how much exquisite goodness there was in his heart that the first words he spoke were, "Thank Heaven!"

The Doctor did not expect that thanksgiving, and he was so startled that he exclaimed, "For what?"

"I have nothing to pity or excuse in the woman I knew and honoured as a mother.   I am not her son—her—"

He stopped short.

"No : but don't be hard on your true mother—poor Nora!"

Leonard staggered and then burst into a sudden paroxysm of tears.

"Oh, my own mother!—my dead mother!   Thou for whom I felt so mysterious a love—thou, from whom I took this poet soul—pardon me, pardon me!   Hard on thee!   Would that thou wert living yet, that I might comfort thee!   What thou must have suffered!"

These words were sobbed forth in broken gasps from the depth of his heart.   Then he caught up the letter again, and his thoughts were changed as his eyes fell upon the writer's shame and fear, as it were, of his very existence.   All his native haughtiness returned to him.   His crest rose, his tears dried.   "Tell her," he said, with a stern, unfaltering voice—"tell Mrs. Avenel that she is obeyed —that I will never seek her roof, never cross her path, never disgrace her wealthy son.   But tell her, also, that I will choose my own way in life—that I will not take from her a bribe for concealment.   Tell her that I am nameless, and will yet make a name."

A name!   Was this but an idle boast, or was it one of those flashes of conviction which are never belied, lighting up our future for one lurid instant, and then fading into darkness?

"I do not doubt it, my prave poy," said Dr. Morgan, growing exceedingly Welsh in his excitement; "and perhaps you may find a father, who—"

"Father—who is he—what is he?   He lives, then!   But he has deserted me—he must have betrayed her!   I need him not.   The law gives me no father."

The last words were said with a return of bitter anguish : then, in a calmer tone, he resumed, "But I should know who he is—as another one whose path I may not cross."

Dr. Morgan looked embarrassed, and paused in deliberation. "Nay," said he, at length, "as you know so much, it is surely best that you should know all."

The Doctor then proceeded to detail with some circumlocution, what we will here repeat from his account more succinctly.

Nora Avenel, while yet very young, left her native village, or rather the house of Lady Lansmere, by whom she had been educated and brought up, in order to accept the place of companion to a lady in London. One evening she suddenly presented herself at her father's house, and at the first sight of her mother's face she fell down insensible. She was carried to bed. Dr. Morgan (then the chief medical practitioner of the town) was sent for. That night Leonard came into the world, and his mother died. She never recovered her senses, never spoke intelligibly from the time she entered the house. "And never, therefore, named your father," said Dr. Morgan. "We knew not who he was."

"And how," cried Leonard, fiercely—"how have they dared to slander this dead mother? How knew they that I—was—was—was not the child of wedlock?"

"There was no wedding-ring on Nora's finger—never any rumour of her marriage—her strange and sudden appearance at her father's house—her emotions on entrance, so unlike those natural to a wife returning to a parent's home; these are all the evidence against her. But Mrs. Avenel deemed them strong, and so did I. You have a right to think we judged too harshly—perhaps we did."

"And no inquiries were ever made?" said Leonard, mournfully, and after long silence—"no inquiries to learn who was the father of the motherless child?"

"Inquiries!—Mrs. Avenel would have died first. Your grandmother's nature is very rigid. Had she come from princes, from Cadwallader himself," said the Welshman, "she could not more have shrunk from the thought of dishonour. Even over her dead child, the child she had loved the best, she thought but how to save that child's name and memory from suspicion. There was luckily no servant in the house, only Mark Fairfield and his wife (Nora's sister): they had arrived the same day on a visit.

"Mrs. Fairfield was nursing her own infant, two or three months old; she took charge of you; Nora was buried and the secret kept. None out of the family knew of it, but myself and the curate of the town—Mr. Dale. The day after your birth, Mrs. Fairfield, to prevent discovery, moved to a village at some distance. There her child died; and when she returned to Hazeldean, where her husband was settled, you passed as the son she had lost. Mark, I know, was as a father to you, for he had loved Nora; they had been children together."

"And she came to London—London is strong and cruel," muttered Leonard. "She was friendless and deceived. I see all—I desire to know no more. This father, he must indeed have been like those whom I have read of in books. To love, to wrong her—*that* I can conceive ; but then to leave, to abandon ; no visit to her grave—no remorse—no search for his own child. Well, well ; Mrs. Avenel was right. Let us think of *him* no more."

The man-servant knocked at the door, and then put in his head. "Sir, the ladies are getting very impatient, and say they'll go."

"Sir," said Leonard, with a strange calm return to the things about him, "I ask your pardon for taking up your time so long. I go now. I will never mention to my moth—I mean to Mrs. Fairfield—what I have learned, nor to any one. I will work my way somehow. If Mr. Prickett will keep me, I will stay with him at present ; but I repeat, I cannot take Mrs. Avenel's money and be bound apprentice. Sir, you have been good and patient with me —Heaven reward you."

The Doctor was too moved to answer. He wrung Leonard's hand, and in another minute the door closed upon the nameless boy. He stood alone in the streets of London ; and the sun flashed on him red and menacing, like the eye of a foe !

CHAPTER XIX.

LEONARD did not appear at the shop of Mr. Prickett that day. Needless it is to say where he wandered—what he suffered—what thought—what felt. All within was storm. Late at night he returned to his solitary lodging. On his table, neglected since the morning, was Helen's rose-tree. It looked parched and fading. His heart smote him : he watered the poor plant—perhaps with his tears.

Meanwhile Dr. Morgan, after some debate with himself, whether or not to apprise Mrs. Avenel of Leonard's discovery and message, resolved to spare her an uneasiness and alarm that might be danger-ous to her health, and unnecessary in itself. He replied shortly, that she need not fear Leonard's coming to her house—that he was disinclined to bind himself an apprentice, but that he was provided for at present ; and in a few weeks, when Dr. Morgan heard more of him through the tradesman by whom he was employed, the

Doctor would write to her from Germany. He then went to Mr. Prickett's—told the willing bookseller to keep the young man for the present—to be kind to him, watch over his habits and conduct, and report to the Doctor in his new home, on the Rhine, what avocation he thought Leonard would be best suited for, and most inclined to adopt. The charitable Welshman divided with the bookseller the salary given to Leonard, and left a quarter of his moiety in advance. It is true that he knew he should be repaid on applying to Mrs. Avenel; but being a man of independent spirit himself, he so sympathized with Leonard's present feelings, that he felt as if he should degrade the boy did he maintain him, even secretly, out of Mrs. Avenel's money—money intended not to raise, but keep him down in life. At the worst, it was a sum the Doctor could afford, and he had brought the boy into the world.

Having thus, as he thought, safely provided for his two young charges, Helen and Leonard, the Doctor then gave himself up to his final preparations for departure. He left a short note for Leonard with Mr. Prickett, containing some brief advice, some kind cheering ; a postscript to the effect that he had not communicated to Mrs. Avenel the information Leonard had acquired, and that it were best to leave her in that ignorance ; and six small powders to be dissolved in water, and a tea-spoonful every fourth hour—" Sovereign against rage and sombre thoughts," wrote the Doctor.

By the evening of the next day Dr. Morgan, accompanied by his pet patient with the chronic tic, whom he had talked into exile, was on the steamboat on his way to Ostend.

Leonard resumed his life at Mr. Prickett's : but the change in him did not escape the bookseller. All his ingenuous simplicity had deserted him. He was very distant and very taciturn ; he seemed to have grown much older. I shall not attempt to analyze meta-physically this change. By the help of such words as Leonard may himself occasionally let fall, the reader will dive into the boy's heart, and see how there the change had worked, and is working still. The happy dreamy peasant-genius, gazing on Glory with inebriate, undazzled eyes, is no more. It is a man, suddenly cut off from the old household holy ties—conscious of great powers, and confronted on all sides by barriers of iron—alone with hard Reality, and scornful London ; and if he catches a glimpse of the lost Helicon, he sees, where he saw the Muse, a pale melancholy spirit veiling its face in shame—the ghost of the mournful mother, whose child has no name, not even the humblest, among the family of men.

On the second evening after Dr. Morgan's departure, as Leonard

was just about to leave the shop, a customer stepped in with a book
in his hand, which he had snatched from the shop-boy, who was
removing the volumes for the night from the booth without.

"Mr. Prickett, Mr. Prickett!" said the customer, "I am ashamed
of you. You presume to put upon this work, in two volumes, the
sum of eight shillings."

Mr. Prickett stepped forth from the Cimmerian gloom of some
recess, and cried, "What! Mr. Burley, is that you? But for your
voice, I should not have known you."

"Man is like a book, Mr. Prickett; the commonalty only look
to his binding. I am better bound, it is very true."

Leonard glanced towards the speaker, who now stood under the
gas-lamp, and thought he recognized his face. He looked again.
Yes; it was the perch-fisher whom he had met on the banks of the
Brent, and who had warned him of the lost fish and the broken line.

MR. BURLEY (continuing).—"But the 'Art of Thinking!'—you
charge eight shillings for the 'Art of Thinking.'"

MR. PRICKETT.—"Cheap enough, Mr. Burley. A very clean
copy."

MR. BURLEY.—"Usurer! I sold it to you for three shillings. .
It is more than 150 per cent. you propose to gain from my 'Art of
Thinking.'"

MR. PRICKETT (stuttering and taken aback).—"*You* sold it to
me! Ah, now I remember. But it was more than three shillings
I gave. You forget—two glasses of brandy-and-water."

MR. BURLEY.—"Hospitality, sir, is not to be priced. If you
sell your hospitality, you are not worthy to possess my 'Art of
Thinking.' I resume it. There are three shillings, and a shiiling
more for interest. No; on second thoughts, instead of that shilling,
I will return your hospitality: and the first time you come my way
you shall have two glasses of brandy-and-water."

Mr. Prickett did not look pleased, but he made no objection; and
Mr. Burley put the book into his pocket, and turned to examine the
shelves. He bought an old jest-book, a stray volume of the Comedies of Destouches—paid for them—put them also into his pocket,
and was sauntering out—when he perceived Leonard, who was now
standing at the doorway.

"Hem! who is that?" he asked, whispering to Mr. Prickett.

"A young assistant of mine, and very clever."

Mr. Burley scanned Leonard from top to toe.

"We have met before, sir. But you look as if you had returned
to the Brent, and been fishing for my perch."

"Possibly, sir," answered Leonard. "But my line is tough, and is not yet broken, though the fish drags it amongst the weeds, and buries itself in the mud."

He lifted his hat, bowed slightly, and walked on.

"He *is* clever," said Mr. Burley to the bookseller: "he understands allegory."

Mr. Prickett.—"Poor youth! He came to town with the idea of turning author: you know what *that* is, Mr. Burley."

Mr. Burley (with an air of superb dignity).—"Bibliopole, yes! An author is a being between gods and men, who ought to be lodged in a palace, and entertained at the public charge upon Ortolans and Tokay. He should be kept lapped in down, and curtained with silken awnings from the cares of life—have nothing to do but to write books upon tables of cedar, and fish for perch from a gilded galley. And that's what will come to pass when the ages lose their barbarism, and know their benefactors. Meanwhile, sir, I invite you to my rooms, and will regale you upon brandy-and-water as long as I can pay for it; and when I cannot—you shall regale me."

Mr. Prickett muttered, "A very bad bargain, indeed," as Mr. Burley, with his chin in the air, stepped into the street.

CHAPTER XX.

AT first, Leonard had always returned home through the crowded thoroughfares—the contact of numbers had animated his spirits. But the last two days, since his discovery of his birth, he had taken his way down the comparatively unpeopled path of the New Road.

He had just gained that part of this outskirt in which the statuaries and tomb-makers exhibit their gloomy wares—furniture alike for gardens and for graves—and, pausing, contemplated a column, on which was placed an urn, half covered with a funeral mantle, when his shoulder was lightly tapped, and, turning quickly, he saw Mr. Burley standing behind him.

"Excuse me, sir, but you understand perch-fishing; and since we find ourselves on the same road, I should like to be better acquainted with you. I hear you once wished to be an author. I am one."

Leonard had never before, to his knowledge, seen an author and a mournful smile passed his lips as he surveyed the perch-fisher.

Mr. Burley was indeed very differently attired since the first interview by the brooklet. He looked much less like an author—but more perhaps like a perch-fisher. He had a new white hat, stuck on one side of his head—a new green overcoat—new gray trousers, and new boots. In his hand was a whalebone stick, with a silver handle. Nothing could be more vagrant, devil-me-carish, and, to use a slang word, *tigrish*, than his whole air. Yet, vulgar as was his costume, he did not himself seem vulgar, but rather eccentric—lawless—something out of the pale of convention. His face looked more pale and more puffed than before, the tip of his nose redder; but the spark in his eye was of livelier light, and there was self-enjoyment in the corners of his sensual humorous lip.

"You are an author, sir," repeated Leonard. "Well. And what is your report of the calling? Yonder column props an urn. The column is tall, and the urn is graceful. But it looks out of place by the roadside: what say you?"

MR. BURLEY.—"It would look better in the churchyard."

LEONARD.—"So I was thinking. And you are an author!"

MR. BURLEY.—"Ah, I said you had a quick sense of allegory. And so you think an author looks better in a churchyard, when you see him but as a muffled urn under the moonshine, than standing beneath the gas-lamp in a white hat, and with a red tip to his nose. Abstractedly, you are right. But, with your leave, the author would rather be where he is. Let us walk on." The two men felt an interest in each other, and they walked some yards in silence.

"To return to the urn," said Mr. Burley—"you think of fame and churchyards. Natural enough, before illusion dies; but I think of the moment, of existence—and I laugh at fame. Fame, sir—not worth a glass of cold without! And as for a glass of warm, with sugar—and five shillings in one's pocket to spend as one pleases— what is there in Westminster Abbey to compare with it?"

"Talk on, sir—I should like to hear you talk. Let me listen and hold my tongue." Leonard pulled his hat over his brows, and gave up his moody, questioning, turbulent mind to his new acquaintance.

And John Burley talked on. A dangerous and fascinating talk it was—the talk of a great intellect fallen. A serpent trailing its length on the ground, and showing bright, shifting, glorious hues, as it grovelled. A serpent, yet without the serpent's guile. If John Burley deceived and tempted, he meant it not—he crawled and glittered alike honestly. No dove could be more simple.

Laughing at fame, he yet dwelt with an eloquent enthusiasm on the joy of composition. "What do I care what men without are to say and think of the words that gush forth on my page?" cried he. "If you think of the public, of urns, and laurels, while you write, you are no genius; you are not fit to be an author. I write because

it rejoices me—because it is my nature. Written, I care no more
what becomes of it than the lark for the effect that the song has on
the peasant it wakes to the plough. The poet, like the lark, sings
'from his watch-tower in the skies.' Is this true?"

"Yes, very true!"

"What can rob us of this joy! The bookseller will not buy:
the public will not read. Let them sleep at the foot of the ladder of
the angels—we climb it all the same. And then one settles down
into such good-tempered Lucianic contempt for men. One wants so
little from them, when one knows what one's self is worth, and what
they are. They are just worth the coin one can extract from them,
in order to live. Our life—*that* is worth so much to us. And then
their joys, so vulgar to them, we can make them golden and kingly.
Do you suppose Burns drinking at the ale-house, with his boors
around him, was drinking, like them, only beer and whiskey? No,
he was drinking nectar—he was imbibing his own ambrosial thoughts
—shaking with laughter of the gods. The coarse human liquid was
just needed to unlock his spirit from the clay—take it from jerkin
and corduroys, and wrap it in the 'singing robes' that floated wide
in the skies: the beer or the whiskey needed but for that, and then
it changed at once into the drink of Hebé. But come, you have
not known this life—you have not seen it. Come, give me this
night. I have moneys about me—I will fling them abroad as liberally
as Alexander himself, when he left to his share but hope. Come!"

"Whither?"

"To my throne. On that throne last sate Edmund Kean—mighty
mime. I am his successor. We will see whether in truth these
wild sons of genius, who are cited but 'to point a moral and adorn
a tale,' were objects of compassion. Sober-suited cits to lament
over a Savage and a Morland—a Porson and a Burns!—"

"Or a Chatterton," said Leonard, gloomily.

"Chatterton was an impostor in all things; he feigned excesses
that he never knew. *He* a bacchanalian—a royster! HE!—No.
We will talk of him. Come!"

Leonard went.

<h2 style="text-align:center">CHAPTER XXI.</h2>

THE ROOM! And the smoke-reek, and the gas glare of
it!—The whitewash of the walls, and the prints thereon
of the actors in their mime-robes, and stage postures;
actors as far back as their own lost Augustan era, when
the stage was a real living influence on the manners and the age!

There was Betterton in wig and gown—as Cato, moralizing on the soul's eternity, and halting between Plato and the dagger. There was Woodward as "The Fine Gentleman," with the inimitable rake-hell air in which the heroes of Wycherly and Congreve and Farquhar live again. There was jovial Quin as Falstaff, with round buckler and "fair round belly." There was Colly Cibber in brocade—taking snuff as with "his Lord," the thumb and forefinger raised in air—and looking at you for applause. There was Macklin as Shylock, with knife in hand: and Kemble in the solemn weeds of the Dane; and Kean in the place of honour over the chimney-piece.

When we are suddenly taken from practical life, with its real workday men, and presented to the portraits of those sole heroes of a world Phantastic and Phantasmal, in the garments wherein they did "strut and fret their hour upon the stage," verily there is something in the sight that moves an inner sense within ourselves—for all of us have an inner sense of some existence, apart from the one that wears away our days: an existence, that afar from St. James's and St. Giles's, the Law Courts and Exchange, goes its way in terror or mirth, in smiles or in tears, through a vague magic land of the poets. There, see those actors—they are the men who lived it—to whom our world was the false one, to whom the Imaginary was the Actual! And did Shakspeare himself, in his life, ever hearken to such applause as thundered round the personators of his airy images? Vague children of the most transient of the arts, fleet shadows on running waters, though thrown down from the steadfast stars, were ye not happier than we who live in the Real? How strange you must feel in the great circuit that ye now take through eternity! No prompt-books, no lamps, no acting Congreve and Shakspeare there! For what parts in the skies have your studies on the earth fitted you? Your ultimate destinies are very puzzling. Hail to your effigies, and pass we on!

There, too, on the whitewashed walls, were admitted the portraits of ruder rivals in the arena of fame—yet they, too, had known an applause warmer than his age gave to Shakspeare; the Champions of the Ring—Cribb, and Molyneux, and Dutch Sam. Interspersed with these was an old print of Newmarket in the early part of the last century, and sundry engravings from Hogarth. But poets, oh! they were there too: poets who might be supposed to have been sufficiently good fellows to be at home with such companions. Shakspeare, of course, with his placid forehead; Ben Jonson, with his heavy scowl; Burns and Byron cheek by jowl. But the strangest of all these heterogeneous specimens of graphic art was a full-length print of William Pitt!—William Pitt, the austere and imperious.

What the deuce did he do there amongst prize-fighters, and actors, and poets? It seemed an insult to his grand memory. Nevertheless there he was, very erect, and with a look of ineffable disgust in his upturned nostrils. The portraits on the sordid walls were very like the crambo in the minds of ordinary men—very like the motley pictures of the FAMOUS hung up in your parlour, O my Public! Actors and prize-fighters, poets and statesmen, all without congruity and fitness, all whom you have been to see or to hear for a moment, and whose names have stared out in your newspapers, O my Public!

And the company? Indescribable! Comedians, from small theatres, out of employ; pale, haggard-looking boys, probably the sons of worthy traders, trying their best to break their fathers' hearts; here and there the marked features of a Jew. Now and then you might see the curious puzzled face of some greenhorn about town, or perhaps a Cantab; and men of grave age, and gray-haired, were there, and amongst them a wondrous proportion of carbuncled faces and bottle noses. And when John Burley entered, there was a shout that made William Pitt shake in his frame. Such stamping and hallooing, and such hurrahs for "Burly John." And the gentleman who had filled the great high leathern chair in his absence gave it up to John Burley; and Leonard, with his grave, observant eye, and lip half sad and half scornful, placed himself by the side of his introducer. There was a nameless expectant stir through the assembly, as there is in the pit of the opera when some great singer advances to the lamps, and begins, "*Di tanti palpiti.*" Time flies. Look at the Dutch clock over the door. Half-an-hour. John Burley begins to warm. A yet quicker light begins to break from his eye; his voice has a mellow luscious roll in it.

"He will be grand to-night," whispered a thin man, who looked like a tailor, seated on the other side of Leonard.

Time flies—an hour! Look again at the Dutch clock. John Burley *is* grand, he is in his zenith, at his culminating point. What magnificent drollery!—what luxuriant humour! How the Rabelais shakes in his easy chair! Under the rush and the roar of this fun, (what word else shall describe it?) the man's intellect is as clear as gold sand under a river. Such wit and such truth, and, at times, such a flood of quick eloquence. All now are listeners—silent, save in applause. And Leonard listened too. Not, as he would some nights ago, in innocent unquestioning delight. No; his mind has passed through great sorrow, great passion, and it comes out unsettled, inquiring, eager, brooding over joy itself as over a problem. And the drink circulates, and faces change; and there are gabbling and babbling; and Burley's head sinks in his bosom, and he is silent. And up starts a wild, dissolute, bacchanalian glee for seven voices. And the smoke-reek grows denser and thicker, and the gas-light looks dizzy through the haze. And John Burley's eyes reel.

Look again at the Dutch clock. Two hours have gone. John Burley has broken out again from his silence, his voice thick and husky, and his laugh cracked; and he talks, O ye Gods! such rubbish and ribaldry; and the listeners roar aloud, and think it finer than before. And Leonard, who had hitherto been measuring himself in his mind, against the giant, and saying inly, " He soars out of my reach," finds the giant shrink smaller and smaller, and saith to himself, " He is but of man's common standard after all ! "

Look again at the Dutch clock. Three hours have passed. Is John Burley now of man's common standard? Man himself seems to have vanished from the scene: his soul stolen from him, his form gone away with the fumes of the smoke, and the nauseous steam from that fiery bowl. And Leonard looked round, and saw but the swine of Circe—some on the floor, some staggering against the walls, some hugging each other on the tables, some fighting, some bawling, some weeping. The divine spark had fled from the human face; the Beast is everywhere growing more and more out of the thing that had been Man. And John Burley, still unconquered, but clean lost to his senses, fancies himself a preacher, and drawls forth the most lugubrious sermon upon the brevity of life that mortal ever heard, accompanied with unctuous sobs; and now and then, in the midst of balderdash, gleams out a gorgeous sentence, that Jeremy Taylor might have envied; drivelling away again into a cadence below the rhetoric of a Muggletonian. And the waiters choked up the doorway, listening and laughing, and prepared to call cabs and coaches; and suddenly some one turned off the gas-light, and all was dark as pitch—howls and laughter, as of the damned, ringing through the Pandemonium. Out from the black atmosphere stept the boy-poet; and the still stars rushed on his sight, as they looked over the grimy roof-tops.

CHAPTER XXII.

WELL, Leonard, this is the first time thou hast shown that thou hast in thee the iron out of which true manhood is forged and shaped. Thou hast *the power to resist*. Forth, unebriate, unpolluted, he came from the orgy, as yon star above him came from the cloud.

He had a latch-key to his lodgings. He let himself in, and walked noiselessly up the creaking, wooden stair. It was dawn. He passed on to his window and threw it open. The green elm-tree from the carpenter's yard looked as fresh and fair as if rooted in solitudes, leagues away from the smoke of Babylon.

"Nature, Nature!" murmured Leonard, "I hear thy voice now. This stills—this strengthens. But the struggle is very dread. Here, despair of life—there, faith in life. Nature thinks of neither, and lives serenely on."

By and by a bird slid softly from the heart of the tree, and dropped on the ground below out of sight. But Leonard heard its carol. It awoke its companions—wings began to glance in the air, and the clouds grew red towards the east.

Leonard sighed and left the window. On the table, near Helen's rose-tree, which he bent over wistfully, lay a letter. He had not observed it before. It was in Helen's hand. He took it to the light, and read it by the pure, healthful gleams of morn :—

"Oh my dear brother Leonard, will this find you well, and (more happy I dare not say, but) less sad than when we parted? I write kneeling, so that it seems to me as if I wrote and prayed at the same time. You may come and see me to-morrow evening, Leonard. Do come, do—we shall walk together in this pretty garden ; and there is an arbour all covered with jessamine and honeysuckle, from which we can look down on London. I have looked from it so many times—so many—trying if I can guess the roofs in our poor little street, and fancying that I do see the dear elm-tree.

"Miss Starke is very kind to me ; and I think after I have seen you, that I shall be happy here—that is, if you are happy.

"Your own grateful sister,
"HELEN.

"Ivy Lodge."

"P.S.—Any one will direct you to our house ; it lies to the left near the top of the hill, a little way down a lane that is overhung on one side with chestnut trees and lilacs. I shall be watching for you at the gate."

Leonard's brow softened, he looked again like his former self. Up from the dark sea at his heart smiled the meek face of a child, and the waves lay still as at the charm of a spirit.

CHAPTER XXIII.

"AND what is Mr. Burley, and what has he written?" asked Leonard of Mr. Prickett, when he returned to the shop.

Let us reply to that question in our own words, for we know more about Mr. Burley than Mr. Prickett does.

John Burley was the only son of a poor clergyman, in a village near Ealing, who had scraped, and saved, and pinched, to send his son to an excellent provincial school in a northern county, and thence to college. At the latter, during his first year, young Burley was remarked by the undergraduates for his thick shoes and coarse linen, and remarkable to the authorities for his assiduity and learning. The highest hopes were entertained of him by the tutors and examiners. At the beginning of the second year his high animal spirits, before kept down by study, broke out. Reading had become easy to him. He knocked off his tasks with a facile stroke, as it were. He gave up his leisure hours to Symposia by no means Socratical. He fell into an idle, hard-drinking set. He got into all kinds of scrapes. The authorities were at first kind and forbearing in their admonitions, for they respected his abilities, and still hoped he might become an honour to the university. But at last he went drunk into a formal examination, and sent in papers, after the manner of Aristophanes, containing capital jokes upon the Dons and Big-wigs themselves. The offence was the greater, and seemed the more premeditated, for being clothed in Greek. John Burley was expelled. He went home to his father's a miserable man, for, with all his follies, he had a good heart. Removed from ill example, his life for a year was blameless. He got admitted as usher into the school in which he had received instruction as a pupil. This school was in a large town. John Burley became member of a club formed among the tradesmen, and spent three evenings a-week there. His astonishing convivial and conversational powers began to declare themselves. He grew the oracle of the club; and, from being the most sober, peaceful assembly in which grave fathers of a family ever smoked a pipe or sipped a glass, it grew, under Mr. Burley's auspices, the parent of revels as frolicking and frantic as those out of which the old Greek Goat Song ever tipsily rose. This would not do. There was a great riot in the streets one night, and the next morning the usher was dismissed. Fortunately for John Burley's conscience, his father had died before this happened —died believing in the reform of his son. During his ushership Mr. Burley had scraped acquaintance with the editor of the county newspaper, and given him some capital political articles; for Burley was, like Parr and Porson, a notable politician. The editor furnished him with letters to the journalists in London, and John came to the metropolis and got employed on a very respectable newspaper. At college he had known Audley Egerton, though but slightly: that gentleman was then just rising into repute in Parliament. Burley sympathized with some question on which Audley had distinguished himself, and wrote a very good article thereon—an article so good that Egerton inquired into the authorship, found out Burley, and resolved in his own mind to provide for him whenever he himself came into office. But Burley was a man whom it was impossible to provide for. He soon lost his connection with the newspaper. First, he was so irregular that he could never be depended upon. Secondly, he had strange honest eccentric twists of thinking, that could coalesce with the thoughts of no party in the long run. An article of his, inadvertently admitted, had horrified all the proprietors, staff, and readers of the paper. It was diametrically opposite to the principles the paper advocated, and compared its pet politician to Cataline. Then John Burley shut himself up and wrote books. He wrote two or three books, very clever, but not at all to the popular taste—abstract and learned, full of whims that were *caviare* to the multitude, and larded with Greek. Nevertheless they obtained for him a little money, and among literary men some reputation. Now Audley Egerton came into power, and got him, though with great difficulty—for there were many prejudices against this scampish, harum-scarum son of the Muses—a place in a public office. He kept it about a month, and then voluntarily resigned it. "My crust of bread and liberty!" quoth John Burley, and he vanished into a garret. From that time to the present he lived—Heaven knows how! Literature is a business, like everything else; John Burley grew more and more incapable of business. "He could not do task-work," he said; he wrote when the whim seized him, or when the last penny was in his pouch, or when he was actually in the spunging house or the Fleet—migrations which occurred to him, on an average, twice a year. He could generally sell what he had actually written, but no one would engage him beforehand. Editors of Magazines and other periodicals were very glad to have his articles, on the condition that they were anonymous; and his style was not necessarily detected, for he could vary it with the facility of a practised pen. Audley Egerton continued his best supporter, for there were certain questions on which no one wrote with such force as John Burley—questions connected with the metaphysics of politics, such as law reform and economical science. And Audley Egerton was the only man John Burley put himself out of the way to serve, and for whom he would give up a drinking bout and do *task-work*; for John Burley was grateful by nature, and he felt that Egerton had really tried to befriend him. Indeed, it was true, as he had stated to Leonard by the Brent, that, even after he had resigned his desk in the London office, he had had the offer of an appointment in Jamaica, and a place in India, from the Minister. But probably there were other charms then than those exercised by the one-eyed perch that kept him to the neighbourhood of London. With all his grave faults of character and conduct, John Burley was not without the fine qualities of a large nature. He was most resolutely his own enemy, it is true, but he could hardly be said to be any one else's. Even when he criticised some more fortunate writer, he was good-humoured in his very satire : he had no bile, no envy. And as for freedom from malignant personalities, he might have been a model to all critics. I must except politics, however, for in these he could be rabid and savage. He had a passion for independence, which, though pushed to excess, was not without grandeur. No lick-platter, no parasite, no toad-eater, no literary beggar, no hunter after patronage and subscrip-tions ; even in his dealings with Audley Egerton, he insisted on naming the price for his labours. He took a price, because, as the papers required by Audley demanded much reading and detail, which was not at all to his taste, he considered himself entitled fairly to something more than the editor of the journal wherein the papers appeared was in the habit of giving. But he assessed this extra price himself, and as he would have done to a bookseller. And when in debt and in prison, though he knew a line to Egerton would have extricated him, he never wrote that line. He would depend alone on his pen—dipped it hastily in the ink, and scrawled himself free. The most debased point about him was certainly the incorrigible vice of drinking, and with it the usual concomitant of that vice—the love of low company. To be King of the Bohemians —to dazzle by his wild humour, and sometimes to exalt by his fanciful eloquence, the rude, gross natures that gathered round him —this was a royalty that repaid him for all sacrifice of solid dignity ; a foolscap crown that he would not have changed for an emperor's diadem. Indeed, to appreciate rightly the talents of John Burley, it was necessary to hear him talk on such occasions. As a writer, after all, he was now only capable of unequal desultory efforts. But as a talker, in his own wild way, he was original and matchless. And the gift of talk is one of the most dangerous gifts a man can possess for his own sake—the applause is so immediate, and gained with so little labour. Lower, and lower, and lower had sunk John Burley, not only in the opinion of all who knew his name, but in

the habitual exercise of his talents. And this seemed wilfully—
from choice. He would write for some unstamped journal of the
populace, out of the pale of the law, for pence, when he could have
got pounds from journals of high repute. He was very fond of
scribbling off penny ballads, and then standing in the street to hear
them sung. He actually once made himself the poet of an adver-
tising tailor, and enjoyed it excessively. But that did not last long,
for John Burley was a Pittite—not a Tory, he used to say, but a
Pittite. And if you had heard him talk of Pitt, you would never
have known what to make of that great statesman. He treated
him as the German commentators do Shakspeare, and invested him
with all imaginary meanings and objects, that would have turned
the grand practical man into a sybil. Well, he was a Pittite; the
tailor a fanatic for Thelwall and Cobbett. Mr. Burley wrote a
poem, wherein Britannia appeared to the tailor, complimented him
highly on the art he exhibited in adorning the persons of her sons;
and, bestowing upon him a gigantic mantle, said that he, and he
alone, might be enabled to fit it to the shoulders of living men.
The rest of the poem was occupied in Mr. Snip's unavailing attempts
to adjust this mantle to the eminent politicians of the day, when just
as he had sunk down in despair, Britannia reappeared to him, and
consoled him with the information that he had done all mortal man
could do, and that she had only desired to convince pigmies that no
human art could adjust to *their* proportions the mantle of William
Pitt. *Sic itur ad astra*—she went back to the stars, mantle and
all! Mr. Snip was exceedingly indignant at this allegorical
effusion, and with wrathful shears cut the tie between himself and
his poet.

Thus, then, the reader has, we trust, a pretty good idea of John
Burley—a specimen of his genius, not very common in any age, and
now happily almost extinct, since authors of all degrees share in the
general improvement in order, economy, and sober decorum, which
has obtained in the national manners. Mr. Prickett, though
entering into less historical detail than we have done, conveyed to
Leonard a tolerably accurate notion of the man, representing him as
a person of great powers and learning, who had thoroughly thrown
himself away.

Leonard did not, however, see how much Mr. Burley himself
was to be blamed for his waste of life; he could not conceive a man
of genius voluntarily seating himself at the lowest step in the social
ladder. He rather supposed he had been thrust down there by
Necessity.

And when Mr. Prickett, concluding, said, "Well, I should think
Burley would cure you of the desire to be an author even more than

Chatterton," the young man answered, gloomily, " Perhaps," and turned to the book-shelves.

With Mr. Prickett's consent, Leonard was released earlier than usual from his task, and a little before sunset he took his way to Highgate. He was fortunately directed to take the new road by the Regent's Park, and so on through a very green and smiling country. The walk, the freshness of the air, the songs of the birds, and, above all, when he had got half-way, the solitude of the road, served to rouse him from his stern and sombre meditations. And when he came into the lane overhung with chestnut trees, and suddenly caught sight of Helen's watchful and then brightening face, as she stood by the wicket, and under the shadow of cool murmurous boughs, the blood rushed gaily through his veins, and his heart beat loud and gratefully.

CHAPTER XXIV.

HE drew him into the garden with such true childlike joy. Now behold them seated in the arbour—a perfect bower of sweets and blossoms ; the wilderness of roof-tops and spires stretching below, broad and far ; London seen dim and silent, as in a dream.

She took his hat from his brows gently, and looked him in the face with tearful penetrating eyes.

She did not say, " You are changed." She said, " Why, why did I leave you ? " and then turned away.

" Never mind me, Helen. I am man, and rudely born—speak of yourself. This lady is kind to you, then ? "

" Does she not let me see you ? Oh ! very kind—and look here."

Helen pointed to fruits and cakes set out on the table. " A feast, brother."

And she began to press her hospitality with pretty winning ways, more playful than was usual to her, and talking very fast, and with forced, but silvery, laughter.

By degrees she stole him from his gloom and reserve ; and though he could not reveal to her the cause of his bitterest sorrow, he owned that he had suffered much. He would not have owned *that* to another living being. And then, quickly turning from this brief confession, with assurances that the worst was over, he sought to amuse her by speaking of his new acquaintance with the perch-fisher. But when he spoke of this man with a kind of reluctant admiration, mixed with compassionate yet gloomy interest, and drew a grotesque, though subdued, sketch of the wild scene in which he had been spectator, Helen grew alarmed and grave.

"Oh, brother, do not go there again—do not see more of this bad man."

"Bad!—no! Hopeless and unhappy, he has stooped to stimulants and oblivion;—but you cannot understand these things, my pretty preacher."

"Yes I do, Leonard. What is the difference between being good and bad? The good do not yield to temptations, and the bad do."

The definition was so simple and so wise that Leonard was more struck with it than he might have been by the most elaborate sermon by Parson Dale.

"I have often murmured to myself since I lost you, 'Helen was my good angel;'—say on. For my heart is dark to myself, and while you speak light seems to dawn on it."

This praise so confused Helen that she was long before she could obey the command annexed to it. But, by little and little, words came to both more frankly. And then he told her the sad tale of Chatterton, and waited, anxious to hear her comments.

"Well," he said, seeing that she remained silent, "how can *I* hope, when this mighty genius laboured and despaired? What did he want save birth and fortune, and friends, and human justice?"

"Did he pray to God?" asked Helen, drying her tears.

Again Leonard was startled. In reading the life of Chatterton, he had not much noted the scepticism, assumed or real, of the ill-fated aspirer to earthly immortality. At Helen's question, that scepticism struck him forcibly.

"Why do you ask that, Helen?"

"Because, when we pray often, we grow so very, very patient," answered the child. "Perhaps, had he been patient a few months more, all would have been won by him, as it will be by you, brother: for you pray, and you will be patient."

Leonard bowed his head in deep thought, and this time the thought was not gloomy. Then out from that awful life there glowed another passage, which before he had not heeded duly, but regarded rather as one of the darkest mysteries in the fate of Chatterton.

At the very time the despairing poet had locked himself up in his garret, to dismiss his soul from its earthly ordeal, his genius had just found its way into the light of renown. Good and learned and powerful men were preparing to serve and save him. Another year—nay, perchance another month—and he might have stood acknowledged and sublime in the foremost ranks of his age.

"Oh, Helen!" cried Leonard, raising his brows from which the cloud had passed, "why, indeed, did you leave me?"

Helen started in her turn as he repeated this regret, and in her turn grew thoughtful. At length she asked him if he had written for the box which had belonged to her father, and been left at the inn.

And Leonard, though a little chafed at what he thought a childish interruption to themes of graver interest, owned, with self-reproach, that he had forgotten to do so. Should he not write now to order the box to be sent to her at Miss Starke's.

"No; let it be sent to you. Take care of it. I should like to know that something of mine is with you; and perhaps I may not stay here long."

"Not stay here? That you must, my dear Helen—at least as long as Miss Starke will keep you, and is kind. By and by (added Leonard, with something of his former sanguine tone) I may yet make my way, and we shall have our cottage to ourselves. But— Oh Helen!—I forgot—you wounded me; you left your money with me. I only found it in my drawers the other day. Fie!—I have brought it back."

"It was not mine—it is yours. We were to share together—you paid all; and how can I want it here, too?"

But Leonard was obstinate; and as Helen mournfully received back all that of fortune her father had bequeathed to her, a tall female figure stood at the entrance of the arbour, and said, in a voice that scattered all sentiment to the winds—"Young man, it is time to go."

CHAPTER XXV.

"ALREADY," said Helen, with faltering accents, as she crept to Miss Starke's side while Leonard rose and bowed. "I am very grateful to you, madam," said he, with the grace that comes from all refinement of idea, "for allowing me to see Miss Helen. Do not let me abuse your kindness."

Miss Starke seemed struck with his look and manner, and made a stiff half-curtsey.

A form more rigid than Miss Starke's it was hard to conceive. She was like the Grim White Woman in the nursery ballads. Yet, apparently, there was a good-nature in allowing the stranger to enter her trim garden, and providing for him and her little charge those fruits and cakes, which belied her aspect. "May I go with him to the gate?" whispered Helen, as Leonard had already passed up the path.

"You may, child: but do not loiter. And then come back, and lock up the cakes and cherries, or Patty will get at them."

Helen ran after Leonard.

"Write to me, brother—write to me; and do not, do not be friends with this man, who took you to that wicked, wicked place."

"Oh, Helen, I go from you strong enough to brave worse dangers than that," said Leonard, almost gaily.

They kissed each other at the little wicket-gate, and parted.

Leonard walked home under the summer moonlight, and on entering his chamber looked first at his rose-tree. The leaves of yesterday's flowers lay strewn round it; but the tree had put forth new buds.

"Nature ever restores," said the young man. He paused a moment, and added, "Is it that Nature is very patient?"

His sleep that night was not broken by the fearful dreams he had lately known. He rose refreshed, and went his way to his day's work —not stealing along the less crowded paths, but with a firm step, through the throng of men. Be bold, adventurer—thou hast more to suffer! Wilt thou sink? I look into thy heart, and I cannot answer.

NOTE ON HOMŒOPATHY.

A gentleman who practises Homœopathy, and who rejoices in the name of Luther, has done me the honour to issue a pamphlet in grave vindication of the art of Hahnemann from what he conceives to be the assault thereon, perpetrated in "My Novel." Luther the First, though as combative as Luther the Second, did not waste his polemical vigour upon giants of his own making. It is true that, though in "My Novel" Dr. Morgan is represented as an able and warm-hearted man there is a joke at his humours—what then? Do I turn the art itself into ridicule? As well might some dignitary of the Church accuse me of satirizing his sacred profession, whenever the reader is invited to a smile at the expense of Parson Dale,—or a country gentleman take up his pen to clear the territorial class from participation in the prejudices assigned to the Squire of Hazeldean. Nay, as well might some literary allopathist address to me a homily on profaning the dignity of the College of Physicians, by the irreverent portraiture of Dr. Dosewell. "My Novel" is intended as a survey of varieties in English life, chiefly through the medium of the prevailing humours in various modifications of character. Like other enthusiasts, Dr. Morgan pushes his favourite idea into humorous extravagance—and must bear the penalty of a good-natured banter. If I were opposed altogether to Homœopathy, I should take a very different mode of dealing with it; and Dr. Morgan, instead of being represented as an experienced practitioner in allopathy, converted to the homœo-pathical theory by honest convictions, and redeeming his foibles by shrewd observation and disinterested benevolence, would be drawn as an ignorant charlatan, and a greedy impostor.

But the fact is that, if I do not think Homœopathy capable of all the wonders ascribed to it by some of its professors, or the only scientific mode of dealing with human infirmities, I sincerely believe that it is often resorted to with very great benefit—nay, I myself have frequently employed, and even advised it, I opine, with advantage. And if it had done nothing else than introduce many notable reforms in allopathical practice, it would be entitled to the profound gratitude of all, with stomachs no longer over irrigated by the apothecary, and veins no longer under-drained by the phlebotomist.

But Dr. Luther assumes that I have no authority for the crotchets ascribed to Dr. Morgan—that it is monstrous in me to assert that Homœopathy professes to have globules for the mind as well as the body, that I have evidently only read some shallow catchpenny treatises on the subject, &c., &c. Unlucky Dr. Luther! Does he profess to be a Homœopathist, and yet forget his JAHR! Will he tell me that Jahr is not the great original manual of the science—the Blackstone of Homœopathy? And what says this master text-book?—I quote therefrom not for the purpose only of justifying Dr. Morgan and myself from the charges so inconsiderately brought against us by Dr. Luther—but also for the purpose of proving to the general reader, that Dr. Morgan has full authority for prescribing CAUSTIC for tears, and AGARICUS MUSCARIUS for the propensity to indulge in verse-making. Nay, I will add that there is not a single prescription for mental disturbance suggested by Dr. Morgan for which, strange as it may seem to the uninitiated, he is not warranted literally by that work by JAHR, which is the groundwork of all homœopathical literature. Imprimis, O too oblivious Luther, does not JAHR assign a large section of his manual to Moral Affections? Open vol. iii. of the Paris Edition, in 4 vols., 1850—go on to page 236. Does not JAHR prescribe arsenic for *la Mélancolie noire*, HELLEBORE for *la Mélancolie douce;* and, with the nice distinction only known to homœopathical philosophy, GOLD for *la Mélancolie religieuse?* If it be the patient's inclination to rest silent, must he not take IGNATIA—if he have a desire to drown himself, should not the globule be PULSATILLA?

For *ill humour* (p. 246) is there no suggestion of ACONITE? If that humour is of the contemptuous character, like Dr. Luther's, is there no injunction to try IPECACUANHA? If it be "*disposition à faire des reproches, à critiquer*" (to quarrel and criticise), does not JAHR give you, Oh frowning Luther, a wide choice from BELLA DONNA to VERATRIUM? Nay, if it be in a close apartment rather than the open air that the attack seizes you—should you not ingurgitate a pin's head of platinum? JAHR, JAHR! O, Dr. Luther, would you have fallen into such a scrape, if you had consulted your JAHR?

Turn to the same volume, p. 30, on *Moral Emotions*, is there not a globule for an *Amour malheureux*—for a lover disappointed are there not HYOS: IGN: PHOS-AC? Nay, to sum up and clench the whole by the very proposition which I undertook to prove, does not JAHR, vol. iii. p. 255, recommend AGARICUS for the disposition *à faire des vers* (to make verses), and more than once or twice throughout the same volume, is not CAUSTIC the remedy, by preference, for a tendency to shed tears, provided, of course, other symptoms invite its application?

And O, Dr. Luther, do you mean to tell us that the enthusiast of an art, to which this book, by JAHR, is an acknowledged text-book, may not, whatever the skill of the man or the excellence of the art, or the value of the text-book, incur every one of the extravagances imputed to Dr. Morgan, or not freely lay himself open to the gall-less pleasantries of a writer in search of the Humorous?

Dr. Morgan is represented as one of the earliest disciples of Hahnemann in this country, and therefore likely, in the zeal of a Tyro, and the passion of a convert, *aprum consumere totum*—which Horatian elegancy our vernacular has debased into the familiar vulgarism, "Go the whole hog." But even in the present day, I assure Dr. Luther, and my readers generally, that I have met, abroad, Homœopathic physicians of considerable eminence, who have seriously contended for the application of globules to the varieties of mental affliction and human vicissitude; who have solemnly declared, that, while the rest of the family have been plunged into despair at the death of its head—one of the bereaved children resorting to Homœopathy has been preserved from the depressing consequences of grief, and been as cheerful as usual; that a lover who meditated suicide at the perfidy of his beloved, has in ten days been homœopathically reduced into felicitous indifference—and that there are secrets in the science professed by Dr. Luther, that cannot be too earnestly urged on his own attention—by which an irritable man may be taught to control his temper, and a dull man to comprehend a joke.

BOOK SEVENTH.

INITIAL CHAPTER.

MR. CAXTON UPON COURAGE AND PATIENCE.

"WHAT is courage?" said my Uncle Roland, rousing himself from a reverie into which he had fallen, after the sixth book in this history had been read to our family circle.

"What is courage?" he repeated more earnestly. "Is it insensibility to fear? *That* may be the mere accident of constitution; and, if so, there is no more merit in being courageous than in being this table."

"I am very glad to hear you speak thus," observed Mr. Caxton, "for I should not like to consider myself a coward; yet I am very sensible to fear in all dangers, bodily and moral."

"La, Austin, how can you say so?" cried my mother, firing up; "was it not only last week that you faced the great bull that was rushing after Blanche and the children?"

Blanche at that recollection stole to my father's chair, and, hanging over his shoulder, kissed his forehead.

MR. CAXTON (sublimely unmoved by these flatteries). — "I don't deny that I faced the bull, but I assert that I was horribly frightened."

ROLAND. — "The sense of honour which conquers fear is the true courage of chivalry: you could not run away when others were looking on—no gentleman could."

MR. CAXTON. — "Fiddledee! It was not on my gentility that I stood, Captain. I should have run fast enough, if it had done any good. I stood upon my understanding. As the bull could run faster than I could, the only chance of escape was to make the brute as frightened as myself."

BLANCHE. — "Ah, you did not think of that; your only thought was to save me and the children."

MR. CAXTON. — "Possibly, my dear—very possibly I might have been afraid for you too;—but I was very much afraid for myself. However, luckily, I had the umbrella, and I sprang it up and spread it forth in the animal's stupid eyes, hurling at him simultaneously the biggest lines I could think of in the First Chorus of the 'Seven against Thebes.' I began with ELEDEMNAS PEDIOPLOKTUPOS; and when I came to the grand howl of 'Ιὼ, ἰὼ, ἰὼ, ἰὼ,—the beast stood appalled as at the roar of a lion. I shall never forget his amazed snort at the Greek. Then he kicked up his hind legs, and went bolt through the gap in the hedge. Thus, armed with Æschylus and the umbrella, I remained master of the field; but, (continued Mr. Caxton, ingenuously,) I should not like to go through that half-minute again."

"No man would," said the Captain, kindly. "I should be sorry to face a bull myself, even with a bigger umbrella than yours, and even though I had Æschylus, and Homer to boot, at my fingers' ends."

MR. CAXTON.—"You would not have minded if it had been a Frenchman with a sword in his hand?"

CAPTAIN.—"Of course not. Rather liked it than otherwise," he added, grimly.

MR. CAXTON.—"Yet many a Spanish matador, who doesn't care a button for a bull, would take to his heels at the first lunge *en carte* from a Frenchman. Therefore, in fact, if courage be a matter of constitution, it is also a matter of custom. We face calmly the dangers we are habituated to, and recoil from those of which we have no familiar experience. I doubt if Marshal Turenne himself would have been quite at his ease on the tight-rope; and a rope-dancer, who seems disposed to scale the heavens with Titanic temerity, might possibly object to charge on a canon."

CAPTAIN ROLAND.—"Still, either this is not the courage I mean, or it is another kind of it. I mean by courage that which is the especial force and dignity of the human character, without which there is no reliance on principle, no constancy in virtue—a something," continued my uncle gallantly, and with a half bow towards my mother, "which your sex shares with our own. When the lover, for instance, clasps the hand of his betrothed, and says, ' Wilt thou be true to me, in spite of absence and time, in spite of hazard and fortune, though my foes malign me, though thy friends may dissuade thee, and our lot in life may be rough and rude?' and when the betrothed answers, 'I will be true,' does not the lover trust to her courage as well as her love?"

"Admirably put, Roland," said my father. "But *à propos* of what do you puzzle us with these queries on courage?"

CAPTAIN ROLAND (with a slight blush).—"I was led to the inquiry (though, perhaps, it may be frivolous to take so much thought of what, no doubt, costs Pisistratus so little) by the last chapters in my nephew's story. I see this poor boy Leonard, alone with his fallen hopes, (though very irrational they were,) and his sense of shame. And I read his heart, I dare say, better than Pisistratus does, for I could feel like that boy if I had been in the same position ; and conjecturing what he and thousands like him must go through, I asked myself, 'What can save him and them?' I answered, as a soldier would answer, 'Courage?' Very well. But pray, Austin, what is courage?"

MR. CAXTON (prudently backing out of a reply).—"*Papæ!* Brother, since you have just complimented the ladies on that quality, you had better address your question to them."

Blanche here leant both hands on my father's chair, and said, looking down at first bashfully, but afterwards warming with the subject, "Do you not think, sir, that little Helen has already suggested, if not what is courage, what at least is the real essence of all courage that endures and conquers, that ennobles, and hallows, and redeems? Is it not PATIENCE, father?—and that is why we women have a courage of our own. Patience does not affect to be superior to fear, but at least it never admits despair."

PISISTRATUS.—"Kiss me, my Blanche, for you have come near to the truth which perplexed the soldier and puzzled the sage."

MR. CAXTON (tartly).—"If you mean me by the sage, I was not puzzled at all. Heaven knows you do right to inculcate patience —it is a virtue very much required in your readers. Nevertheless," added my father, softening with the enjoyment of his joke— "nevertheless, Blanche and Helen are quite right. Patience is the courage of the conqueror ; it is the virtue, *par excellence*, of Man against Destiny—of the One against the World, and of the Soul against Matter. Therefore this is the courage of the Gospel ; and its importance, in a social view—its importance to races and institutions—cannot be too earnestly inculcated. What is it that distinguishes the Anglo-Saxon from all other branches of the human family, peoples deserts with his children, and consigns to them the heritage of rising worlds ? What but his faculty to brave, to suffer, to endure—the patience that resists firmly, and innovates slowly. Compare him with the Frenchman. The Frenchman has plenty of valour—that there is no denying ; but as for fortitude, he has not enough to cover the point of a pin. He is ready to rush out of the world if he is bitten by a flea."

CAPTAIN ROLAND.—"There was a case in the papers the other day, Austin, of a Frenchman who actually did destroy himself because he was so teased by the little creatures you speak of. He left a paper on his table, saying that 'life was not worth having at the price of such torments.'"[1]

MR. CAXTON (solemnly).—"Sir, their whole political history, since the great meeting of the Tiers Etat, has been the history of men who would rather go to the devil than be bitten by a flea. It is the record of human impatience, that seeks to force time, and expects to grow forests from the spawn of a mushroom. Wherefore, running through all extremes of constitutional experiment, when they are nearest to democracy they are next door to a despot; and all they have really done is to destroy whatever constitutes the foundation of every tolerable government. A constitutional monarchy cannot exist without aristocracy, nor a healthful republic endure with corruption of manners. The cry of Equality is incompatible with civilization, which, of necessity, contrasts poverty with wealth —and, in short, whether it be an emperor or a mob[2] that is to rule, Force is the sole hope of order, and the government is but an army.

"Impress, O Pisistratus! impress the value of patience as regards man and men. You touch there on the kernel of the social system —the secret that fortifies the individual and disciplines the million. I care not, for my part, if you are tedious so long as you are earnest. Be minute and detailed. Let the real Human Life, in its war with Circumstance, stand out. Never mind if one can read you but slowly—better chance of being less quickly forgotten. Patience, patience! By the soul of Epictetus, your readers shall set you an example!"

CHAPTER II.

EONARD had written twice to Mrs. Fairfield, twice to Riccabocca, and once to Mr. Dale; and the poor proud boy could not bear to betray his humiliation. He wrote as with cheerful spirits—as if perfectly satisfied with his prospects. He said that he was well employed, in the midst of books, and that he had found kind friends. Then he turned from

[1] Fact. In a work by M. GIBERT, a celebrated French physician, on diseases of the skin, he states that that minute troublesome kind of rash, known by the name of *prurigo*, though not dangerous in itself, has often driven the individual afflicted by it to—suicide. I believe that our more varying climate, and our more heating drinks and aliments, render this skin complaint more common in England than in France, yet I doubt if any English physician could state that it had ever driven one of his *English* patients to suicide.

[2] Published more-than a year before the date of the French empire under Louis Napoleon.

himself to write about those whom he addressed, and the affairs and interests of the quiet world wherein they lived. He did not give his own address, nor that of Mr. Prickett. He dated his letters from a small coffee-house near the bookseller's, to which he occasionally went for his simple meals. He had a motive in this. He did not desire to be found out. Mr. Dale replied for himself and for Mrs. Fairfield, to the epistles addressed to these two. Riccabocca wrote also. Nothing could be more kind than the replies of both. They came to Leonard in a very dark period in his life, and they strengthened him in the noiseless battle with despair.

If there be a good in the world that we do without knowing it, without conjecturing the effect it may have upon a human soul, it is when we show kindness to the young in the first barren footpath up the mountain of life.

Leonard's face resumed its serenity in his intercourse with his employer; but he did not recover his boyish ingenuous frankness. The under-currents flowed again pure from the turbid soil and the splintered fragments uptorn from the deep; but they were still too strong and too rapid to allow transparency to the surface. And now he stood in the sublime world of books, still and earnest as a seer who invokes the dead. And thus, face to face with knowledge, hourly he discovered how little he knew. Mr. Prickett lent him such works as he selected and asked to take home with him. He spent whole nights in reading, and no longer desultorily. He read no more poetry, no more Lives of Poets. He read what poets must read if they desire to be great—*Sapere principium et fons*—strict reasonings on the human mind: the relations between motive and conduct, thought and action; the grave and solemn truths of the past world; antiquities, history, philosophy. He was taken out of himself. He was carried along the ocean of the universe. In that ocean, O seeker, study the law of the tides; and seeing Chance nowhere—Thought presiding over all,—Fate, that dread phantom, shall vanish from creation, and Providence alone be visible in heaven and on earth!

CHAPTER III.

THERE was to be a considerable book-sale at a country house one day's journey from London. Mr. Prickett meant to have attended it on his own behalf, and that of several gentlemen who had given him commissions for purchase; but, on the morning fixed for his departure, he was seized with a severe return of his old foe, the rheumatism. He requested Leonard to attend instead of himself. Leonard went, and was absent for the three days during which the sale lasted. He returned late in the evening, and went at once to Mr. Prickett's house. The shop was closed ; he knocked at the private entrance ; a strange person opened the door to him, and, in reply to his question if Mr. Prickett was at home, said, with a long and funereal face—"Young man, Mr. Prickett senior is gone to his long home, but Mr. Richard Prickett will see you."

At this moment a very grave-looking man, with lank hair, looked forth from the side-door communicating between the shop and the passage, and then stepped forward—"Come in, sir ; you are my late uncle's assistant, Mr. Fairfield, I suppose ?"

"Your late uncle ! Heavens, sir, do I understand aright—can Mr. Prickett be dead since I left London ?"

"Died, sir, suddenly, last night. It was an affection of the heart. The Doctor thinks the rheumatism attacked that organ. He had small time to provide for his departure, and his account-books seem in sad disorder : I am his nephew and executor."

Leonard had now followed the nephew into the shop. There, still burned the gas-lamp. The place seemed more dingy and cavernous than before. Death always makes its presence felt in the house it visits.

Leonard was greatly affected—and yet more, perhaps, by the utter want of feeling which the nephew exhibited. In fact, the deceased had not been on friendly terms with this person, his nearest relative and heir-at-law, who was also a bookseller.

"You were engaged but by the week, I find, young man, on reference to my late uncle's papers. He gave you £1 a-week—a monstrous sum ! I shall not require your services any further. I shall move these books to my own house. You will be good enough to send me a list of those you bought at the sale, and your account of travelling expenses, &c. What may be due to you shall be sent to your address. Good evening."

Leonard went home, shocked and saddened at the sudden death of his kind employer. He did not think much of himself that night ; but, when he rose the next day, he suddenly felt that the world of London lay before him, without a friend, without a calling, without an occupation for bread.

This time it was no fancied sorrow, no poetic dream disappointed. Before him, gaunt and palpable, stood Famine.

Escape !—yes. Back to the village : his mother's cottage ; the exile's garden ; the radishes and the fount. Why could he not escape? Ask why civilization cannot escape its ills, and fly back to the wild and the wigwam.

Leonard could not have returned to the cottage, even if the Famine that faced had already seized him with her skeleton hand. London releases not so readily her fated step-sons.

CHAPTER IV.

ONE day three persons were standing before an old book-stall in a passage leading from Oxford Street into Tottenham Court Road. Two were gentlemen; the third, of the class and appearance of those who more habitually halt at old book-stalls.

"Look," said one of the gentlemen to the other, "I have discovered here what I have searched for in vain the last ten years—the Horace of 1580, the Horace of the Forty Commentators—a perfect treasury of learning, and marked only fourteen shillings!"

"Hush, Norreys," said the other, "and observe what is yet more worth your study;" and he pointed to the third bystander, whose face, sharp and attenuated, was bent with an absorbed, and, as it were, with a hungering attention over an old worm-eaten volume.

"What is the book, my lord?" whispered Mr. Norreys.

His companion smiled, and replied by another question, "What is the man who reads the book?"

Mr. Norreys moved a few paces, and looked over the student's shoulder. "Preston's translation of BOETHIUS *The Consolations of Philosophy*," he said, coming back to his friend.

"He looks as if he wanted all the consolations Philosophy can give him, poor boy."

At this moment a fourth passenger paused at the book-stall, and, recognizing the pale student, placed his hand on his shoulder, and said, "Aha, young sir, we meet again. So poor Prickett is dead. But you are still haunted by associations. Books—books—magnets to which all iron minds move insensibly. What is this? BOETHIUS! Ah, a book written in prison, but a little time before the advent of the only philosopher who solves to the simplest understanding every mystery of life—"

"And that philosopher?"

"Is death!" said Mr. Burley. "How can you be dull enough to ask? Poor Boethius, rich, nobly born, a consul, his sons consuls —the world one smile to the Last Philosopher of Rome. Then suddenly, against this type of the old world's departing WISDOM, stands frowning the new world's grim genius, FORCE—Theodoric the Ostrogoth condemning Boethius the Schoolman ; and Boethius, in his Pavian dungeon, holding a dialogue with the shade of Athenian Philosophy. It is the finest picture upon which lingers the glimmering of the Western golden day, before night rushes over time."

"And," said Mr. Norreys, abruptly, "Boethius comes back to us with the faint gleam of returning light, translated by Alfred the Great. And, again, as the sun of knowledge bursts forth in all its splendour, by Queen Elizabeth. Boethius influences us as we stand in this passage ; and that is the best of all the Consolations of Philosophy—eh, Mr. Burley?"

Mr. Burley turned and bowed.

The two men looked at each other ; you could not see a greater contrast. Mr. Burley, his gay green dress already shabby and soiled, with a rent in the skirts, and his face speaking of habitual night-cups. Mr. Norreys, neat and somewhat precise in dress, with firm lean figure, and quiet, collected, vigorous energy in his eye and aspect.

"If," replied Mr. Burley, "a poor devil like me may argue with a gentleman who may command his own price with the booksellers, I should say it is no consolation at all, Mr. Norreys. And I should like to see any man of sense accept the condition of Boethius in his prison, with some strangler or headsman waiting behind the door, upon the promised proviso that he should be translated, centuries afterwards, by Kings and Queens, and help indirectly to influence the minds of Northern barbarians, babbling about him in an alley, jostled by passers-by who never heard the name of Boethius, and who don't care a fig for philosophy. Your servant, sir—young man, come and talk."

Burley hooked his arm within Leonard's, and led the boy passively away.

"That is a clever man," said Harley L'Estrange. "But I am sorry to see yon young student, with his bright earnest eyes, and his lip that has the quiver of passion and enthusiasm, leaning on the arm of a guide who seems disenchanted of all that gives purpose to learning, and links philosophy with use to the world. Who, and what is this clever man whom you call Burley?"

"A man who might have been famous, if he had condescended to be respectable! The boy listening to us both so attentively interested *me* too—I should like to have the making of him. But I must buy this Horace."

The shopman, lurking within his hole like a spider for flies, was now called out. And when Mr. Norreys had bought the Horace, and given an address where to send it, Harley asked the shopman if he knew the young man who had been reading Boethius.

"Only by sight. He has come here every day the last week, and spends hours at the stall. When once he fastens on a book, he reads it through."

"And never buys?" said Mr. Norreys.

"Sir," said the shopman, with a good-natured smile, "they who buy seldom read. The poor boy pays me twopence a-day to read as long as he pleases. I would not take it, but he is proud."

"I have known men amass great learning in that way," said Mr. Norreys. "Yes, I should like to have that boy in my hands. And now, my lord, I am at your service, and we will go to the studio of your artist."

The two gentlemen walked on towards one of the streets out of Fitzroy Square.

In a few minutes more Harley L'Estrange was in his element, seated carelessly on a deal table, smoking his cigar, and discussing art with the gusto of a man who honestly loved, and the taste of a man who thoroughly understood it. The young artist, in his dressing-robe, adding slow touch upon touch, paused often to listen the better. And Henry Norreys, enjoying the brief respite from a life of great labour, was gladly reminded of idle hours under rosy skies ; for these three men had formed their friendship in Italy, where the bands of friendship are woven by the hands of the Graces.

CHAPTER V.

LEONARD and Mr. Burley walked on into the suburbs round the north road from London, and Mr. Burley offered to find literary employment for Leonard—an offer eagerly accepted.

Then they went into a public-house by the way-side. Burley demanded a private room, called for pen, ink, and paper ; and placing these implements before Leonard, said, "Write what you please in prose, five sheets of letter-paper, twenty-two lines to a page —neither more nor less."

"I cannot write so."

"Tut, 'tis for bread."

The boy's face crimsoned.

" I must forget that," said he.

" There is an arbour in the garden, under a weeping ash," returned Burley. " Go there, and fancy yourself in Arcadia."

Leonard was too pleased to obey. He found out the little arbour at one end of a deserted bowling-green. All was still—the hedgerow shut out the sight of the inn. The sun lay warm on the grass, and glinted pleasantly through the leaves of the ash. And Leonard there wrote the first essay from his hand as Author by profession. What was it that he wrote? His dreamy impressions of London? an anathema on its streets, and its hearts of stone? murmurs against poverty? dark elegies on fate?

Oh no! little knowest thou true genius, if thou askest such questions, or thinkest that there, under the weeping ash, the taskwork for bread was remembered; or that the sunbeam glinted but over the practical world, which, vulgar and sordid, lay around. Leonard wrote a fairy tale—one of the loveliest you can conceive, with a delicate touch of playful humour—in a style all flowered over with happy fancies. He smiled as he wrote the last word—he was happy. In rather more than an hour Mr. Burley came to him, and found him with that smile on his lips.

Mr. Burley had a glass of brandy-and-water in his hand; it was his third. He too smiled—he too looked happy. He read the paper aloud and well. He was very complimentary. "You will do!" said he, clapping Leonard on the back. " Perhaps some day you will catch my one-eyed perch." Then he folded up the MS., scribbled off a note, put the whole in one envelope—and they returned to London.

Mr. Burley disappeared within a dingy office near Fleet Street, on which was inscribed—" Office of the *Beehive*," and soon came forth with a golden sovereign in his hand—Leonard's first-fruits. Leonard thought Peru lay before him. He accompanied Mr. Burley to that gentleman's lodging in Maida Hill. The walk had been very long; Leonard was not fatigued. He listened with a livelier attention than before to Burley's talk. And when they reached the apartments of the latter, and Mr. Burley sent to the cookshop, and their joint supper was taken out of the golden sovereign, Leonard felt proud, and for the first time for weeks he laughed the heart's laugh. The two writers grew more and more intimate and cordial. And there was a vast deal in Burley by which any young man might be made the wiser. There was no apparent evidence of poverty in the apartments—clean, new, well-furnished; but all things in the most horrible litter—all speaking of the huge literary sloven.

For several days Leonard almost lived in those rooms. He wrote continuously—save when Burley's conversation fascinated him into idleness. Nay, it was not idleness—his knowledge grew larger as he listened ; but the cynicism of the talker began slowly to work its way. That cynicism in which there was no faith, no hope, no vivifying breath from Glory—from Religion. The cynicism of the Epicurean, more degraded in his stye than ever was Diogenes in his tub ; and yet presented with such ease and such eloquence—with such art and such mirth—so adorned with illustration and anecdote, so unconscious of debasement !

Strange and dread philosophy—that made it a maxim to squander the gifts of mind on the mere care for matter, and fit the soul to live but as from day to day, with its scornful cry, "A fig for immortality and laurels !" An author for bread ! Oh, miserable calling ! was there something grand and holy, after all, even in Chatterton's despair !

CHAPTER VI.

THE villainous *Beehive!* Bread was worked out of it, certainly ; but fame, but hope for the future—certainly not. Milton's *Paradise Lost* would have perished without a sound had it appeared in the *Beehive.*

Fine things were there in a fragmentary crude state, composed by Burley himself. At the end of a week they were dead and forgotten —never read by one man of education and taste ; taken simultaneously and indifferently with shallow politics and wretched essays, yet selling, perhaps, twenty or thirty thousand copies—an immense sale ;—and nothing got out of them but bread and brandy !

"What more would you have ?" cried John Burley. "Did not stern old Sam Johnson say he could never write but from want ?"

"He might say it," answered Leonard ; "but he never meant posterity to believe him. And he would have died of want, I suspect, rather than have written *Rasselas* for the *Beehive!* Want is a grand thing," continued the boy, thoughtfully. "A parent of grand things. Necessity is strong, and should give us its own strength ; but Want should shatter asunder, with its very writhings, the walls of our prison-house, and not sit contented with the allowance the jail gives us in exchange for our work."

"There is no prison-house to a man who calls upon Bacchus— stay—I will translate to you Schiller's Dithyramb. 'Then see I Bacchus—then up come Cupid and Phœbus, and all the Celestials are filling my dwelling.'"

Breaking into impromptu careless rhymes, Burley threw off a rude, but spirited translation of that divine lyric.

"O materialist!" cried the boy, with his bright eyes suffused. "Schiller calls on the gods to take him to their heaven with him; and you would debase the gods to a gin palace."

"Ho, ho!" cried Burley, with his giant laugh. "Drink, and you will understand the Dithyramb."

CHAPTER VII.

SUDDENLY one morning, as Leonard sate with Burley, a fashionable cabriolet, with a very handsome horse, stopped at the door—a loud knock—a quick step on the stairs, and Randal Leslie entered. Leonard recognized him and started. Randal glanced at him in surprise, and then, with a tact that showed he had already learned to profit by London life, after shaking hands with Burley, approached, and said, with some successful attempt at ease, "Unless I am not mistaken, sir, we have met before. If you remember me, I hope all boyish quarrels are forgotten?"

Leonard bowed, and his heart was still good enough to be softened.

"Where could you two ever have met?" asked Burley.

"In a village green, and in single combat," answered Randal, smiling; and he told the story of the Battle of the Stocks, with a well-bred jest on himself. Burley laughed at the story. "But," said he, when this laugh was over, "my young friend had better have remained guardian of the village stocks, than come to London in search of such fortune as lies at the bottom of an ink-horn."

"Ah," said Randal, with the secret contempt which men elaborately cultivated are apt to feel for those who seek to educate themselves—"ah, you make literature your calling, sir? At what school did you conceive a taste for letters—not very common at our great public schools."

"I am at school now for the first time," answered Leonard, dryly.

"Experience is the best school-mistress," said Burley; "and that was the maxim of Goethe, who had book-learning enough, in all conscience."

Randal slightly shrugged his shoulders, and, without wasting another thought on Leonard, peasant-born and self-taught, took his seat, and began to talk to Burley upon a political question, which made then the war-cry between the two great Parliamentary parties.

It was a subject in which Burley showed much general knowledge ;
and Randal, seeming to differ from him, drew forth alike his information and his argumentative powers.   The conversation lasted more
than an hour.

"I can't quite agree with you," said Randal, taking his leave ;
"but you must allow me to call again—will the same hour to-morrow
suit you ?"

"Yes," said Burley.

Away went the young man in his cabriolet.   Leonard watched
him from the window.

For five days, consecutively, did Randal call and discuss the
question in all its bearings ; and Burley, after the second day, got
interested in the matter, looked up his authorities—refreshed his
memory—and even spent an hour or two in the Library of the British
Museum.

By the fifth day, Burley had really exhausted all that could well
be said on his side of the question.

Leonard, during these colloquies, had sate apart seemingly absorbed
in reading, and secretly stung by Randal's disregard of his presence.
For indeed that young man, in his superb self-esteem, and in the
absorption of his ambitious projects, scarce felt even curiosity as to
Leonard's rise above his earlier station, and looked on him as a mere
journeyman of Burley's.   But the self-taught are keen and quick
observers.   And Leonard had remarked that Randal seemed more
as one playing a part for some private purpose, than arguing in
earnest ; and that, when he rose and said, "Mr. Burley, you have
convinced me," it was not with the modesty of a sincere reasoner,
but the triumph of one who has gained his end.   But so struck,
meanwhile, was our unheeded and silent listener, with Burley's power
of generalization, and the wide surface over which his information
extended, that when Randal left the room the boy looked at the
slovenly purposeless man, and said aloud—"True ; knowledge is
not power."

"Certainly not," said Burley, dryly—"the weakest thing in the
world."

"Knowledge is power," muttered Randal Leslie, as, with a smile
on his lip, he drove from the door.

Not many days after this last interview there appeared a short
pamphlet ; anonymous, but one which made a great impression on
the town.   It was on the subject discussed between Randal and
Burley.   It was quoted at great length in the newspapers.   And
Burley started to his feet one morning, and exclaimed, "My own
thoughts !—my very words !   Who the devil is this pamphleteer ?"

Leonard took the newspaper from Burley's hand. The most flattering encomiums preceded the extracts, and the extracts were as stereotypes of Burley's talk.

"Can you doubt the author?" cried Leonard, in deep disgust and ingenuous scorn. "The young man who came to steal your brains, and turn your knowledge—"

"Into power," interrupted Burley, with a laugh, but it was a laugh of pain. "Well, this was very mean; I shall tell him so when he comes."

"He will come no more," said Leonard. Nor did Randal come again. But he sent Mr. Burley a copy of the pamphlet with a polite note, saying, with candid but careless acknowledgment, that "he had profited much by Mr. Burley's hints and remarks."

And now it was in all the papers, that the pamphlet which had made so great a noise was by a very young man, Mr. Audley Egerton's relation. And high hopes were expressed of the future career of Mr. Randal Leslie.

Burley still attempted to laugh, and still his pain was visible. Leonard most cordially despised and hated Randal Leslie, and his heart moved to Burley with noble but perilous compassion. In his desire to soothe and comfort the man whom he deemed cheated out of fame, he forgot the caution he had hitherto imposed on himself, and yielded more and more to the charm of that wasted intellect. He accompanied Burley now to the haunts to which his friend went to spend his evenings; and more and more—though gradually, and with many a recoil and self-rebuke—there crept over him the cynic's contempt for glory, and miserable philosophy of debased content.

Randal had risen into grave repute upon the strength of Burley's knowledge. But, had Burley written the pamphlet, would the same repute have *attended him?* Certainly not. Randal Leslie brought to that knowledge qualities all his own—a style, simple, strong, and logical; a certain tone of good society, and allusions to men and to parties that showed his connection with a cabinet minister, and proved that he had profited no less by Egerton's talk than Burley's.

Had Burley written the pamphlet, it would have showed more genius, it would have had humour and wit, but have been so full of whims and quips, sins against taste, and defects in earnestness, that it would have failed to create any serious sensation. Here, then, there was something else besides knowledge, by which knowledge became power. Knowledge must not smell of the brandy bottle.

Randal Leslie might be mean in his plagiarism, but he turned the useless into use. And so far he was original.

But one's admiration, after all, rests where Leonard's rested—with the poor, riotous, lawless, big, fallen man.

Burley took himself off to the Brent, and fished again for the one-eyed perch. Leonard accompanied him. His feelings were indeed different from what they had been when he had reclined under the old tree, and talked with Helen of the future. But it was almost pathetic to see how Burley's nature seemed to alter, as he strayed along the banks of the rivulet, and discoursed of his own boyhood. The man then seemed restored to something of the innocence of the child. He cared, in truth, little for the perch, which continued intractable, but he enjoyed the air and the sky, the rustling grass and the murmuring waters. These excursions to the haunts of youth seemed to rebaptize him, and then his eloquence took a pastoral character, and Isaak Walton himself would have loved to hear him. But as he got back into the smoke of the metropolis, and the gas-lamps made him forget the ruddy sunset, and the soft evening star, the gross habits reassumed their sway ; and on he went with his swaggering reckless step to the orgies in which his abused intellect flamed forth, and then sank into the socket quenched and rayless.

CHAPTER VIII.

HELEN was seized with profound and anxious sadness. Leonard had been three or four times to see her, and each time she saw a change in him that excited all her fears. He seemed, it is true, more shrewd, more worldly-wise, more fitted, it might be, for coarse daily life : but, on the other hand, the freshness and glory of his youth were waning slowly. His aspirings drooped earthward. He had not mastered the Practical, and moulded its uses with the strong hand of the Spiritual Architect, of the Ideal Builder ; the Practical was overpowering himself. She grew pale when he talked of Burley, and shuddered, poor little Helen ! when she found he was daily and almost nightly in a companionship which, with her native honest prudence, she saw so unsuited to strengthen him in his struggles, and aid him against temptation. She almost groaned when, pressing him as to his pecuniary means, she found his old terror of debt seemed fading away, and the solid healthful principles he had taken from his village were loosening fast. Under all, it is true, there was what a wiser and older person than Helen would have hailed as the redeeming promise. But that something was *grief*—a sublime grief in his own sense of falling—in his own impotence against the Fate he had pro-voked and coveted. The sublimity of that grief Helen could not detect ; she saw only that it *was* grief, and she grieved with it, letting it excuse every fault—making her more anxious to comfort, in order that she might save. Even, from the first, when Leonard had exclaimed, "Ah, Helen, why did you ever leave me?" she had revolved the idea of return to him ; and when in the boy's last visit he told her that Burley, persecuted by duns, was about to fly from his present lodgings, and take his abode with Leonard in the room she had left vacant, all doubt was over. She resolved to sacrifice the safety and shelter of the home assured her. She resolved to come back and share Leonard's penury and struggles, and save the old room, wherein she had prayed for him, from the tempter's dangerous presence. Should she burden him? No ; she had assisted her father by many little female arts in needle and fancy work. She had improved herself in these during her sojourn with Miss Starke. She could bring her share to the common stock. Possessed with this idea, she determined to realize it before the day on which Leonard had told her Burley was to move his quarters. Accordingly she rose very early one morning ; she wrote a pretty and grateful note to Miss Starke, who was fast asleep, left it on the table, and, before any one was astir, stole from the house, her little bundle on her arm. She lingered an instant at the garden-gate, with a re-morseful sentiment—a feeling that she had ill-repaid the cold and prim protection that Miss Starke had shown her. But sisterly love carried all before it. She closed the gate with a sigh, and went on.

She arrived at the lodging-house before Leonard was up, took possession of her old chamber, and presenting herself to Leonard, as he was about to go forth, said, (story-teller that she was,)—"I am sent away, brother, and I have come to you to take care of me. Do not let us part again. But you must be very cheerful and very happy, or I shall think that I am sadly in your way."

Leonard at first did look cheerful, and even happy ; but then he thought of Burley, and then of his own means of supporting Helen, and was embarrassed, and began questioning her as to the possibility of reconciliation with Miss Starke. And Helen said gravely, " Impossible—do not ask it, and do not go near her."

Then Leonard thought she had been humbled and insulted, and remembered that she was a gentleman's child, and felt for her wounded pride—he was so proud himself. Yet still he was embarrassed.

"Shall I keep the purse again, Leonard?" said Helen, coaxingly.

"Alas!" replied Leonard, "the purse is empty."

"That is very naughty in the purse," said Helen, "since you put so much into it."

"I?"

"Did not you say that you made, at least, a guinea a-week?"

"Yes; but Burley takes the money; and then, poor fellow! as I owe all to him, I have not the heart to prevent him spending it as he likes."

"Please, I wish you could settle the month's rent," said the landlady, suddenly showing herself. She said it civilly, but with firmness.

Leonard coloured. "It shall be paid to-day."

Then he pressed his hat on his head, and, putting Helen gently aside, went forth.

"Speak to *me* in future, kind Mrs. Smedley," said Helen, with the air of a housewife. "*He* is always in study, and must not be disturbed."

The landlady—a good woman, though she liked her rent—smiled benignly. She was fond of Helen, whom she had known of old.

"I am so glad you are come back; and perhaps now the young man will not keep such late hours. I meant to give him warning, but—"

"But he will be a great man one of these days, and you must bear with him now." And Helen kissed Mrs. Smedley, and sent her away half inclined to cry.

Then Helen busied herself in the rooms. She found her father's box, which had been duly forwarded. She re-examined its contents, and wept as she touched each humble and pious relic. But her father's memory itself thus seemed to give this home a sanction which the former had not; and she rose quietly and began mechanically to put things in order, sighing as she saw all so neglected, till she came to the rose-tree, and that alone showed heed and care. "Dear Leonard!" she murmured, and the smile resettled on her lips.

CHAPTER IX.

NOTHING, perhaps, could have severed Leonard from Burley but Helen's return to his care. It was impossible for him, even had there been another room in the house vacant, (which there was not,) to install this noisy riotous son of the Muse by Bacchus, talking at random, and smelling of spirits, in the same dwelling with an innocent, delicate, timid, female child. And Leonard could not leave her alone all the twenty-four hours. She restored a home to him and imposed its duties. He therefore told Mr. Burley that in future he should write and study in his own room, and hinted, with many a blush, and as delicately as he could, that it seemed to him that whatever he obtained from his pen ought to be halved with Burley, to whose interest he owed the employment, and from whose books or whose knowledge he took what helped to maintain it ; but that the other half, if his, he could no longer afford to spend upon feasts or libations. He had another life to provide for.

Burley pooh-poohed the notion of taking half his coadjutor's earning, with much grandeur, but spoke very fretfully of Leonard's sober appropriation of the other half; and, though a good-natured warm-hearted man, felt extremely indignant at the sudden interposition of poor Helen. However, Leonard was firm ; and then Burley grew sullen, and so they parted. But the rent was still to be paid. How? Leonard for the first time thought of the pawnbroker. He had clothes to spare, and Riccabocca's watch. No ; that last he shrank from applying to such base uses.

He went home at noon, and met Helen at the street-door. She too had been out, and her soft cheek was rosy red with unwonted exercise and the sense of joy. She had still preserved the few gold pieces which Leonard had taken back to her on his first visit to Miss Starke's. She had now gone out and bought wools and implements for work ; and meanwhile she had paid the rent.

Leonard did not object to the work, but he blushed deeply when he knew about the rent, and was very angry. He paid back to her that night what she had advanced ; and Helen wept silently at his pride, and wept more when she saw the next day a woeful hiatus in his wardrobe.

But Leonard now worked at home, and worked resolutely ; and Helen sate by his side, working too ; so that next day, and the next, slipped peacefully away, and in the evening of the second he asked her to walk out in the fields. She sprang up joyously at the invitation, when bang went the door, and in reeled John Burley—drunk : —and *so* drunk.

CHAPTER X.

AND with Burley there reeled in another man—a friend of his—a man who had been a wealthy trader and once well to do,—but who, unluckily, had literary tastes, and was fond of hearing Burley talk. So, since he had known the wit, his business had fallen from him, and he had passed through the Bankrupt Court.   A very shabby-looking dog he was, indeed, and his nose was redder than Burley's.

John made a drunken dash at poor Helen.   "So you are the Pentheus in petticoats who defies Bacchus," cried he ; and therewith he roared out a verse from Euripides.   Helen ran away, and Leonard interposed.

"For shame, Burley !"

"He's drunk," said Mr. Douce, the bankrupt trader—"very drunk—don't mind—him.   I say, sir, I hope we don't intrude.   Sit still, Burley, sit still, and talk, do—that's a good man.   You should hear him—ta—ta—talk, sir."

Leonard meanwhile had got Helen out of the room, into her own, and begged her not to be alarmed, and keep the door locked.   He then returned to Burley, who had seated himself on the bed, trying wondrous hard to keep himself upright; while Mr. Douce was striving to light a short pipe that he carried in his button-hole— —without having filled it—and naturally failing in that attempt, was now beginning to weep.

Leonard was deeply shocked and revolted for Helen's sake ; but it was hopeless to make Burley listen to reason.   And how could the boy turn out of his room the man to whom he was under obligations?

Meanwhile there smote upon Helen's shrinking ears loud jarring talk and maudlin laughter, and cracked attempts at jovial songs. Then she heard Mrs. Smedley in Leonard's room, remonstrating ; and Burley's laugh was louder than before, and Mrs. Smedley, who was a meek woman, evidently got frightened, and was heard in precipitate retreat.   Long and loud talk recommenced, Burley's great voice predominant, Mr. Douce chiming in with hiccupy broken treble.   Hour after hour this lasted, for want of the drink that would have brought it to a premature close.   And Burley gradually began to talk himself somewhat sober.   Then Mr. Douce was heard descending the stairs, and silence followed. At dawn, Leonard knocked at Helen's door.   She opened it at once, for she had not gone to bed.

"Helen," said he, very sadly, "you cannot continue here.   I must find out some proper home for you.   This man has served me when all London was friendless, and he tells me that he has nowhere else to go—that the bailiffs are after him.   He has now fallen asleep.   I will go and find you some lodging close at hand—for I cannot expel him who has protected me ; and yet you cannot be under the same roof with him.   My own good angel, I must lose you."

He did not wait for her answer, but hurried down the stairs.

The morning looked through the shutterless panes in Leonard's garret, and the birds began to chirp from the elm-tree, when Burley rose and shook himself and stared round. He could not quite make out where he was. He got hold of the water-jug, which he emptied at three draughts, and felt greatly refreshed. He then began to reconnoitre the chamber—looked at Leonard's MSS.—peeped into the drawers—wondered where the devil Leonard himself had gone to—and finally amused himself by throwing down the fire-irons, ringing the bell, and making all the noise he could, in the hopes of attracting the attention of somebody or other, and procuring himself his morning dram.

In the midst of this *charivari* the door opened softly, but as if with a resolute hand, and the small quiet form of Helen stood before the threshold. Burley turned round, and the two looked at each other for some moments with silent scrutiny.

BURLEY (composing his features into their most friendly expression).—"Come hither, my dear. So you are the little girl whom I saw with Leonard on the banks of the Brent, and you have come back to live with him—and I have come to live with him too. You shall be our little housekeeper, and I will tell you the story of Prince Prettyman, and a great many others not to be found in *Mother Goose*. Meanwhile, my dear little girl, here's sixpence—just run out and change this for its worth in rum."

HELEN (coming slowly up to Mr. Burley, and still gazing earnestly into his face).—"Ah, sir, Leonard says you have a kind heart, and that you have served him—he cannot ask you to leave the house; and so I, who have never served him, am to go hence and live alone."

BURLEY (moved).—"You go, my little lady?—and why? Can we not all live together?"

HELEN.—"No, sir. I left everything to come to Leonard, for we had met first at my father's grave. But you rob me of him, and I have no other friend on earth."

BURLEY (discomposed).—"Explain yourself. Why must you leave him because I come?"

Helen looks at Mr. Burley again, long and wistfully, but makes no answer.

BURLEY (with a gulp).—"Is it because he thinks I am not fit company for you?"

Helen bowed her head.

Burley winced, and after a moment's pause said—"He is right."

HELEN (obeying the impulse at her heart, springs forward and takes Burley's hand).—"Ah, sir," she cried, "before he knew you he was so different : then he was cheerful—then, even when his first disappointment came, I grieved and wept : but I felt he would conquer still—for his heart was so good and pure. Oh, sir, don't think I reproach you ; but what is to become of him if—if—No, it is not for myself I speak. I know that if I was here, that if he had me to care for, he would come home early—and work patiently—and—and—that I might save him. But now when I am gone, and you live with him—you to whom he is grateful, you whom he would follow against his own conscience (you must see that, sir)—what is to become of him ? "

Helen's voice died in sobs.

Burley took three or four long strides through the room ;—he was greatly agitated. "I am a demon," he murmured. "I never saw it before—but it is true—I should be this boy's ruin." Tears stood in his eyes, he paused abruptly, made a clutch at his hat, and turned to the door.

Helen stopped the way, and taking him gently by the arm, said, —"Oh, sir, forgive me—I have pained you ; " and looked up at him with a compassionate expression, that indeed made the child's sweet face as that of an angel.

Burley bent down as if to kiss her, and then drew back—perhaps with a sentiment that his lips were not worthy to touch that innocent brow.

"If I had had a sister—a child like you, little one," he muttered, "perhaps I too might have been saved in time. Now—"

" Ah, now you may stay, sir ; I don't fear you any more."

" No, no ; you would fear me again ere night-time, and I might not be always in the right mood to listen to a voice like yours, child. Your Leonard has a noble heart and rare gifts. He should rise yet, and he shall. I will not drag him into the mire. Good-bye—you will see me no more." He broke from Helen, cleared the stairs with a bound, and was out of the house.

When Leonard returned he was surprised to hear his unwelcome guest was gone—but Helen did not venture to tell him of her interposition. She knew instinctively how such officiousness would mortify and offend the pride of man—but she never again spoke harshly of poor Burley. Leonard supposed that he should either see or hear of the humorist in the course of the day. Finding he did not, he went in search of him at his old haunts ! but no trace. He inquired at the *Beehive* if they knew there of his new address, but no tidings of Burley could be obtained.

As he came home disappointed and anxious, for he felt uneasy as to the disappearance of his wild friend, Mrs. Smedley met him at the door.

"Please, sir, suit yourself with another lodging," said she. "I can have no such singings and shoutings going on at night in my house. And that poor little girl, too! you should be ashamed of yourself."

Leonard frowned, and passed by.

CHAPTER XI.

MEANWHILE, on leaving Helen, Burley strode on; and, as if by some better instinct, for he was unconscious of his own steps, he took the way towards the still green haunts of his youth. When he paused at length, he was already before the door of a rural cottage, standing alone in the midst of fields, with a little farmyard at the back; and far through the trees in front was caught a glimpse of the winding Brent.

With this cottage Burley was familiar; it was inhabited by a good old couple who had known him from a boy. There he habitually left his rods and fishing-tackle; there, for intervals in his turbid, riotous life, he had sojourned for two or three days together—fancying the first day that the country was a heaven, and convinced before the third that it was a purgatory.

An old woman, of neat and tidy exterior, came forth to greet him.

"Ah, Master John," said she, clasping his nerveless hand—"well, the fields be pleasant now—I hope you are come to stay a bit? Do; it will freshen you: you lose all the fine colour you had once, in Lunnon town."

"I will stay with you, my kind friend," said Burley, with unusual meekness—"I can have the old room, then?"

"Oh, yes, come and look at it. I never let it now to any one but you—never have let it since the dear beautiful lady with the angel's face went away. Poor thing, what could have become of her?"

Thus speaking, while Burley listened not, the old woman drew him within the cottage, and led him up the stairs into a room that might have well become a better house, for it was furnished with taste, and even elegance. A small cabinet piano-forte stood opposite the fireplace, and the window looked upon pleasant meads and tangled hedgerows, and the narrow windings of the blue rivulet. Burley sank down exhausted, and gazed wistfully from the casement.

"You have not breakfasted?" said the hostess, anxiously.

"No."

"Well, the eggs are fresh laid, and you would like a rasher

of bacon, Master John?   And if you *will* have brandy in your tea,
I have some that you left long ago in your own bottle."

Burley shook his head.   "No brandy, Mrs. Goodyer; only fresh
milk.   I will see whether I can yet coax Nature."

Mrs. Goodyer did not know what was meant by coaxing Nature,
but she said, "Pray do, Master John," and vanished.

That day Burley went out with his rod, and he fished hard for
the one-eyed perch : but in vain.   Then he roved along the stream
with his hands in his pockets, whistling.   He returned to the
cottage at sunset, partook of the fare provided for him, abstained
from the brandy, and felt dreadfully low.   He called for pen, ink,
and paper, and sought to write, but could not achieve two lines.
He summoned Mrs. Goodyer.   "Tell your husband to come and
sit and talk."

Up came old Jacob Goodyer, and the great wit bade him tell him
all the news of the village.   Jacob obeyed willingly, and Burley at
last fell asleep.   The next day it was much the same, only at dinner
he had up the brandy bottle, and finished it ; and he did *not* have
up Jacob, but he contrived to write.

The third day it rained incessantly.   "Have you no books, Mrs.
Goodyer?" asked poor John Burley.

"Oh, yes, some that the dear lady left behind her ; and perhaps
you would like to look at some papers in her own writing?"

"No, not the papers—all women scribble, and all scribble the
same things.   Get me the books."

The books were brought up—poetry and essays—John knew
them by heart.   He looked out on the rain, and at evening the rain
had ceased.   He rushed to his hat and fled.

"Nature, Nature !" he exclaimed, when he was out in the air
and hurrying by the dripping hedgerows, "you are not to be coaxed
by me !   I have jilted you shamefully, I own it ; you are a female,
and unforgiving.   I don't complain.   You may be very pretty, but
you are the stupidest and most tiresome companion that ever I met
with.   Thank Heaven, I am not married to you."

Thus John Burley made his way into town, and paused at the
first public-house.   Out of that house he came with a jovial air, and
on he strode towards the heart of London.   Now he is in Leicester
Square, and he gazes on the foreigners who stalk that region, and
hums a tune ; and now from yonder alley two forms emerge, and
dog his careless footsteps ; now through the maze of passages towards
St. Martin's he threads his path, and, anticipating an orgy as he
nears his favourite haunts, jingles the silver in his pockets ; and now
the two forms are at his heels.

"Hail to thee, O Freedom!" muttered John Burley, "thy dwelling is in cities, and thy palace is the tavern."

"In the king's name," quoth a gruff voice: and John Burley feels the horrid and familiar tap on the shoulder.

The two bailiffs who dogged have seized their prey.

"At whose suit?" asked John Burley, falteringly.

"Mr. Cox, the wine-merchant."

"Cox! A man to whom I gave a cheque on my bankers not three months ago!"

"But it warn't cashed."

"What does that signify?—the intention was the same. A good heart takes the will for the deed. Cox is a monster of ingratitude, and I withdraw my custom."

"Sarve him right. Would your honour like a jarvey?"

"I would rather spend the money on something else," said John Burley. "Give me your arm, I am not proud. After all, thank Heaven, I shall not sleep in the country."

And John Burley made a night of it in the Fleet.

CHAPTER XII.

MISS STARKE was one of those ladies who pass their lives in the direst of all civil strife—war with their servants. She looked upon the members of that class as the unrelenting and sleepless enemies of the unfortunate householders condemned to employ them. She thought they ate and drank to their villainous utmost, in order to ruin their benefactors—that they lived in one constant conspiracy with one another and the tradesmen, the object of which was to cheat and pilfer. Miss Starke was a miserable woman. As she had no relations or friends who cared enough for her to share her solitary struggle against her domestic foes; and her income, though easy, was an annuity that died with herself, thereby reducing various nephews, nieces, or cousins, to the strict bounds of a natural affection—that did not exist; and as she felt the want of some friendly face amidst this world of distrust and hate, so she had tried the resource of venal companions. But the venal companions had never stayed long—either they disliked Miss Starke, or Miss Starke disliked them. Therefore the poor woman had resolved upon bringing up some little girl whose heart, as she said to herself, would be fresh and uncorrupted, and from whom she might expect gratitude. She had been contented, on the whole, with Helen, and had meant to keep that child in her house as long as she (Miss Starke) remained upon the earth—perhaps some thirty years longer ; and then, having carefully secluded her from marriage, and other friendship, to leave her nothing but the regret of having lost so kind a benefactress. Conformably with this notion, and in order to secure the affections of the child, Miss Starke had relaxed the frigid austerity natural to her manner and mode of thought, and been kind to Helen in an iron way. She had neither slapped nor pinched her, neither had she starved. She had allowed her to see Leonard, according to the agreement made with Dr. Morgan, and had laid out tenpence on cakes, besides contributing fruit from her garden for the first interview—a hospitality she did not think it fit to renew on subsequent occasions. In return for this, she conceived she had purchased the right to Helen bodily and spiritually, and nothing could exceed her indignation when she rose one morning and found the child had gone. As it never had occurred to her to ask Leonard's address, though she suspected Helen had gone to him, she was at a loss what to do, and remained for twenty-four hours in a state of inane depression. But ·then she began to miss the child so much that her energies woke, and she persuaded herself that she was actuated by the purest benevolence in trying to reclaim this poor creature from the world into which Helen had thus rashly plunged.

Accordingly she put an advertisement into the *Times*, to the following effect, liberally imitated from one by which, in former years, she had recovered a favourite Blenheim :—

TWO GUINEAS REWARD.

STRAYED, from Ivy Cottage, Highgate, a Little Girl—answers to the name of Helen ; with blue eyes and brown hair ; white muslin frock, and straw hat with blue ribbons. Whoever will bring the same to Ivy Cottage, shall receive the above Reward.

N.B.—Nothing more will be offered.

Now, it so happened that Mrs. Smedley had put an advertisement in the *Times* on her own account, relative to a niece of hers who was coming from the country, and for whom she desired to find a situation. So, contrary to her usual habit, she sent for the newspaper, and, close by her own advertisement, she saw Miss Starke's.

It was impossible that she could mistake the description of Helen ; and as this advertisement caught her eye the very day after the whole house had been disturbed and scandalized by Burley's noisy visit, and on which she had resolved to get rid of a lodger who received such visitors, the good-hearted woman was delighted to think that she could restore Helen to some safe home. While thus thinking, Helen herself entered the kitchen where Mrs. Smedley sate, and the landlady had the imprudence to point out the advertisement, and talk, as she called it, "seriously" to the little girl.

Helen in vain and with tears entreated her to take no step in reply to the advertisement. Mrs. Smedley felt it was an affair of duty, and was obdurate, and shortly afterwards put on her bonnet and left the house. Helen conjectured that she was on her way to Miss Starke's, and her whole soul was bent on flight. Leonard had gone to the office of the *Beehive* with his MSS.; but she packed up all their joint effects, and, just as she had done so, he returned. She communicated the news of the advertisement, and said she should be so miserable if compelled to go back to Miss Starke's, and implored him so pathetically to save her from such sorrow, that he at once assented to her proposal of flight. Luckily, little was owing to the landlady—that little was left with the maidservant; and, profiting by Mrs. Smedley's absence, they escaped without scene or conflict. Their effects were taken by Leonard to a stand of hackney vehicles, and then left at a coach-office while they went in search of lodgings. It was wise to choose an entirely new and remote district; and before night they were settled in an attic in Lambeth.

CHAPTER XIII.

AS the reader will expect, no trace of Burley could Leonard find: the humorist had ceased to communicate with the *Beehive*. But Leonard grieved for Burley's sake; and, indeed, he missed the intercourse of the large wrong mind. But he settled down by degrees to the simple loving society of his child companion, and in that presence grew more tranquil. The hours in the daytime that he did not pass at work, he spent as before, picking up knowledge at book-stalls; and at dusk he and Helen would stroll out—sometimes striving to escape from the long suburb into fresh rural air; more often wandering to and fro the bridge that led to glorious Westminster—London's classic land—and watching the vague lamps reflected on the river. This haunt suited the musing melancholy boy. He would stand long and with wistful silence by the balustrade—seating Helen thereon, that she too might look along the dark mournful waters which, dark though they be, still have their charm of mysterious repose.

As the river flowed between the world of roofs, and the roar of human passions on either side, so in those two hearts flowed Thought—and all they knew of London was its shadow.

CHAPTER XIV.

THERE appeared in the *Beehive* certain very truculent political papers—papers very like the tracts in the Tinker's bag. Leonard did not heed them much, but they made far more sensation in the public that read the *Beehive* than Leonard's papers, full of rare promise though the last were. They greatly increased the sale of the periodical in the manufacturing towns, and began to awake the drowsy vigilance of the Home Office. Suddenly a descent was made upon the *Beehive*, and all its papers and plant. The editor saw himself threatened with a criminal prosecution, and a certainty of two years' imprisonment: he did not like the prospect, and disappeared. One evening, when Leonard, unconscious of these mischances, arrived at the door of the office, he found it closed. An agitated mob was before it, and a voice that was not new to his ear was haranguing the bystanders, with many imprecations against "tyrants." He looked, and, to his amaze, recognized in the orator Mr. Sprott the Tinker.

The police came in numbers to disperse the crowd, and Mr. Sprott prudently vanished. Leonard learned, then, what had befallen, and again saw himself without employment and the means of bread.

Slowly he walked back. "O knowledge, knowledge!—powerless, indeed!" he murmured.

As he thus spoke, a handbill in large capitals met his eyes on a dead wall—"Wanted, a few smart young men for India."

A crimp accosted him—"You would make a fine soldier, my man. You have stout limbs of your own."

Leonard moved on.

"It has come back, then, to this. Brute physical force after all! O Mind, despair! O Peasant, be a machine again!"

He entered his attic noiselessly, and gazed upon Helen as she sate at work, straining her eyes by the open window—with tender and deep compassion. She had not heard him enter, nor was she aware of his presence. Patient and still she sate, and the small fingers plied busily. He gazed, and saw that her cheek was pale and hollow and the hands looked so thin! His heart was deeply touched, and at that moment he had not one memory of the baffled Poet, one thought that proclaimed the Egotist.

He approached her gently, laid his hand on her shoulder—"Helen, put on your shawl and bonnet, and walk out—I have much to say."

In a few moments she was ready, and they took their way to their favourite haunt upon the bridge. Pausing in one of the recesses, or nooks, Leonard then began,—"Helen, we must part."

"Part?—Oh, brother!"

"Listen. All work that depends on mind is over for me—nothing remains but the labour of thews and sinews. I cannot go back to my village and say to all, 'My hopes were self-conceit, and my intellect a delusion!' I cannot. Neither in this sordid city can I turn menial or porter. I might be born to that drudgery, but my mind has, it may be unhappily, raised me above my birth. What, then, shall I do? I know not yet—serve as a soldier, or push my way to some wilderness afar, as an emigrant, perhaps. But whatever my choice, I must henceforth be alone; I have a home no more. But there is a home for you, Helen, a very humble one, (for you, too, so well born,) but very safe—the roof of—of—my peasant mother. She will love you for my sake, and—and—"

Helen clung to him trembling, and sobbed out, "Anything, anything you will. But I can work; I can make money, Leonard. I do, indeed, make money—you do not know how much—but enough for us both till better times come to you. Do not let us part."

"And I—a man, and born to labour, to be maintained by the work of an infant! No, Helen, do not so degrade me."

She drew back as she looked on his flushed brow, bowed her head submissively, and murmured, "Pardon."

"Ah!" said Helen, after a pause, "if now we could but find my poor father's friend! I never so much cared for it before."

"Yes, he would surely provide for you."

"For *me*!" repeated Helen, in a tone of soft deep reproach, and she turned away her head to conceal her tears.

"You are sure you would remember him, if we met him by chance?"

"Oh yes. He was so different from all we see in this terrible city, and his eyes were like yonder stars, so clear and so bright; yet the light seemed to come from afar off, as the light does in yours, when your thoughts are away from all things round you. And then, too, his dog, whom he called Nero—I could not forget that."

"But his dog may not be always with him."

"But the bright clear eyes are! Ah, now you look up to heaven, and yours seem to dream like his."

Leonard did not answer, for his thoughts were indeed less on earth than struggling to pierce into that remote and mysterious heaven.

Both were silent long; the crowd passed them by unheedingly. Night deepened over the river, but the reflection of the lamp-lights on its waves was more visible than that of the stars. The beams showed the darkness of the strong current, and the craft that lay eastward on the tide, with sail-less spectral masts and black dismal hulks, looked deathlike in their stillness.

Leonard looked down, and the thought of Chatterton's grim suicide came back to his soul; and a pale scornful face, with luminous haunting eyes, seemed to look up from the stream, and murmur from livid lips—"Struggle no more against the tides on the surface—all is calm and rest within the deep."

Starting in terror from the gloom of his reverie, the boy began to talk fast to Helen, and tried to soothe her with descriptions of the lowly home which he had offered.

He spoke of the light cares which she would participate with his mother, (for by that name he still called the widow,) and dwelt, with an eloquence that the contrast round him made sincere and strong, on the happy rural life, the shadowy woodlands, the rippling corn-fields, the solemn lone church-spire soaring from the tranquil landscape. Flatteringly he painted the flowery terraces of the Italian exile, and the playful fountain that, even as he spoke, was flinging up its spray to the stars, through serene air untroubled by the smoke of cities, and untainted by the sinful sighs of men. He promised her the love and protection of natures akin to the happy scene : the simple affectionate mother—the gentle pastor—the exile wise and kind—Violante, with dark eyes full of the mystic thoughts that solitude calls from childhood,—Violante should be her companion.

"And, oh!" cried Helen, "if life be thus happy there, return with me, return—return!"

"Alas!" murmured the boy, "if the hammer once strike the spark from the anvil, the spark must fly upward ; it cannot fall back to earth until light has left it. Upward still, Helen—let me go upward still!"

CHAPTER XV.

THE next morning Helen was very ill—so ill that, shortly after rising, she was forced to creep back to bed. Her frame shivered—her eyes were heavy—her hand burned like fire. Fever had set in. Perhaps she might have caught cold on the bridge—perhaps her emotions had proved too much for her frame. Leonard, in great alarm, called in the nearest apothecary. The apothecary looked grave, and said there was danger. And danger soon declared itself—Helen became delirious. For several days she lay in this state, between life and death. Leonard then felt that all the sorrows of earth are light, compared with the fear of losing what we love. How valueless the envied laurel seemed beside the dying rose.

Thanks, perhaps, more to his heed and tending than to medical skill, she recovered sense at last—immediate peril was over. But she was very weak and reduced—her ultimate recovery doubtful—convalescence, at best, likely to be very slow.

But when she learned how long she had been thus ill, she looked anxiously at Leonard's face as he bent over her, and faltered forth, —" Give me my work ; I am strong enough for that now—it would amuse me."

Leonard burst into tears.

Alas ! he had no work himself; all their joint money had melted away. The apothecary was not like good Dr. Morgan ; the medicines were to be paid for—and the rent. Two days before, Leonard had pawned Riccabocca's watch ; and when the last shilling thus raised was gone, how should he support Helen ? Nevertheless he conquered his tears, and assured her that he had employment ; and that so earnestly that she believed him, and sank into soft sleep. He listened to her breathing, kissed her forehead, and left the room. He turned into his own neighbouring garret, and, leaning his face on his hands, collected all his thoughts.

He must be a beggar at last. He must write to Mr. Dale for money—Mr. Dale, too, who knew the secret of his birth. He would rather have begged of a stranger—it seemed to add a new dishonour to his mother's memory for the child to beg of one who was acquainted with her shame. Had he himself been the only one to want and to starve, he would have sunk inch by inch into the grave of famine, before he would have so subdued his pride. But Helen, there on that bed—Helen needing, for weeks perhaps, all support, and illness making luxuries themselves like necessaries! Beg he must. And when he so resolved, had you but seen the proud bitter soul he conquered, you would have said—"This, which he thinks is degradation—this is heroism." Oh strange human heart! no epic ever written achieves the Sublime and the Beautiful which are graven, unread by human eye, in thy secret leaves. Of whom else should he beg? His mother had nothing, Riccabocca was poor, and the stately Violante, who had exclaimed, "Would that I were a man!" —he could not endure the thought that she should pity him, and despise. The Avenels! No—thrice No. He drew towards him hastily ink and paper, and wrote rapid lines, that were wrung from him as from the bleeding strings of life.

But the hour for the post had passed—the letter must wait till the next day; and three days at least would elapse before he could receive an answer. He left the letter on the table, and, stifling as for air, went forth. He crossed the bridge—he passed on mechanic- ally—and was borne along by a crowd pressing towards the doors of Parliament. A debate that excited popular interest was fixed for that evening, and many bystanders collected in the street to see the members pass to and fro, or hear what speakers had yet risen to take part in the debate, or try to get orders for the gallery.

He halted amidst these loiterers, with no interest, indeed, in common with them, but looking over their heads abstractedly towards the tall Funeral Abbey—imperial Golgotha of Poets, and Chiefs, and Kings.

Suddenly his attention was diverted to those around by the sound of a name—displeasingly known to him. "How are you, Randal Leslie?—coming to hear the debate?" said a member, who was passing through the street.

"Yes; Mr. Egerton promised to get me under the gallery. He is to speak himself to-night, and I have never heard him. As you are going into the House, will you remind him of his promise to me?"

"I can't now, for he is speaking already—and well too. I hurried from the Athenæum, where I was dining, on purpose to be in time, as I heard that his speech was making a great effect."

"This is very unlucky," said Randal. "I had no idea he would speak so early."

"C—— brought him up by a direct personal attack. But follow me; perhaps I can get you into the House; and a man like you, Leslie, from whom we expect great things some day, I can tell you, should not miss any such opportunity of knowing what this House of ours is on a field night. Come on!"

The member hurried towards the door; and as Randal followed him, a bystander cried—"That is the young man who wrote the famous pamphlet—Egerton's relation."

"Oh, indeed!" said another. "Clever man, Egerton—I am waiting for him."

"So am I."

"Why, you are not a constituent as I am."

"No; but he has been very kind to my nephew, and I must thank him. You are a constituent—he is an honour to your town."

"So he is: enlightened man!"

"And so generous!"

"Brings forward really good measures," quoth the politician.

"And clever young men," said the uncle.

Therewith one or two others joined in the praise of Audley Egerton, and many anecdotes of his liberality were told.

Leonard listened at first listlessly, at last with thoughtful attention. He had heard Burley, too, speak highly of this generous statesman, who, without pretending to genius himself, appreciated it in others. He suddenly remembered, too, that Egerton was half-brother to the Squire. Vague notions of some appeal to this eminent person, not for charity, but employment to his mind, gleamed across him— inexperienced boy that he yet was! And, while thus meditating, the door of the House opened and out came Audley Egerton himself. A partial cheering, followed by a general murmur, apprised Leonard of the presence of the popular statesman. Egerton was caught hold of by some five or six persons in succession; a shake of the hand, a nod, a brief whispered word or two, sufficed the practised member for graceful escape; and soon, free from the crowd, his tall, erect figure passed on, and turned towards the bridge. He paused at the angle and took out his watch, looking at it by the lamp-light.

"Harley will be here soon," he muttered—"he is always punctual; and now that I have spoken, I can give him an hour or so. That is well."

As he replaced his watch in his pocket, and rebuttoned his coat over his firm, broad chest, he lifted his eyes, and saw a young man standing before him.

"Do you want me?" asked the statesman, with the direct brevity of his practical character.

"Mr. Egerton," said the young man, with a voice that slightly trembled, and yet was manly amidst emotion, "you have a great name, and great power—I stand here in these streets of London without a friend, and without employment. I believe that I have it in me to do some nobler work than that of bodily labour, had

I but one friend—one opening for my thoughts. And now I have
said this, I scarcely know how, or why, but from despair, and the
sudden impulse which that despair took from the praise that follows
your success—I have nothing more to add."

Audley Egerton was silent for a moment, struck by the tone and
address of the stranger; but the consummate and wary man of the
world, accustomed to all manner of strange applications, and all
varieties of imposture, quickly recovered from a passing and slight
effect.

"Are you a native of —— ?" (naming the town which the statesman represented.)

"No, sir."

"Well, young man, I am very sorry for you; but the good sense
you must possess (for I judge of that by the education you have
evidently received) must tell you that a public man, whatever be
his patronage, has it too fully absorbed by claimants who have a
right to demand it, to be able to listen to strangers."

He paused a moment, and, as Leonard stood silent, added, with
more kindness than most public men so accosted would have
showed—

"You say you are friendless;—poor fellow. In early life that
happens to many of us, who find friends enough before the close.
Be honest, and well-conducted: lean on yourself, not on strangers;
work with the body if you can't with the mind; and, believe me,
that advice is all I can give you, unless this trifle,"—and the minister
held out a crown piece.

Leonard bowed, shook his head sadly, and walked away. Egerton
looked after him with a slight pang.

"Pooh!" said he to himself, "there must be thousands in the
same state in these streets of London. I cannot redress the necessities of civilization. Well educated! It is not from ignorance
henceforth that society will suffer—it is from over-educating the
hungry thousands who, thus unfitted for manual toil, and with no
career for mental, will some day or other stand like that boy in our
streets, and puzzle wiser ministers than I am."

As Egerton thus mused, and passed on to the bridge, a bugle-
horn rang merrily from the box of a gay four-in-hand. A drag-
coach with superb blood-horses rattled over the causeway, and in
the driver Egerton recognized his nephew—Frank Hazeldean.

The young Guardsman was returning, with a lively party of men,
from dining at Greenwich; and the careless laughter of these children
of pleasure floated far over the still river; it vexed the ear of the
careworn statesman—sad, perhaps, with all his greatness, lonely

amidst all his crowd of friends.   It reminded him, perhaps, of his own youth, when such parties and companionships were familiar to him, though through them all he had borne an ambitious, aspiring soul—"*Le jeu, vaut-il la chandelle ?*" said he, shrugging his shoulders.

The coach rolled rapidly past Leonard, as he stood leaning against the corner of the bridge, and the mire of the kennel splashed over him from the hoofs of the fiery horses.   The laughter smote on his ear more discordantly than on the minister's, but it begot no envy.

"Life is a dark riddle," said he, smiting his breast.

And he walked slowly on, gained the recess where he had stood several nights before with Helen, and, dizzy with want of food, and worn out for want of sleep, he sank down into the dark corner ; while the river that rolled under the arch of stone muttered dirge-like in his ear—as under the social keystone wails and rolls on for ever the mystery of Human Discontent.   Take comfort, O Thinker by the stream !   'Tis the river that founded and gave pomp to the city ; and without the discontent, where were progress—what were Man?   Take comfort, O Thinker !   wherever the stream over which thou bendest, or beside which thou sinkest, weary and deso-late, frets the arch that supports thee ;—never dream that, by destroying the bridge, thou canst silence the moan of the wave !

CHAPTER XVI.

BEFORE a table, in the apartments appropriated to him in his father's house at Knightsbridge, sate Lord L'Estrange, sorting or destroying letters and papers—an ordinary symptom of change of residence.   There are certain trifles by which a shrewd observer may judge of a man's disposition. Thus, ranged on the table, with some elegance, but with soldier-like precision, were sundry little relics of former days, hallowed by some sentiment of memory, or perhaps endeared solely by custom ; which, whether he was in Egypt, Italy, or England, always made part of the furniture of Harley's room.   Even the small, old-fashioned, and somewhat inconvenient inkstand into which he dipped the pen as he labelled the letters he put aside, belonging to the writing-desk which had been his pride as a schoolboy.   Even the books that lay scattered round were not new works, not those to which we turn to satisfy the curiosity of an hour, or to distract our graver thoughts ; they were chiefly either Latin or Italian poets, with many a pencil-mark on the margin ; or books which, making severe demand on thought, require slow and frequent perusal, and become companions. Somehow or other, in remarking that even in dumb, inanimate things the man was averse to change, and had the habit of attaching himself to whatever was connected with old associations, you might guess that he clung with pertinacity to affections more important, and you could better comprehend the freshness of his friendship for one so dissimilar in pursuits and character as Audley Egerton. An affection once admitted into the heart of Harley L'Estrange, seemed never to be questioned or reasoned with ; it became tacitly fixed, as it were, into his own nature ; and little less than a revolution of his whole system could dislodge or disturb it.

Lord L'Estrange's hand rested now upon a letter in a stiff, legible Italian character ; and instead of disposing of it at once as he had done with the rest, he spread it before him, and re-read the con-tents. It was a letter from Riccabocca, received a few weeks since, and ran thus :—

Letter from Signor Riccabocca to Lord L'Estrange.

"I thank you, my noble friend, for judging of me with faith in my honour, and respect for my reverses.

"No, and thrice no, to all concessions, all overtures, all treaty with Giulio Franzini. I write the name, and my emotions choke me. I must pause, and cool back into disdain. It is over. Pass from that subject. But you have alarmed me. This sister ! I have not seen her since her childhood ; but she was brought up under *his* influence—she can but work as his agent. She wish to learn my residence ! It can be but for some hostile and malignant purpose. I may trust in you—I know that. You say I may trust equally in the discretion of your friend. Pardon me—my confidence is not so elastic. A word may give the clue to my retreat. But, if discovered, what harm can ensue? An English roof protects me from Austrian despotism : true ; but not the brazen tower of Danaë could protect me from Italian craft. And, were there nothing worse, it would be intolerable to me to live under the eyes of a relentless spy. Truly saith our proverb, 'He sleeps ill for whom the enemy wakes.' Look you, my friend, I have done with my old life—I wish to cast it from me as a snake its skin. I have denied myself all that exiles deem consolation. No pity for misfortune, no messages from sympathizing friendship, no news from a lost and bereaved country follow me to my hearth under the skies of the stranger. From all these I have voluntarily cut myself off. I am as dead to the life I once lived as if the Styx rolled between *it* and me. With that sternness which is admissible only to the afflicted, I have denied myself even the consolation of your visits. I have told you fairly and simply that your presence would unsettle all my enforced and infirm philosophy, and remind me only of the past, which I seek to blot from remembrance. You have complied on the one condition, that whenever I really want your aid I will ask it ; and, meanwhile, you have generously sought to obtain me justice from the cabinets of ministers and in the courts of kings. I did not refuse your heart this luxury ; for I have a child—(Ah ! I have taught that child already to revere your name, and in her prayers it is not forgotten.) But now that you are convinced that even your zeal is unavailing, I ask you to discontinue attempts which may but bring the spy upon my track, and involve me in new misfortunes. Believe me, O brilliant Englishman, that I am satisfied and contented with my lot. I am sure it would not be for my happiness to change it, 'Chi non ha provato il male non conosce il bene.' (One does not know when one is well off till one has known misfortune.) You ask me how I live—I answer, *alla giornata*, (to the day)—not for the morrow, as I did once. I have accustomed myself to the calm existence of a village. I take interest in its details. There is my wife, good creature, sitting opposite to me, never asking what I write, or to whom, but ready to throw aside her work and talk the moment the pen is out of my hand. Talk—and what about ? Heaven knows ! But I would rather hear that talk, though on the affairs of a hamlet, than babble again with recreant nobles and blundering professors about commonwealths and constitutions. When I want to see how little those last influence the happiness of wise men, have I not Machiavelli and Thucydides? Then, by and by, the Parson will drop in, and we argue. He never knows when he is beaten, so the argument is everlasting. On fine days I ramble out by a winding rill with my Violante, or stroll to my friend the Squire's, and see how healthful a thing is true pleasure ; and on wet days I shut myself up, and mope, perhaps, till, hark ! a gentle tap at the door, and in comes Violante, with her dark eyes, that shine out through reproachful tears—reproachful that I should mourn alone, while she is under my roof—so she puts her arms round me, and in five minutes all is sunshine within. What care we for your English gray clouds without ?

"Leave me, my dear Lord—leave me to this quiet happy passage towards old age, serener than the youth that I wasted so wildly : and guard well the secret on which my happiness depends.

"Now to yourself, before I close. Of that same *yourself* you speak too little, as of me too much. But I so well comprehend the profound melancholy that lies underneath the wild and fanciful humour with which you but suggest, as in sport, what you feel so in earnest. The laborious solitude of cities weighs on you. You are flying back to the *dolce far niente*—to friends few, but intimate ; to life monotonous, but unrestrained ; and even there the sense of loneliness will again seize upon you ; and you do not seek, as I do, the annihilation of memory ; your dead passions are turned to ghosts that haunt you, and unfit you for the living world. I see it all—I see it still, in your hurried fantastic lines, as I saw it when we two sat amidst the pines and beheld the blue lake stretched below ;—I troubled by the shadow of the Future, you disturbed by that of the Past.

"Well, but you say, half seriously, half in jest, 'I *will* escape from this prison-house of memory ; I will form new ties, like other men, and before it be too late ; I *will* marry—Ay, but I must love—there is the difficulty'—difficulty—yes, and Heaven be thanked for it ! Recall all the unhappy marriages that have come to your knowledge —pray have not eighteen out of twenty been marriages for love? It always has been so, and it always will. Because, whenever we love deeply, we exact so much and forgive so little. Be content to find some one with whom your hearth and your honour are safe. You will grow to love what never wounds your heart—you will soon grow out of love with what must always disappoint your imagination. *Cospetto!* I wish my Jemima had a younger sister for you. Yet it was with a deep groan that I settled myself to a—Jemima.

"Now, I have written you a long letter, to prove how little I need of your compassion or your zeal. Once more let there be long silence between us. It is not easy for me to correspond with a man of your rank, and not incur the curious gossip of my still little pool of a world which the splash of a pebble can break into circles. I must take this over to a post-town some ten miles off, and drop it into the box by stealth.

"Adieu, dear and noble friend, gentlest heart and s btlest fancy that I have met in my walk through life. Adieu. Write me word when you have abandoned a day-dream and found a Jemima.

"ALPHONSO.

"*P.S.*—For Heaven's sake, caution and recaution your friend the minister not to drop a word to this woman that may betray my hiding-place."

"Is he really happy?" murmured Harley, as he closed the letter ; and he sank for a few moments into a reverie.

"This life in a village—this wife in a lady who puts down her work to talk about villages—what a contrast to Audley's full existence. And I cannot envy nor comprehend either—yet my own existence—what is it?"

He rose, and moved towards the window, from which a rustic stair descended to a green lawn—studded with larger trees than are often found in the grounds of a suburban residence. There were calm and coolness in the sight, and one could scarcely have supposed that London lay so near.

The door opened softly, and a lady past middle age entered; and, approaching Harley, as he still stood musing by the window, laid her hand on his shoulder. What character there is in a hand! Hers was a hand that Titian would have painted with elaborate care! Thin, white and delicate—with the blue veins raised from the surface. Yet there was something more than mere patrician elegance in the form and texture. A true physiologist would have said at once, "There are intellect and pride in that hand, which seems to fix a hold where it rests; and, lying so lightly, yet will not be as lightly shaken off."

"Harley," said the lady—and Harley turned—"you do not deceive me by that smile," she continued, sadly; "you were not smiling when I entered."

"It is rarely that we smile to ourselves, my dear mother; and I have done nothing lately so foolish as to cause me to smile *at* myself."

"My son," said Lady Lansmere, somewhat abruptly, but with great earnestness, "you come from a line of illustrious ancestors; and methinks they ask from their tombs why the last of their race has no aim and no object—no interest—no home in the land which they served, and which rewarded them with its honours."

"Mother," said the soldier, simply, "when the land was in danger I served it as my forefathers served—and my answer would be the scars on my breast."

"Is it only in danger that a country is served—only in war that duty is fulfilled? Do you think that your father, in his plain manly life of country gentleman, does not fulfil, though perhaps too obscurely, the objects for which aristocracy is created, and wealth is bestowed?"

"Doubtless he does, ma'am—and better than his vagrant son ever can."

"Yet his vagrant son has received such gifts from nature—his youth was so rich in promise—his boyhood so glowed at the dream of glory!—"

"Ay," said Harley, very softly, "it is possible—and all to be buried in a single grave!"

The Countess started, and withdrew her hand from Harley's shoulder.

Lady Lansmere's countenance was not one that much varied in expression. She had in this, as in her cast of feature, little resemblance to her son.

Her features were slightly aquiline—the eyebrows of that arch which gives a certain majesty to the aspect : the lines round the mouth were habitually rigid and compressed. Her face was that of one who had gone through great emotion and subdued it. There was something formal, and even ascetic, in the character of her beauty, which was still considerable—in her air and in her dress. She might have suggested to you the idea of some Gothic baroness of old, half chatelaine, half abbess ; you would see at a glance that she did not live in the light world around her, and disdained its fashion and its mode of thought ; yet with all this rigidity it was still the face of the woman who has known human ties and human affections. And now, as she gazed long on Harley's quiet, saddened brow, it was the face of a mother.

"A single grave," she said, after a long pause. "And you were then but a boy, Harley! Can such a memory influence you even to this day! It is scarcely possible : it does not seem to me within the realities of man's life—though it might be of woman's."

"I believe," said Harley, half soliloquizing, "that I have a great deal of the woman in me. Perhaps men who live much alone, and care not for men's objects, do grow tenacious of impressions, as your sex does. But oh," he cried, aloud, and with a sudden change of countenance, "Oh, the hardest and the coldest man would have felt as I do, had he known *her*—had he loved *her*. She was like no other woman I have ever met. Bright and glorious creature of another sphere? She descended on this earth and darkened it when she passed away. It is no use striving. Mother, I have as much courage as our steel-clad fathers ever had. I have dared in battle and in deserts—against man and the wild beast—against the storm and the ocean—against the rude powers of Nature—dangers as dread as ever pilgrim or Crusader rejoiced to brave. But courage against that one memory! no, I have none!"

"Harley, Harley, you break my heart!" cried the Countess, clasping her hands.

"It is astonishing," continued her son, so wrapped in his own thoughts that he did not, perhaps, hear her outcry. "Yea, verily, it is astonishing, that considering the thousands of women I have seen and spoken with, I never see a face like hers—never hear a voice so sweet. And all this universe of life cannot afford me one look and one tone that can restore me to man's privilege—love. Well, well, well, life has other things yet—Poetry and Art live still—still smiles the heaven, and still wave the trees. Leave me to happiness in my own way."

The Countess was about to reply, when the door was thrown hastily open, and Lord Lansmere walked in.

The Earl was some years older than the Countess, but his placid face showed less wear and tear—a benevolent, kindly face, without any evidence of commanding intellect, but with no lack of sense in its pleasant lines. His form not tall, but upright, and with an air of consequence—a little pompous, but good-humouredly so. The pomposity of the *Grand Seigneur*, who has lived much in provinces —whose will has been rarely disputed, and whose importance has been so felt and acknowledged as to react insensibly on himself ;— an excellent man ; but when you glanced towards the high brow and dark eye of the Countess, you marvelled a little how the two had come together, and, according to common report, lived so happily in the union.

"Ho, ho ! my dear Harley," cried Lord Lansmere, rubbing his hands with an appearance of much satisfaction, "I have just been paying a visit to the Duchess."

"What Duchess, my dear father?"

"Why, your mother's first cousin, to be sure—the Duchess of Knaresborough, whom, to oblige me, you condescended to call upon ; and delighted I am to hear that you admire Lady Mary—"

"She is very high bred, and rather—high-nosed," answered Harley.—Then, observing that his mother looked pained, and his father disconcerted, he added seriously, "But handsome, certainly."

"Well, Harley," said the Earl, recovering himself, "the Duchess, taking advantage of our connection to speak freely, has intimated to me that Lady Mary has been no less struck with yourself ; and, to come to the point, since you allow that it is time you should think of marrying, I do not know a more desirable alliance.—What do you say, Katherine ?"

"The Duke is of a family that ranks in history before the Wars of the Roses," said Lady Lansmere, with an air of deference to her husband ; "and there has never been one scandal in its annals, nor one blot in its scutcheon. But I am sure my dear Lord must think that the Duchess should not have made the first overture—even to a friend and a kinsman ?"

"Why, we are old-fashioned people," said the Earl, rather embarrassed, "and the Duchess is a woman of the world."

"Let us hope," said the Countess, mildly, "that her daughter is not."

"I would not marry Lady Mary, if all the rest of the female sex were turned into apes," said Lord L'Estrange, with deliberate fervour.

"Good heavens!" cried the Earl, "what extraordinary language is this? And pray why, sir?"

HARLEY.—"I can't say—there is no why in these cases. But, my dear father, you are not keeping faith with me."

LORD LANSMERE.—"How?"

HARLEY.—"You and my Lady, here, entreat me to marry—I promise to do my best to obey you; but on one condition—that I choose for myself, and take my time about it. Agreed on both sides. Whereon, off goes your Lordship—actually before noon, at an hour when no lady, without a shudder, could think of cold blonde and damp orange flowers—off goes your Lordship, I say, and commits poor Lady Mary and your unworthy son to a mutual admiration —which neither of us ever felt. Pardon me, my father—but this is grave. Again let me claim your promise—full choice for myself, and no reference to the Wars of the Roses. What war of the roses like that between Modesty and Love upon the cheek of the virgin!"

LADY LANSMERE.—"Full choice for yourself, Harley:—so be it. But we, too, named a condition.—Did we not, Lansmere?"

The EARL (puzzled).—"Eh—Did we? Certainly we did."

HARLEY.—"What was it?"

LADY LANSMERE.—"The son of Lord Lansmere can only marry the daughter of a gentleman."

The EARL.—"Of course—of course."

The blood rushed over Harley's fair face, and then as suddenly left it pale.

He walked away to the window; his mother followed him, and again laid her hand on his shoulder.

"You were cruel," said he, gently, and in a whisper, as he winced under the touch of the hand. Then turning to the Earl, who was gazing at him in blank surprise—(it never occurred to Lord Lansmere that there could be a doubt of his son's marrying beneath the rank modestly stated by the Countess)—Harley stretched forth his hand, and said, in his soft winning tone, "You have ever been most gracious to me, and most forbearing; it is but just that I should sacrifice the habits of an egotist, to gratify a wish which you so warmly entertain. I agree with you, too, that our race should not close in me—*Noblesse oblige*. But you know I was ever romantic; and I must love where I marry—or, if not love, I must feel that my wife is worthy of all the love I could once have bestowed. Now, as to the vague word 'gentleman' that my mother employs—word that means so differently on different lips—I confess that I have a prejudice against young ladies brought up in the 'excellent foppery of the world,' as the daughters of gentlemen of our rank mostly are. I crave, therefore, the most liberal interpretation of this word 'gentleman.' And so long as there be nothing mean or sordid in the birth, habits, and education of the father of this bride to be, I trust you will both agree to demand nothing more—neither titles nor pedigree."

"Titles, no—assuredly," said Lady Lansmere; "they do not make gentlemen."

"Certainly not," said the Earl, "many of our best families are untitled."

"Titles—no," repeated Lady Lansmere; "but ancestors—yes."

"Ah, my mother," said Harley, with his most sad and quiet smile, "it is fated that we shall never agree. The first of our race is ever the one we are most proud of; and pray, what ancestors had he? Beauty, virtue, modesty, intellect—if these are not nobility enough for a man, he is a slave to the dead."

With these words Harley took up his hat and made towards the door.

"You said yourself, '*Noblesse oblige*,'" said the Countess, following him to the threshold; "we have nothing more to add."

Harley slightly shrugged his shoulders, kissed his mother's hand, whistled to Nero, who started up from a doze by the window, and went his way.

"Does he really go abroad next week?" said the Earl.

"So he says."

"I am afraid there is no chance for Lady Mary," resumed Lord Lansmere, with a slight but melancholy smile.

"She has not intellect enough to charm him. She is not worthy of Harley," said the proud mother.

"Between you and me," rejoined the Earl, rather timidly, "I don't see what good his intellect does him. He could not be more unsettled and useless if he were the merest dunce in the three kingdoms. And so ambitious as he was when a boy! Katherine, I sometimes fancy that you know what changed him."

"I! Nay, my dear Lord, it is a common change enough with the young, when of such fortunes; who find, when they enter life, that there is really little left for them to strive for. Had Harley been a poor man's son, it might have been different."

"I was born to the same fortunes as Harley," said the Earl, shrewdly, "and yet I flatter myself I am of some use to old England."

The Countess seized upon the occasion, complimented her Lord, and turned the subject.

CHAPTER XVII.

HARLEY spent his day in his usual desultory, lounging manner—dined in his quiet corner at his favourite club —Nero, not admitted into the club, patiently waited for him outside the door. The dinner over, dog and man, equally indifferent to the crowd, sauntered down that thoroughfare which, to the few who can comprehend the Poetry of London, has associations of glory and of woe sublime as any that the ruins of the dead elder world can furnish—thoroughfare that traverses what was once the courtyard of Whitehall, having to its left the site of the palace that lodged the royalty of Scotland—gains, through a narrow strait, that old isle of Thorney, in which Edward the Confessor received the ominous visit of the Conqueror—and, widening once more by the Abbey and the Hall of Westminster, then loses itself, like all memories of earthly grandeur, amidst humble passages and mean defiles.

Thus thought Harley L'Estrange—ever less amidst the actual world around him, than the images invoked by his own solitary soul—as he gained the Bridge, and saw the dull, lifeless craft sleeping on the "Silent Way," once loud and glittering with the gilded barks of the antique Seignorie of England.

It was on that bridge that Audley Egerton had appointed to meet L'Estrange, at an hour when he calculated he could best steal a respite from debate. For Harley, with his fastidious dislike to all the resorts of his equals, had declined to seek his friend in the crowded regions of Bellamy's.

Harley's eye, as he passed along the bridge, was attracted by a still form, seated on the stones in one of the nooks, with its face covered by its hands. "If I were a sculptor," said he to himself, "I should remember that image whenever I wished to convey the idea of *Despondency!*" He lifted his looks and saw, a little before him in the midst of the causeway, the firm erect figure of Audley Egerton. The moonlight was full on the bronzed countenance of the strong public man—with its lines of thought and care, and its vigorous, but cold expression of intense self-control.

"And looking yonder," continued Harley's soliloquy, "I should remember that form, when I wished to hew out from the granite the idea of *Endurance*."

"So you are come, and punctually," said Egerton, linking his arm in Harley's.

HARLEY.—"Punctually, of course, for I respect your time, and I will not detain you long, I presume you will speak to-night?"

EGERTON.—"I have spoken."

HARLEY (with interest).—"And well, I hope?"

EGERTON.—"With effect, I suppose, for I have been loudly cheered, which does not always happen to me."

HARLEY.—"And that gave you pleasure?"

EGERTON (after a moment's thought).—"No, not the least."

HARLEY.—"What, then, attaches you so much to this life—constant drudgery, constant warfare—the more pleasurable faculties dormant, all the harsher ones aroused, if even its rewards (and I take the best of those to be applause) do not please you?"

EGERTON.—"What? Custom."

HARLEY.—"Martyr."

EGERTON.—"You say it. But turn to yourself: you have decided, then, to leave England next week?"

HARLEY (moodily).—"Yes. This life in a capital, where all are so active, myself so objectless, preys on me like a low fever. Nothing here amuses me, nothing interests, nothing comforts and consoles. But I am resolved, before it be too late, to make one great struggle out of the Past, and into the natural world of men. In a word, I have resolved to marry."

EGERTON.—"Whom?"

HARLEY (seriously).—"Upon my life, my dear fellow, you are a great philosopher. You have hit the exact question. You see I cannot marry a dream; and where, out of dreams, shall I find this 'whom?'"

EGERTON.—"You do not search for her."

HARLEY.—"Do we ever search for love? Does it not flash upon us when we least expect it? Is it not like the inspiration to the muse? What poet sits down and says, 'I will write a poem?' What man looks out and says, 'I will fall in love?' No! Happiness, as the great German tells us, 'falls suddenly from the bosom of the gods;' so does love."

EGERTON.—"You remember the old line in Horace: 'The tide flows away while the boor sits on the margin and waits for the ford.'"

HARLEY.—"An idea which incidentally dropped from you some weeks ago, and which I had before half-meditated, has since haunted me. If I could but find some child with sweet dispositions and fair intellect not yet formed, and train her up, according to my ideal. I am still young enough to wait a few years. And meanwhile I shall have gained what I so sadly want—an object in life."

EGERTON.—"You are ever the child of romance. But what—"

Here the minister was interrupted by a messenger from the House of Commons, whom Audley had instructed to seek him on the bridge should his presence be required—"Sir, the Opposition are taking advantage of the thinness of the House to call for a division. Mr. —— is put up to speak for time, but they won't hear him."

Egerton turned hastily to Lord L'Estrange—"You see, you must excuse me now. To-morrow I must go to Windsor for two days : but we shall meet on my return."

"It does not matter," answered Harley; "I stand out of the pale of your advice, O practical man of sense. And if," added Harley, with affectionate and mournful sweetness—"if I weary you with complaints which you cannot understand, it is only because of old schoolboy habits. I can have no trouble that I do not confide to you."

Egerton's hand trembled as it pressed his friend's ; and, without a word, he hurried away abruptly. Harley remained motionless for some seconds, in deep and quiet reverie ; then he called to his dog, and turned back towards Westminster.

He passed the nook in which had sate the still figure of Despondency. But the figure had now risen, and was leaning against the balustrade. The dog, who preceded his master, passed by the solitary form, and sniffed it suspiciously.

"Nero, sir, come here," said Harley.

"Nero," that was the name by which Helen had said that her father's friend had called his dog. And the sound startled Leonard as he leant, sick at heart, against the stone. He lifted his head and looked wistfully, eagerly into Harley's face. Those eyes, bright, clear, yet so strangely deep and absent, which Helen had described, met his own, and chained them. For L'Estrange halted also ; the boy's countenance was not unfamiliar to him. He returned the inquiring look fixed on his own, and recognized the student by the bookstall.

"The dog is quite harmless, sir," said L'Estrange, with a smile.

"And you call him 'Nero?'" said Leonard, still gazing on the stranger.

Harley mistook the drift of the question.

"Nero, sir; but he is free from the sanguinary propensities of his Roman namesake." Harley was about to pass on, when Leonard said, falteringly,—

"Pardon me, but can it be possible that you are one whom I have sought in vain, on behalf of the child of Captain Digby?"

Harley stopped short. "Digby!" he exclaimed, "where is he? He should have found me easily. I gave him an address."

"Ah, Heaven be thanked!" cried Leonard. "Helen is saved—she will not die," and he burst into tears.

A very few moments, and a very few words sufficed to explain to Harley the state of his old fellow-soldier's orphan. And Harley himself soon stood in the young sufferer's room, supporting her burning temples on his breast, and whispering into ears that heard him as in a happy dream, "Comfort, comfort; your father yet lives in me."

And then Helen, raising her eyes, said, "But Leonard is my brother—more than brother—and he needs a father's care more than I do."

"Hush, hush, Helen. I need no one—nothing now!" cried Leonard and his tears gushed over the little hand that clasped his own.

CHAPTER XVIII.

ARLEY L'ESTRANGE was a man whom all things that belong to the romantic and poetic side of our human life deeply impressed. When he came to learn the ties between these two Children of Nature, standing side by side, alone amidst the storms of fate, his heart was more deeply moved than it had been for many years. In those dreary attics, overshadowed by the smoke and reek of the humble suburb—the workday world in its harshest and tritest forms below and around them—he recognized that divine poem which comes out from all union between the mind and the heart. Here, on the rough deal table, (the ink scarcely dry,) lay the writings of the young wrestler for fame and bread; there, on the other side of the partition, on that mean pallet, lay the boy's sole comforter—the all that warmed his heart with living mortal affection. On one side the wall, the world of imagination; on the other this world of grief and of love. And in both, a spirit equally sublime—unselfish devotion—"the something afar from the sphere of our sorrow." [1]

He looked round the room into which he had followed Leonard,

[1] SHELLEY.

on quitting Helen's bedside.   He noted the MSS. on the table,
and, pointing to them, said gently, " And these are the labours by
which you supported the soldier's orphan?—soldier yourself in a
hard battle ! "

"The battle was lost—I could not support her," replied Leonard,
mournfully.

"But you did not desert her.   When Pandora's box was opened,
they say Hope lingered last——"

"False, false," said Leonard ; "a heathen's notion.   There are
deities that linger behind Hope—Gratitude, Love, and Duty."

"Yours is no common nature," exclaimed Harley, admiringly,
"but I must sound it more deeply hereafter : at present I hasten
for the physician; I shall return with him.   We must move that
poor child from this low close air as soon as possible.   Meanwhile,
let me qualify your rejection of the old fable.   Wherever Gratitude,
Love, and Duty remain to man, believe me that Hope is there too,
though she may be often invisible, hidden behind the sheltering
wings of the nobler deities."

Harley said this with that wondrous smile of his, which cast a
brightness over the whole room—and went away.

Leonard stole softly towards the grimy window ; and looking up
towards the stars that shone pale over the roof-tops, he murmured,
"O Thou, the All-seeing and All-merciful !—how it comforts me
now to think that, though my dreams of knowledge may have sometimes obscured the Heavens, I never doubted that Thou wert there !
—as luminous and everlasting, though behind the cloud !"   So, for
a few minutes, he prayed silently—then passed into Helen's room,
and sate beside her motionless, for she slept.   She woke just as
Harley returned with a physician ; and then Leonard, returning to
his own room, saw amongst his papers the letter he had written to
Mr. Dale, and muttering, " I need not disgrace my calling—I need
not be the mendicant now "—held the letter to the flame of the
candle.   And while he said this, and as the burning tinder dropped
on the floor, the sharp hunger, unfelt during his late anxious emotions, gnawed at his entrails.   Still, even hunger could not reach
that noble pride which had yielded to a sentiment nobler than itself
—and he smiled as he repeated, " No mendicant !—the life that
I was sworn to guard is saved.   I can raise against Fate the front
of Man once more."

CHAPTER XIX.

A FEW days afterwards, and Helen, removed to a pure air, and under the advice of the first physicians, was out of all danger.

It was a pretty detached cottage, with its windows looking over the wild heaths of Norwood, to which Harley rode daily to watch the convalescence of his young charge : an object in life was already found. As she grew better and stronger, he coaxed her easily into talking, and listened to her with pleased surprise. The heart so infantine, and the sense so womanly, struck him much by its rare contrast and combination. Leonard, whom he had insisted on placing also in the cottage, had stayed there willingly till Helen's recovery was beyond question. Then he came to Lord L'Estrange, as the latter was about one day to leave the cottage, and said, quietly, " Now, my Lord, that Helen is safe, and now that she will need me no more, I can no longer be a pensioner on your bounty. I return to London."

" You are my visitor, not my pensioner, foolish boy," said Harley, who had already noticed the pride which spoke in that farewell ; " come into the garden and let us talk."

Harley seated himself on a bench on the little lawn ; Nero crouched at his feet ; Leonard stood beside him.

" So," said Lord L'Estrange, " you would return to London? What to do ? "

" Fulfil my fate."

" And that ? "

" I cannot guess. Fate is the Isis whose veil no mortal can ever raise."

" You should be born for great things," said Harley, abruptly. " I am sure that you write well. I have seen that you study with passion. Better than writing and better than study, you have a noble heart, and the proud desire of independence. Let me see your MSS., or any copies of what you have already printed. Do not hesitate—I ask but to be a reader. I don't pretend to be a patron : it is a word I hate."

Leonard's eyes sparkled through their sudden moisture. He brought out his portfolio, placed it on the bench beside Harley, and then went softly to the further part of the garden. Nero looked after him, and then rose and followed him slowly. The boy seated himself on the turf and Nero rested his dull head on the loud heart of the poet.

Harley took up the various papers before him, and read them through leisurely. Certainly he was no critic. He was not accustomed to analyze what pleased or displeased him; but his perceptions were quick, and his taste exquisite. As he read, his countenance, always so genuinely expressive, exhibited now doubt and now admiration. He was soon struck by the contrast, in the boy's writings, between the pieces that sported with fancy, and those that grappled with thought. In the first, the young poet seemed so unconscious of his own individuality. His imagination, afar and aloft from the scenes of his suffering, ran riot amidst a paradise of happy golden creations. But in the last, the THINKER stood out alone and mournful, questioning, in troubled sorrow, the hard world on which he gazed. All in the thought was unsettled, tumultuous; all in the fancy serene and peaceful. The genius seemed divided into twain shapes; the one bathing its wings amidst the starry dews of heaven; the other wandering "melancholy, slow," amidst desolate and boundless sands. Harley gently laid down the paper and mused a little while. Then he rose and walked to Leonard, gazing on his countenance as he neared the boy, with a new and a deeper interest.

"I have read your papers," he said, "and recognize in them two men, belonging to two worlds, essentially distinct."

Leonard started, and murmured, "True, true!"

"I apprehend," resumed Harley, "that one of these men must either destroy the other, or that the two must become fused and harmonized into a single existence. Get your hat, mount my groom's horse, and come with me to London; we will converse by the way. Look you, I believe you and I agree in this, that the first object of every nobler spirit is independence. It is towards this independence that I alone presume to assist you, and this is a service which the proudest man can receive without a blush."

Leonard lifted his eyes towards Harley's, and those eyes swam with grateful tears; but his heart was too full to answer.

"I am not one of those," said Harley, when they were on the road, "who think that because a young man writes poetry he is fit for nothing else, and that he must be a poet or a pauper. I have said that in you there seem to me to be two men, the man of the Actual world, the man of the Ideal. To each of these men I can offer a separate career. The first is perhaps the more tempting. It is the interest of the state to draw into its service all the talent and industry it can obtain; and under his native state every citizen of a free country should be proud to take service. I have a friend who is a minister, and who is known to encourage talent—Audley

Egerton. I have but to say to him, 'There is a young man who will well repay to the government whatever the government bestows on him;' and you will rise to-morrow independent in means, and with fair occasions to attain to fortune and distinction. This is one offer—what say you to it?"

Leonard thought bitterly of his interview with Audley Egerton, and the minister's proffered crown-piece. He shook his head, and replied—

"Oh, my Lord, how have I deserved such kindness? Do with me what you will; but if I have the option, I would rather follow my own calling. This is not the ambition that inflames me."

"Hear, then, the other offer. I have a friend with whom I am less intimate than Egerton, and who has nothing in his gift to bestow. I speak of a man of letters—Henry Norreys—of whom you have doubtless heard, who, I should say, conceived an interest in you when he observed you reading at the bookstall. I have often heard him say, 'that literature as a profession is misunderstood, and that rightly followed, with the same pains and the same prudence which are brought to bear on other professions, a competence at least can be always ultimately obtained.' But the way may be long and tedious—and it leads to no power but over thought; it rarely attains to wealth; and, though *reputation* may be certain, *Fame*, such as poets dream of, is the lot of few. What say you to this course?"

"My Lord, I decide," said Leonard firmly; and then, his young face lighting up with enthusiasm, he exclaimed, "Yes, if, as you say, there be two men within me, I feel that were I condemned wholly to the mechanical and practical world, one would indeed destroy the other. And the conqueror would be the ruder and the coarser. Let me pursue those ideas that, though they have but flitted across me, vague and formless—have ever soared towards the sunlight. No matter whether or not they lead to fortune or to fame, at least they will lead me upward! Knowledge for itself I desire—what care I if it be not power!"

"Enough," said Harley, with a pleased smile at his young companion's outburst. "As you decide so shall it be settled. And now permit me, if not impertinent, to ask you a few questions. Your name is Leonard Fairfield?"

The boy blushed deeply, and bowed his head as if in assent.

"Helen says you are self-taught; for the rest she refers me to you—thinking, perhaps, that I should esteem you less—rather than yet more highly—if she said you were, as I presume to conjecture, of humble birth."

"My birth," said Leonard, slowly, "is very—very—humble."

"The name of Fairfield is not unknown to me. There was one of that name who married into a family in Lansmere—married an Avenel," continued Harley, and his voice quivered. "You change countenance. Oh, could your mother's name have been Avenel?"

"Yes," said Leonard, between his set teeth. Harley laid his hand on the boy's shoulder. "Then, indeed, I have a claim on you—then, indeed, we are friends. I have a right to serve any of that family."

Leonard looked at him in surprise—"For," continued Harley, recovering himself, "they always served my family; and my recollections of Lansmere, though boyish, are indelible." He spurred on his horse as the words closed—and again there was a long pause; but from that time Harley always spoke to Leonard in a soft voice, and often gazed on him with earnest and kindly eyes.

They reached a house in a central, though not fashionable street. A man-servant of a singularly grave and awful aspect opened the door—a man who had lived all his life with authors. Poor fellow, he was indeed prematurely old! The care on his lip and the pomp on his brow—no mortal's pen can describe!

"Is Mr. Norreys at home?" asked Harley.

"He is at home—to his friends, my Lord," answered the man, majestically; and he stalked across the hall with the step of a Dangeau ushering some Montmorenci into the presence of *Louis le Grand*.

"Stay—show this gentleman into another room. I will go first into the library; wait for me, Leonard." The man nodded, and conducted Leonard into the dining-room. Then pausing before the door of the library, and listening an instant, as if fearful to disturb some mood of inspiration, opened it very softly. To his ineffable disgust, Harley pushed before, and entered abruptly. It was a large room, lined with books from the floor to the ceiling. Books were on all the tables—books were on all the chairs. Harley seated himself on a folio of Raleigh's History of the World, and cried—

"I have brought you a treasure!"

"What is it?" said Norreys, good-humouredly, looking up from his desk.

"A mind!"

"A mind!" echoed Norreys, vaguely. "Your own?"

"Pooh—I have none—I have only a heart and a fancy. Listen. You remember the boy we saw reading at the bookstall. I have caught him for you, and you shall train him into a man. I have the warmest interest in his future—for I know some of his family—and one of that family was very dear to me. As for money, he has not a shilling, and not a shilling would he accept gratis from you or me either. But he comes with bold heart to work—and work you must find him." Harley then rapidly told his friend of the two offers he had made to Leonard—and Leonard's choice.

"This promises very well; for letters a man must have a strong vocation as he should have for law—I will do all that you wish."

Harley rose with alertness—shook Norreys cordially by the hand —hurried out of the room, and returned with Leonard.

Mr. Norreys eyed the young man with attention. He was naturally rather severe than cordial in his manner to strangers— contrasting in this, as in most things, the poor vagabond Burley. But he was a good judge of the human countenance, and he liked Leonard's. After a pause he held out his hand.

"Sir," said he, "Lord L'Estrange tells me that you wish to enter literature as a calling, and no doubt to study it as an art. I may help you in this, and you meanwhile can help me. I want an amanuensis—I offer you that place. The salary will be proportioned to the services you will render me. I have a room in my house at your disposal. When I first came up to London, I made the same choice that I hear you have done. I have no cause, even in a worldly point of view, to repent my choice. It gave me an income larger than my wants. I trace my success to these maxims, which are applicable to all professions—1st, Never to trust to genius for what can be obtained by labour; 2dly, Never to profess to teach what we have not studied to understand; 3dly, Never to engage our word to what we do not our best to execute.

"With these rules, literature—provided a man does not mistake his vocation for it, and will, under good advice, go through the preliminary discipline of natural powers, which all vocations re- quire—is as good a calling as any other. Without them, a shoe- black's is infinitely better."

"Possibly enough," muttered Harley; "but there have been great writers who observed none of your maxims."

"Great writers, probably, but very unenviable men. My Lord, my Lord, don't corrupt the pupil you bring to me." Harley smiled and took his departure, and left Genius at school with Common Sense and Experience.

CHAPTER XX.

WHILE Leonard Fairfield had been obscurely wrestling against poverty, neglect, hunger, and dread temptation, bright had been the opening day, and smooth the upward path, of Randal Leslie. Certainly no young man, able and ambitious, could enter life under fairer auspices ; the connection and avowed favourite of a popular and energetic statesman, the brilliant writer of a political work, that had lifted him at once into a station of his own—received and courted in those highest circles, to which neither rank nor fortune alone suffices for a familiar passport—the circles above fashion itself—the circles of POWER—with every facility of augmenting information, and learning the world betimes through the talk of its acknowledged masters,—Randal had but to move straight onward, and success was sure. But his tortuous spirit delighted in scheme and intrigue for their own sake. In scheme and intrigue he saw shorter paths to fortune, if not to fame. His besetting sin was also his besetting weakness. He did not aspire—he *coveted*. Though in a far higher social position than Frank Hazeldean, despite the worldly prospects of his old school-fellow, he coveted the very things that kept Frank Hazeldean below him—coveted his idle gaieties, his careless pleasures, his very waste of youth. Thus, also, Randal less aspired to Audley Egerton's repute than he coveted Audley Egerton's wealth and pomp, his princely expenditure, and his Castle Rackrent in Grosvenor Square. It was the misfortune of his birth to be so near to both these fortunes—near to that of Leslie, as the future head of that fallen house,—near even to that of Hazeldean, since, as we have seen before, if the Squire had had no son, Randal's descent from the Hazeldeans suggested himself as the one on whom these broad lands should devolve. Most young men, brought into intimate contact with Audley Egerton, would have felt for that personage a certain loyal and admiring, if not very affectionate, respect. For there was something grand in Egerton—something that commands and fascinates the young. His determined courage, his energetic will, his almost regal liberality, contrasting a simplicity in personal tastes and habits that was almost austere—his rare and seemingly unconscious power of charming even the women most wearied of homage, and persuading even the men most obdurate to counsel—all served to invest the practical man with those spells which are usually confined to the ideal one. But, indeed, Audley Egerton was an Ideal—the ideal of the Practical. Not the mere vulgar, plodding, red-tape machine of petty business, but the man of strong sense, inspired by inflexible energy, and guided to definite earthly objects. In a dissolute and corrupt form of government, under a decrepit monarchy, or a vitiated republic, Audley Egerton might have been a most dangerous citizen : for his ambition was so resolute, and his sight to its ends was so clear. But there is something in public life in England which compels the really ambitious man to honour, unless his eyes are jaundiced and oblique, like Randal Leslie's. It is so necessary in England to be a gentleman. And thus Egerton was emphatically considered a *gentleman*. Without the least pride in other matters, with little apparent sensitiveness, touch him on the point of gentleman, and no one so sensitive and so proud. As Randal saw more of him, and watched his moods with the lynx-eyes of the household spy, he could perceive that this hard mechanical man was subject to fits of melancholy, even of gloom ; and though they did not last long, there was even in his habitual coldness an evidence of something compressed, latent, painful, lying deep within his memory. This would have interested the kindly feelings of a grateful heart. But Randal detected and watched it only as a clue to some secret it might profit him to gain. For Randal Leslie hated Egerton ; and hated him the more because, with all his book knowledge and his conceit in his own talents, he could not despise his patron—because he had not yet succeeded in making his patron the mere tool or stepping-stone—because he thought that Egerton's keen eye saw through his wily heart, even while, as if in profound disdain, the minister helped the *protégé*. But this last suspicion was unsound. Egerton had not detected Leslie's corrupt and treacherous nature. He might have other reasons for keeping him at a certain distance, but he inquired too little into Randal's feelings towards himself to question the attachment, or doubt the sincerity, of one who owed to him so much. But that which more than all embittered Randal's feelings towards Egerton, was the careful and deliberate frankness with which the latter had, more than once, repeated and enforced the odious announcement, that Randal had nothing to expect from the minister's—WILL ;— nothing to expect from that wealth which glared in the hungry eyes of the pauper heir to the Leslies of Rood. To whom, then, could Egerton mean to devise his fortune? To whom but Frank Hazeldean. Yet Audley took so little notice of his nephew—seemed so indifferent to him, that that supposition, however natural, was exposed to doubt. The astuteness of Randal was perplexed. Meanwhile, however, the less he himself could rely upon Egerton for fortune, the more he revolved the possible chances of ousting Frank from the inheritance of Hazeldean—in part, at least, if not wholly. To one less scheming, crafty, and remorseless than Randal Leslie such a project would have seemed the wildest delusion. But there was something fearful in the manner in which this young man sought to turn knowledge into power, and make the study of all weakness in others subservient to his own ends. He wormed himself thoroughly into Frank's confidence. He learned, through Frank, all the Squire's peculiarities of thought and temper, and pondered over each word in the father's letters, which the son gradually got into the habit of showing to the perfidious eyes of his friend. Randal saw that the Squire had two characteristics, which are very common amongst proprietors, and which might be invoked as antagonists to his warm fatherly love. First, the Squire was as fond of his estate as if it were a living thing, and part of his own flesh and blood; and in his lecture to Frank upon the sin of extravagance, the Squire always let out this foible :—" What was to become of the estate if it fell into the hands of a spendthrift? No man should make ducks and drakes of Hazeldean; let Frank beware of *that*," &c. Secondly, the Squire was not only fond of his lands, but he was jealous of them—that jealousy which even the tenderest fathers sometimes entertain towards their natural heirs. He could not bear the notion that Frank should count on his death; and he seldom closed an admonitory letter without repeating the information that Hazeldean was not entailed; that it was his to do with as he pleased through life and in death. Indirect menace of this nature rather wounded and galled than intimidated Frank; for the young man was extremely generous and high-spirited by nature, and was always more disposed to some indiscretion after such warnings to his self-interest, as if to show that those were the last kinds of appeal likely to influence him. By the help of such insights into the character of father and son, Randal thought he saw gleams of daylight illumining his own chance to the lands of Hazeldean. Meanwhile it appeared to him obvious that, come what might of it, his own interests could not lose, and might most probably gain, by whatever could alienate the Squire from his natural heir. Accordingly, though with consummate tact, he instigated Frank towards the very excesses most calculated to irritate the Squire, all the while appearing rather to give the counter advice, and never sharing in any of the follies to which he conducted his thoughtless friend. In this he worked chiefly through others, introducing Frank to every acquaintance most dangerous to youth, either from the wit that laughs at prudence, or the spurious magnificence that subsists so handsomely upon bills endorsed by friends of "great expectations."

The minister and his *protégé* were seated at breakfast, the first reading the newspaper, the last glancing over his letters ; for Randal had arrived to the dignity of receiving many letters—ay, and notes, too, three-cornered and fantastically embossed. Egerton uttered an exclamation, and laid down the newspaper. Randal looked up from his correspondence. The minister had sunk into one of his absent reveries.

After a long silence, observing that Egerton did not return to the newspaper, Randal said, "Ehem—sir, I have a note from Frank Hazeldean, who wants much to see me ; his father has arrived in town unexpectedly."

"What brings him here?" asked Egerton, still abstractedly.

"Why, it seems that he has heard some vague reports of poor Frank's extravagance, and Frank is rather afraid, or ashamed, to meet him."

"Ay—a very great fault extravagance in the young !—destroys independence ; ruins or enslaves the future. Great fault—very ! And what does youth want that it should be extravagant ? Has it not everything in itself, merely because it *is ?* Youth is youth— what needs it more ?"

Egerton rose as he said this, and retired to his writing-table, and in his turn opened his correspondence. Randal took up the newspaper, and endeavoured, but in vain, to conjecture what had excited the minister's exclamation, and the reverie that succeeded it.

Egerton suddenly and sharply turned round in his chair—" If you have done with the *Times,* have the goodness to place it here."

Randal had just obeyed, when a knock at the street door was heard, and presently Lord L'Estrange came into the room, with somewhat a quicker step, and somewhat a gayer mien than usual.

Audley's hand, as if mechanically, fell upon the newspaper—fell upon that part of the columns devoted to births, deaths, and marriages. Randal stood by, and noted ; then, bowing to L'Estrange, left the room.

"Audley," said L'Estrange, "I have had an adventure since I saw you—an adventure that re-opened the Past, and may influence my future."

"How ?"

"In the first place, I have met with a relation of—of—the Avenels."

"Indeed ! Whom—Richard Avenel ?"

"Richard—Richard—who is he ? Oh, I remember, the wild lad who went off to America ; but that was when I was a mere child."

"That Richard Avenel is now a rich thriving trader, and his marriage is in this newspaper—married to an Honourable Mrs.

M'Catchley.   Well—in this country—who should plume himself on birth?"

"You did not say so always, Egerton," replied Harley, with a tone of mournful reproach.

"And I say so now, pertinently to a Mrs. M'Catchley, not to the heir of the L'Estranges.   But no more of these—these Avenels."

"Yes, more of them.   I tell you I have met a relation of theirs—a nephew of—of—"

"Of Richard Avenel's?" interrupted Egerton; and then added in the slow, deliberate, argumentative tone in which he was wont to speak in public, "Richard Avenel the trader!   I saw him once—a presuming and intolerable man!"

"The nephew has not those sins.   He is full of promise, of modesty, yet of pride.   And his countenance—oh, Egerton, he has *her* eyes."

Egerton made no answer, and Harley resumed—

"I had thought of placing him under your care.   I knew you would provide for him."

"I will.   Bring him hither," cried Egerton, eagerly.   "All that I can do to prove my—regard for a wish of yours."

Harley pressed his friend's hand warmly.

"I thank you from my heart; the Audley of my boyhood speaks now.   But the young man has decided otherwise; and I do not blame him.   Nay, I rejoice that he chooses a career in which, if he find hardship, he may escape dependence."

"And that career is—"

"Letters."

"Letters—Literature!" exclaimed the statesman.   "Beggary! No, no, Harley, this is your absurd romance."

"It will not be beggary, and it is not my romance: it is the boy's. Leave him alone, he is my care and my charge henceforth.   He is of *her* blood, and I said that he had *her* eyes."

"But you are going abroad; let me know where he is; I will watch over him."

"And unsettle a right ambition for a wrong one?   No—you shall know nothing of him till he can proclaim himself.   I think that day will come."

Audley mused a moment, and then said, "Well, perhaps you are right.   After all, as you say, independence is a great blessing, and my ambition has not rendered myself the better or the happier."

"Yet, my poor Audley, you ask me to be ambitious."

"I only wish you to be consoled," cried Egerton, with passion.

"I will try to be so; and by the help of a milder remedy than yours. I said that my adventure might influence my future; it brought me acquainted not only with the young man I speak of, but the most winning, affectionate child—a girl."

"Is this child an Avenel too?"

"No, she is of gentle blood—a soldier's daughter; the daughter of that Captain Digby on whose behalf I was a petitioner to your patronage. He is dead, and in dying, my name was on his lips. He meant me, doubtless, to be the guardian to his orphan. I shall be so. I have at last an object in life."

"But can you seriously mean to take this child with you abroad?"

"Seriously, I do."

"And lodge her in your own house?"

"For a year or so while she is yet a child. Then, as she approaches youth, I shall place her elsewhere."

"You may grow to love her. Is it clear that she will love you?—not mistake gratitude for love? It is a very hazardous experiment."

"So was William the Norman's—still he was William the Conqueror. Thou biddest me move on from the Past, and be consoled, yet thou wouldst make me as inapt to progress as the mule in Slawkenbergius's tale, with thy cursed interlocutions, 'Stumbling, by St. Nicholas, every step. Why, at this rate, we shall be all night in getting into—' *Happiness!* Listen," continued Harley, setting off, full pelt, into one of his wild whimsical humours. "One of the sons of the prophets in Israel, felling wood near the river Jordan, his hatchet forsook the helve, and fell to the bottom of the river; so he prayed to have it again (it was but a small request, mark you); and having a strong faith, he did not throw the hatchet after the helve, but the helve after the hatchet. Presently two great miracles were seen. Up springs the hatchet from the bottom of the water, and fixes itself to its old acquaintance, the helve. Now, had he wished to coach it up to heaven in a fiery chariot, like Elias, be as rich as Job, strong as Samson, and beautiful as Absalom, would he have obtained the wish, do you think? In truth, my friend, I question it very much."

"I can't comprehend what you mean. Sad stuff you are talking."

"I cannot help that; Rabelais is to be blamed for it. I am quoting him, and it is to be found in his Prologue to the Chapters on the Moderation of Wishes. And apropos of 'moderate wishes in point of hatchet,' I want you to understand that I ask but little from Heaven. I fling but the helve after the hatchet that has sunk into the silent stream. I want the other half of the weapon that is buried fathom deep, and for want of which the thick woods darken round me by the Sacred River, and I can catch not a glimpse of the stars."

"In plain English," said Audley Egerton, "you want—" he stopped short, puzzled.

"I want my purpose and my will, and my old character, and the nature God gave me. I want the half of my soul which has fallen from me. I want such love as may replace to me the vanished affections. Reason not—I throw the helve after the hatchet."

CHAPTER XXI.

RANDAL LESLIE, on leaving Audley, repaired to Frank's lodgings, and after being closeted with the young Guardsman an hour or so, took his way to Limmer's hotel, and asked for Mr. Hazeldean. He was shown into the coffee-room, while the waiter went up-stairs with his card, to see if the Squire was within, and disengaged. The *Times* newspaper lay sprawling on one of the tables, and Randal, leaning over it, looked with attention into the column containing births, deaths, and marriages. But in that long and miscellaneous list, he could not conjecture the name which had so excited Mr. Egerton's interest.

"Vexatious!" he muttered; "there is no knowledge which has power more useful than that of the secrets of men."

He turned as the waiter entered, and said that Mr. Hazeldean would be glad to see him.

As Randal entered the drawing-room, the Squire, shaking hands with him, looked towards the door as if expecting some one else, and his honest face assumed a blank expression of disappointment when the door closed, and he found that Randal was unaccompanied.

"Well," said he, bluntly, "I thought your old schoolfellow, Frank, might have been with you."

"Have not you seen him yet, sir?"

"No, I came to town this morning; travelled outside the mail; sent to his barracks, but the young gentleman does not sleep there—has an apartment of his own; he never told me that. We are a plain family, the Hazeldeans—young sir; and I hate being kept in the dark, by my own son, too."

Randal made no answer, but looked sorrowful. The Squire, who had never before seen his kinsman, had a vague idea that it was not polite to entertain a stranger, though a connection to himself, with his family troubles, and so resumed good-naturedly,

"I am very glad to make your acquaintance at last, Mr. Leslie. You know, I hope, that you have good Hazeldean blood in your veins?"

RANDAL (smiling).—"I am not likely to forget that; it is the boast of our pedigree."

SQUIRE (heartily).—"Shake hands again on it, my boy. You don't want a friend, since my grandee of a half-brother has taken you up; but if ever you should, Hazeldean is not very far from Rood. Can't get on with your father at all, my lad—more's the pity, for I think I could have given him a hint or two as to the improvement of his property. If he would plant those ugly commons —larch and fir soon come into profit, sir; and there are some low lands about Rood that would take mighty kindly to draining."

RANDAL.—"My poor father lives a life so retired, and you cannot wonder at it. Fallen trees lie still, and so do fallen families."

SQUIRE.—"Fallen families can get up again, which fallen trees can't."

RANDAL.—"Ah, sir, it often takes the energy of generations to repair the thriftlessness and extravagance of a single owner."

SQUIRE (his brow lowering).—"That's very true. Frank *is* d——d extravagant; treats me very coolly, too—not coming; near three o'clock. By the bye, I suppose he told you where I was, otherwise how did you find me out?"

RANDAL (reluctantly).—"Sir, he did; and to speak frankly, I am not surprised that he has not yet appeared."

SQUIRE.—"Eh!"

RANDAL.—"We have grown very intimate."

SQUIRE.—"So he writes me word—and I am glad of it. Our member, Sir John, tells me you are a very clever fellow, and a very steady one. And Frank says that he wishes he had your prudence, if he can't have your talents. He has a good heart, Frank," added the father, relentingly. "But zounds, sir, you say you are not surprised he has not come to welcome his own father!"

"My dear sir," said Randal, "you wrote word to Frank that you had heard from Sir John and others of his goings-on, and that you were not satisfied with his replies to your letters."

"Well."

"And then you suddenly come up to town."

"Well."

"Well. And Frank is ashamed to meet you. For, as you say, he has been extravagant, and he has exceeded his allowance; and knowing my respect for you, and my great affection for himself, he

has asked me to prepare you to receive his confession and forgive
him. I know I am taking a great liberty. I have no right to
interfere between father and son; but pray—pray think I mean for
the best."

"Humph !" said the Squire, recovering himself very slowly, and
showing evident pain, "I knew already that Frank had spent more
than he ought; but I think he should not have employed a third
person to prepare me to forgive him. (Excuse me—no offence.)
And if he wanted a third person, was not there his own mother?
What the devil!—(firing up)—am I a tyrant—a bashaw—that my
own son is afraid to speak to me? Gad, I'll give it him !"

"Pardon me, sir," said Randal, assuming at once that air of
authority which superior intellect so well carries off and excuses,
"but I strongly advise you not to express any anger at Frank's
confidence in me. At present I have influence over him. Whatever you may think of his extravagance, I have saved him from
many an indiscretion, and many a debt—a young man will listen to
one of his own age so much more readily than even to the kindest
friend of graver years. Indeed, sir, I speak for your sake as well
as for Frank's. Let me keep this influence over him; and don't
reproach him for the confidence he placed in me. Nay, let him
rather think that I have softened any displeasure you might otherwise
have felt."

There seemed so much good sense in what Randal said, and the
kindness of it seemed so disinterested, that the Squire's native
shrewdness was deceived.

"You are a fine young fellow," said he, "and I am very much
obliged to you. Well, I suppose there is no putting old heads upon
young shoulders; and I promise you I'll not say an angry word to
Frank. I dare say, poor boy, he is very much afflicted, and I long
to shake hands with him. So, set his mind at ease."

"Ah, sir," said Randal, with much apparent emotion, "your
son may well love you: and it seems to be a hard matter for so
kind a heart as yours to preserve the proper firmness with him."

"Oh, I can be firm enough," quoth the Squire—"especially
when I don't see him—handsome dog that he is : very like his
mother—don't you think so ?"

"I never saw his mother, sir."

"Gad ! Not seen my Harry ? No more you have; you must
come and pay us a visit. I suppose my half-brother will let you
come ?"

"To be sure, sir. Will you not call on him while you are in
town ?"

"Not I. He would think I expected to get something from the Government. Tell him the ministers must go on a little better, if they want my vote for their member. But go. I see you are impatient to tell Frank that all's forgot and forgiven. Come and dine with him here at six, and let him bring his bills in his pocket. Oh, I shan't scold him."

"Why, as to that," said Randal smiling, "I think (forgive me still) that you should not take it too easily ; just as I think that you had better not blame him for his very natural and praiseworthy shame in approaching you, so I think, also, that you should do nothing that would tend to diminish that shame—it is such a check on him. And therefore, if you can contrive to affect to be angry with him for his extravagance, it will do good."

"You speak like a book, and I'll try my best."

"If you threaten, for instance, to take him out of the army, and settle him in the country, it would have a very good effect."

"What ! would he think it so great a punishment to come home and live with his parents ? "

"I don't say that ; but he is naturally so fond of London. At his age, and with his large inheritance, *that* is natural."

"Inheritance !" said the Squire, moodily—"inheritance ! he is not thinking of that, I trust ? Zounds, sir, I have as good a life as his own. Inheritance !—to be sure the Casino property is entailed on him ; but as for the rest, sir, I am no tenant for life. I could leave the Hazeldean lands to my ploughman, if I chose it. Inheritance, indeed ! "

"My dear sir, I did not mean to imply that Frank would entertain the unnatural and monstrous idea of calculating on your death ; and all we have to do is to get him to sow his wild oats as soon as possible —marry and settle down into the country. For it would be a thousand pities if his town habits and tastes grew permanent—a bad thing for the Hazeldean property, that ! And," added Randal, laughing, "I feel an interest in the old place, since my grandmother comes of the stock. So, just force yourself to seem angry, and grumble a little when you pay the bills."

"Ah, ah, trust me," said the Squire, doggedly, and with a very altered air. "I am much obliged to you for these hints, my young kinsman." And his stout hand trembled a little as he extended it to Randal.

Leaving Limmer's, Randal hastened to Frank's rooms in St. James's Street. "My dear fellow," said he, when he entered, "it is very fortunate that I persuaded you to let me break matters to your father. You might well say he was rather passionate ; but I have contrived to soothe him. You need not fear that [he will not pay your debts."

"I never feared that," said Frank, changing colour; "I only feared his anger. But, indeed, I fear his kindness still more. What a reckless hound I have been! However, it shall be a lesson to me. And my debts once paid, I will turn as economical as yourself."

"Quite right, Frank. And, indeed, I am a little afraid that, when your father knows the total, he may execute a threat that would be very unpleasant to you."

"What's that?"

"Make you sell out, and give up London."

"The devil!" exclaimed Frank, with fervent emphasis; "that would be treating me like a child."

"Why, it *would* make you seem rather ridiculous to your set, which is not a very rural one. And you, who like London so much, and are so much the fashion."

"Don't talk of it," cried Frank, walking to and fro the room in great disorder.

"Perhaps, on the whole, it might be well not to say all you owe, at once. If you named half the sum, your father would let you off with a lecture; and really I tremble at the effect of the total."

"But how shall I pay the other half?"

"Oh, you must save from your allowance; it is a very liberal one; and the tradesmen are not pressing."

"No—but the cursed bill-brokers—"

"Always renew to a young man of your expectations. And if I get into an office, I can always help you, my dear Frank."

"Ah, Randal, I am not so bad as to take advantage of your friendship," said Frank, warmly. "But it seems to me mean, after all, and a sort of a lie, indeed, disguising the real state of my affairs. I should not have listened to the idea from any one else. But you are such a sensible, kind, honourable fellow."

"After epithets so flattering, I shrink from the responsibility of advice. But apart from your own interests, I should be glad to save your father the pain he would feel at knowing the whole extent of the scrape you have got into. And if it entailed on you the necessity to lay by—and give up Hazard, and not be security for other men—why it would be the best thing that could happen. Really, too, it seems hard upon Mr. Hazeldean, that he should be the only sufferer, and quite just that you should bear half your own burdens."

"So it is, Randal; that did not strike me before. I will take your counsel; and now I will go at once to Limmer's. My dear father! I hope he is looking well?"

"Oh, very. Such a contrast to the sallow Londoners! But I think you had better not go till dinner. He has asked me to meet you at six. I will call for you a little before, and we can go together. This will prevent a great deal of *gêne* and constraint. Good-bye till then.—Ha! by the way, I think if I were you, I would not take the matter too seriously and penitentially. You see the best of fathers like to keep their sons under their thumb, as the saying is. And if you want at your age to preserve your independence, and not be hurried off and buried in the country, like a schoolboy in disgrace, a little manliness of bearing would not be amiss. You can think over it."

The dinner at Limmer's went off very differently from what it ought to have done. Randal's words had sunk deep, and rankled sorely in the Squire's mind; and that impression imparted a certain coldness to his manner which belied the hearty, forgiving, generous impulse with which he had come up to London, and which even Randal had not yet altogether whispered away. On the other hand, Frank, embarrassed both by the sense of disingenuousness, and a desire "not to take the thing too seriously," seemed to the Squire ungracious and thankless.

After dinner the Squire began to hum and haw, and Frank to colour up and shrink. Both felt discomposed by the presence of a third person; till, with an art and address worthy of a better cause, Randal himself broke the ice, and so contrived to remove the restraint he had before imposed, that at length each was heartily glad to have matters made clear and brief by his dexterity and tact.

Frank's debts were not, in reality, large; and when he named the half of them—looking down in shame—the Squire, agreeably surprised, was about to express himself with a liberal heartiness that would have opened his son's excellent heart at once to him. But a warning look from Randal checked the impulse; and the Squire thought it right, as he had promised, to affect an anger he did not feel, and let fall the unlucky threat, "that it was all very well once in a way to exceed his allowance; but if Frank did not, in future, show more sense than to be led away by a set of London sharks and coxcombs, he must cut the army, come home, and take to farming."

Frank imprudently exclaimed, "Oh, sir, I have no taste for farming. And after London, at my age, the country would be so horribly dull."

"Aha!" said the Squire, very gimly—and he thrust back into

his pocket-book some extra bank-notes which his fingers had itched to add to those he had already counted out. "The country is terribly dull, is it? Money goes there not upon follies and vices, but upon employing honest labourers, and increasing the wealth of the nation. It does not please you to spend money in that way: it is a pity you should ever be plagued with such duties."

"My dear father—"

"Hold your tongue, you puppy. Oh, I dare say, if you were in my shoes, you would cut down the oaks, and mortgage the property —sell it, for what I know—all go on a cast of the dice! Aha, sir —very well, very well—the country is horribly dull, is it? Pray stay in town."

"My dear Mr. Hazeldean," said Randal, blandly, and as if with the wish to turn off into a joke what threatened to be serious, "you must not interpret a hasty expression so literally. Why you would make Frank as bad as Lord A——, who wrote word to his steward to cut down more timber; and when the steward replied, 'There are only three sign-posts left on the whole estate,' wrote back, '*They've* done growing at all events—down with them!' You ought to know Lord A——, sir; so witty; and—Frank's particular friend."

"Your particular friend, Master Frank? Pretty friends!"—and the Squire buttoned up the pocket, to which he had transferred his note-book, with a determined air.

"But I'm his friend, too," said Randal, kindly; "and I preach to him properly, I can tell you." Then, as if delicately anxious to change the subject, he began to ask questions upon crops, and the experiment of bone manure. He spoke earnestly, and with *gusto*, yet with the deference of one listening to a great practical authority. Randal had spent the afternoon in cramming the subject from agricultural journals and Parliamentary reports; and like all practised readers, had really learnt in a few hours more than many a man, unaccustomed to study, could gain from books in a year. The Squire was surprised and pleased at the young scholar's information and taste for such subjects.

"But, to be sure," quoth he, with an angry look at poor Frank, "you have good Hazeldean blood in you, and know a bean from a turnip."

"Why, sir," said Randal ingenuously, "I am training myself for public life; and what is a public man worth if he do not study the agriculture of his country?"

"Right—what is he worth? Put that question, with my compliments, to my half-brother. What stuff he did talk, the other night, on the malt-tax, to be sure!"

"Mr. Egerton has had so many other things to think of, that we must excuse his want of information upon one topic, however important. With his strong sense he must acquire that information, sooner or later; for he is fond of power; and, sir, knowledge is power!"

"Very true;—very fine saying," quoth the poor Squire, unsuspiciously, as Randal's eye rested on Mr. Hazeldean's open face, and then glanced towards Frank, who looked sad and bored.

"Yes," repeated Randal, "knowledge is power;" and he shook his head wisely, as he passed the bottle to his host.

Still, when the Squire, who meant to return to the Hall next morning, took leave of Frank, his heart warmed to his son; and still more for Frank's dejected looks. It was not Randal's policy to push estrangement too far at first, and in his own presence.

"Speak to poor Frank—kindly now, sir—do," whispered he, observing the Squire's watery eyes, as he moved to the window.

The Squire, rejoiced to obey, thrust out his hand to his son—"My dear boy," said he, "there, don't fret—pshaw!—it was but a trifle after all. Think no more of it."

Frank took the hand, and suddenly threw his arm round his father's broad shoulder.

"Oh, sir, you are too good—too good." His voice trembled so, that Randal took alarm, passed by him, and touched him meaningly.

The Squire pressed his son to his heart—heart so large, that it seemed to fill the whole width under his broadcloth.

"My dear Frank," said he, half blubbering, "it is not the money; but, you see, it so vexes your poor mother; you must be careful in future; and, zounds, boy, it will be all yours one day; only don't calculate on it; I could not bear *that*—I could not, indeed."

"Calculate!" cried Frank. "Oh, sir, can you think it?"

"I am so delighted that I had some slight hand in your complete reconciliation with Mr. Hazeldean," said Randal, as the young men walked from the hotel. "I saw that you were disheartened, and I told him to speak to you kindly."

"Did you? Ah—I am sorry he needed telling."

"I know his character so well already," said Randal, "that I flatter myself I can always keep things between you as they ought to be. What an excellent man!"

"The best man in the world," cried Frank, heartily; and then, as his accents drooped, "yet I have deceived him. I have a great mind to go back—"

"And tell him to give you twice as much money as you had asked for. He would think you had only seemed so affectionate in order to take him in. No, no, Frank—save—lay by—economize; and then tell him that you have paid half your own debts. Something high-minded in that."

"So there is. Your heart is as good as your head. Good-night."

"Are you going home so early? Have you no engagements?"

"None that I shall keep."

"Good-night, then."

They parted, and Randal walked into one of the fashionable clubs. He neared a table, where three or four young men (younger sons, who lived in the most splendid style, Heaven knew how) were still over their wine.

Leslie had little in common with these gentlemen, but he forced his nature to be agreeable to them, in consequence of a very excellent piece of worldly advice given to him by Audley Egerton. "Never let the dandies call you a prig," said the statesman. "Many a clever fellow fails through life, because the silly fellows, whom half a word well spoken could make his *claqueurs*, turn him into ridicule. Whatever you are, avoid the fault of most reading men : in a word, don't be a prig!"

"I have just left Hazeldean," said Randal. "What a good fellow he is!"

"Capital!" said the Honourable George Borrowell. "Where is he?"

"Why, he is gone to his rooms. He has had a little scene with his father, a thorough, rough, country squire. It would be an act of charity if you would go and keep him company, or take him with you to some place a little more lively than his own lodgings."

"What! the old gentleman has been teasing him!—a horrid shame! Why Frank is not extravagant, and he will be very rich —eh?"

"An immense property," said Randal, "and not a mortgage on it : an only son," he added, turning away.

Among these young gentlemen there was a kindly and most benevolent whisper, and presently they all rose, and walked away towards Frank's lodgings.

"The wedge is in the tree," said Randal to himself, "and there is a gap already between the bark and the wood."

CHAPTER XXII.

HARLEY L'ESTRANGE is seated beside Helen at the lattice-window in the cottage at Norwood. The bloom of reviving health is on the child's face, and she is listening with a smile, for Harley is speaking of Leonard with praise, and of Leonard's future with hope. "And thus," he continued, "secure from his former trials, happy in his occupation, and pursuing the career he has chosen, we must be content, my dear child, to leave him."

"Leave him!" exclaimed Helen, and the rose on her cheek faded.

Harley was not displeased to see her emotion. He would have been disappointed in her heart if it had been less susceptible to affection.

"It is hard on you, Helen," said he, "to be separated from one who has been to you as a brother. Do not hate me for doing so. But I consider myself your guardian, and your home as yet must be mine. We are going from this land of cloud and mist, going as into the world of summer. Well, that does not content you. You weep, my child; you mourn your own friend, but do not forget your father's. I am alone, and often sad, Helen; will you not comfort me? You press my hand, but you must learn to smile on me also. You are born to be the Comforter. Comforters are not egotists; they are always cheerful when they console."

The voice of Harley was so sweet, and his words went so home to the child's heart, that she looked up and smiled in his face as he kissed her ingenuous brow. But then she thought of Leonard, and felt so solitary—so bereft—that tears burst forth again. Before these were dried, Leonard himself entered, and, obeying an irresistible impulse, she sprang to his arms, and leaning her head on his shoulder, sobbed out, "I am going from you, brother—do not grieve—do not miss me."

Harley was much moved: he folded his arms, and contemplated them both silently—and his own eyes were moist. "This heart," thought he, "will be worth the winning!"

He drew aside Leonard, and whispered, "Soothe, but encourage and support her. I leave you together; come to me in the garden later."

It was nearly an hour before Leonard joined Harley.

"She was not weeping when you left her?" asked L'Estrange.

"No; she has more fortitude than we might suppose. Heaven knows how that fortitude has supported mine. I have promised to write to her often."

Harley took two strides across the lawn, and then, coming back to Leonard, said, "Keep your promise, and write often for the first year. I would then ask you to let the correspondence drop gradually."

"Drop!—Ah! my lord!"

"Look you, my young friend, I wish to lead this fair mind wholly from the sorrows of the Past. I wish Helen to enter, not abruptly, but step by step into a new life. You love each other now, as do two children—as brother and sister. But later, if encouraged, would the love be the same? And is it not better for both of you, that youth should open upon the world with youth's natural affections free and unforestalled?"

"True! And she is so above me," said Leonard, mournfully.

"No one is above him who succeeds in your ambition, Leonard. It is not *that*, believe me."

Leonard shook his head.

"Perhaps," said Harley, with a smile, "I rather feel that you are above me. For what vantage-ground is so high as youth? Perhaps I may become jealous of you. It is well that she should learn to like one who is to be henceforth her guardian and protector. Yet, how can she like me as she ought, if her heart is to be full of you?"

The boy bowed his head; and Harley hastened to change the subject, and speak of letters and of glory. His words were eloquent and his voice kindling : for he had been an enthusiast for fame in his boyhood ; and in Leonard's, his own seemed to him to revive. But the poet's heart gave back no echo—suddenly it seemed void and desolate. Yet when Leonard walked back by the moonlight, he muttered to himself, "Strange—strange—so mere a child ;— this cannot be love ! Still what else to love is there left to me?"

And so he paused upon the bridge where he had so often stood with Helen, and on which he had found the protector that had given to her a home—to himself a career. And life seemed very long, and fame but a dreary phantom. Courage, still, Leonard ! These are the sorrows of the heart that teach thee more than all the precepts of sage and critic.

Another day, and Helen had left the shores of England, with her fanciful and dreaming guardian. Years will pass before our tale re-opens. Life in all the forms we have seen it travels on. And the Squire farms and hunts ; and the Parson preaches and chides and soothes. And Riccabocca reads his Machiavelli, and sighs and smiles as he moralizes on Men and States. And Violante's dark eyes grow deeper and more spiritual in their lustre; and her beauty takes thought from solitary dreams. And Mr. Richard Avenel has his house in London, and the Honourable Mrs. Avenel her opera-box; and hard and dire is their struggle into fashion, and hotly does the new man, scorning the aristocracy, pant to become aristocrat. And Audley Egerton goes from the office to the Parliament, and drudges, and debates, and helps to govern the empire in which the sun never sets. Poor Sun, how tired he must be—but not more tired than the Government! And Randal Leslie has an excellent place in the bureau of a minister, and is looking to the time when he shall resign it to come into Parliament, and on that large arena turn knowledge into power. And meanwhile, he is much where he was with Audley Egerton; but he has established intimacy with the Squire, and visited Hazeldean twice, and examined the house and the map of the property—and very nearly fallen a second time into the Ha-ha, and the Squire believes that Randal Leslie alone can keep Frank out of mischief, and has spoken rough words to his Harry about Frank's continued extravagance. And Frank does continue to pursue pleasure, and is very miserable, and horribly in debt. And Madame di Negra has gone from London to Paris, and taken a tour into Switzerland, and come back to London again, and has grown very intimate with Randal Leslie; and Randal has introduced Frank to her; and Frank thinks her the loveliest woman in the world, and grossly slandered by certain evil tongues. And the brother of Madame di Negra is expected in England at last; and what with his repute for beauty and for wealth, people anticipate a sensation. And Leonard, and Harley, and Helen? Patience—they will all re-appear.

BOOK EIGHTH.

INITIAL CHAPTER.

THE ABUSE OF INTELLECT.

THERE is at present so vehement a flourish of trumpets, and so prodigious a roll of the drum, whenever we are called upon to throw up our hats, and cry "Huzza" to the "March of Enlightenment," that, out of that very spirit of contradiction natural to all rational animals, one is tempted to stop one's ears, and say, "Gently, gently; LIGHT is noiseless; how comes 'Enlightenment' to make such a clatter? Meanwhile if it be not impertinent, pray, where is Enlightenment marching to?" Ask that question of any six of the loudest bawlers in the procession, and I'll wager tenpence to California that you get six very unsatisfactory answers. One respectable gentleman, who, to our great astonishment, insists upon calling himself "a slave," but has a remarkably free way of expressing his opinions, will reply—"Enlightenment is marching towards the seven points of the Charter." Another, with his hair *à la jeune France*, who has taken a fancy to his friend's wife, and is rather embarrassed with his own, asserts that Enlightenment is proceeding towards the Rights of Women, the reign of Social Love, and the annihilation of Tyrannical Prejudice. A third, who has the air of a man well to do in the middle class, more modest in his hopes, because he neither wishes to have his head broken by his errand-boy, nor his wife carried off to an Agapemoné by his apprentice, does not take Enlightenment a step farther than a siege on Debrett, and a cannonade on the Budget. Illiberal man! the march that he swells will soon trample *him* under foot. No one fares so ill in a crowd as the man who is wedged in the middle. A fourth, looking wild and dreamy, as if he had come out of the cave of Trophonius, and who is a mesmeriser and a mystic, thinks Enlightenment is in full career towards the good old days of alchemists and necromancers. A fifth, whom one might take for a Quaker, asserts that the march of Enlightenment is a crusade for universal philanthropy, vegetable diet, and the perpetuation of peace by means of speeches, which certainly do produce a very contrary effect from the

Philippics of Demosthenes ! The sixth—(good fellow without a rag on his back)—does not care a straw where the march goes. He can't be worse off than he is; and it is quite immaterial to him whether he goes to the dog-star above, or the bottomless pit below. I say nothing, however, against the march, while we take it altogether. Whatever happens, one is in good company; and though I am somewhat indolent by nature, and would rather stay at home with Locke and Burke, (dull dogs though they were,) than have my thoughts set off helter-skelter with those cursed trumpets and drums, blown and dub-a-dubbed by fellows whom I vow to heaven I would not trust with a five-pound note—still, if I must march, I must ; and so deuce take the hindmost. But when it comes to individual marchers upon their own account—privateers and condottieri of Enlightenment—who have filled their pockets with lucifer-matches, and have a sublime contempt for their neighbours' barns and hayricks, I don't see why I should throw myself into the seventh heaven of admiration and ecstasy.

If those who are eternally rhapsodizing on the celestial blessings that are to follow Enlightenment, Universal Knowledge, and so forth, would just take their eyes out of their pockets, and look about them, I would respectfully inquire if they have never met any very knowing and enlightened gentleman, whose acquaintance is by no means desirable. If not, they are monstrous lucky. Every man must judge by his own experience ; and the worst rogues I have ever encountered were amazingly well-informed clever fellows ! From dunderheads and dunces we can protect ourselves, but from your sharp-witted gentleman, all enlightenment and no prejudice, we have but to cry, "Heaven defend us !" It is true, that the rogue (let him be ever so enlightened) usually comes to no good himself, (though not before he has done harm enough to his neighbours.) But that only shows that the world wants something else in those it rewards, besides intelligence *per se* and in the abstract ; and is much too old a world to allow any Jack Horner to pick out its plums for his own personal gratification. Hence a man of very moderate intelligence, who believes in God, suffers his heart to beat with human sympathies, and keeps his eyes off your strong-box, will perhaps gain a vast deal more power than knowledge ever gives to a rogue.

Wherefore, though I anticipate an outcry against me on the part of the blockheads, who, strange to say, are the most credulous idolaters of enlightenment, and, if knowledge were power, would rot on a dunghill ; yet, nevertheless, I think all really enlightened men will agree with me, that when one falls in with detached sharp-

shooters from the general March of Enlightenment, it is no reason
that we should make ourselves a target, because Enlightenment has
furnished them with a gun. It has, doubtless, been already remarked
by the judicious reader, that of the numerous characters introduced
into this work, the larger portion belong to that species which we
call the INTELLECTUAL—that through them are analyzed and developed human intellect, in various forms and directions. So that
this History, rightly considered, is a kind of humble familiar Epic,
or, if you prefer it, a long Serio-Comedy, upon the Varieties of
English Life in this our Century, set in movement by the intelligences
most prevalent. And where more ordinary and less refined types of
the species round and complete the survey of our passing generation,
they will often suggest, by contrast, the deficiencies which mere
intellectual culture leaves in the human being. Certainly, I have no
spite against intellect and enlightenment. Heaven forbid I should
be such a Goth! I am only the advocate for common sense and
fair play. I don't think an able man necessarily an angel; but I
think if his heart match his head, and both proceed in the Great
March under the divine Oriflamme, he goes as near to the angel as
humanity will permit: if not, if he has but a penn'orth of heart to a
pound of brains, I say, "*Bon jour, mon ange!* I see not the starry
upward wings, but the grovelling cloven-hoof." I'd rather be
offuscated by the Squire of Hazeldean, than enlightened by Randal
Leslie. Every man to his taste. But intellect itself (not in the
philosophical but the ordinary sense of the term) is rarely, if ever,
one completed harmonious agency: it is not one faculty, but a compound of many, some of which are often at war with each other, and
mar the concord of the whole. Few of us but have some predominant
faculty, in itself a strength; but which, usurping unseasonably
dominion over the rest, shares the lot of all tyranny, however brilliant, and leaves the empire weak against disaffection within, and
invasion from without. Hence, intellect may be perverted in a man
of evil disposition, and sometimes merely wasted in a man of excellent
impulses, for want of the necessary discipline, or of a strong ruling
motive. I doubt if there be one person in the world, who has
obtained a high reputation for talent, who has not met somebody
much cleverer than himself, which said somebody has never obtained
any reputation at all! Men like Audley Egerton are constantly seen
in the great positions of life; while men like Harley L'Estrange,
who could have beaten them hollow in anything equally striven for
by both, float away down the stream, and, unless some sudden
stimulant arouse their dreamy energies, vanish out of sight into silent
graves. If Hamlet and Polonius were living now, Polonius would

have a much better chance of being a Cabinet Minister, though Hamlet would unquestionably be a much more intellectual character. What would become of Hamlet? Heaven knows! Dr. Arnold said, from his experience of a school, that the difference between one man and another was not mere ability—it was energy. There is a great deal of truth in that saying.

Submitting these hints to the judgment and penetration of the sagacious, I enter on the fresh division of this work, and see already Randal Leslie gnawing his lips on the back-ground. The German poet observes, that the Cow of Isis is to some the divine symbol of knowledge, to others but the milch cow, only regarded for the pounds of butter she will yield. O tendency of our age, to look on Isis as the milch cow! O prostitution of the grandest desires to the basest uses! Gaze on the goddess, Randal Leslie, and get ready thy churn and thy scales. Let us see what the butter will fetch in the market.

CHAPTER II.

 NEW Reign has commenced. There has been a general election; the unpopularity of the Administration has been apparent at the hustings. Audley Egerton, hitherto returned by vast majorities, has barely escaped defeat—thanks to a majority of five. The expenses of his election are said to have been prodigious. "But who can stand against such wealth as Egerton's—no doubt backed, too, by the Treasury purse?" said the defeated candidate. It is towards the close of October; London is already full; Parliament will meet in less than a fortnight.

In one of the principal apartments of that hotel in which foreigners may discover what is meant by English comfort, and the price which foreigners must pay for it, there sat two persons side by side, engaged in close conversation. The one was a female, in whose pale clear complexion and raven hair—in whose eyes, vivid with a power of expression rarely bestowed on the beauties of the north, we recognize Beatrice, Marchesa di Negra. Undeniably handsome as was the Italian lady, her companion, though a man, and far advanced into middle age, was yet more remarkable for personal advantages. There was a strong family likeness between the two; but there was also a striking contrast in air, manner, and all that stamps on the physiognomy the idiosyncrasies of character. There was something of gravity, of earnestness and passion, in Beatrice's countenance when carefully examined: her smile at times might be false, but it was rarely ironical, never cynical. Her gestures, though graceful, were unrestrained and frequent. You could see she was a daughter of the south. Her companion, on the contrary, preserved on the fair, smooth face, to which years had given scarcely a line or wrinkle, something that might have passed, at first glance, for the levity and thoughtlessness of a gay and youthful nature ; but the smile, though exquisitely polished, took at times the derision of a sneer. In his manners he was as composed and as free from gesture as an Englishman. His hair was of that red brown with which the Italian painters produce such marvellous effects of colour ; and if here and there a silver thread gleamed through the locks, it was lost at once amidst their luxuriance. His eyes were light, and his complexion, though without much colour, was singularly transparent. His beauty, indeed, would have been rather womanly than masculine, but for the height and sinewy spareness of a frame in which muscular strength was rather adorned than concealed by an admirable elegance of proportion. You would never have guessed this man to be an Italian ; more likely you would have supposed him a Parisian. He conversed in French, his dress was of French fashion, his mode of thought seemed French. Not that he was like the Frenchman of the present day—an animal, either rude or reserved ; but your ideal of the *Marquis* of the old *régime*—the *roué* of the Regency.

Italian, however, he was, and of a race renowned in Italian history. But, as if ashamed of his country and his birth, he affected to be a citizen of the world. Heaven help the world if it hold only such citizens !

"But, Giulio," said Beatrice di Negra, speaking in Italian, "even granting that you discover this girl, can you suppose that her father will ever consent to your alliance? Surely you know too well the nature of your kinsman?"

"*Tu te trompes, ma sœur*," replied Giulio Franzini, Count di Peschiera, in French, as usual—"*tu te trompes ;* I knew it before he had gone through exile and penury. How can I know it now? But comfort yourself, my too anxious Beatrice, I shall not care for his consent, till I've made sure of his daughter's."

"But how win that in despite of the father?"

"*Eh, mordieu !*" interrupted the Count, with true French gaiety ; "what would become of all the comedies ever written, if marriages were not made in despite of the father? Look you," he resumed, with a very slight compression of his lip, and a still slighter movement in his chair—"look you, this is no question of ifs and buts ! it is a question of must and shall—a question of existence to you and to me. When Danton was condemned to the guillotine, he said, flinging a pellet of bread at the nose of his respectable judge—

' *Mon individu sera bientôt dans le néant*'—*My* patrimony is there already! I am loaded with debts. I see before me, on the one side, ruin or suicide; on the other side, wedlock and wealth."

"But from those vast possessions which you have been permitted to enjoy so long, have you really saved nothing against the time when they might be reclaimed at your hands?"

"My sister," replied the Count, "do I look like a man who saved? Besides, when the Austrian Emperor, unwilling to raze from his Lombard domains a name and a house so illustrious as our kinsman's, and desirous, while punishing that kinsman's rebellion, to reward my adherence, forbore the peremptory confiscation of those vast possessions at which my mouth waters while we speak, but, annexing them to the crown during pleasure, allowed me, as the next of male kin, to retain the revenues of one-half for the same very indefinite period—had I not every reason to suppose, that, before long, I could so influence his Imperial Majesty or his minister, as to obtain a decree that might transfer the whole, unconditionally and absolutely, to myself? And methinks I should have done so, but for this accursed, intermeddling English Milord, who has never ceased to besiege the court or the minister with alleged extenuations of our cousin's rebellion, and proofless assertions that I shared it in order to entangle my kinsman, and betrayed it in order to profit by his spoils. So that, at last, in return for all my services, and in answer to all my claims, I received from the minister himself this cold reply—' Count of Peschiera, your aid was important, and your reward has been large. That reward it would not be for your honour to extend, and justify the ill opinion of your Italian countrymen by formally appropriating to yourself all that was forfeited by the treason you denounced. A name so noble as yours should be dearer to you than fortune itself.'"

"Ah, Giulio," cried Beatrice, her face lighting up, changed in its whole character—"those were words that might make the demon that tempts to avarice fly from your breast in shame."

The Count opened his eyes in great amaze; then he glanced round the room and said, quietly—

"Nobody else hears you, my dear Beatrice; talk common sense. Heroics sound well in mixed society; but there is nothing less suited to the tone of a family conversation."

Madame di Negra bent down her head abashed, and that sudden change in the expression of her countenance which had seemed to betray susceptibility to generous emotion, faded as suddenly away.

"But still," she said, coldly, "you enjoy one-half of those ample revenues—why talk, then, of suicide and ruin?"

"I enjoy them at the pleasure of the crown ; and what if it be the pleasure of the crown to recall our cousin, and reinstate him in his possessions ? "

"There is a *probability*, then, of that pardon ? When you first employed me in your researches, you only thought there was a *possibility*."

"There is a great probability of it, and therefore I am here. I learned some little time since that the question of such recall had been suggested by the Emperor, and discussed in Council. The danger to the State which might arise from our cousin's wealth, his alleged abilities—(abilities ! bah !)—and his popular name, deferred any decision on the point ; and, indeed, the difficulty of dealing with myself must have embarrassed the minister. But it is a mere question of time. He cannot long remain excluded from the general amnesty already extended to the other refugees. The person who gave me this information is high in power, and friendly to myself ; and he added a piece of advice on which I acted. 'It was intimated,' said he, 'by one of the partisans of your kinsman, that the exile could give a hostage for his loyalty in the person of his daughter and heiress ; that she had arrived at marriageable age ; that if she were to wed, with the Emperor's consent, some one whose attachment to the Austrian crown was unquestionable, there would be a guarantee both for the faith of the father, and for the transmission of so important a heritage to safe and loyal hands. Why not ' continued my friend) 'apply to the Emperor for his consent to that alliance for yourself?—you, on whom he can depend ;—you who, if the daughter should die, would be the legal heir to those lands ?' On that hint I spoke."

"You saw the Emperor ? "

"And after combating the unjust prepossessions against me, I stated, that so far from my cousin having any fair cause of resentment against me, when all was duly explained to him, I did not doubt that he would willingly give me the hand of his child."

"You did ! " cried the Marchesa, amazed.

"And," continued the Count imperturbably, as he smoothed, with careless hand, the snowy plaits of his shirt front—"and that I should thus have the happiness of becoming myself the guarantee of my kinsman's loyalty—the agent for the restoration of his honours, while, in the eyes of the envious and malignant, I should clear up my own name from all suspicion that I had wronged him."

"And the Emperor consented ? "

"*Pardieu*, my dear sister, what else could his majesty do ? My proposition smoothed every obstacle, and reconciled policy with mercy. It remains, therefore, only to find out what has hitherto baffled all our researches, the retreat of our dear kinsfolk, and to make myself a welcome lover to the demoiselle. There is some disparity of years, I own; but—unless your sex and my glass flatter me overmuch—I am still a match for many a gallant of five-and-twenty."

The Count said this with so charming a smile, and looked so preeminently handsome, that he carried off the coxcombry of the words as gracefully as if they had been spoken by some dazzling hero of the grand old comedy of Parisian life.

Then interlacing his fingers, and lightly leaning his hands, thus clasped, upon his sister's shoulder, he looked into her face, and said slowly—"And now, my sister, for some gentle but deserved reproach. Have you not sadly failed me in the task I imposed on your regard for my interests? Is it not some years since you first came to England on the mission of discovering these worthy relations of ours? Did I not entreat you to seduce into your toils the man whom I knew to be my enemy, and who was indubitably acquainted with our cousin's retreat—a secret he has hitherto locked within his bosom? Did you not tell me, that though he was then in England, you could find no occasion even to meet him, but that you had obtained the friendship of the statesman to whom I directed your attention, as his most intimate associate? And yet you, whose charms are usually so irresistible, learn nothing from the statesman, as you see nothing of *Milord*. Nay, baffled and misled, you actually suppose that the quarry has taken refuge in France. You go thither —you pretend to search the capital—the provinces, Switzerland, *que sais-je?*—all in vain,—though—*foi de gentilhomme*—your police cost me dearly—you return to England—the same chase, and the same result. *Palsambleu ma sœur*, I do too much credit to your talents not to question your zeal. In a word, have you been in earnest—or have you not had some womanly pleasure in amusing yourself and abusing my trust?"

"Giulio," answered Beatrice, sadly, "you know the influence you have exercised over my character and my fate. Your reproaches are not just. I made such inquiries as were in my power, and I have now cause to believe that I know one who is possessed of this secret, and can guide us to it."

"Ah, you do!" exclaimed the Count. Beatrice did not heed the exclamation, and hurried on.

"But grant that my heart shrunk from the task you imposed on me, would it not have been natural? When I first came to England, you informed me that your object in discovering the exiles was one which I could honestly aid. You naturally wished first to know if the daughter lived ; if not, you were the heir. If she did, you assured me you desired to effect, through my mediation, some liberal compromise with Alphonso, by which you would have sought to obtain his restoration, provided he would leave you for life in possession of the grant you hold from the crown. While these were your objects, I did my best, ineffectual 'as it was, to obtain the information required."

" And what made me lose so important, though so ineffectual an ally?" asked the Count, still smiling ; but a gleam that belied the smile shot from his eye.

" What! when you bade me receive and co-operate with the miserable spies—the false Italians—whom you sent over, and seek to entangle this poor exile, when found, in some rash correspondence to be revealed to the court ;—when you sought to seduce the daughter of the Count of Peschiera, the descendant of those who had ruled in Italy, into the informer, the corrupter, and the traitress : No, Giulio —then I recoiled ; and then, fearful of your own sway over me, I retreated into France. I have answered you frankly."

The Count removed his hands from the shoulder on which they had reclined so cordially.

" And this," said he, " is your wisdom, and this your gratitude. You, whose fortunes are bound up in mine—you, who subsist on my bounty—you, who——"

" Hold," cried the Marchesa, rising, and with a burst of emotion, as if stung to the utmost, and breaking into revolt from the tyranny of years—" hold—gratitude! bounty! Brother, brother—what, indeed, do I owe to you? The shame and the misery of a life. While yet a child, you condemned me to marry against my will— against my heart—against my prayers—and laughed at my tears when I knelt to you for mercy. I was pure then, Giulio—pure and innocent as the flowers in my virgin crown. And now—now— "

Beatrice stopped abruptly, and clasped her hands before her face.

" Now you upbraid me," said the Count, unruffled by her sudden passion, " because I gave you in marriage to a man young and noble ? "

" Old in vices, and mean of soul! The marriage I forgave you. You had the right, according to the customs of our country, to dispose of my hand. But I forgave you not the consolations that you whispered in the ear of a wretched and insulted wife."

" Pardon me the remark," replied the Count, with a courtly bend of his head, " but those consolations were also conformable to the customs of our country, and I was not aware till now that you had wholly disdained them. And," continued the Count, " you were not so long a wife that the gall of the chain should smart still. You were soon left a widow—free, childless, young, beautiful."

"And penniless."

"True, Di Negra was a gambler, and very unlucky; no fault of mine. I could neither keep the cards from his hands, nor advise him how to play them."

"And my own portion? Oh Giulio, I knew but at his death why you had condemned me to that renegade Genoese. He owed you money, and, against honour, and I believe against law, you had accepted my fortune in discharge of the debt."

"He had no other way to discharge it—a debt of honour must be paid—old stories these. What matters? Since then my purse has been open to you."

"Yes, not as your sister, but your instrument—your spy! Yes, your purse has been open—with a niggard hand."

"*Un peu de conscience, ma chère,* you are so extravagant. But come, be plain. What would you?"

"I would be free from you."

"That is, you would form some second marriage with one of these rich island lords. *Ma foi,* I respect your ambition."

"It is not so high. I aim but to escape from slavery—to be placed beyond dishonourable temptation. I desire," cried Beatrice, with increased emotion—"I desire to re-enter the life of woman."

"Eno'!" cried the Count, with a visible impatience; "is there anything in the attainment of your object that should render you indifferent to mine? You desire to marry, if I comprehend you right. And to marry, as becomes you, you should bring to your husband not debts, but a dowry. Be it so. I will restore the portion that I saved from the spendthrift clutch of the Genoese— the moment that it is mine to bestow—the moment that I am husband to my kinsman's heiress. And now, Beatrice, you imply that my former notions revolted your conscience; my present plan should content it; for by this marriage shall our kinsman regain his country, and repossess, at least, half his lands. And if I am not an excellent husband to the demoiselle, it will be her own fault. I have sown my wild oats. *Je suis bon prince,* when I have things a little my own way. It is my hope and my intention, and certainly it will be my interest, to become *digne époux et irréprochable père de famille.* I speak lightly—'tis my way. I mean seriously. The little girl will be very happy with me, and I shall succeed in sooth-ing all resentment her father may retain. Will you aid me then— yes or no? Aid me, and you shall indeed be free. The magician will release the fair spirit he has bound to his will. Aid me not, *mia chère*, and mark, I do not threaten—I do but warn—aid me not; grant that I become a beggar, and ask yourself what is to become of you—still young, still beautiful, and still penniless? Nay, worse than penniless; you have done me the honour, (and here the Count, looking on the table, drew a letter from a portfolio emblazoned with his arms and coronet,) you have done me the honour to consult me as to your debts."

"You will restore my fortune?" said the Marchesa, irresolutely —and averting her head from an odious schedule of figures.

"When my own, with your aid, is secured."

"But do you not overrate the value of my aid?"

"Possibly," said the Count, with a caressing suavity—and he kissed his sister's forehead. "Possibly; but, by my honour, I wish to repair to you any wrong, real or supposed, I may have done you in past times. I wish to find again my own dear sister. I may overvalue your aid, but not the affection from which it comes. Let us be friends, *cara Beatrice mia*," added the Count, for the first time employing Italian words.

The Marchesa laid her head on his shoulder and her tears flowed softly. Evidently this man had great influence over her—and evidently, whatever her cause for complaint, her affection for him was still sisterly and strong. A nature with fine flashes of generosity, spirit, honour, and passion, was hers—but uncultured, unguided— spoilt by the worst social examples—easily led into wrong—not always aware where the wrong was—letting affections good or bad whisper away her conscience or blind her reason. Such women are often far more dangerous when induced to wrong, than those who are thoroughly abandoned—such women are the accomplices men like the Count of Peschiera most desire to obtain.

"Ah, Giulio," said Beatrice, after a pause, and looking up at him through her tears, "when you speak to me thus, you know you can .do with me what you will. Fatherless and motherless, whom had my childhood to love and obey but you?"

"Dear Beatrice," murmured the Count, tenderly—and he again kissed her forehead. "So," he continued, more carelessly—"so the reconciliation is effected, and our interests and our hearts re- allied. Now, alas! to descend to business. You say that you know some one whom you believe to be acquainted with the lurking- place of my father-in-law—that is to be!"

"I think so. You remind me that I have an appointment with him this day: it is near the hour—I must leave you."

"To learn the secret?—Quick—quick. I have no fear of your success, if it is by his heart that you lead him!"

"You mistake; on his heart I have no hold. But he has a friend who loves me, and honourably, and whose cause he pleads. I think here that I have some means to control or persuade him. If not—ah, he is of a character that perplexes me in all but his worldly ambition; and how can we foreigners influence him through *that?*"

"Is he poor, or is he extravagant?"

"Not extravagant, and not positively poor, but dependent."

"Then we have him," said the Count, composedly. "If his assistance be worth buying, we can bid high for it. *Sur mon âme*, I never yet knew money fail with any man who was both worldly and dependent. I put him and myself in your hands."

Thus saying, the Count opened the door, and conducted his sister with formal politeness to her carriage. He then returned, reseated himself, and mused in silence. As he did so, the muscles of his countenance relaxed. The levity of the Frenchman fled from his visage, and in his eye, as it gazed abstractedly into space, there was that steady depth so remarkable in the old portraits of Florentine diplomatist or Venetian Oligarch. Thus seen, there was in that face, despite all its beauty, something that would have awed back even the fond gaze of love; something hard, collected, inscrutable, remorseless. But this change of countenance did not last long. Evidently thought, though intense for the moment, was not habitual to the man. Evidently he had lived the life which takes all things lightly—so he rose with a look of fatigue, shook and stretched himself, as if to cast off, or grow out of, an unwelcome and irksome mood. An hour afterwards, the Count of Peschiera was charming all eyes, and pleasing all ears, in the saloon of a high-born beauty, whose acquaintance he had made at Vienna, and whose charms, according to that old and never-truth-speaking oracle, Polite Scandal, were now said to have attracted to London the brilliant foreigner.

CHAPTER III.

THE Marchesa regained her house, which was in Curzon Street, and withdrew to her own room, to readjust her dress, and remove from her countenance all trace of the tears she had shed.

Half-an-hour afterwards she was seated in her drawing-room, composed and calm; nor, seeing her then, could you have guessed that she was capable of so much emotion and so much weakness. In that stately exterior, in that quiet attitude, in that elaborate and finished elegance which comes alike from the arts of the toilet and the conventional repose of rank, you could see but the woman of the world and the great lady.

A knock at the door was heard, and in a few moments there entered a visitor, with the easy familiarity of intimate acquaintance —a young man, but with none of the bloom of youth. His hair, fine as a woman's, was thin and scanty, but it fell low over the forehead, and concealed that noblest of our human features. "A gentleman," says Apuleius, "ought to wear his whole mind on his forehead."[1] The young visitor would never have committed so frank an imprudence. His cheek was pale, and in his step and his movements there was a languor that spoke of fatigued nerves or delicate health. But the light of the eye and the tone of the voice were those of a mental temperament controlling the bodily—vigorous and energetic. For the rest, his general appearance was distinguished by a refinement alike intellectual and social. Once seen, you would not easily forget him. And the reader, no doubt, already recognizes Randal Leslie. His salutation, as I before said, was that of intimate familiarity; yet it was given and replied to with that unreserved openness which denotes the absence of a more tender sentiment.

Seating himself by the Marchesa's side, Randal began first to converse on the fashionable topics and gossip of the day; but it was observable that while he extracted from her the current anecdote and scandal of the great world, neither anecdote nor scandal did he communicate in return. Randal Leslie had already learned the art not to commit himself, nor to have quoted against him one ill-natured remark upon the eminent. Nothing more injures the man who would rise beyond the fame of the *salons*, than to be considered backbiter and gossip; "yet it is always useful," thought Randal Leslie, "to know the foibles—the small social and private springs by which the great are moved. Critical occasions may arise in which such knowledge may be power." And hence, perhaps, (besides a more private motive, soon to be perceived,) Randal did not consider his time thrown away in cultivating Madame di Negra's friendship. For, despite much that was whispered against her, she had succeeded in dispelling the coldness with which she had at first been received in the London circles. Her beauty, her grace, and her high birth, had raised her into fashion, and the homage of men of the first station, while it perhaps injured her reputation as woman, added to her celebrity as fine lady. So much do we cold English, prudes though we be, forgive to the foreigner what we avenge on the native.

[1] "Hominem liberum et magnificum debere, si queat, in primori fronte, animum gestare."

Sliding at last from these general topics into very well-bred and elegant personal compliment, and reciting various eulogies, which Lord this and the Duke of that had passed on the Marchesa's charms, Randal laid his hand on hers, with the license of admitted friendship, and said—

"But since you have deigned to confide in me, since when (happily for me, and with a generosity of which no *coquette* could have been capable) you, in good time, repressed into friendship feelings that might else have ripened into those you are formed to inspire and disdain to return, you told me with your charming smile, 'Let no one speak to me of love who does not offer me his hand, and with it the means to supply tastes that I fear are terribly extravagant;'—since thus you allowed me to divine your natural objects, and upon that understanding our intimacy has been founded, you will pardon me for saying that the admiration you excite amongst these *grands seigneurs* I have named, only serves to defeat your own purpose, and scare away admirers less brilliant, but more in earnest. Most of these gentlemen are unfortunately married; and they who are not belong to those members of our aristocracy who, in marriage, seek more than beauty and wit—namely, connections to strengthen their political station, or wealth to redeem a mortgage and sustain a title."

"My dear Mr. Leslie," replied the Marchesa—and a certain sadness might be detected in the tone of the voice and the droop of the eye—"I have lived long enough in the real world to appreciate the baseness and the falsehood of most of those sentiments which take the noblest names. I see through the hearts of the admirers you parade before me, and know that not one of them would shelter with his ermine the woman to whom he talks of his heart. Ah," continued Beatrice, with a softness of which she was unconscious, but which might have been extremely dangerous to youth less steeled and self-guarded than was Randal Leslie's—"Ah, I am less ambitious than you suppose. I have dreamed of a friend, a companion, a protector, with feelings still fresh, undebased by the low round of vulgar dissipation and mean pleasures—of a heart so new, that it might restore my own to what it was in its happy spring. I have seen in your country some marriages, the mere contemplation of which has filled my eyes with delicious tears. I have learned in England to know the value of home. And with such a heart as I describe, and such a home, I could forget that I ever knew a less pure ambition."

"This language does not surprise me," said Randal; "yet it does not harmonize with your former answer to me."

"To you," repeated Beatrice, smiling, and regaining her lighter manner: "to you—true. But I never had the vanity to think that your affection for me could bear the sacrifices it would cost you in marriage; that you, with your ambition, could bound your dreams of happiness to home. And then, too," said she, raising her head, and with a certain grave pride in her air—"and *then*, I could not have consented to share my fate with one whom my poverty would cripple. I could not listen to my heart, if it had beat for a lover without fortune, for to him I could then have brought but a burden, and betrayed him into a union with poverty and debt. *Now*, it may be different. Now I may have the dowry that befits my birth. And now I may be free to choose according to my heart as woman, not according to my necessities, as one poor, harassed, and despairing."

"Ah," said Randal, interested, and drawing still closer towards his fair companion—"ah, I congratulate you sincerely; you have cause, then, to think that you shall be—rich?"

The Marchesa paused before she answered, and during that pause Randal relaxed the web of the scheme which he had been secretly weaving, and rapidly considered whether, if Beatrice di Negra would indeed be rich, she might answer to himself as a wife; and in what way, if so, he had best change his tone from that of friendship into that of love. While thus reflecting, Beatrice answered—

"Not rich for an Englishwoman; for an Italian, yes. My fortune should be half a million—"

"Half a million!" cried Randal, and with difficulty he restrained himself from falling at her feet in adoration.

"Of francs!" continued the Marchesa.

"Francs! Ah," said Randal, with a long-drawn breath, and recovering from his sudden enthusiasm, "about twenty thousand pounds?—eight hundred a-year at four per cent. A very handsome portion, certainly (Genteel poverty! he murmured to himself. What an escape I have had! but I see—I see. This will smooth all difficulties in the way of my better and earlier project. I see)—a very handsome portion," he repeated aloud—"not for a *grand seigneur*, indeed, but still for a gentleman of birth and expectations worthy of your choice, if ambition be not your first object. Ah, while you spoke with such endearing eloquence of feelings that were fresh, of a heart that was new, of the happy English home, you might guess that my thoughts ran to my friend who loves you so devotedly, and who so realizes your idol. Proverbially, with us, happy marriages and happy homes are found not in the gay circles of London fashion, but at the hearths of our rural nobility—our un-titled country gentlemen. And who, amongst all your adorers, can offer you a lot so really enviable as the one whom, I see by your blush, you already guess that I refer to?"

"Did I blush?" said the Marchesa, with a silvery laugh. "Nay, I think that your zeal for your friend misled you. But I will own frankly, I have been touched by his honest ingenuous love—so evident, yet rather looked than spoken. I have contrasted the love that honours me with the suitors that seek to degrade; more I cannot say. For though I grant that your friend is handsome, high-spirited, and generous, still he is not what—"

"You mistake, believe me," interrupted Randal. "You shall not finish your sentence. He *is* all that you do not yet suppose him; for his shyness, and his very love, his very respect for your superiority, do not allow his mind and his nature to appear to advantage. You, it is true, have a taste for letters and poetry rare among your countrywomen. He has not at present—few men have. But what Cimon would not be refined by so fair an Iphigenia? Such frivolities as he now shows belong but to youth and inexperience of life. Happy the brother who could see his sister the wife of Frank Hazeldean."

The Marchesa leant her cheek on her hand in silence. To her, marriage was more than it usually seems to dreaming maiden or to disconsolate widow. So had the strong desire to escape from the control of her unprincipled and remorseless brother grown a part of her very soul—so had whatever was best and highest in her very mixed and complex character been galled and outraged by her friendless and exposed position, the equivocal worship rendered to her beauty, the various debasements to which pecuniary embarrassments had subjected her—(not without design on the part of the Count, who though grasping, was not miserly, and who by precarious and seemingly capricious gifts at one time, and refusals of all aid at another, had involved her in debt in order to retain his hold on her)—so utterly painful and humiliating to a woman of her pride and her birth was the station that she held in the world—that in marriage she saw liberty, life, honour, self-redemption; and these thoughts, while they compelled her to co-operate with the schemes, by which the Count, on securing to himself a bride, was to bestow on herself a dower, also disposed her now to receive with favour Randal Leslie's pleadings on behalf of his friend.

The advocate saw that he had made an impression, and with the marvellous skill which his knowledge of those natures that engaged his study bestowed on his intelligence, he continued to improve his cause by such representations as were likely to be most effective. With what admirable tact he avoided panegyric of Frank as the mere individual, and drew him rather as the type, the ideal of what a woman in Beatrice's position might desire, in the safety, peace, and honour of a home, in the trust, and constancy, and honest confiding love of its partner! He did not paint an elysium; he described a haven; he did not glowingly delineate a hero of romance —he soberly portrayed that Representative of the Respectable and the Real which a woman turns to when romance begins to seem to her but delusion. Verily, if you could have looked into the heart of the person he addressed, and heard him speak, you would have cried admiringly, "Knowledge *is* power; and this man, if as able on a larger field of action, should play no mean part in the history of his time."

Slowly Beatrice roused herself from the reveries which crept over her as he spoke—slowly, and with a deep sigh, and said—

"Well, well, grant all you say; at least before I can listen to so honourable a love, I must be relieved from the base and sordid pressure that weighs on me. I cannot say to the man who woos me, 'Will you pay the debts of the daughter of Franzini, and the widow of di Negra?'"

"Nay, your debts, surely, make no slight portion of your dowry."

"But the dowry has to be secured;" and here, turning the tables upon her companion, as the apt proverb expresses it, Madame di Negra extended her hand to Randal, and said in the most winning accents, "You are, then, truly and sincerely my friend?"

"Can you doubt it?"

"I prove that I do not, for I ask your assistance."

"Mine? How?"

"Listen; my brother has arrived in London—"

"I see that arrival announced in the papers."

"And he comes, empowered by the consent of the Emperor, to ask the hand of a relation and countrywoman of his; an alliance that will heal long family dissensions, and add to his own fortunes those of an heiress. My brother, like myself, has been extravagant. The dowry which by law he still owes me it would distress him to pay till this marriage be assured."

"I understand," said Randal. "But how can I aid this marriage?"

"By assisting us to discover the bride. She, with her father, sought refuge and concealment in England."

"The father had, then, taken part in some political disaffections, and was proscribed?"

"Exactly; and so well has he concealed himself, that he has baffled all our efforts to discover his retreat. My brother can obtain him his pardon in cementing this alliance—"

" Proceed."

" Ah, Randal, Randal, is this the frankness of friendship? You know that I have before sought to obtain the secret of our relation's retreat—sought in vain to obtain it from Mr. Egerton, who assuredly knows it—"

" But who communicates no secrets to living man," said Randal, almost bitterly; " who, close and compact as iron, is as little malleable to me as to you."

" Pardon me. I know you so well that I believe you could attain to any secret you sought earnestly to acquire. Nay, more, I believe that you know already that secret which I ask you to share with me."

" What on earth makes you think so?"

" When, some weeks ago, you asked me to describe the personal appearance and manners of the exile, which I did partly from the recollections of my childhood, partly from the description given to me by others, I could not but notice your countenance, and remark its change; in spite," said the Marchesa, smiling, and watching Randal while she spoke—" in spite of your habitual self-command. And when I pressed you to own that you had actually seen some one who tallied with that description, your denial did not deceive me. Still more, when returning recently, of your own accord, to the subject, you questioned me so shrewdly as to my motives in seeking the clue to our refugees, and I did not then answer you satisfactorily, I could detect—"

" Ha, ha," interrupted Randal with the low soft laugh by which occasionally he infringed upon Lord Chesterfield's recommendations to shun a merriment so natural as to be ill-bred—" Ha, ha, you have the fault of all observers too minute and refined. But even granting that I may have seen some Italian exiles, (which is likely enough,) what could be more natural than my seeking to compare your description with their appearance; and granting that I might suspect some one amongst them to be the man you search for, what more natural also, than that I should desire to know if you meant him harm or good in discovering his 'whereabout?' For ill," added Randal, with an air of prudery—"ill would it become me to betray, even to friendship, the retreat of one who would hide from persecution; and even if I did so—for honour itself is a weak safeguard against your fascinations—such indiscretion might be fatal to my future career."

" How?"

" Do you not say that Egerton knows the secret, yet will not communicate?—and is he a man who would ever forgive in me

an imprudence that committed himself? My dear friend, I will tell
you more. When Audley Egerton first noticed my growing intimacy
with you, he said, with his usual dryness of counsel, 'Randal, I do
not ask you to discontinue acquaintance with Madame di Negra—
for an acquaintance with women like her forms the manners, and
refines the intellect; but charming women are dangerous, and
Madame di Negra is—a charming woman.'"

The Marchesa's face flushed. Randal resumed: "'Your fair
acquaintance' (I am still quoting Egerton) 'seeks to discover the
home of a countryman of hers. She suspects that I know it. She
may try to learn it through you. Accident may possibly give you
the information she requires. Beware how you betray it. By one
such weakness I should judge of your general character. He from
whom a woman can extract a secret will never be fit for public life.'
Therefore, my dear Marchesa, even supposing I possess this secret,
you would be no true friend of mine to ask me to reveal what would
imperil all my prospects. For as yet," added Randal, with a
gloomy shade on his brow—"as yet, I do not stand alone and erect
—I *lean ;*—I am dependent."

"There may be a way," replied Madame di Negra, persisting,
"to communicate this intelligence, without the possibility of Mr.
Egerton's tracing our discovery to yourself; and, though I will not
press you farther, I add this—You urge me to accept your friend's
hand ; you seem interested in the success of his suit, and you plead
it with a warmth that shows how much you regard what you suppose
is his happiness ; I will never accept his hand till I can do so without blush for my penury—till my dowry is secured, and that can
only be by my brother's union with the exile's daughter. For your
friend's sake, therefore, think well how you can aid me in the first
step to that alliance. The young lady once discovered, and my
brother has no fear for the success of his suit."

"And you would marry Frank if the dower was secured?"

"Your arguments in his favour seem irresistible," replied Beatrice,
looking down.

A flash went from Randal's eyes, and he mused a few moments.

Then slowly rising and drawing on his gloves, he said—

"Well, at least you so far reconcile my honour towards aiding
your research, that you now inform me you mean no ill to the exile."

"Ill !—the restoration to fortune, honours, his native land."

"And you so far enlist my heart on your side, that you inspire
me with the hope to contribute to the happiness of two friends
whom I dearly love. I will, therefore, diligently try to ascertain
if, among the refugees I have met with, lurk those whom you seek ;

and if so, I will thoughtfully consider how to give you the clue.
Meanwhile, not one incautious word to Egerton."

"Trust me—I am a woman of the world."

Randal now had gained the door. He paused, and renewed
carelessly—

"This young lady must be heiress to great wealth, to induce
a man of your brother's rank to take so much pains to discover her."

"Her wealth *will* be vast," replied the Marchesa; "and if anything from wealth or influence in a foreign state could be permitted
to prove my brother's gratitude—"

"Ah, fie!" interrupted Randal; and, approaching Madame di
Negra, he lifted her hand to his lips, and said gallantly—

"This is reward enough to your *preux chevalier*."

With those words he took his leave.

CHAPTER IV.

WITH his hands behind him, and his head drooping on his
breast—slow, stealthy, noiseless, Randal Leslie glided
along the streets on leaving the Italian's house. Across
the scheme he had before revolved, there glanced another
yet more glittering, for its gain might be more sure and immediate.
If the exile's daughter were heiress to such wealth, might he himself hope ——. He stopped short even in his own soliloquy, and
his breath came quick. Now, in his last visit to Hazeldean, he
had come in contact with Riccabocca, and been struck by the
beauty of Violante. A vague suspicion had crossed him that these
might be the persons of whom the Marchesa was in search, and
the suspicion had been confirmed by Beatrice's description of the
refugee she desired to discover. But as he had not then learned
the reason for her inquiries, nor conceived the possibility that he
could have any personal interest in ascertaining the truth, he had
only classed the secret in question among those the farther research
into which might be left to time and occasion. Certainly the
reader will not do the unscrupulous intellect of Randal Leslie the
injustice to suppose that he was deterred from confiding to his fair
friend all that he knew of Riccabocca, by the refinement of honour
to which he had so chivalrously alluded. He had correctly stated
Audley Egerton's warning against any indiscreet confidence, though
he had forborne to mention a more recent and direct renewal of the
same caution. His first visit to Hazeldean had been paid without
consulting Egerton. He had been passing some days at his father's

house, and had gone over thence to the Squire's. On his return to London, he had, however, mentioned this visit to Audley, who had seemed annoyed and even displeased at it, though Randal knew sufficient of Egerton's character to guess that such feelings could scarce be occasioned merely by his estrangement from his half-brother. This dissatisfaction. had, therefore, puzzled the young man. But, as it was necessary to his views to establish intimacy with the Squire, he did not yield the point with his customary deference to his patron's whims. Accordingly he observed, that he should be very sorry to do anything displeasing to his benefactor, but that his father had been naturally anxious that he should not appear positively to slight the friendly overtures of Mr. Hazeldean.

"Why naturally?" asked Egerton.

"Because you know that Mr. Hazeldean is a relation of mine—that my grandmother was a Hazeldean."

"Ah!" said Egerton, who, as it has been before said, knew little and cared less, about the Hazeldean pedigree, "I was either not aware of that circumstance, or had forgotten it. And your father thinks that the Squire may leave you a legacy?"

"Oh, sir, my father is not so mercenary—such an idea never entered his head. But the Squire himself has indeed said—'Why, if anything happened to Frank, you would be next heir to my lands, and therefore we ought to know each other.' But—"

"Enough," interrupted Egerton. "I am the last man to pretend to the right of standing between you and a single chance of fortune, or of aid to it. And whom did you meet at Hazeldean?"

"There was no one there, sir; not even Frank."

"Hum. Is the Squire not on good terms with his parson? Any quarrel about tithes?"

"Oh, no quarrel. I forgot Mr. Dale; I saw him pretty often. He admires and praises you very much, sir."

"Me—and why? What did he say of me?"

"That your heart was as sound as your head; that he had once seen you about some old parishioners of his, and that he had been much impressed with the depth of feeling he could not have antici- pated in a man of the world, and a statesman."

"Oh, that was all; some affair when I was member for Lans-mere?"

"I suppose so."

Here the conversation had broken off; but the next time Randal was led to visit the Squire he had formally asked Egerton's consent, who, after a moment's hesitation, had as formally replied, "I have no objection."

On returning from this visit, Randal mentioned that he had seen Riccabocca : and Egerton, a little startled at first, said, composedly, "Doubtless one of the political refugees ; take care not to set Madame di Negra on his track. Remember, she is suspected of being a spy of the Austrian government."

"Rely on me, sir," said Randal ; "but I should think this poor Doctor can scarcely be the person she seeks to discover."

"That is no affair of ours," answered Egerton : "we are English gentlemen, and make not a step towards the secrets of another."

Now, when Randal revolved this rather ambiguous answer, and recalled the uneasiness with which Egerton had first heard of his visit to Hazeldean, he thought that he was indeed near the secret which Egerton desired to conceal from him and from all—viz., the incognito of the Italian whom Lord L'Estrange had taken under his protection.

"My cards," said Randal to himself, as with a deep-drawn sigh he resumed his soliloquy, "are become difficult to play. On the one hand, to entangle Frank into marriage with this foreigner, the Squire could never forgive him. On the other hand, if she will not marry him without the dowry—and that depends on her brother's wedding this countrywoman—and that countrywoman be, as I surmise, Violante—and Violante be this heiress, and to be won by me ! Tush, tush. Such delicate scruples in a woman so placed and so constituted as Beatrice di Negra must be easily talked away. Nay, the loss itself of this alliance to her brother, the loss of her own dowry—the very pressure of poverty and debt—would compel her into the sole escape left to her option. I will then follow up the old plan ; I will go down to Hazeldean, and see if there be any substance in the new one ;—and then to reconcile both. Aha—the House of Leslie shall rise yet from its ruin—and—"

Here he was startled from his reverie by a friendly slap on the shoulder, and an exclamation—"Why, Randal, you are more absent than when you used to steal away from the cricket-ground, muttering Greek verses, at Eton."

"My dear Frank," said Randal, "you—you are so *brusque*, and I was just thinking of you."

"Were you? And kindly, then, I am sure," said Frank Hazeldean, his honest, handsome face lighted up with the unsuspecting genial trust of friendship ; "and Heaven knows," he added, with a sadder voice, and a graver expression on his eye and lip,—"Heaven knows I want all the kindness you can give me !"

"I thought," said Randal, "that your father's last supply, of which I was fortunate enough to be the bearer would clear off your more pressing debts.   I don't pretend to preach, but really I must say, once more, you should not be so extravagant."

FRANK (seriously).—"I have done my best to reform.   I have sold off my horses, and I have not touched dice nor card these six months; I would not even put into the raffle for the last Derby." This last was said with the air of a man who doubted the possibility of obtaining belief to some assertion of preternatural abstinence and virtue.

RANDAL.—"Is it possible?   But, with such self-conquest, how is it that you cannot contrive to live within the bounds of a very liberal allowance?"

FRANK (despondingly).—"Why, when a man once gets his head under water, it is so hard to float back again on the surface.   You see, I attribute all my embarrassments to that first concealment of my debts from my father, when they could have been so easily met, and when he came up to town so kindly."

"I am sorry, then, that I gave you that advice."

"Oh, you meant it so kindly, I don't reproach you; it was all my own fault."

"Why, indeed, I did urge you to pay off that moiety of your debts left unpaid, with your allowance.   Had you done so, all had been well."

"Yes; but poor Borrowell got into such a scrape at Goodwood— I could not resist him; a debt of honour—*that* must be paid; so when I signed another bill for him, he could not pay it, poor fellow! Really he would have shot himself, if I had not renewed it.   And now it is swelled to such an amount with that cursed interest, that *he* never can pay it; and one bill, of course, begets another—and to be renewed every three months; 'tis the devil and all!   So little as I ever got for all I have borrowed," added Frank, with a kind of rueful amaze.   "Not £1500 ready money; and the interest would cost me almost as much yearly—if I had it."

"Only £1500!"

"Well—besides seven large chests of the worst cigars you ever smoked, three pipes of wine that no one would drink; and a great bear that had been imported from Greenland for the sake of its grease."

"That should, at least, have saved you a bill with your hair-dresser."

"I paid his bill with it," said Frank, "and very good-natured he was to take the monster off my hands—it had already hugged two soldiers and one groom into the shape of a flounder.   I tell you what," resumed Frank, after a short pause, "I have a great mind even now to tell my father honestly all my embarrassments."

RANDAL (solemnly).—"Hum!"

FRANK.—"What? don't you think it would be the best way? I never can save enough—never can pay off what I owe? and it rolls like a snowball."

RANDAL.—"Judging by the Squire's talk, I think that with the first sight of your affairs you would forfeit his favour for ever; and your mother would be so shocked, especially after supposing that the sum I brought you so lately sufficed to pay off every claim on you. If you had not assured her of that it might be different; but she who so hates an untruth, and who said to the Squire, 'Frank says this will clear him; and with all his faults, Frank never yet told a lie!'"

"Oh, my dear mother!—I fancy I hear her!" cried Frank, with deep emotion. "But I did not tell a lie, Randal; I did not say that that sum would clear me."

"You empowered and begged me to say so," replied Randal, with grave coldness; "and don't blame me if I believed you."

"No, no! I only said it would clear me for the moment."

"I misunderstood you, then, sadly; and such mistakes involve my own honour. Pardon me, Frank; don't ask my aid in future. You see with the best intentions, I only compromise myself."

"If you forsake me, I may as well go and throw myself into the river," said Frank, in a tone of despair; "and sooner or later, my father must know my necessities. The Jews threaten to go to him already; and the longer the delay, the more terrible the explanation."

"I don't see why your father should ever learn the state of your affairs; and it seems to me that you could pay off these usurers, and get rid of these bills, by raising money on comparatively easy terms—"

"How?" cried Frank, eagerly.

"Why, the Casino property is entailed on you, and you might obtain a sum upon that, not to be paid till the property becomes yours."

"At my poor father's death? Oh, no—no! I cannot bear the idea of this cold-blooded calculation on a father's death. I know it is not uncommon; I know other fellows who have done it, but they never had parents so kind as mine; and even in them it shocked and revolted me. The contemplating a father's death, and profiting by the contemplation,—it seems a kind of parricide: it is not natural, Randal. Besides, don't you remember what the Governor said—he actually wept while he said it—'Never calculate on my death; I could not bear that.' Oh, Randal, don't speak of it!"

"I respect your sentiments; but still, all the post-obits you could raise could not shorten Mr. Hazeldean's life by a day. However, dismiss that idea ; we must think of some other device. Ha, Frank ! you are a handsome fellow, and your expectations are great—why don't you marry some woman with money ? "

"Pooh ! " exclaimed Frank, colouring. "You know, Randal, that there is but one woman in the world I can ever think of ; and I love her so devotedly, that, though I was as gay as most men before, I really feel as if the rest of her sex had lost every charm. I was passing through the street now—merely to look up at her windows."

"You speak of Madame di Negra ? I have just left her. Certainly she is two or three years older than you ; but if you can get over that misfortune, why not marry her ? "

"Marry her ! " cried Frank, in amaze, and all his colour fled from his cheeks. "Marry her ! Are you serious ? "

"Why not ? "

"But even if she, who is so accomplished, so admired—even if she would accept me, she is, you know, poorer than myself. She has told me so frankly. That woman has such a noble heart ! and —and—my father would never consent, nor my mother either. I know they would not."

"Because she is a foreigner ? "

"Yes—partly."

"Yet the Squire suffered his cousin to marry a foreigner."

"That was different. He had no control over Jemima ; and a daughter-in-law is so different ; and my father is so English in his notions ; and Madame di Negra, you see, is altogether so foreign. Her very graces would be against her in his eyes."

"I think you do both your parents injustice. A foreigner of low birth—an actress or singer, for instance—of course would be highly objectionable ; but a woman, like Madame di Negra, of such high birth and connections—"

Frank shook his head. "I don't think the Governor would care a straw about her connections, if she were a king's daughter. He considers all foreigners pretty much alike. And then, you know " (Frank's voice sank into a whisper)—"you know that one of the very reasons why she is so dear to me, would be an insuperable objection to the old-fashioned folks at home."

"I don't understand you, Frank."

"I love her the more," said young Hazeldean, raising his front with a noble pride, that seemed to speak of his descent from a race of cavaliers and gentlemen—"I love her the more because the world has slandered her name—because I believe her to be pure and wronged. But would they at the Hall—they who do not see with a lover's eyes—they who have all the stubborn English notions about the indecorum and license of Continental manners, and will so readily credit the worst?—Oh, no—I love, I cannot help it—but I have no hope."

"It is very possible that you may be right," exclaimed Randal, as if struck and half convinced by his companion's argument—"very possible; and certainly I think that the homely folks at the Hall would fret and fume at first, if they heard you were married to Madame di Negra. Yet still, when your father learned that you had done so, not from passion alone, but to save him from all pecuniary sacrifice—to clear yourself of debt—to—"

"What do you mean?" exclaimed Frank, impatiently.

"I have reason to know that Madame di Negra will have as large a portion as your father could reasonably expect you to receive with any English wife. And when this is properly stated to the Squire, and the high position and rank of your wife fully established and brought home to him—for I must think that these would tell, despite your exaggerated notions of his prejudices—and then, when he really sees Madame di Negra, and can judge of her beauty and rare gifts, upon my word, I think, Frank, that there would be no cause for fear. After all, too, you are his only son. He will have no option but to forgive you; and I know how anxiously both your parents wish to see you settled in life."

Frank's whole countenance became illuminated. "There is no one who understands the Squire like you, certainly," said he, with lively joy. "He has the highest opinion of your judgment. And you really believe you could smooth matters?"

"I believe so; but I should be sorry to induce you to run any risk; and if, on cool consideration, you think that risk is incurred, I strongly advise you to avoid all occasion of seeing the poor Marchesa. Ah, you wince; but I say it for her sake as well as your own. First you must be aware, that, unless you have serious thoughts of marriage, your attentions can but add to the very rumours that, equally groundless, you so feelingly resent; and, secondly, because I don't think any man has a right to win the affections of a woman—especially a woman who seems to me likely to love with her whole heart and soul—merely to gratify his own vanity."

"Vanity! Good heavens! can you think so poorly of me? But as to the Marchesa's affections," continued Frank, with a faltering voice, "do you really and honestly believe that they are to be won by me?"

"I fear lest they may be half won already," said Randal, with a smile and a shake of the head; but she is too proud to let you see any effect you may produce on her, especially when, as I take it for granted, you have never hinted at the hope of obtaining her hand."

"I never till now conceived such a hope. My dear Randal, all my cares have vanished—I tread upon air—I have a great mind to call on her at once."

"Stay, stay," said Randal. "Let me give you a caution. I have just informed you that Madame di Negra will have, what you suspected not before, a fortune suitable to her birth. Any abrupt change in your manner at present might induce her to believe that you were influenced by that intelligence."

"Ah!" exclaimed Frank, stopping short, as if wounded to the quick. "And I feel guilty—feel as if I *was* influenced by that intelligence. So I am, too, when I reflect," he continued, with a *naïveté* that was half pathetic; "but I hope she will not be *very* rich—if so, I'll not call."

"Make your mind easy, it is but a portion of some twenty or thirty thousand pounds, that would just suffice to discharge all your debts, clear away all obstacle to your union, and in return for which you could secure a more than adequate jointure and settlement on the Casino property. Now I am on that head, I will be yet more communicative. Madame di Negra has a noble heart, as you say, and told me herself, that, until her brother on his arrival had assured her of this dowry, she would never have consented to marry you— never crippled with her own embarrassments the man she loves. Ah! with what delight she will hail the thought of assisting you to win back your father's heart! But be guarded meanwhile. And now, Frank, what say you—would it not be well if I ran down to Hazeldean to sound your parents? It is rather inconvenient to me, to be sure, to leave town just at present; but I will do more than that to render you a smaller service. Yes, I'll go to Rood Hall to-morrow, and thence to Hazeldean. I am sure your father will press me to stay, and I shall have ample opportunities to judge of the manner in which he would be likely to regard your marriage with Madame di Negra—supposing always it were properly put to him. We can then act accordingly."

"My dear, dear Randal, how can I thank you? If ever a poor fellow like me can serve you in return—but that's impossible."

"Why certainly, I will never ask you to be security to a bill of mine," said Randal, laughing. "I practise the economy I preach."

"Ah!" said Frank, with a groan, "that is because your mind is cultivated—you have so many resources; and all my faults have come from idleness. If I had had anything to do on a rainy day, I should never have got into these scrapes."

"Oh! you will have enough to do some day managing your property. We who have no property must find one in knowledge. Adieu, my dear Frank—I must go home now. By the way, you have never, by chance, spoken of the Riccaboccas to Madame di Negra?"

"The Riccaboccas? No. That's well thought of. It may interest her to know that a relation of mine has married her countryman. Very odd that I never did mention it; but, to say truth, I really do talk so little to her: she is so superior, and I feel positively shy with her."

"Do me the favour, Frank," said Randal, waiting patiently till this reply ended—for he was devising all the time what reason to give for his request—"never to allude to the Riccaboccas either to her or to her brother, to whom you are sure to be presented."

"Why not allude to them?"

Randal hesitated a moment. His invention was still at fault, and, for a wonder, he thought it the best policy to go pretty near the truth.

"Why, I will tell you. The Marchesa conceals nothing from her brother, and he is one of the few Italians who are in high favour with the Austrian court."

"Well!"

"And I suspect that poor Dr. Riccabocca fled his country from some mad experiment at revolution, and is still hiding from the Austrian police."

"But they can't hurt him here," said Frank, with an Englishman's dogged inborn conviction of the sanctity of his native island. "I should like to see an Austrian pretend to dictate to us whom to receive and whom to reject."

"Hum—that's true and constitutional, no doubt; but Riccabocca may have excellent reasons—and, to speak plainly, I know he has (perhaps as affecting the safety of friends in Italy)—for preserving his incognito, and we are bound, to respect those reasons without inquiring further."

"Still I cannot think so meanly of Madame di Negra," persisted Frank (shrewd here, though credulous elsewhere, and both from his sense of honour), "as to suppose that she would descend to be a spy, and injure a poor countryman of her own, who trusts to the same hospitality she receives herself at our English hands. Oh! if I thought that, I could not love her!" added Frank, with energy.

"Certainly you are right. But see in what a false position you would place both her brother and herself. If they knew Riccabocca's secret, and proclaimed it to the Austrian Government, as you say, it would be cruel and mean ; but if they knew it and concealed it, it might involve them both in the most serious consequences. You know the Austrian policy is proverbially so jealous and tyrannical ? "

" Well, the newspapers say so, certainly."

" And, in short, your discretion can do no harm, and your indiscretion may. Therefore, give me your word, Frank. I can't stay to argue now."

" I'll not allude to the Riccaboccas, upon my honour," answered Frank ; "still, I am sure that they would be as safe with the Marchesa as with——"

" I rely on your honour," interrupted Randal, hastily, and hurried off.

CHAPTER V.

OWARDS the evening of the following day, Randal Leslie walked slowly from a village in the main road (about two miles from Rood Hall), at which he had got out of the coach. He passed through meads and cornfields, and by the skirts of woods which had formerly belonged to his ancestors, but had been long since alienated. He was alone amidst the haunts of his boyhood, the scenes in which he had first invoked the grand Spirit of Knowledge, to bid the Celestial Still One minister to the commands of an earthly and turbulent ambition. He paused often in his path, especially when the undulations of the ground gave a glimpse of the gray church tower, or the gloomy firs that rose above the desolate wastes of Rood.

" Here," thought Randal, with a softening eye—"here, how often, comparing the fertility of the lands passed away from the inheritance of my fathers, with the forlorn wilds that are left to their mouldering Hall—here, how often have I said to myself—'I will rebuild the fortunes of my house.' And straightway Toil lost its aspect of drudge, and grew kingly, and books became as living armies to serve my thought. Again—again—O thou haughty Past, brace and strengthen me in the battle with the Future." His pale lips writhed as he soliloquized, for his conscience spoke to him while he thus addressed his will, and its voice was heard more audibly in the quiet of the rural landscape, than amidst the turmoil and din of that armed and sleepless camp which we call a city.

Doubtless, though Ambition have objects more vast and beneficent than the restoration of a name,—*that* in itself is high and chivalrous, and appeals to a strong interest in the human heart. But all emotions, and all ends, of a nobler character, had seemed to filter themselves free from every golden grain in passing through the mechanism of Randal's intellect, and came forth at last into egotism clear and unalloyed. Nevertheless, it is a strange truth that, to a man of cultivated mind, however perverted and vicious, there are vouchsafed gleams of brighter sentiments, irregular perceptions of moral beauty, denied to the brutal unreasoning wickedness of uneducated villainy —which perhaps ultimately serve as his punishment—according to the old thought of the satirist, that there is no greater curse than to perceive virtue yet adopt vice. And as the solitary schemer walked slowly on, and his childhood—innocent at least in deed—came distinct before him through the halo of bygone dreams—dreams far purer than those from which he now rose each morning to the active world of Man—a profound, melancholy crept over him, and suddenly he exclaimed aloud, " *Then* I aspired to be renowned and great— *now*, how is it that, so advanced in my career, all that seemed lofty in the end has vanished from me, and the only means that I contemplate are those which my childhood would have called poor and vile? Ah! is it that I then read but books, and now my knowledge has passed onward, and men contaminate more than books? But," he continued, in a lower voice, as if arguing with himself,—"if power is only so to be won—and of what use is knowledge if it be not power—does not success in life justify all things? And who prizes the wise man if he fails?" He continued his way, but still the soft tranquillity around rebuked him, and still his reason was dissatisfied, as well as his conscience. There are times when Nature, like a bath of youth, seems to restore to the jaded soul its freshness—times from which some men have emerged, as if re-born. The crises of life are very silent. Suddenly the scene opened on Randal Leslie's eyes. The bare desert common—the dilapidated church—the old house, partially seen in the dank dreary hollow, into which it seemed to Randal to have sunken deeper and lowlier than when he saw it last. And on the common were some young men playing at hockey. That old-fashioned game, now very uncommon in England, except at schools, was still preserved in the primitive vicinity of Rood by the young yeomen and farmers. Randal stood by the stile and looked on, for among the players he recognized his brother Oliver. Presently the ball was struck towards Oliver, and the group instantly gathered round that young gentleman and snatched him from Randal's eye; but the elder brother heard

a displeasing din, a derisive laughter. Oliver had shrunk from the
danger of the thick clubbed sticks that plied around him, and received
some stroke across the legs, for his voice rose whining, and was
drowned by shouts of, "Go to your mammy. That's Noll Leslie—
all over. Butter shins."

Randal's sallow face became scarlet. "The jest of boors—a
Leslie!" he muttered, and ground his teeth. He sprang over the
stile and walked erect and haughtily across the ground. The
players cried out indignantly. Randal raised his hat, and they
recognized him, and stopped the game. For him at least a certain
respect was felt. Oliver turned round quickly, and ran up to him.
Randal caught his arm firmly, and without saying a word to the
rest, drew him away towards the house. Oliver cast a regretful,
lingering look behind him, rubbed his shins, and then stole a timid
glance towards Randal's severe and moody countenance.

"You are not angry that I was playing at hockey with our neighbours," said he deprecatingly, observing that Randal would not
break the silence.

"No," replied the elder brother; "but, in associating with his
inferiors, a gentleman still knows how to maintain his dignity.
There is no harm in playing with inferiors, but it is necessary to a
gentleman to play so that he is not the laughing-stock of clowns."

Oliver hung his head, and made no answer. They came into the
slovenly precincts of the court, and the pigs stared at them from the
palings, as their progenitors had stared, years before, at Frank
Hazeldean.

Mr. Leslie senior, in a shabby straw-hat, was engaged in feeding
the chickens before the threshold, and he performed even that
occupation with a maundering lackadaisical slothfulness, dropping
down the grains almost one by one from his inert dreamy fingers.

Randal's sister, her hair still and for ever hanging about her ears,
was seated on a rush-bottom chair, reading a tattered novel; and
from the parlour window was heard the querulous voice of Mrs.
Leslie, in high fidget and complaint.

Somehow or other, as the young heir to all this helpless poverty
stood in the courtyard, with his sharp, refined, intelligent features,
and his strange elegance of dress and aspect, one better comprehended how, left solely to the egotism of his knowledge and his
ambition, in such a family, and without any of the sweet nameless
lessons of Home, he had grown up into such close and secret solitude
of soul—how the mind had taken so little nutriment from the heart,
and how that affection and respect which the warm circle of the
hearth usually calls forth had passed with him to the graves of dead

fathers, growing, as it were, bloodless and ghoul-like amidst the charnels on which they fed.

"Ha, Randal, boy," said Mr. Leslie, looking up, lazily, "how d'ye do? Who could have expected you? My dear—my dear," he cried, in a broken voice, and as if in helpless dismay, "here's Randal, and he'll be wanting dinner, or supper, or something." But, in the meanwhile, Randal's sister Juliet had sprung up and thrown her arms round her brother's neck, and he had drawn her aside caressingly, for Randal's strongest human affection was for this sister."

"You are growing very pretty, Juliet," said he, smoothing back her hair; "why do yourself such injustice—why not pay more attention to your appearance, as I have so often begged you to do?"

"I did not expect you, dear Randal; you always come so suddenly, and catch us *en dish-a-bill.*"

"Dish-abill!" echoed Randal, with a groan. "*Dishabille!*—you ought never to be so caught!"

"No one else does so catch us—nobody else ever comes—Heigho!" and the young lady sighed very heartily.

"Patience, patience; my day is coming, and then yours, my sister," replied Randal, with genuine pity, as he gazed upon what a little care could have trained into so fair a flower, and what now looked so like a weed.

Here Mrs. Leslie, in a state of intense excitement—having rushed through the parlour—leaving a fragment of her gown between the yawning brass of the never-mended Brummagem work-table—tore across the hall—whirled out of the door, scattering the chickens to the right and left, and clutched hold of Randal in her motherly embrace. "La, how you do shake my nerves," she cried, after giving him a most hasty and uncomfortable kiss. "And you are hungry too, and nothing in the house but cold mutton! Jenny, Jenny—I say, Jenny! Juliet, have you seen Jenny? Where's Jenny? Out with the odd man, I'll be bound."

"I am not hungry, mother," said Randal; "I wish for nothing but tea." Juliet, scrambling up her hair, darted into the house to prepare the tea, and also to "tidy herself." She dearly loved her fine brother, but she was greatly in awe of him.

Randal seated himself on the broken pales. "Take care they don't come down," said Mr. Leslie, with some anxiety.

"Oh, sir, I am very light; nothing comes down with me."

The pigs stared up, and grunted in amaze at the stranger.

"Mother," said the young man, detaining Mrs. Leslie, who wanted to set off in chase of Jenny—"Mother, you should not let

Oliver associate with those village boors. It is time to think of a profession for him."

"Oh, he eats us out of house and home—such an appetite! But as to a profession—what is he fit for! He will never be a scholar."

Randal nodded a moody assent; for, indeed Oliver had been sent to Cambridge, and supported there out of Randal's income from his official pay; and Oliver had been plucked for his Little Go.

"There is the army," said the elder brother—"a gentleman's calling. How handsome Juliet ought to be—but—I left money for masters—and she pronounces French like a chambermaid."

"Yet she is fond of her book too. She's always reading, and good for nothing else."

"Reading!—those trashy novels!"

"So like you—you always come to scold, and make things unpleasant," said Mrs. Leslie, peevishly. "You are grown too fine for us, and I am sure we suffer affronts enough from others, not to want a little respect from our own children."

"I did not mean to affront you," said Randal, sadly. "Pardon me. But who else has done so?"

Then Mrs. Leslie went into a minute and most irritating catalogue of all the mortifications and insults she had received; the grievances of a petty provincial family, with much pretension and small power; of all people, indeed, without the disposition to please—without the ability to serve—who exaggerate every offence, and are thankful for no kindness. Farmer Jones had insolently refused to send his waggon twenty miles for coals. Mr. Giles, the butcher, requesting the payment of his bill, had stated that the custom at Rood was too small for him to allow credit. Squire Thornhill, who was the present owner of the fairest slice of the old Leslie domains, had taken the liberty to ask permission to shoot over Mr. Leslie's land, since Mr. Leslie did not preserve. Lady Spratt (new people from the city, who hired a neighbouring country-seat) had taken a discharged servant of Mrs. Leslie's without applying for the character. The Lord-Lieutenant had given a ball, and had not invited the Leslies. Mr. Leslie's tenants had voted against their landlord's wish at the recent election. More than all, Squire Hazeldean and his Harry had called at Rood, and though Mrs. Leslie had screamed out to Jenny, "Not at home," she had been seen at the window, and the Squire had actually forced his way in, and caught the whole family "in a state not fit to be seen." That was a trifle, but the Squire had presumed to instruct Mr. Leslie how to manage his property, and Mrs. Hazeldean had actually told Juliet to hold up her head, and tie up her hair, "as if we were her cottagers!" said Mrs. Leslie, with the pride of a Montfydget.

All these, and various other annoyances, though Randal was too sensible not to perceive their insignificance, still galled and mortified the listening heir of Rood. They showed, at least, even to the well-meant officiousness of the Hazeldeans, the small account in which the fallen family was held. As he sat still on the moss-grown pales, gloomy and taciturn, his mother standing beside him, with her cap awry, Mr. Leslie shamblingly sauntered up, and said in a pensive, dolorous whine—

"I wish we had a good sum of money, Randal, boy!"

To do Mr. Leslie justice, he seldom gave vent to any wish that savoured of avarice. His mind must be singularly aroused, to wander out of its normal limits of sluggish, dull content.

So Randal looked at him in surprise, and said, "Do you, sir? —why?"

"The manors of Rood and Dulmansberry, and all the lands therein, which my great-grandfather sold away, are to be sold again when Squire Thornhill's eldest son comes of age, to cut off the entail. Sir John Spratt talks of buying them. I should like to have them back again! 'Tis a shame to see the Leslie estates hawked about, and bought by Spratts and people. I wish I had a great—great sum of ready money."

The poor gentleman extended his helpless fingers as he spoke, and fell into a dejected reverie.

Randal sprang from the paling, a movement which frightened the contemplative pigs, and set them off squalling and scampering, "When does young Thornhill come of age?"

"He was nineteen last August. I know it, because the day he was born I picked up my fossil of the sea-horse, just by Dulmans-berry church, when the joy-bells were ringing. My fossil sea-horse! It will be an heirloom, Randal——"

"Two years—nearly two years—yet—ah, ah!" said Randal; and his sister now appearing, to announce that tea was ready, he threw his arm round her neck and kissed her. Juliet had arranged her hair and trimmed up her dress. She looked very pretty, and she had now the air of a gentlewoman—something of Randal's own refinement in her slender proportions and well-shaped head.

"Be patient, patient still, my dear sister," whispered Randal, " and keep your heart whole for two years longer."

The young man was gay and good-humoured over his simple meal, while his family grouped round him. When it was over, Mr. Leslie lighted his pipe, and called for his brandy-and-water.

Mrs. Leslie began to question about London and Court, and the new King and the new Queen, and Mr. Audley Egerton, and hoped Mr. Egerton would leave Randal all his money, and that Randal would marry a rich woman, and that the King would make him a prime-minister one of these days; and then she should like to see if Farmer Jones would refuse to send his waggon for coals! And, every now and then, as the word "riches" or "money" caught Mr. Leslie's ears, he shook his head, drew his pipe from his mouth, "A Spratt should not have what belonged to my great-great-grandfather. If I had a good sum of ready money!—the old family estates!" Oliver and Juliet sat silent, and on their good behaviour; and Randal, indulging his own reveries, dreamily heard the words "money," "Spratt," "great-great-grandfather," "rich wife," "family estates;" and they sounded to him vague and afar off, like whispers from the world of romance and legend—weird prophecies of things to be.

Such was the hearth which warmed the viper that nestled and gnawed at the heart of Randal, poisoning all the aspirations that youth should have rendered pure, ambition lofty, and knowledge beneficent and divine.

CHAPTER VI.

WHEN the rest of the household were in deep sleep, Randal stood long at his open window, looking over the dreary, comfortless scene—the moon gleaming from skies half-autumnal, half-wintry, upon squalid decay, through the ragged fissures of the firs; and when he lay down to rest, his sleep was feverish, and troubled by turbulent dreams.

However, he was up early, and with an unwonted colour in his cheeks, which his sister ascribed to the country air. After breakfast, he took his way towards Hazeldean, mounted upon a tolerable horse, which he borrowed of a neighbouring farmer who occasionally hunted. Before noon, the garden and terrace of the Casino came in sight. He reined in his horse, and by the little fountain at which Leonard had been wont to eat his radishes and con his book, he saw Riccabocca seated under the shade of the red umbrella. And by the Italian's side stood a form that a Greek of old might have deemed the Naïad of the Fount; for in its youthful beauty there was something so full of poetry—something at once so sweet and so stately—that it spoke to the imagination while it charmed the sense.

Randal dismounted, tied his horse to the gate, and, walking down a trellised alley, came suddenly to the spot. His dark shadow fell over the clear mirror of the fountain just as Riccabocca had said, "All here is so secure from evil!—the waves of the fountain are never troubled like those of the river!" and Violante had answered in her soft native tongue, and lifting her dark, spiritual eyes—"But the fountain would be but a lifeless pool, oh, my father, if the spray did not mount towards the skies!"

CHAPTER VII.

RANDAL advanced—"I fear, Signor Riccabocca, that I am guilty of some want of ceremony."

"To dispense with ceremony is the most delicate mode of conferring a compliment," replied the urbane Italian, as he recovered from his first surprise at Randal's sudden address, and extended his hand.

Violante bowed her graceful head to the young man's respectful salutation. "I am on my way to Hazeldean," resumed Randal, "and, seeing you in the garden, could not resist this intrusion."

RICCABOCCA.—"You come from London? Stirring times for you English, but I do not ask you the news. No news can affect us."

RANDAL (softly).—"Perhaps yes."

RICCABOCCA (startled).—"How?"

VIOLANTE.—"Surely he speaks of Italy, and news from that country affects you still, my father."

RICCABOCCA.—"Nay, nay, nothing affects me like this country; its east winds might affect a pyramid! Draw your mantle round you, child, and go in; the air has suddenly grown chill."

Violante smiled on her father, glanced uneasily towards Randal's grave brow, and went slowly towards the house.

Riccabocca, after waiting some moments in silence, as if expecting Randal to speak, said, with affected carelessness, "So you think that you have news that might affect me? *Corpo di Bacco!* I am curious to learn what!"

"I may be mistaken—that depends on your answer to one question. Do you know the Count of Peschiera?"

Riccabocca winced, and turned pale. He could not baffle the watchful eye of the questioner.

"Enough," said Randal; "I see that I am right. Believe in my sincerity. I speak but to warn and to serve you. The Count seeks to discover the retreat of a countryman and kinsman of his own."

"And for what end?" cried Riccabocca, thrown off his guard, and his breast dilated, his crest rose, and his eye flashed; valour and defiance broke from habitual caution and self-control. "But —pooh!" he added, striving to regain his ordinary and half-ironical calm, "it matters not to me. I grant, sir, that I know the Count di Peschiera; but what has Dr. Riccabocca to do with the kinsman of so grand a personage?"

"Dr. Riccabocca—nothing. But—" here Randal put his lip close to the Italian's ear, and whispered a brief sentence. Then retreating a step, but laying his hand on the exile's shoulder, he added—"Need I say that your secret is safe with me?"

Riccabocca made no answer. His eyes rested on the ground musingly.

Randal continued—"And I shall esteem it the highest honour you can bestow on me, to be permitted to assist you in forestalling danger."

RICCABOCCA (slowly).—"Sir, I thank you; you have my secret, and I feel assured it is safe, for I speak to an English gentleman. There may be family reasons why I should avoid the Count di Peschiera; and, indeed, he is safest from shoals who steers clearest of his—relations."

The poor Italian regained his caustic smile as he uttered that wise villainous Italian maxim.

RANDAL.—"I know little of the Count of Peschiera save from the current talk of the world. He is said to hold the estates of a kinsman who took part in a conspiracy against the Austrian power."

RICCABOCCA.—"It is true. Let that content him; what more does he desire? You spoke of forestalling danger; what danger? I am on the soil of England, and protected by its laws."

RANDAL.—"Allow me to inquire if, had the kinsman no child, the Count di Peschiera would be legitimate and natural heir to the estates he holds?"

RICCABOCCA.—"He would—What then?"

RANDAL.—"Does that thought suggest no danger to the child of the kinsman?"

Riccabocca recoiled, and gasped forth, "The child! You do not mean to imply that this man, infamous though he be, can contemplate the crime of an assassin?"

Randal paused perplexed. His ground was delicate. He knew not what causes of resentment the exile entertained against the Count. He knew not whether Riccabocca would not assent to an alliance that might restore him to his country—and he resolved to feel his way with precaution.

"I did not," said he, smiling gravely, "mean to insinuate so horrible a charge against a man whom I have never seen. He seeks you—that is all I know. I imagine, from his general character, that in this search he consults his interest. Perhaps all matters might be conciliated by an interview!"

"An interview!" exclaimed Riccabocca; "there is but one way we should meet—foot to foot, and hand to hand."

"Is it so? Then you would not listen to the Count if he proposed some amicable compromise—if, for instance, he was a candidate for the hand of your daughter?"

The poor Italian, so wise and so subtle in his talk, was as rash and blind when it came to action, as if he had been born in Ireland, and nourished on potatoes and Repeal. He bared his whole soul to the merciless eye of Randal.

"My daughter!" he exclaimed. "Sir, your very question is an insult."

Randal's way became clear at once. "Forgive me," he said, mildly; "I will tell you frankly all that I know. I am acquainted with the Count's sister. I have some little influence over her. It was she who informed me that the Count had come here, bent upon discovering your refuge, and resolved to wed your daughter. This is the danger of which I spoke. And when I asked your permission to aid in forestalling it, I only intended to suggest that it might be wise to find some securer home, and that I, if permitted to know that home, and to visit you, could apprise you from time to time of the Count's plans and movements."

"Sir, I thank you sincerely," said Riccabocca, with emotion; "but am I not safe here?"

"I doubt it. Many people have visited the Squire in the shooting season, who will have heard of you—perhaps seen you, and who are likely to meet the Count in London. And Frank Hazeldean, too, who knows the Count's sister——"

"True, true," interrupted Riccabocca. "I see, I see. I will consider. I will reflect. Meanwhile you are going to Hazeldean. Do not say a word to the Squire. He knows not the secret you have discovered."

With those words Riccabocca turned slightly away, and Randal took the hint to depart.

"At all times command and rely on me," said the young traitor, and he regained the pale to which he had fastened his horse.

As he remounted, he cast his eyes towards the place where he had left Riccabocca. The Italian was still standing there. Presently the form of Jackeymo was seen emerging from the shrubs.

Riccabocca turned hastily round, recognized his servant, uttered an exclamation loud enough to reach Randal's ear, and then, catching Jackeymo by the arm, disappeared with him amidst the deep recesses of the garden.

"It will be indeed in my favour," thought Randal, as he rode on, "if I can get them into the neighbourhood of London—all occasion there to woo, and if expedient, to win—the heiress."

CHAPTER VIII.

"BY the Lord, Harry!" cried the Squire, as he stood with his wife in the park, on a visit of inspection to some first-rate South-Downs just added to his stock—"By the Lord, if that is not Randal Leslie trying to get into the park at the back gate! Hollo, Randal! you must come round by the lodge, my boy," said he. "You see this gate is locked, to keep out trespassers."

"A pity," said Randal. "I like short cuts, and you have shut up a very short one."

"So the trespassers said," quoth the Squire; "but Stirn insisted on it;—valuable man, Stirn. But ride round to the lodge. Put up your horse, and you'll join us before we can get to the house."

Randal nodded and smiled, and rode briskly on.

The Squire rejoined his Harry.

"Ah, William," said she, anxiously, "though certainly Randal Leslie means well, I always dread his visits."

"So do I, in one sense," quoth the Squire, "for he always carries away a bank-note for Frank."

"I hope he is really Frank's friend," said Mrs. Hazeldean.

"Who's else can he be? Not his own, poor fellow, for he will never accept a shilling from me, though his grandmother was as good a Hazeldean as I am. But, zounds, I like his pride, and his economy too. As for Frank—"

"Hush, William!" cried Mrs. Hazeldean, and put her fair hand before the Squire's mouth. The Squire was softened, and kissed the fair hand gallantly—perhaps he kissed the lips too : at all events, the worthy pair were walking lovingly arm-in-arm when Randal joined them.

He did not affect to perceive a certain coldness in the manner of Mrs. Hazeldean, but began immediately to talk to her about Frank ; praise that young gentleman's appearance ; expatiate on his health, his popularity, and his good gifts, personal and mental—and this with so much warmth, that any dim and undeveloped suspicions Mrs. Hazeldean might have formed soon melted away.

Randal continued to make himself thus agreeable, until the Squire, persuaded that his young kinsman was a first-rate agriculturalist, insisted upon carrying him off to the home farm; and Harry turned towards the house, to order Randal's room to be got ready: "For," said Randal, "knowing that you will excuse my morning dress, I venture to invite myself to dine and sleep at the Hall."

On approaching the farm-buildings, Randal was seized with the terror of an impostor; for, despite all the theoretical learning on Bucolics and Georgics with which he had dazzled the Squire, poor Frank, so despised, would have beat him hollow when it came to the judging of the points of an ox, or the show of a crop.

"Ha, ha!" cried the Squire, chuckling, "I long to see how you'll astonish Stirn. Why, you'll guess in a moment where we put the top-dressing; and when you come to handle my short-horns, I dare swear you'll know to a pound how much oil-cake has gone into their sides."

"Oh, you do me too much honour—indeed you do. I only know the general principles of agriculture; the details are eminently interesting, but I have not had the opportunity to acquire them."

"Stuff!" cried the Squire. "How can a man know general principles unless he has first studied the details? You are too modest, my boy. Ho! there's Stirn looking out for us!"

Randal saw the grim visage of Stirn peering out of a cattle-shed, and felt undone. He made a desperate rush towards changing the Squire's humour.

"Well, sir, perhaps Frank may soon gratify your wish, and turn farmer himself."

"Eh!" quoth the Squire, stopping short—"what now?"

"Suppose he were to marry?"

"I'd give him the two best farms on the property rent free. Ha, ha! Has he seen the girl yet? I'd leave him free to choose; sir, I chose for myself—every man should. Not but what Miss Sticktorights is an heiress, and, I hear, a very decent girl, and that would join the two properties, and put an end to that lawsuit about the right of way, which began in the reign of King Charles the Second, and is likely otherwise to last till the day of judgment. But never mind her; let Frank choose to please himself."

"I'll not fail to tell him so, sir. I did fear you might have some prejudices. But here we are at the farmyard."

"Burn the farmyard! How can I think of farmyards when you talk of Frank's marriage? Come on—this way. What were you saying about prejudices?"

"Why you might wish him to marry an Englishwoman, for instance."

"English! Good heavens, sir, does he mean to marry a Hindoo?"

"Nay, I don't know that he means to marry at all: I am only surmising; but if he did fall in love with a foreigner—"

"A foreigner! Ah, then Harry was—" The Squire stopped short.

"Who might, perhaps," observed Randal—not truly, if he referred to Madame di Negra—"who might, perhaps, speak very little English?"

"Lord ha' mercy!"

"And a Roman Catholic—"

"Worshipping idols, and roasting people who don't worship them."

"Signor Riccabocca is not so bad as that."

"Rickeybockey! Well, if it was his daughter! But not speak English! and not go to the parish church! By George, if Frank thought of such a thing, I'd cut him off with a shilling. Don't talk to me, sir; I would. I'm a mild man, and an easy man; but when I say a thing, I say it, Mr. Leslie. Oh, but it is a jest—you are laughing at me. There's no such painted good-for-nothing creature in Frank's eye—eh?"

"Indeed, sir, if ever I find there is, I will give you notice in time. At present, I was only trying to ascertain what you wished for a daughter-in-law. You said you had no prejudice."

"No more I have—not a bit of it."

"You don't like a foreigner and a Catholic?"

"Who the devil would?"

"But if she had rank and title?"

"Rank and title! Bubble and squeak! No, not half so good as bubble and squeak. English beef and good cabbage. But foreign rank and title!—foreign cabbage and beef!—foreign bubble and foreign squeak!" And the Squire made a wry face, and spat forth his disgust and indignation.

"You must have an Englishwoman?"

"Of course."

"Money?"

"Don't care, provided she is a tidy, sensible, active lass, with a good character for her dower."

"Character—ah, that is indispensable?"

"I should think so, indeed. A Mrs. Hazeldean of Hazeldean— You frighten me. He's not going to run off with a divorced woman, or a—"

The Squire stopped, and looked so red in the face that Randal feared he might be seized with apoplexy before Frank's crimes had made him alter his will.

Therefore he hastened to relieve Mr. Hazeldean's mind, and assured him that he had been only talking at random; that Frank was in the habit, indeed, of seeing foreign ladies occasionally, as all persons in the London world were; but that he was sure Frank would never marry without the full consent and approval of his parents. He ended by repeating his assurance, that he would warn the Squire if ever it became necessary. Still, however, he left Mr. Hazeldean so disturbed and uneasy that that gentleman forgot all about the farm, and went moodily on in the opposite direction, re-entering the park at its farther extremity. As soon as they approached the house, the Squire hastened to shut himself with his wife in full parental consultation; and Randal, seated upon a bench on the terrace, revolved the mischief he had done, and its chances of success.

While thus seated, and thus thinking, a footstep approached cautiously, and a low voice said, in broken English, "Sare, sare, let me speak vid you."

Randal turned in surprise, and beheld a swarthy saturnine face, with grizzled hair and marked features. He recognized the figure that had joined Riccabocca in the Italian's garden.

"Speak-a you Italian?" resumed Jackeymo.

Randal, who had made himself an excellent linguist, nodded assent; and Jackeymo, rejoiced, begged him to withdraw into a more private part of the grounds.

Randal obeyed, and the two gained the shade of a stately chestnut avenue.

"Sir," then said Jackeymo, speaking in his native tongue, and expressing himself with a certain simple pathos, "I am but a poor man; my name is Giacomo. You have heard of me; servant to the Signore whom you saw to-day—only a servant; but he honours me with his confidence. We have known danger together; and of all his friends and followers, I alone came with him to the stranger's land."

"Good, faithful fellow," said Randal, examining the man's face, "say on. Your master confides in you? He has confided that which I told him this day?"

"He did. Ah, sir; the Padrone was too proud to ask you to explain more—too proud to show fear of another. But he does fear —he ought to fear—he shall fear," (continued Jackeymo, working himself up to passion)—"for the Padrone has a daughter, and his enemy is a villain. Oh, sir, tell me all that you did not tell to the Padrone. You hinted that this man might wish to marry the Signora. Marry her!—I could cut his throat at the altar!"

"Indeed," said Randal;—"I believe that such is his object."

"But why? He is rich—she is penniless;—no, not quite that, for we have saved—but penniless, compared to him."

"My good friend, I know not yet his motives; but I can easily learn them. If, however, this Count be your master's enemy, it is surely well to guard against him, whatever his designs; and, to do so, you should move into London or its neighbourhood. I fear that, while we speak, the Count may get upon his track."

"He had better not come here!" cried the servant, menacingly, and putting his hand where the knife was *not*.

"Beware of your own anger, Giacomo. One act of violence, and you would be transported from England, and your master would lose a friend."

Jackeymo seemed struck by this caution.

"And if the Padrone were to meet him, do you think the Padrone would meekly say, '*Come stà sa Signoria?*' The Padronè would strike him dead!"

"Hush—hush! You speak of what in England is called murder, and is punished by the gallows. If you really love your master, for Heaven's sake get him from this place—get him from all chance of such passion and peril. I go to town to-morrow; I will find him a house that shall be safe from all spies—all discovery. And there, too, my friend, I can do—what I cannot at this distance—watch over him, and keep watch also on his enemy."

Jackeymo seized Randal's hand, and lifted it towards his lip; then, as if struck by a sudden suspicion, dropped the hand, and said bluntly, "Signore, I think you have seen the Padrone twice. Why do you take this interest in him?"

"Is it so uncommon to take interest even in a stranger who is menaced by some peril?"

Jackeymo, who believed little in general philanthropy, shook his head sceptically.

"Besides," continued Randal, suddenly bethinking himself of a more plausible reason—"besides, I am a friend and connection of Mr. Egerton; and Mr. Egerton's most intimate friend is Lord L'Estrange; and I have heard that Lord L'Estrange—"

"The good Lord! Oh, now I understand," interrupted Jack-eymo, and his brow cleared. "Ah, if *he* were in England! But you will let us know when he comes?"

"Certainly. Now, tell me, Giacomo, is this Count really un-principled and dangerous? Remember I know him not personally."

"He has neither heart nor conscience."

"That defect makes him dangerous to men; perhaps not less so to women. Could it be possible, if he obtained any interview with the Signora, that he could win her affections?"

Jackeymo crossed himself rapidly and made no answer.

"I have heard that he is still very handsome."

Jackeymo groaned.

Randal resumed—"Enough; persuade the Padrone to come to town."

"But if the Count is in town?"

"That makes no difference; the safest place is always the largest city. Everywhere else, a foreigner is in himself an object of attention and curiosity."

"True."

"Let your master, then, come to London, or rather, into its neighbourhood. He can reside in one of the suburbs most remote from the Count's haunts. In two days I will have found him a lodging and write to him. You trust to me now?"

"I do indeed—I do, Excellency. Ah, if the Signorina were married, we would not care!"

"Married! But she looks so high!"

"Alas! not now—not here!"

Randal sighed heavily. Jackeymo's eyes sparkled. He thought he had detected a new motive for Randal's interest—a motive to an Italian the most natural, the most laudable of all.

"Find the house, Signore—write to the Padrone. He shall come. I'll talk to him. I can manage him. Holy San Giacomo, bestir thyself now—'tis long since I troubled thee!"

Jackeymo strode off through the fading trees, smiling and mutter-ing as he went.

The first dinner-bell rang, and on entering the drawing-room, Randal found Parson Dale and his wife, who had been invited in haste to meet the unexpected visitor.

The preliminary greetings over, Mr. Dale took the opportunity afforded by the Squire's absence to inquire after the health of Mr. Egerton.

"He is always well," said Randal. "I believe he is made of iron."

"His heart is of gold," said the Parson.

"Ah," said Randal, inquisitively, "you told me you had come in contact with him once, respecting, I think, some of your old parishioners at Lansmere?"

The Parson nodded, and there was a moment's silence.

"Do you remember your battle by the stocks, Mr. Leslie?" said Mr. Dale, with a good-humoured laugh.

"Indeed, yes. By the way, now you speak of it, I met my old opponent in London the first year I went up to it."

"You did!—where?"

"At a literary scamp's—a cleverish man called Burley."

"Burley! I have seen some burlesque verses in Greek by a Mr. Burley."

"No doubt, the same person. He has disappeared—gone to the dogs, I dare say. Burlesque Greek is not a knowledge very much in power at present."

"Well, but Leonard Fairfield?—you have seen him since?"

"No."

"Nor heard of him?"

"No!—have you?"

"Strange to say, not for a long time. But I have reason to believe that he must be doing well."

"You surprise me! Why?"

"Because two years ago he sent for his mother. She went to him."

"Is that all?"

"It is enough; for he would not have sent for her if he could not maintain her."

Here the Hazeldeans entered, arm-in-arm, and the fat butler announced dinner.

The Squire was unusually taciturn—Mrs. Hazeldean thoughtful—Mrs. Dale languid and headachy. The Parson, who seldom enjoyed the luxury of converse with a scholar, save when he quarrelled with Dr. Riccabocca, was animated by Randal's repute for ability, into a great desire for argument.

"A glass of wine, Mr. Leslie. You were saying, before dinner, that burlesque Greek is not a knowledge very much in power at present. Pray, sir, what knowledge is in power?"

RANDAL (laconically).—"Practical knowledge."

PARSON.—"What of?"

RANDAL.—"Men."

PARSON (candidly).—"Well, I suppose that is the most available sort of knowledge, in a worldly point of view. How does one learn it? Do books help?"

RANDAL.—"According as they are read, they help or injure."

PARSON.—"How should they be read in order to help?"

RANDAL.—"Read specially to apply to purposes that lead to power."

PARSON (very much struck with Randal's pithy and Spartan logic), —"Upon my word, sir, you express yourself very well. I must own that I began these questions in the hope of differing from you; for I like an argument."

"That he does," growled the Squire; "the most contradictory creature!"

PARSON.—"Argument is the salt of talk. But now I am afraid I must agree with you, which I was not at all prepared for."

Randal bowed and answered—"No two men of our education can dispute upon the application of knowledge."

PARSON (pricking up his ears).—"Eh?—what to?"

RANDAL.—"Power, of course."

PARSON (overjoyed).—"Power!—the vulgarest application of it, or the loftiest? But you mean the loftiest?"

RANDAL (in his turn interested and interrogative).—"What do you call the loftiest, and what the vulgarest?"

PARSON.—"The vulgarest, self-interest; the loftiest, beneficence."

Randal suppressed the half-disdainful smile that rose to his lip.

"You speak, sir, as a clergyman should do. I admire your sentiment, and adopt it; but I fear that the knowledge which aims only at beneficence very rarely in this world gets any power at all."

SQUIRE (seriously).—"That's true; I never get my own way when I want to do a kindness, and Stirn always gets his when he insists on something diabolically brutal and harsh."

PARSON.—"Pray, Mr. Leslie, what does intellectual power refined to the utmost, but entirely stripped of beneficence, most resemble?"

RANDAL.—"Resemble?—I can hardly say. Some very great man—almost any very great man—who has baffled all his foes, and attained all his ends."

PARSON.—"I doubt if any man has ever become very great who has not meant to be beneficent, though he might err in the means. Cæsar was naturally beneficent, and so was Alexander. But intellectual power refined to the utmost, and wholly void of beneficence, resembles only one being, and that, sir, is the Principle of Evil."

RANDAL (startled).—"Do you mean the Devil?"

PARSON.—"Yes, sir—the Devil; and even he, sir, did not succeed! Even he, sir, is what your great men would call a most decided failure."

Mrs. Dale.—"My dear—my dear!"

Parson.—"Our religion proves it, my love; he was an angel, and he fell."

There was a solemn pause. Randal was more impressed than he liked to own to himself. By this time the dinner was over, and the servants had retired. Harry glanced at Carry. Carry smoothed her gown and rose.

The gentlemen remained over their wine; and the Parson, satisfied with what he deemed a clencher upon his favourite subject of discussion, changed the subject to lighter topics, till, happening to fall upon tithes, the Squire struck in, and by dint of loudness of voice, and truculence of brow, fairly overwhelmed both his guests, and proved to his own satisfaction that tithes were an unjust and unchristianlike usurpation on the part of the Church generally, and a most especial and iniquitous infliction upon the Hazeldean estates in particular.

CHAPTER IX.

ON entering the drawing-room, Randal found the two ladies seated close together, in a position much more appropriate to the familiarity of their school-days, than to the politeness of the friendship now existing between them. Mrs. Hazeldean's hand hung affectionately over Carry's shoulder, and both those fair English faces were bent over the same book. It was pretty to see these sober matrons, so different from each other in character and aspect, thus unconsciously restored to the intimacy of happy maiden youth by the golden link of some Magician from the still land of Truth or Fancy—brought together in heart, as each eye rested on the same thought;—closer and closer, as sympathy, lost in the actual world, grew out of that world which unites in one bond of feeling the readers of some gentle book.

"And what work interests you so much?" asked Randal, pausing by the table.

"One you have read, of course," replied Mrs. Dale, putting a book-mark embroidered by herself into the page, and handing the volume to Randal. "It has made a great sensation, I believe."

Randal glanced at the title of the work. "True," said he, "I have heard much of it in London, but I have not yet had time to read it."

Mrs. Dale.—"I can lend it to you, if you like to look over it to-night, and you can leave it for me with Mrs. Hazeldean."

PARSON (approaching).—"Oh! that book !—yes, you must read it. I do not know a work more instructive."

RANDAL.—"Instructive ! Certainly I will read it then. But I thought it was a mere work of amusement—of fancy. It seems so as I look over it."

PARSON.—"So is the *Vicar of Wakefield;* yet what book more instructive ?"

RANDAL.—"I should not have said *that* of the *Vicar of Wake-field.* A pretty book enough, though the story is most improbable. But how is it instructive ?"

PARSON.—"By its results : it leaves us happier and better. What can any instruction do more? Some works instruct through the head, some through the heart. The last reach the widest circle, and often produce the most genial influence on the character. This book belongs to the last. You will grant my proposition when you have read it."

Randal smiled and took the volume.

MRS. DALE.—"Is the author known yet ?"

RANDAL.—"I have heard it ascribed to many writers, but I believe no one has claimed it."

PARSON.—"I think it must have been written by my old college friend, Professor Moss, the naturalist—its descriptions of scenery are so accurate."

MRS. DALE.—"La, Charles, dear! that snuffy, tiresome, prosy professor? How can you talk such nonsense? I am sure the author must be young—there is so much freshness of feeling."

MRS. HAZELDEAN (positively).—"Yes, certainly, young."

PARSON (no less positively).—"I should say just the contrary. Its tone is too serene, and its style too simple, for a young man. Besides I don't know any young man who would send me his book, and this book has been sent me—very handsomely bound, too, you see. Depend upon it Moss is the man—quite his turn of mind."

MRS. DALE.—"You are too provoking, Charles dear ! Mr. Moss is so remarkably plain, too."

RANDAL.—"Must an author be handsome ?"

PARSON.—"Ha ! ha ! Answer that if you can, Carry."

Carry remained mute and disdainful.

SQUIRE (with great *naïveté*).—"Well, I don't think there's much in the book, whoever wrote it ; for I've read it myself, and understand every word of it."

MRS. DALE.—"I don't see why you should suppose it was written by a man at all. For my part, I think it must be a woman."

MRS. HAZELDEAN.—"Yes, there's a passage about maternal affection, which only a woman could have written."

PARSON.—"Pooh! pooh! I should like to see a woman who could have written that description of an August evening before a thunderstorm; every wildflower in the hedgerow exactly the flowers of August—every sign in the air exactly those of the month. Bless you! a woman would have filled the hedge with violets and cowslips. Nobody else but my friend Moss could have written that description."

SQUIRE.—"I don't know; there's a simile about the waste of corn-seed in hand-sowing, which makes me think he must be a farmer!"

MRS. DALE (scornfully).—"A farmer! In hobnailed shoes, I suppose! I say it is a woman."

MRS. HAZELDEAN.—"A WOMAN, and A MOTHER!"

PARSON.—"A middle-aged man, and a naturalist."

SQUIRE.—"No, no, Parson—certainly a young man; for that love-scene puts me in mind of my own young days, when I would have given my ears to tell Harry how handsome I thought her; and all I could say was, 'Fine weather for the crops, Miss.' Yes, a young man and a farmer. I should not wonder if he had held the plough himself."

RANDAL (who had been turning over the pages).—"This sketch of Night in London comes from a man who has lived the life of cities and looked at wealth with the eyes of poverty. Not bad! I will read the book."

"Strange," said the Parson, smiling, "that this little work should so have entered into our minds, suggested to all of us different ideas, yet equally charmed all—given a new and fresh current to our dull country life—animated us as with the sight of a world in our breasts we had never seen before save in dreams: a little work like this by a man we don't know and never may! Well, *that* knowledge *is* power, and a noble one!"

"A sort of power, certainly, sir," said Randal, candidly; and that night, when Randal retired to his own room, he suspended his schemes and projects, and read, as he rarely did, without an object to gain by the reading.

The work surprised him by the pleasure it gave. Its charm lay in the writer's calm enjoyment of the beautiful. It seemed like some happy soul sunning itself in the light of its own thoughts. Its power was so tranquil and even, that it was only a critic who could perceive how much force and vigour were necessary to sustain the wing that floated aloft with so imperceptible an effort. There was no one

faculty predominating tyrannically over the others ; all seemed proportioned in the felicitous symmetry of a nature rounded, integral,
and complete. And when the work was closed, it left behind it a
tender warmth that played round the heart of the reader and vivified
feelings which seemed unknown before. Randal laid down the
book softly ; and for five minutes the ignoble and base purposes to
which his own knowledge was applied, stood before him, naked and
unmasked.

"Tut !" said he, wrenching himself violently away from the
benign influence, "it was not to sympathize with Hector, but to
conquer with Achilles, that Alexander of Macedon kept Homer under
his pillow. Such should be the true use of books to him who has
the practical world to subdue ; let parsons and women construe it
otherwise, as they may ! "

And the Principle of Evil descended again upon the intellect, from
which the guide of Beneficence was gone.

CHAPTER X.

RANDAL rose at the sound of the first breakfast bell, and
on the staircase met Mrs. Hazeldean. He gave her back
the book ; and as he was about to speak, she beckoned
to him to follow her into a little morning-room appropriated to herself. No boudoir of white and gold, with pictures by
Watteau, but lined with large walnut-tree presses, that held the old
heirloom linen, strewed with lavender—stores for the housekeeper,
and medicines for the poor.

Seating herself on a large chair in this sanctum, Mrs. Hazeldean
looked formidably at home.

"Pray," said the lady, coming at once to the point, with her
usual straightforward candour, "what is all this you have been
saying to my husband as to the possibility of Frank's marrying a
foreigner ?"

RANDAL.—" Would you be as averse to such a notion as Mr.
Hazeldean is ?"

MRS. HAZELDEAN.—" You ask me a question, instead of answering mine."

Randal was greatly put out in his fence by these rude thrusts. For
indeed he had a double purpose to serve—first, thoroughly to know
if Frank's marriage with a woman like Madame di Negra would
irritate the Squire sufficiently to endanger the son's inheritance ;

and, secondly, to prevent Mr. and Mrs. Hazeldean believing seriously that such a marriage was to be apprehended, lest they should prematurely address Frank on the subject, and frustrate the marriage itself. Yet, withal, he must so express himself, that he could not be afterwards accused by the parents of disguising matters. In his talk to the Squire the preceding day, he had gone a little too far—farther than he would have done but for his desire of escaping the cattle-shed and short-horns.   While he mused, Mrs. Hazeldean observed him with her honest sensible eyes, and finally exclaimed—

"Out with it, Mr. Leslie!"

"Out with what, my dear madam? The Squire has sadly exaggerated the importance of what was said mainly in jest. But I will own to ycu plainly, that Frank has appeared to me a little smitten with a certain fair Italian."

"Italian!" cried Mrs. Hazeldean. "Well, I said so from the first.   Italian!—that's all, is it?" and she smiled.

Randal was more and more perplexed. The pupil of his eye contracted, as it does when we retreat into ourselves, and think, watch, and keep guard.

"And perhaps," resumed Mrs. Hazeldean, with a very sunny expression of countenance, "you have noticed this in Frank since he was here?"

"It is true," murmured Randal; "but I think his heart or his fancy was touched even before."

"Very natural," said Mrs. Hazeldean; "how could he help it? —such a beautiful creature! Well, I must not ask you to tell Frank's secrets; but I guess the object of attraction; and though she will have no fortune to speak of—and it is not such a match as he might form—still she is so amiable, and has been so well brought up, and is so little like one's general notions of a Roman Catholic, that I think I could persuade Hazeldean into giving his consent."

"Ah," said Randal, drawing a long breath, and beginning with his practised acuteness to detect Mrs. Hazeldean's error, "I am very much relieved and rejoiced to hear this; and I may venture to give Frank some hope, if I find him disheartened and desponding, poor fellow!"

"I think you may," replied Mrs. Hazeldean, laughing pleasantly. "But you should not have frightened poor William so, hinting that the lady knew very little English. She has an accent, to be sure; but she speaks our tongue very prettily. I always forget that she's not English born! Ha, ha, poor William!"

RANDAL.—"Ha, ha!"

MRS. HAZELDEAN.—"We had once thought of another match for Frank—a girl of good English family."

RANDAL.—"Miss Sticktorights?"

MRS. HAZELDEAN.—"No; that's an old whim of Hazeldean's. But I doubt if the Sticktorights would ever merge their property in ours. Bless you, it would be all off the moment they came to settlements, and had to give up the right of way. We thought of a very different match; but there's no dictating to young hearts, Mr. Leslie."

RANDAL.—"Indeed no, Mrs. Hazeldean. But since we now understand each other so well, excuse me if I suggest that you had better leave things to themselves, and not write to Frank on the subject. Young hearts, you know, are often stimulated by apparent difficulties, and grow cool when the obstacle vanishes."

MRS. HAZELDEAN.—"Very possibly; it was not so with Hazeldean and me. But I shall not write to Frank on the subject for a different reason—though I would consent to the match, and so would William; yet we both would rather, after all, that Frank married an Englishwoman, and a Protestant. We will not, therefore, do anything to encourage the idea. But if Frank's happiness becomes really at stake, *then* we will step in. In short, we would neither encourage nor oppose. You understand?"

"Perfectly."

"And in the meanwhile, it is quite right that Frank should see the world, and try to distract his mind, or at least to know it. And I dare say it has been some thought of that kind which has prevented his coming here."

Randal, dreading a farther and plainer *éclaircissement*, now rose, and saying, "Pardon me, but I must hurry over breakfast, and be back in time to catch the coach"—offered his arm to his hostess, and led her into the breakfast-parlour. Devouring his meal, as if in great haste, he then mounted his horse, and, taking cordial leave of his entertainers, trotted briskly away.

All things favoured his project—even chance had befriended him in Mrs. Hazeldean's mistake. She had, not unnaturally, supposed Violante to have captivated Frank on his last visit to the Hall. Thus, while Randal had certified his own mind that nothing could more exasperate the Squire than an alliance with Madame di Negra, he could yet assure Frank that Mrs. Hazeldean was all on his side. And when the error was discovered, Mrs. Hazeldean would only have to blame herself for it. Still more successful had his diplomacy proved with the Riccaboccas: he had ascertained the secret he had come to discover; he should induce the Italian to remove to the neighbourhood of London ; and if Violante were the great heiress he suspected her to prove, whom else of her own age would she see but him ?   And the old Leslie domains, to be sold in two years—a portion of the dowry might purchase them ! Flushed by the triumph of his craft, all former vacillations of conscience ceased.   In high and fervent spirits he passed the Casino, the garden of which was solitary and deserted, reached his home, and, telling Oliver to be studious, and Juliet to be patient, walked thence to meet the coach and regain the capital.

CHAPTER XI.

IOLANTE was seated in her own little room, and looking from the window on the terrace that stretched below. The day was warm for the time of year.   The orange-trees had been removed under shelter for the approach of winter ; but where they had stood sate Mrs. Riccabocca at work. In the Belvedere, Riccabocca himself was conversing with his favourite servant.   But the casements and the door of the Belvedere were open ; and where they sate, both wife and daughter could see the Padrone leaning against the wall, with his arms folded, and his eyes fixed on the floor ; while Jackeymo, with one finger on his master's arm, was talking to him with visible earnestness.   And the daughter from the window, and the wife from her work, directed tender, anxious eyes towards the still thoughtful form so dear to both.   For the last day or two, Riccabocca had been peculiarly abstracted, even to gloom.   Each felt there was something stirring at his heart— neither, as yet, knew what.

Violante's room silently revealed the nature of the education by which her character had been formed.   Save a sketch-book, which lay open on a desk at hand, and which showed talent exquisitely taught (for in this Riccabocca had been her teacher), there was nothing that spoke of the ordinary female accomplishments.   No piano stood open, no harp occupied yon nook, which seemed made for one ; no broidery-frame, nor implements of work, betrayed the usual and graceful resources of a girl ; but ranged on shelves against the wall were the best writers in English, Italian, and French ; and these betokened an extent of reading, that he who wishes for a companion to his mind in the sweet commune of woman, which softens and refines all it gives and takes in interchange, will never condemn as masculine.   You had but to look into Violante's face to see how noble was the intelligence that brought soul to those lovely features. Nothing hard, nothing dry and stern was there. Even as you detected knowledge, it was lost in the gentleness of grace. In fact, whatever she gained in the graver kinds of information, became transmuted, through her heart and her fancy, into spiritual golden stores. Give her some tedious and arid history, her imagination seized upon beauties other readers had passed by, and, like the eye of the artist, detected everywhere the Picturesque. Something in her mind seemed to reject all that was mean and commonplace, and to bring out all that was rare and elevated in whatever it received. Living so apart from all companions of her age, she scarcely belonged to the Present time. She dwelt in the Past, as Sabrina in her crystal well. Images of chivalry—of the Beautiful and the Heroic—such as, in reading the silvery line of Tasso, rise before us, softening force and valour into love and song —haunted the reveries of the fair Italian maid.

Tell us not that the Past, examined by cold Philosophy, was no better and no loftier than the Present : it is not thus seen by pure and generous eyes. Let the Past perish, when it ceases to reflect on its magic mirror the beautiful Romance which is its noblest reality, though perchance but the shadow of Delusion.

Yet Violante was not merely the dreamer. In her, life was so puissant and rich, that action seemed necessary to its glorious development—action, but still in the woman's sphere—action to bless and to refine and to exalt all around her, and to pour whatever else of ambition was left unsatisfied into sympathy with the aspirations of man. Despite her father's fears of the bleak air of England, in that air she had strengthened the delicate health of her childhood. Her elastic step—her eyes full of sweetness and light—her bloom, at once soft and luxuriant—all spoke of the vital powers fit to sustain a mind of such exquisite mould, and the emotions of a heart that, once aroused, could ennoble the passions of the South with the purity and devotion of the North.

Solitude makes some natures more timid, some more bold. Violante was fearless. When she spoke, her eyes frankly met your own ; and she was so ignorant of evil, that as yet she seemed nearly unacquainted with shame. From this courage, combined with affluence of idea, came a delightful flow of happy converse. Though possessing so imperfectly the accomplishments ordinarily taught to young women, and which may be cultured to the utmost, and yet leave the thoughts so barren, and the talk so vapid—she had that accomplishment which most pleases the taste, and commands the love, of the man of talent ; especially if his talent be not so actively employed as to make him desire only relaxation where he seeks companionship—the accomplishment of facility in intellectual inter-change—the charm that clothes in musical words beautiful womanly ideas.

"I hear him sigh at this distance," said Violante, softly, as she still watched her father; "and methinks this is a new grief; and not for his country.   He spoke twice yesterday of that dear English friend, and wished that he were here."

As she said this, unconsciously the virgin blushed, her hands drooped on her knee, and she fell herself into thought as profound as her father's, but less gloomy.   From her arrival in England, Violante had been taught a grateful interest in the name of Harley L'Estrange.   Her father, preserving a silence, that seemed disdain, of all his old Italian intimates, had been pleased to converse with open heart of the Englishman who had saved where countrymen had betrayed.   He spoke of the soldier, then in the full bloom of youth, who, unconsoled by fame, had nursed the memory of some hidden sorrow amidst the pine-trees that cast their shadow over the sunny Italian lake; how Riccabocca, then honoured and happy, had courted from his seclusion the English Signore, then the mourner and the voluntary exile; how they had grown friends amidst the landscapes in which her eyes had opened to the day; how Harley had vainly warned him from the rash schemes in which he had sought to reconstruct in an hour the ruins of weary ages; how, when abandoned, deserted, proscribed, pursued, he had fled for life —the infant Violante clasped to his bosom—the English soldier had given him refuge, baffled the pursuers, armed his servants, accom-panied the fugitive at night towards the defile in the Apennines, and, when the emissaries of a perfidious enemy, hot in the chase, came near, had said, "You have your child to save! Fly on! Another league, and you are beyond the borders.   We will delay the foes with parley; they will not harm us."   And not till escape was gained did the father know that the English friend had delayed the foe, not by parley, but by the sword, holding the pass against numbers, with a breast as dauntless as Bayard's on the glorious bridge.

And since then, the same Englishman had never ceased to vindicate his name, to urge his cause; and if hope yet remained of restoration to land and honours, it was in that untiring zeal.

Hence, naturally and insensibly, this secluded and musing girl had associated all that she read in tales of romance and chivalry with the image of the brave and loyal stranger.   He it was who animated her dreams of the Past, and seemed born to be, in the destined hour, the deliverer of the Future.   Around this image grouped all the.

charms that the fancy of virgin woman can raise from the enchanted
lore of old Heroic Fable. Once in her early girlhood, her father
(to satisfy her curiosity, eager for general description) had drawn
from memory a sketch of the features of the Englishman—drawn
Harley, as he was in that first youth, flattered and idealized, no
doubt, by art, and by partial gratitude—but still resembling him as
he was then, while the deep mournfulness of recent sorrow yet
shadowed and concentrated all the varying expressions of his
countenance ; and to look on him was to say—"So sad, yet so
young!" Never did Violante pause to remember that the same
years which ripened herself from infancy into woman, were passing
less gently over that smooth cheek and dreamy brow—that the
world might be altering the nature as time the aspect. To her the
hero of the Ideal remained immortal in bloom and youth. Bright
illusion, common to us all, where Poetry once hallows the human
form! Whoever thinks of Petrarch as the old time-worn man?
Who does not see him as when he first gazed on Laura?—

> "Ogni altra cosa ogni pensier va fore ;
> E sol ivi con voi rimansi Amore !"

CHAPTER XII.

AND Violante, thus absorbed in reverie, forgot to keep
watch on the Belvedere. And the Belvedere was now
deserted. The wife, who had no other ideal to distract
her thoughts, saw Riccabocca pass into the house.

The exile entered his daughter's room, and she started to feel his
hand upon her locks and his kiss upon her brow.

"My child !" cried Riccabocca, seating himself, "I have resolved
to leave for a time this retreat, and to seek the neighbourhood of
London."

"Ah, dear father, *that*, then, was your thought? But what can
be your reason? Do not turn away ; you know how carefully I have
obeyed your command and kept your secret. Ah, you will confide
in me."

"I do, indeed," returned Riccabocca, with emotion. "I leave
this place, in the fear lest my enemies discover me. I shall say to
others that you are of an age to require teachers, not to be obtained
here. But I should like none to know where we go."

The Italian said these last words through his teeth, and hanging
his head. He said them in shame.

"My mother—(so Violante always called Jemima)—my mother—you have spoken to her?"

"Not yet. *There* is the difficulty."

"No difficulty, for she loves you so well," replied Violante, with soft reproach. "Ah, why not also confide in her? Who so true? so good?"

"Good—I grant it!" exclaimed Riccabocca. "What then? '*Da cattiva Donna guardati, ed alla buona non fidar niente,*' (from the bad woman, guard thyself; to the good woman trust nothing). And if you must trust," added the abominable man, "trust her with anything but a secret!"

"Fie," said Violante, with arch reproach, for she knew her father's humours too well to interpret his horrible sentiments literally —"fie on your consistency, *Padre carissimo*. Do you not trust your secret to me?"

"You! A kitten is not a cat, and a girl is not a woman. Besides, the secret was already known to you, and I had no choice. Peace, Jemima will stay here for the present. See to what you wish to take with you; we shall leave to-night."

Not waiting for an answer, Riccabocca hurried away, and with a firm step strode the terrace, and approached his wife.

"*Anima mia,*" said the pupil of Machiavelli, disguising in the tenderest words the cruellest intentions—for one of his most cherished Italian proverbs was to the effect, that there is no getting on with a mule or a woman unless you coax them,—"*Anima mia*, soul of my being, you have already seen that Violante mopes herself to death here."

"She, poor child! Oh no!"

"She does, core of my heart—she does—and is as ignorant of music as I am of tent-stitch."

"She sings beautifully."

"Just as birds do, against all the rules, and in defiance of gamut. Therefore, to come to the point, O treasure of my soul! I am going to take her with me for a short time, perhaps to Cheltenham or Brighton. We shall see."

"All places with you are the same to me, Alphonso. When shall we go?"

"*We* shall go to-night; but terrible as it is to part from you—you—"

"Ah!" interrupted the wife, and covered her face with her hands.

Riccabocca, the wiliest and most relentless of men in his maxims, melted into absolute uxorial imbecility at the sight of that mute distress. He put his arm round his wife's waist, with genuine affection, and without a single proverb at his heart—"*Carissima*, do not grieve so; we shall be back soon, and travelling is expensive; rolling stones gather no moss, and there is so much to see to at home."

Mrs. Riccabocca gently escaped from her husband's arm. She withdrew her hands from her face and brushed away the tears that stood in her eyes.

"Alphonso," she said, touchingly, "hear me! What you think good, that shall ever be good to me. But do not think that I grieve solely because of our parting. No; I grieve to think that, despite all these years in which I have been the partner of your hearth, and slept on your breast—all these years in which I have had no thought but, however humbly, to do my duty to you and yours, and could have wished that you had read my heart, and seen there but yourself and your child—*I* grieve to think that you still deem me as unworthy your trust as when you stood by my side at the altar."

"Trust!" repeated Riccabocca, startled and conscience-stricken: "why do you say 'trust?' In what have I distrusted you? I am sure," he continued, with the artful volubility of guilt, "that I never doubted your fidelity—hook-nosed, long-visaged foreigner though I be; never pried into your letters; never inquired into your solitary walks; never heeded your flirtations with that good-looking Parson Dale; never kept the money; and never looked into the account books!" Mrs. Riccabocca refused even a smile of contempt at these revolting evasions; nay, she seemed scarcely to hear them.

"Can you think," she resumed, pressing her hand on her heart to still its struggles for relief in sobs—"can you think that I could have watched, and thought, and taxed my poor mind so constantly, to conjecture what might best soothe or please you, and not seen, long since, that you have secrets known to your daughter—your servant—not to me? Fear not—the secrets cannot be evil, or you would not tell them to your innocent child. Besides, do I not know your nature? and do I not love you because I know it?—it is for something connected with those secrets that you leave your home. You think that I should be incautious—imprudent. You will not take me with you. Be it so. I go to prepare for your departure. Forgive me if I have displeased you, husband."

Mrs. Riccabocca turned away; but a soft hand touched the Italian's arm. "O father, can you resist this? Trust her! trust her!—I am a woman like her! I answer for her woman's faith. Be yourself—ever nobler than all others, my own father."

"*Diavolo!* Never one door shuts but another opens," groaned Riccabocca. "Are you a fool, child? Don't you see that it was for your sake only I feared—and would be cautious?" ·

"For mine! O then do not make me deem myself mean, and the cause of meanness. For mine! Am I not your daughter—the descendant of men who never feared?"

Violante looked sublime while she spoke; and as she ended she led her father gently on towards the door, which his wife had now gained.

"Jemima—wife mine!—pardon, pardon," cried the Italian, whose heart had been yearning to repay such tenderness and devotion,— "come back to my breast—it has been long closed—it shall be open to you now and for ever."

In another moment the wife was in her right place—on her husband's bosom; and Violante, beautiful peacemaker, stood smiling awhile at both, and then lifted her eyes gratefully to Heaven, and stole away.

CHAPTER XIII.

ON Randal's return to town, he heard mixed and contradictory rumours in the streets, and at the clubs, of the probable downfall of the Government at the approaching session of Parliament. These rumours had sprung up suddenly, as if in an hour. True that, for some time, the sagacious had shaken their heads and said, "Ministers could not last." True, that certain changes in policy, a year or two before, had divided the party on which the Government depended, and strengthened that which opposed it. But still the more important members of that Government had been so long identified with official station, and there seemed so little power in the Opposition to form a cabinet of names familiar to official ears, that the general public had anticipated, at most, a few partial changes. Rumour now went far beyond this. Randal, whose whole prospects at present were but reflections from the greatness of his patron, was alarmed. He sought Egerton, but the minister was impenetrable, and seemed calm, confident, and imperturbed. Somewhat relieved, Randal then set himself to work to find a safe home for Riccabocca; for the greater need to succeed in obtaining fortune there, if he failed in getting it through Egerton. He found a quiet house, detached and secluded, in the neighbourhood of Norwood. No vicinity more secure from espionage and remark. He wrote to Riccabocca, and communicated the address, adding fresh assurances of his own power to be of use. The next morning he was seated in his office, thinking very little of the details, that he mastered, however, with mechanical precision, when the minister who presided over that department of the public service, sent for him into his private room, and begged him to take a letter to Egerton, with whom he wished to consult relative to a very important point to be decided in the Cabinet that day. "I want you to take it," said the minister smiling, (the minister was a frank homely man,) "because you are in Mr. Egerton's confidence, and he may give you some verbal message besides a written reply. Egerton is often *over* cautious and brief in the *litera scripta*."

Randal went first to Egerton's neighbouring office—Egerton had not been there that day. He then took a cabriolet and drove to Grosvenor Square. A quiet-looking chariot was at the door. Mr. Egerton was at home; but the servant said, "Dr. F. is with him, sir; and perhaps he may not like to be disturbed."

"What—is your master ill?"

"Not that I know of, sir. He never says he is ill. But he has looked poorly the last day or two."

Randal hesitated a moment; but his commission might be important, and Egerton was a man who so held the maxim, that health and all else must give way to business, that he resolved to enter; and, unannounced and unceremoniously, as was his wont, he opened the door of the library. He started as he did so. Audley Egerton was leaning back on the sofa, and the doctor, on his knees before him, was applying the stethoscope to his breast. Egerton's eyes were partially closed as the door opened. But at the noise he sprang up, nearly oversetting the doctor. "Who's that?—How dare you?" he exclaimed, in a voice of great anger. Then recognizing Randal, he changed colour, bit his lip, and muttered dryly, "I beg pardon for my abruptness; what do you want, Mr. Leslie?"

"This letter from Lord ——; I was told to deliver it immediately into your own hands. I beg pardon—"

"There is no cause," said Egerton, coldly. "I have had a slight attack of bronchitis; and as Parliament meets so soon, I must take advice from my doctor, if I would be heard by the reporters. Lay the letter on the table, and be kind enough to wait for my reply."

Randal withdrew. He had never seen a physician in that house before, and it seemed surprising that Egerton should even take a medical opinion upon a slight attack. While waiting in the ante-room there was a knock at the street door, and presently a gentleman, exceedingly well dressed, was shown in, and honoured Randal with an easy and half-familiar bow. Randal remembered to have met this personage at dinner, and at the house of a young nobleman of high fashion, but had not been introduced to him, and did not even know him by name. _ The visitor was better informed.

"Our friend Egerton is busy, I hear, Mr. Leslie," said he, arranging the camellia in his button-hole.

"Our friend Egerton!" It must be a very great man to say, "Our friend Egerton."

"He will not be engaged long, I dare say," returned Randal, glancing his shrewd inquiring eye over the stranger's person.

"I trust not; my time is almost as precious as his own. I was not so fortunate as to be presented to you when we met at Lord Spendquick's. Good fellow, Spendquick; and decidedly clever."

Lord Spendquick was usually esteemed a gentleman without three ideas.

Randal smiled.

In the meanwhile the visitor had taken out a card from an embossed morocco case, and now presented it to Randal, who read thereon, "Baron Levy, No. —, Bruton St."

The name was not unknown to Randal. It was a name too often on the lips of men of fashion not to have reached the ears of an *habitué* of good society.

Mr. Levy had been a solicitor by profession. He had of late years relinquished his ostensible calling: and not long since, in consequence of some services towards the negotiation of a loan, had been created a baron by one of the German kings. The wealth of Mr. Levy was said to be only equalled by his good nature to all who were in want of a temporary loan, and with sound expectations of repaying it some day or other.

You seldom saw a finer-looking man than Baron Levy—about the same age as Egerton, but looking younger: so well preserved—such magnificent black whiskers—such superb teeth! Despite his name and his dark complexion, he did not, however, resemble a Jew—at least externally; and, in fact, he was not a Jew on the father's side, but the natural son of a rich English *grand seigneur*, by a Hebrew lady of distinction—in the opera. After his birth, this lady had married a German trader of her own persuasion, and her husband had been prevailed upon, for the convenience of all parties, to adopt his wife's son, and accord to him his own Hebrew name. Mr. Levy, senior, was soon left a widower, and then the real father, though never actually owning the boy, had shown him great attention—had him frequently at his house—initiated him betimes into his own high-born society, for which the boy showed great taste. But when my Lord died, and left but a moderate legacy to the younger Levy, who was then about eighteen, that ambiguous person was articled to an attorney by his putative sire, who shortly afterwards returned to his native land, and was buried at Prague, where his tombstone may yet be seen. Young Levy, however, contrived to do very well without him. His real birth was generally known, and rather advantageous to him in a social point of view. His legacy enabled him to become a partner where he had been a clerk, and his practice became great amongst the fashionable classes of society. Indeed he was so useful, so pleasant, so much a man of the world, that he grew intimate with his clients —chiefly young men of rank ; was on good terms with both Jew and Christian ; and being neither one nor the other, resembled (to use Sheridan's incomparable simile) the blank page between the Old and the New Testament.

Vulgar, some might call Mr. Levy, from his assurance, but it was not the vulgarity of a man accustomed to low and coarse society— rather the *mauvais ton* of a person not sure of his own position, but who has resolved to swagger into the best one he can get. When it is remembered that he had made his way in the world, and gleaned together an immense fortune, it is needless to add that he was as sharp as a needle, and as hard as a flint. No man had had more friends, and no man had stuck by them more firmly—so long as there was a pound in their pockets !

Something of this character had Randal heard of the Baron, and he now gazed, first at his card, and then at him with—admiration.

"I met a friend of yours at Borrowell's the other day," resumed the Baron—"Young Hazeldean. Careful fellow—quite a man of the world."

As this was the last praise poor Frank deserved, Randal again smiled.

The Baron went on—"I hear, Mr. Leslie, that you have much influence over this same Hazeldean. His affairs are in a sad state. I should be very happy to be of use to him, as a relation of my friend Egerton's ; but he understands business so well that he despises my advice."

"I am sure you do him injustice."

"Injustice ! I honour his caution. I say to every man, 'Don't come to me—I can get you money on much easier terms than any one else ; and what's the result ! You come so often that you ruin yourself ; whereas a regular usurer without conscience frightens you. "Cent. per cent.," you say ; "oh, I must pull in."' If you have influence over your friend, tell him to stick to his bill-brokers, and have nothing to do with Baron Levy."

Here the minister's bell rung, and Randal, looking through the window, saw Dr. F. walking to his carriage, which had made way for Baron Levy's splendid cabriolet—a cabriolet in the most perfect taste—Baron's coronet on the dark-brown panels—horse black, with such action!—harness just relieved with plating. The servant now entered, and requested Randal to step in; and addressing the Baron, assured him that he would not be detained a minute.

"Leslie," said the minister, sealing a note, "take this back to Lord ——, and say that I shall be with him in an hour."

"No other message—he seemed to expect one."

"I dare say he did. Well, my letter is official, my message is not: beg him to see Mr. —— before we meet—he will understand —all rests upon that interview."

Egerton then, extending the letter, resumed gravely—"Of course, you will not mention to any one that Dr. F. was with me: the health of public men is not to be suspected. Hum—were you in your own room or the ante-room?"

"The ante-room, sir."

Egerton's brow contracted slightly. "And Mr. Levy was there, eh?"

"Yes—the Baron."

"Baron! true. Come to plague me about the Mexican loan, I suppose. I will keep you no longer."

Randal, much meditating, left the house, and re-entered his hack cab. The Baron was admitted to the statesman's presence.

CHAPTER XIV.

EGERTON had thrown himself at full length on the sofa, a position exceedingly rare with him; and about his whole air and manner, as Levy entered, there was something singularly different from that stateliness of port common to the austere legislator. The very tone of his voice was different. It was as if the statesman—the man of business—had vanished; it was rather the man of fashion and the idler, who, nodding languidly to his visitor, said, "Levy, what money can I have for a year?"

"The estate will bear very little more. My dear fellow, that last election was the very devil. You cannot go on thus much longer."

"My dear fellow!" Baron Levy hailed Audley Egerton as "my dear fellow." And Audley Egerton, perhaps, saw nothing strange in the words, though his lip curled.

"I shall not want to go on thus much longer," answered Egerton, as the curl on his lip changed to a gloomy smile. "The estate must, meanwhile, bear £5000 more."

"A hard pull on it. You had really better sell."

"I cannot afford to sell at present. I cannot afford men to say, 'Audley Egerton is done up—his property is for sale.'"

"It is very sad when one thinks what a rich man you have been —and may be yet !"

"Be yet ! How ?"

Baron Levy glanced towards the thick mahogany doors—thick and impervious as should be the doors of statesmen. "Why, you know that, with three words from you, I could produce an effect upon the stocks of three nations, that might give us each a hundred thousand pounds. We would go shares."

"Levy," said Egerton, coldly, though a deep flush overspread his face, "you are a scoundrel ; that is your look-out. I interfere with no man's tastes and conscience. I don't intend to be a scoundrel myself. I have told you that long ago."

The usurer's brows darkened, but he dispelled the cloud with an easy laugh.

"Well," said he, "you are neither wise nor complimentary, but you shall have the money. But yet, would it not be better," added Levy, with emphasis, "to borrow it without interest, of your friend L'Estrange ?"

Egerton started as if stung.

"You mean to taunt me, sir !" he exclaimed, passionately. "I accept pecuniary favours from Lord L'Estrange !—I !"

"Tut, my dear Egerton, I dare say my Lord would not think so ill now of that act in your life which—"

"Hold !" exclaimed Egerton, writhing. "Hold !"

He stopped, and paced the room, muttering, in broken sentences, "To blush before this man ! Chastisement, chastisement !"

Levy gazed on him with hard and sinister eyes. The minister turned abruptly.

"Look you, Levy," said he, with forced composure—"you hate me—why, I know not."

"Hate you ! How have I shown hatred? Would you ever have lived in this palace, and ruled this country as one of the most influential of its ministers, but for my management—my whispers to the wealthy Miss Leslie? Come, but for me what would you have been—perhaps a beggar ?"

"What shall I be now, if I live? And this fortune which my marriage brought to me—it has passed for the main part into your hands. Be patient, you will have it all ere long. But there is one man in the world who has loved me from a boy, and woe to you if ever he learn that he has the right to despise me !"

"Egerton, my good fellow," said Levy, with great composure, "you need not threaten me, for what interest can I possibly have in tale-telling to Lord L'Estrange? Again, dismiss from your mind the absurd thought that I hate you. True, you snub me in private, you cut me in public, you refuse to come to my dinners, you'll not ask me to your own; still, there is no man I like better, nor would more willingly serve. When do you want the £5000?"

"Perhaps in one month, perhaps not for three or four. Let it be ready when required."

"Enough; depend on it. Have you any other commands?"

"None."

"I will take my leave, then. By the bye, what do you suppose the Hazeldean rental is worth—net?"

"I don't know, nor care. You have no designs upon *that* too?"

"Well, I like keeping up family connections. Mr. Frank seems a liberal young gentleman."

Before Egerton could answer, the Baron had glided to the door, and, nodding pleasantly, vanished with that nod.

Egerton remained, standing on his solitary hearth. A drear, single man's room it was, from wall to wall, despite its fretted ceilings and official pomp of Bramah escritoires and red boxes. Drear and cheerless—no trace of woman's habitation—no vestige of intruding, happy children. There stood the austere man alone. And then with a deep sigh he muttered, "Thank Heaven, not for long—it will not last long."

Repeating those words, he mechanically locked up his papers, and pressed his hand to his heart for an instant, as if a spasm had shot through it.

"So—I must shun all emotion!" said he, shaking his head gently.

In five minutes more, Audley Egerton was in the streets, his mien erect, and his step firm as ever.

"That man is made of Bronze," said a leader of the Opposition to a friend as they rode past the minister. "What would I not give for his nerves!"

BOOK NINTH.

INITIAL CHAPTER.

ON PUBLIC LIFE.

NOW that I am fairly in the heart of my story, these pre-liminary chapters must shrink into comparatively small dimensions, and not encroach upon the space required by the various personages whose acquaintance I have picked up here and there, and who are now all crowding upon me like poor relations to whom one has unadvisedly given a general invitation, and who descend upon one simultaneously about Christmas time. Where they are to be stowed, and what is to become of them all, Heaven knows; in the meanwhile, the reader will have already observed that the Caxton Family themselves are turned out of their own rooms, sent a-packing, in order to make way for the new comers.

But to proceed.—Note the heading to the present Chapter "ON PUBLIC LIFE,"—a thesis pertinent to this portion of my narrative, and if somewhat trite in itself, the greater is the stimulus to suggest thereon some original hints for reflection.

Were you ever in public life, my dear reader? I don't mean, by that question, to ask whether you were ever Lord Chancellor, Prime Minister, Leader of the Opposition, or even a member of the House of Commons. An author hopes to find readers far beyond that very egregious but very limited segment of the Great Circle. Were you ever a busy man in your vestry, active in a municipal corporation, one of a committee for furthering the interests of an enlightened candidate for your native burgh, town, or shire?—in a word, did you ever resign your private comforts as men in order to share the public troubles of mankind? If ever you have so far departed from the Lucretian philosophy, just look back—was it life at all that you lived?—were you an individual distinct existence—a passenger in the railway?—or were you merely an indistinct portion of that common flame which heated the boiler and generated the steam that set off the monster train?—very hot, very active, very useful, no doubt ; but all your identity fused in flame, and all your forces vanishing in gas.

And do you think the people in the railway carriages care for you?—do you think that the gentleman in the worsted wrapper is saying to his neighbour with the striped rug on his comfortable knees, " How grateful we ought to be for that fiery particle which is crackling and hissing under the boiler ! It helps us on a fraction of an inch from Vauxhall to Putney !" Not a bit of it. Ten to one but he is saying—" Not sixteen miles an hour ! What the deuce is the matter with the stoker?"

Look at our friend Audley Egerton. You have just had a glimpse of the real being that struggles under the huge copper ;—you have heard the hollow sound of the rich man's coffers under the tap of Baron Levy's friendly knuckle—heard the strong man's heart give out its dull warning sound to the scientific ear of Dr. F——. And away once more vanishes the separate existence, lost again in the flame that heats the boiler, and the smoke that curls into air from the grimy furnace.

Look to it, O Public Man, whoever thou art, and whatsoever thy degree—see if thou canst not compound matters, so as to keep a little nook apart for thy private life ; that is, for *thyself!* Let the Great Popkins Question not absorb wholly the individual soul of thee, as Smith or Johnson. Don't so entirely consume thyself under that insatiable boiler, that when thy poor little monad rushes out from the sooty furnace, and arrives at the stars, thou mayest find no vocation for thee there, and feel as if thou hadst nothing to do amidst the still splendours of the Infinite. I don't deny to thee the uses of " Public Life ;" I grant that it is much to have helped to carry that great Popkins Question ; but Private Life, my friend, is the life of thy private soul ; and there may be matters concerned with that which, on consideration, thou mayest allow, cannot be wholly mixed up with the Great Popkins Question—and were not finally settled when thou didst exclaim—" I have not lived in vain— the Popkins Question is carried at last !" Oh, immortal soul, for one quarter of an hour *per diem*—de-Popkinize thine immortality !

CHAPTER II.

IT had not been without much persuasion on the part of Jackeymo, that Riccabocca had consented to settle himself in the house which Randal had recommended to him. Not that the exile conceived any suspicion of the young man beyond that which he might have shared with Jackeymo, viz., that Randal's interest in the father was increased by a very natural and excusable admiration of the daughter. But the Italian had the pride common to misfortune,—he did not like to be indebted to others, and he shrank from the pity of those to whom it was known that he had held a higher station in his own land. These scruples gave way to the strength of his affection for his daughter and his dread of his foe. Good men, however able and brave, who have suffered from the wicked, are apt to form exaggerated notions of the power that has prevailed against them. Jackeymo had conceived a superstitious terror of Peschiera ; and Riccabocca, though by no means addicted to superstition, still had a certain creep of the flesh whenever he thought of his foe.

But Riccabocca—than whom no man was more physically brave, and no man, in some respects, more morally timid—feared the Count less as a foe than as a gallant. He remembered his kinsman's surpassing beauty—the power he had obtained over women. He knew him versed in every art that corrupts, and wholly void of the conscience that deters. And Riccabocca had unhappily nursed himself into so poor an estimate of the female character, that even the pure and lofty nature of Violante did not seem to him a sufficient safeguard against the craft and determination of a practised and remorseless intriguer. But of all the precautions he could take, none appeared more likely to conduce to safety, than his establishing a friendly communication with one who professed to be able to get at all the Count's plans and movements, and who could apprise Riccabocca at once should his retreat be discovered. "Forewarned is forearmed," said he to himself, in one of the proverbs common to all nations. However, as with his usual sagacity he came to reflect upon the alarming intelligence conveyed to him by Randal, viz., that the Count sought his daughter's hand, he divined that there was some strong personal interest under such ambition ; and what could be that interest save the probability of Riccabocca's ultimate admission to the Imperial grace, and the Count's desire to assure himself of the heritage to an estate that he might be permitted to retain no more ? Riccabocca was not indeed aware of the condition (not according to usual customs in Austria) on which the Count held the forfeited domains. He knew not that they had been granted merely on pleasure ; but he was too well aware of Peschiera's nature to suppose that he would woo a bride without a dower, or be moved by remorse in any overture of reconciliation. He felt assured too— and this increased all his fears—that Peschiera would never venture to seek an interview with himself ; all the Count's designs on Violante would be dark, secret, and clandestine. He was perplexed and tormented by the doubt, whether or not to express openly to Violante his apprehensions of the nature of the danger to be apprehended. He had told her vaguely that it was for her sake that he desired secrecy and concealment. But that might mean anything : what danger to himself would not menace her? Yet to say more was so contrary to a man of his Italian notions and Machia-vellian maxims! To say to a young girl, "There is a man come over to England on purpose to woo and win you. For Heaven's sake take care of him ; he is diabolically handsome ; he never fails where he sets his heart."—"*Cospetto!*" cried the Doctor, aloud, as these admonitions shaped themselves to speech in the camera-obscura of his brain ; "such a warning would have undone a Cornelia while she was yet an innocent spinster." No, he resolved to say nothing to Violante of the Count's intention, only to keep guard, and make himself and Jackeymo all eyes and all ears.

The house Randal had selected pleased Riccabocca at first glance. It stood alone, upon a little eminence ; its upper windows commanded the high road. It had been a school, and was surrounded by high walls, which contained a garden and lawn sufficiently large for exercise. The garden doors were thick, fortified by strong bolts, and had a little wicket lattice, shut and opened at pleasure, from which Jackeymo could inspect all visitors before he permitted them to enter.

An old female servant from the neighbourhood was cautiously hired ; Riccabocca renounced his Italian name, and abjured his origin. He spoke English sufficiently well to think he could pass as an Englishman. He called himself Mr. Richmouth (a liberal translation of Riccabocca). He bought a blunderbuss, two pair of pistols, and a huge house-dog. Thus provided for, he allowed Jackeymo to write a line to Randal and communicate his arrival.

Randal lost no time in calling. With his usual adaptability, and his powers of dissimulation, he contrived easily to please Mrs. Riccabocca, and to increase the good opinion the exile was disposed to form of him. He engaged Violante in conversation on Italy and its poets. He promised to bring her books. He began, though more distantly than he could have desired—for her sweet stateliness awed him—the preliminaries of courtship. He established himself at once as a familiar guest, riding down daily in the dusk of evening, after the toils of office, and retiring at night. In four or five days he thought he had made great progress with all. Riccabocca watched him narrowly, and grew absorbed in thought after every visit. At length one night, when he and Mrs. Riccabocca were alone in the drawing-room, Violante having retired to rest, he thus spoke as he filled his pipe :—

"Happy is the man who has no children! Thrice happy he who has no girls!"

"My dear Alphonso!" said the wife, looking up from the wristband to which she was attaching a neat mother-o'-pearl button. She said no more; it was the sharpest rebuke she was in the custom of administering to her husband's cynical and odious observations. Riccabocca lighted his pipe with a thread paper, gave three great puffs, and resumed.

"One blunderbuss, four pistols, and a house-dog called Pompey, who would have made mincemeat of Julius Cæsar!"

"He certainly eats a great deal, does Pompey!" said Mrs. Riccabocca, simply. "But if he relieves your mind!"

"He does not relieve it in the least, ma'am," groaned Riccabocca; "and that is the point I was coming to. This is a most harassing life, and a most undignified life. And I who have only asked from Heaven dignity and repose! But, if Violante were once married, I should want neither blunderbuss, pistol, nor Pompey. And it is that which would relieve my mind, *cara mia*,—Pompey only relieves my larder!"

Now Riccabocca had been more communicative to Jemima than he had been to Violante. Having once trusted her with one secret, he had every motive to trust her with another; and he had accordingly spoken out his fears of the Count di Peschiera. Therefore she answered, laying down the work, and taking her husband's hand tenderly—

"Indeed, my love, since you dread so much (though I own that I must think unreasonably) this wicked, dangerous man, it would be the happiest thing in the world to see dear Violante well married; because, you see, if she is married to one person she cannot be married to another; and all fear of this Count, as you say, would be at an end."

"You cannot express yourself better. It is a great comfort to unbosom one's-self to a wife, after all," quoth Riccabocca.

"But," said the wife, after a grateful kiss—"but, where and how can we find a husband suitable to the rank of your daughter?"

"There—there—there," cried Riccabocca, pushing back his chair to the farther end of the room—"that comes of unbosoming one's-self! Out flies one's secret; it is opening the lid of Pandora's box; one is betrayed, ruined, undone!"

"Why, there's not a soul that can hear us!" said Mrs. Riccabocca, soothingly.

"That's chance, ma'am! If you once contract the habit of blabbing out a secet when nobody's by, how on earth can you resist it when you have the pleasurable excitement of telling it to all the world? Vanity, vanity—woman's vanity! Woman never could withstand rank—never!" The Doctor went on railing for a quarter of an hour, and was very reluctantly appeased by Mrs. Riccabocca's repeated and tearful assurances that she would never even whisper to herself that her husband had ever held any other rank than that of Doctor. Riccabocca, with a dubious shake of the head, renewed—

"I have done with all pomp and pretension. Besides, the young man is a born gentleman : he seems in good circumstances ; he has energy and latent ambition ; he is akin to L'Estrange's intimate friend : he seems attached to Violante. I don't think it probable that we could do better. Nay, if Peschiera fears that I shall be restored to my country, and I learn the wherefore, and the ground to take, through this young man—why, gratitude is the first virtue of the noble !"

"You speak, then, of Mr. Leslie?"

"To be sure—of whom else?"

Mrs. Riccabocca leaned her cheek on her hand thoughtfully. "Now you have told me *that*, I will observe him with different eyes."

"*Anima mia*, I don't see how the difference of your eyes will alter the object they look upon !" grumbled Riccabocca, shaking the ashes out of his pipe.

"The object alters when we see it in a different point of view !" replied Jemima, modestly. "This thread does very well when I look at it in order to sew on a button, but I should say it would never do to tie up Pompey in his kennel."

"Reasoning by illustration, upon my soul !" ejaculated Riccabocca, amazed.

"And," continued Jemima, "when I am to regard one who is to constitute the happiness of that dear child, and for life, can I regard him as I would the pleasant guest of an evening? Ah, trust me, Alphonso ; I don't pretend to be wise like you ; but, when a woman considers what a man is likely to prove to woman—his sincerity— his honour—his heart—oh, trust me, she is wiser than the wisest man !"

Riccabocca continued to gaze on Jemima with unaffected admiration and surprise. And, certainly, to use his phrase, since he had unbosomed himself to his better half—since he had confided in her, consulted with her, her sense had seemed to quicken—her whole mind to expand."

"My dear," said the sage, "I vow and declare that Machiavelli was a fool to you. And I have been as dull as the chair I sit upon, to deny myself so many years the comfort and counsel of such a —— but, *corpo di Bacco!* forget all about rank ; and so now to bed. —One must not holloa till one's out of the wood," muttered the ungrateful, suspicious villain, as he lighted the chamber candle.

CHAPTER III.

RICCABOCCA could not confine himself to the precincts within the walls to which he condemned Violante. Resuming his spectacles, and wrapped in his cloak, he occasionally sallied forth upon a kind of outwatch or reconnoitring expedition—restricting himself, however, to the immediate neighbourhood, and never going quite out of sight of his house. His favourite walk was to the summit of a hillock overgrown with stunted bush-wood. Here he would sit himself musingly, often till the hoofs of Randal's horse rang on the winding road, as the sun set, over fading herbage, red and vaporous, in autumnal skies. Just below the hillock, and not two hundred yards from his own house, was the only other habitation in view—a charming, thoroughly English cottage, though somewhat imitated from the Swiss—with gable ends, thatched roof, and pretty, projecting casements, opening through creepers and climbing roses. From his height he commanded the gardens of this cottage, and his eye of artist was pleased, from the first sight, with the beauty which some exquisite taste had given to the ground. Even in that cheerless season of the year, the garden wore a summer smile ; the evergreens were so bright and various, and the few flowers, still left, so hardy and so healthful. Facing the south, a colonnade, or covered gallery, of rustic wood-work had been formed, and creeping plants, lately set, were already beginning to clothe its columns. Opposite to this colonnade there was a fountain which reminded Riccabocca of his own at the deserted Casino. It was indeed singularly like it ; the same circular shape, the same girdle of flowers around it. But the jet from it varied every day—fantastic and multiform, like the sports of a Naïad— sometimes shooting up like a tree, sometimes shaped as a convolvu- lus, sometimes tossing from its silver spray a flower of vermilion, or a fruit of gold—as if at play with its toy like a happy child. And near the fountain was a large aviary, large enough to enclose a tree. The Italian could just catch a gleam of rich colour from the wings of the birds, as they glanced to and fro within the network, and could hear their songs, contrasting the silence of the freer populace of air, whom the coming winter had already stilled.

Riccabocca's eye, so alive to all aspects of beauty, luxuriated in the view of this garden. Its pleasantness had a charm that stole him from his anxious fear and melancholy memories.

He never saw but two forms within the demesnes, and he could not distinguish their features. One was a woman, who seemed to him of staid manner and homely appearance: she was seen but rarely. The other a man, often pacing to and fro the colonnade, with frequent pauses before the playful fountain, or the birds that sang louder as he approached. This latter form would then disappear within a room, the glass door of which was at the extreme end of the colonnade; and if the door were left open, Riccabocca could catch a glimpse of the figure bending over a table covered with books.

Always, however, before the sun set, the man would step forth more briskly, and occupy himself with the garden, often working at it with good heart, as if at a task of delight; and then, too, the woman would come out, and stand by as if talking to her companion. Riccabocca's curiosity grew aroused. He bade Jemima inquire of the old maid-servant who lived at the cottage, and heard that its owner was a Mr. Oran—a quiet gentleman, and fond of his book.

While Riccabocca thus amused himself, Randal had not been prevented, either by his official cares or his schemes on Violante's heart and fortune, from furthering the project that was to unite Frank Hazeldean and Beatrice di Negra. Indeed, as to the first, a ray of hope was sufficient to fire the ardent and unsuspecting lover. And Randal's artful misrepresentation of his conference with Mrs. Hazeldean, removed all fear of parental displeasure from a mind always too disposed to give itself up to the temptation of the moment. Beatrice, though her feelings for Frank were not those of love, became more and more influenced by Randal's arguments and representations, the more especially as her brother grew morose, and even menacing, as days slipped on, and she could give no clue to the retreat of those whom he sought for. Her debts, too, were really urgent. As Randal's profound knowledge of human infirmity had shrewdly conjectured, the scruples of honour and pride, that had made her declare she would not bring to a husband her own encumbrances, began to yield to the pressure of necessity. She listened already, with but faint objections, when Randal urged her not to wait for the uncertain discovery that was to secure her dowry, but by a private marriage with Frank escape at once into freedom and security. While, though he had first held out to young Hazeldean the inducement of Beatrice's dowry as a reason of self-justification in the eyes of the Squire, it was still easier to drop that inducement, which had always rather damped than fired the high spirit and generous heart of the poor Guardsman. And Randal could conscientiously say, that when he had asked the Squire if he expected fortune with Frank's bride, the Squire had replied—"I don't care."   Thus encouraged by his friend and his own heart, and the softening manner of a woman who might have charmed many a colder, and fooled many a wiser man, Frank rapidly yielded to the snares held out for his perdition.   And though as yet he honestly shrank from proposing to Beatrice or himself a marriage without the consent, and even the knowledge, of his parents, yet Randal was quite content to leave a nature, however good, so thoroughly impulsive and undisciplined, to the influences of the first strong passion it had ever known.   Meanwhile, it was so easy to dissuade Frank from even giving a hint to the folks at home.   "For," said the wily and able traitor, "though we may be sure of Mrs. Hazeldean's consent, and her power over your father, when the step is once taken, yet we cannot count for certain on the Squire—he is so choleric and hasty.   He might hurry to town—see Madame di Negra, blurt out some passionate, rude expressions, which would wake her resentment, and cause her instant rejection.   And it might be too late if he repented afterwards —as he would be sure to do."

Meanwhile Randal Leslie gave a dinner at the Clarendon Hotel, (an extravagance most contrary to his habits,) and invited Frank, Mr. Borrowell, and Baron Levy.

But this house-spider, which glided with so much ease after its flies, through webs so numerous and mazy, had yet to amuse Madame di Negra with assurances that the fugitives sought for would sooner or later be discovered.   Though Randal baffled and eluded her suspicion that he was already acquainted with the exiles, ("the persons he had thought of were," he said, "quite different from her description;" and he even presented to her an old singing-master, and a sallow-faced daughter, as the Italians who had caused this mistake,) it was necessary for Beatrice to prove the sincerity of the aid she had promised to her brother, and to introduce Randal to the Count.   It was no less desirable to Randal to know, and even win the confidence of this man—his rival.

The two met at Madame di Negra's house.   There is something very strange, and almost mesmerical, in the *rapport* between two evil natures.   Bring two honest men together, and it is ten to one if they recognize each other as honest; differences in temper, manner, even politics, may make each misjudge the other.   But bring together two men, unprincipled and perverted—men who, if born in a cellar, would have been food for the hulks or gallows—and they understand each other by instant sympathy. The eyes of Franzini, Count of Peschiera, and Randal Leslie no sooner met, than a gleam of intelligence shot from both. They talked on indifferent subjects—weather, gossip, politics—what not. They bowed and they smiled; but, all the while, each was watching, plumbing the other's heart, each measuring his strength with his companion; each inly saying, "This is a very remarkable rascal; am I a match for him?" It was at dinner they met; and following the English fashion, Madame di Negra left them alone with their wine.

Then, for the first time, Count di Peschiera cautiously and adroitly made a covered push towards the object of the meeting.

"You have never been abroad, my dear sir? You must contrive to visit me at Vienna. I grant the splendour of your London world; but, honestly speaking, it wants the freedom of ours—a freedom which unites gaiety with polish. For as your society is mixed, there are pretension and effort with those who have no right to be in it, and artificial condescension and chilling arrogance with those who have to keep their inferiors at a certain distance. With us, all being of fixed rank and acknowledged birth, familiarity is at once established. Hence," added the Count, with his French lively smile—"hence there is no place like Vienna for a young man—no place like Vienna for *bonnes fortunes*."

"Those make the paradise of the idle," replied Randal, "but the purgatory of the busy. I confess frankly to you, my dear Count, that I have as little of the leisure which becomes the aspirer to *bonnes fortunes* as I have the personal graces which obtain them without an effort;" and he inclined his head as in compliment.

"So," thought the Count, "woman is not his weak side. What is?"

"*Morbleu!* my dear Mr. Leslie—had I thought as you do some years since, I had saved myself from many a trouble. After all, Ambition is the best mistress to woo; for with her there is always the hope, and never the possession."

"Ambition, Count," replied Randal, still guarding himself in dry sententiousness, "is the luxury of the rich, and the necessity of the poor."

"Aha," thought the Count, "it comes, as I anticipated from the first—comes to the bribe." He passed the wine to Randal, filling his own glass, and draining it carelessly: "*Sur mon âme mon cher,*" said the Count, "luxury is ever pleasanter than necessity; and I am resolved at least to give Ambition a trial—*je vais me réfugier dans le sein du bonheur domestique*—a married life and a settled home. *Peste!* If it were not for ambition, one would die of ennui. Apropos, my dear sir, I have to thank you for promising my sister your aid in finding a near and dear kinsman of mine, who has taken refuge in your country, and hides himself even from me."

"I should be most happy to assist in your search. As yet, however, I have only to regret that all my good wishes are fruitless. I should have thought, however, that a man of such rank had been easily found, even through the medium of your own ambassador."

"Our own ambassador is no very warm friend of mine ; and the rank would be no clue, for it is clear that my kinsman has never assumed it since he quitted his country."

"He quitted it, I understand, not exactly from choice," said Randal, smiling. "Pardon my freedom and curiosity, but will you explain to me a little more than I learn from English rumour, (which never accurately reports upon foreign matters still more notorious,) how a person who had so much to lose, and so little to win, by revolution, could put himself into the same crazy boat with a crew of hair-brained adventurers and visionary professors."

"Professors !" repeated the Count ; "I think you have hit on the very answer to your question ; not but what men of high birth were as mad as the *canaille.* I am the more willing to gratify your curiosity, since it will perhaps serve to guide your kind search in my favour. You must know, then, that my kinsman was not born the heir to the rank he obtained. He was but a distant relation to the head of the house which he afterwards represented. Brought up in an Italian university, he was distinguished for his learning and his eccentricities. There too, I suppose, brooding over old wives' tales about freedom, and so forth, he contracted his *carbonaro,* chimerical notions for the independence of Italy. Suddenly, by three deaths, he was elevated, while yet young, to a station and honours which might have satisfied any man in his senses. *Que diable!* what could the independence of Italy do for *him!* He and I were cousins ; we had played together as boys ; but our lives had been separated till his succession to rank brought us necessarily together. We became exceedingly intimate. And you may judge how I loved him," said the Count, averting his eyes slightly from Randal's quiet, watchful gaze, "when I add, that I forgave him for enjoying a heritage that, but for him, had been mine."

"Ah, you were next heir ?"

"And it is a hard trial to be very near a great fortune, and yet just to miss it."

"True," cried Randal, almost impetuously. The Count now raised his eyes, and again the two men looked into each other's souls.

"Harder still, perhaps," resumed the Count, after a short pause —"harder still might it have been to some men to forgive the rival as well as the heir."

"Rival ! how ?"

"A lady, who had been destined by her parents to myself, though we had never, I own, been formally betrothed, became the wife of my kinsman."

"Did he know of your pretensions ?"

"I do him the justice to say he did not. He saw and fell in love with the young lady I speak of. Her parents were dazzled. Her father sent for me. He apologized—he explained; he set before me, mildly enough, certain youthful imprudences or errors of my own, as an excuse for his change of mind ; and he asked me not only to resign all hope of his daughter, but to conceal from her new suitor that I had ever ventured to hope."

"And you consented ?"

"I consented."

"That was generous. You must indeed have been much attached to your kinsman. As a lover, I cannot comprehend it ; perhaps, my dear Count, you may enable me to understand it better—as a man of the world."

"Well," said the Count, with his most *roué* air, "I suppose we *are* both men of the world ?"

"*Both!* certainly," replied Randal, just in the tone which Peachum might have used in courting the confidence of Lockit.

"As a man of the world, then, I own," said the Count, playing with the rings on his fingers, that if I could not marry the lady myself, (and that seemed to me clear,) it was very natural that I should wish to see her married to my wealthy kinsman."

"Very natural ; it might bring your wealthy kinsman and yourself still closer together."

"This is really a very clever fellow !" thought the Count, but he made no direct reply.

"*Enfin*, to cut short a long story, my cousin afterwards got entangled in attempts, the failure of which is historically known. His projects were detected—himself denounced. He fled, and the Emperor, in sequestrating his estates, was pleased, with rare and singular clemency, to permit me, as his nearest kinsman, to enjoy the revenues of half those estates during the royal pleasure ; nor was the other half formally confiscated. It was no doubt his Majesty's desire not to extinguish a great Italian name ; and if my cousin and his child died in exile, why, of that name, I, a loyal subject of Austria—I, Franzini, Count di Peschiera, would become the representative. Such, in a similar case, has been sometimes the Russian policy towards Polish insurgents."

"I comprehend perfectly; and I can also conceive that you, in profiting so largely, though so justly, by the fall of your kinsman, may have been exposed to much unpopularity—even to painful suspicion."

"*Entre nous, mon cher*, I care not a stiver for popularity; and as to suspicion, who is he that can escape from the calumny of the envious? But, unquestionably, it would be most desirable to unite the divided members of our house; and this union I can now effect, by the consent of the Emperor to my marriage with my kinsman's daughter. You see, therefore, why I have so great an interest in this research?"

"By the marriage articles you could no doubt secure the retention of the half you hold; and if you survive your kinsman you would enjoy the whole. A most desirable marriage; and, if made, I suppose that would suffice to obtain your cousin's amnesty and grace?"

"You say it."

"But even without such marriage, since the Emperor's clemency has been extended to so many of the proscribed, it is perhaps probable that your cousin might be restored?"

"It once seemed to me possible," said the Count, reluctantly; "but since I have been in England, I think not. The recent revolution in France, the democratic spirit rising in Europe, tend to throw back the cause of a proscribed rebel. England swarms with revolutionists; my cousin's residence in this country is in itself suspicious. The suspicion is increased by his strange seclusion. There are many Italians here who would aver that they had met with him, and that he was still engaged in revolutionary projects."

"Aver—untruly?"

"*Ma foi*—it comes to the same thing; *les absens ont toujours tort*. I speak to a man of the world. No; without some such guarantee for his faith, as his daughter's marriage with myself would give, his recall is improbable. By the heaven above us, it shall be *impossible!*" The Count rose as he said this—rose as if the mask of simulation had fairly fallen from the visage of crime—rose tall and towering, a very image of masculine power and strength, beside the slight, bended form and sickly face of the intellectual schemer. And had you seen them thus confronted and contrasted, you would have felt that if ever the time should come when the interest of the one would compel him openly to denounce or boldly to expose the other, the odds were that the brilliant and audacious reprobate would master the weaker nerve but superior wit of the furtive traitor. Randal was startled; but rising also, he said, carelessly—

"What if this guarantee can no longer be given?—what if, in despair of return, and in resignation to his altered fortunes, your cousin has already married his daughter to some English suitor?"

"Ah, that would indeed be, next to my own marriage with her, the most fortunate thing that could happen to myself."

"How? I don't understand!"

"Why, if my cousin has so abjured his birthright, and forsworn his rank—if this heritage, which is so dangerous from its grandeur, pass, in case of his pardon, to some obscure Englishman—a foreigner—a native of a country that has no ties with ours—a country that is the very refuge of levellers and Carbonari—*mort de ma vie*—do you think that such would not annihilate all chance of my cousin's restoration, and be an excuse even in the eyes of Italy for formally conferring the sequestrated estates on an Italian? No; unless, indeed, the girl were to marry an Englishman of such name and birth and connection as would in themselves be a guarantee (and how in poverty is this likely?) I should go back to Vienna with a light heart, if I could say, 'My kinswoman is an Englishman's wife—shall her children be the heirs to a house so renowned for its lineage, and so formidable for its wealth?' *Parbleu!* if my cousin were but an adventurer, or merely a professor, he had been pardoned long ago. The great enjoy the honour not to be pardoned easily."

Randal fell into deep but brief thought. The Count observed him, not face to face, but by the reflection of an opposite mirror. "This man knows something; this man is deliberating; this man can help me," thought the Count.

But Randal said nothing to confirm these hypotheses. Recovering from his abstraction, he expressed courteously his satisfaction at the Count's prospects, either way. "And since, after all," he added, "you mean so well to your cousin, it occurs to me that you might discover him by a very simple English process."

"How?"

"Advertise that, if he will come to some place appointed, he will hear of something to his advantage."

The Count shook his head. "He would suspect me, and not come."

"But he was intimate with you. He joined an insurrection;—you were more prudent. You did not injure him, though you may have benefited yourself. Why should he shun you?"

"The conspirators forgive none who do not conspire; besides, to speak frankly, he thought I injured him."

"Could you not conciliate him through his wife—whom—you resigned to him?"

" She is dead—died before he left the country."

" Oh, that is unlucky!   Still I think an advertisement might do good.   Allow me to reflect on that subject.   Shall we now join *Madame la Marquise?*"

On re-entering the drawing-room, the gentlemen found Beatrice in full dress, seated by the fire, and reading so intently that she did not remark them enter.

" What so interests you, *ma sœur?*—the last novel by Balzac, no doubt?"

Beatrice started, and, looking up, showed eyes that were full of tears.   "Oh, no! no picture of miserable, vicious, Parisian life. This is beautiful; there is *soul* here."

Randal took up the book which the Marchesa laid down; it was the same which had charmed the circle at Hazeldean—charmed the innocent and fresh-hearted—charmed now the wearied and tempted votaress of the world.

"Hum," murmured Randal; "the Parson was right.   This is power—a sort of a power."

"How I should like to know the author!   Who can he be—can you guess?"

"Not I.   Some old pedant in spectacles."

"I think not—I am sure not.—Here beats a heart I have ever sighed to find, and never found."

"Oh, *la naïve enfant!*" cried the Count; "*comme son imagination s'égare en rêves enchantés.*   And to think that, while you talk like an Arcadian, you are dressed like a princess."

"Ah, I forgot—the Austrian ambassador's.   I shall not go to-night.   This book unfits me for the artificial world."

"Just as you will, my sister.   I shall go.   I dislike the man, and he me; but ceremonies before men!"

"You are going to the Austrian Embassy?" said Randal.   "I, too, shall be there.   We shall meet."   And he took his leave.

"I like your young friend prodigiously," said the Count, yawning.   "I am sure that he knows of the lost birds, and will stand to them like a pointer, if I can but make it his interest to do so.   We shall see."

CHAPTER IV.

RANDAL arrived at the ambassador's before the Count, and contrived to mix with the young noblemen attached to the embassy, and to whom he was known. Standing among these was a young Austrian, on his travels, of very high birth, and with an air of noble grace that suited the ideal of the old German chivalry. Randal was presented to him, and, after some talk on general topics, observed, "By the way, Prince, there is now in London a countryman of yours, with whom you are, doubtless, familiarly acquainted—the Count di Peschiera."

"He is no countryman of mine. He is an Italian. I know him but by sight and by name," said the Prince, stiffly.

"He is of very ancient birth, I believe."

"Unquestionably. His ancestors were gentlemen."

"And very rich."

"Indeed! I have understood the contrary. He enjoys, it is true, a large revenue."

A young *attaché*, less discreet than the Prince, here observed, "Oh, Peschiera!—Poor fellow, he is too fond of play to be rich."

"And there is some chance that the kinsman whose revenue he holds may obtain his pardon, and re-enter into possession of his fortunes—so I hear, at least," said Randal, artfully.

"I shall be glad if it be true," said the Prince with decision; "and I speak the common sentiment at Vienna. That kinsman had a noble spirit, and was, I believe, equally duped and betrayed. Pardon me, sir; but we Austrians are not so bad as we are painted. Have you ever met in England the kinsman you speak of?"

"Never, though he is supposed to reside here; and the Count tells me that he has a daughter."

"The Count—ha! I heard something of a scheme—a wager of that—that Count's;—a daughter! Poor girl! I hope she will escape his pursuit; for, no doubt, he pursues her."

"Possibly she may already have married an Englishman."

"I trust not," said the Prince, seriously; "that might at present be a serious obstacle to her father's return."

"You think so?"

"There can be no doubt of it," interposed the *attaché*, with a grand and positive air; "unless, indeed, the Englishman were of a rank equal to her own."

Here there was a slight, well-bred murmur and buzz at the door;

for the Count di Peschiera himself was announced ; and as he entered, his presence was so striking, and his beauty so dazzling, that whatever there might be to the prejudice of his character, it seemed instantly effaced or forgotten in that irresistible admiration which it is the prerogative of personal attributes alone to create.

The Prince, with a slight curve of his lip at the groups that collected round the Count, turned to Randal, and said, "Can you tell me if a distinguished countryman of yours is in England—Lord L'Estrange?"

"No, Prince—he is not. You know him?"

"Well."

"He is acquainted with the Count's kinsman ; and perhaps from him you have learned to think so highly of that kinsman?"

The Prince bowed, and answered as he moved away, "When one man of high honour vouches for another, he commands the belief of all."

"Certainly," soliloquized Randal, "I must not be precipitate. I was very near falling into a terrible trap. If I were to marry the girl, and only, by so doing, settle away her inheritance on Peschiera ! —How hard it is to be sufficiently cautious in this world !"

While thus meditating, a member of Parliament tapped him on the shoulder.

"Melancholy, Leslie ! I lay a wager I guess your thoughts."

"Guess," answered Randal.

"You were thinking of the place you are so soon to lose."

"Soon to lose ! "

"Why, if ministers go out, you could hardly keep it, I suppose."

This ominous and horrid member of Parliament, Squire Hazeldean's favourite county member, Sir John, was one of those legislators especially odious to officials—an independent "large-acred" member, who would no more take office himself than he would cut down the oaks in his park, and who had no bowels of human feeling for those who had opposite tastes and less magnificent means.

"Hem ! " said Randal, rather surlily. "In the first place, Sir John, ministers are not going out."

"Oh yes, they will go. You know I vote with them generally, and would willingly keep them in ; but they are men of honour and spirit ; and if they can't carry their measures, they must resign ; otherwise, by Jove, I would turn round, and vote them out myself ! "

"I have no doubt you would, Sir John ; you are quite capable of it ; that rests with you and your constituents. But even if ministers did go out, I am but a poor subaltern in a public office. I am no minister—why should I go out too?"

"Why? Hang it, Leslie, you are laughing at me. A young fellow like you could never be mean enough to stay in, under the very men who drove out your friend Egerton?"

"It is not usual for those in the public offices to retire with every change of Government."

"Certainly not ; but always those who are the relations of a retiring minister—always those who have been regarded as politicians, and who mean to enter Parliament, as of course you will do at the next election. But you know that as well as I do—you who are so decided a politician—the writer of that admirable pamphlet ! I should not like to tell my friend Hazeldean, who has a sincere interest in you, that you ever doubted on a question of honour as plain as your A, B, C."

"Indeed, Sir John," said Randal, recovering his suavity, while he inly breathed a dire anathema on his county member, "I am so new to these things, that what you say never struck me before. No doubt you must be right ; at all events I cannot have a better guide and adviser than Mr. Egerton himself."

Sir John.—"No, certainly—perfect gentleman, Egerton ! I wish we could make it up with him and Hazeldean."

Randal (sighing).—"Ah, I wish we could !"

Sir John.—"And some chance of it now ; for the time is coming when all true men of the old school must stick together."

Randal.—"Wisely, admirably said, my dear Sir John. But, pardon me, I must pay my respects to the ambassador."

Randal escaped, and passing on, saw the ambassador himself in the next room, conferring in a corner with Audley Egerton. The ambassador seemed very grave—Egerton calm and impenetrable, as usual. Presently the Count passed by, and the ambassador bowed to him very stiffly.

As Randal, some time later, was searching for his cloak below, Audley Egerton unexpectedly joined him.

"Ah, Leslie," said the minister, with more kindness than usual, "if you don't think the night air too cold for you, let us walk home together. I have sent away the carriage."

This condescension in his patron was so singular, that it quite startled Randal, and gave him a presentiment of some evil. When they were in the street, Egerton, after a pause, began—

"My dear Mr. Leslie, it was my hope and belief that I had provided for you at least a competence ; and that I might open to you, later, a career yet more brilliant. Hush! I don't doubt your gratitude ; let me proceed. There is a possible chance, after certain decisions that the Government have come to, that we may be beaten in the House of Commons, and of course resign. I tell you this beforehand, for I wish you to have time to consider what, in that case, would be your best course. My power of serving you may then probably be over. It would, no doubt, (seeing our close connection, and my views with regard to your future being so well known,)—no doubt, be expected that you should give up the place you hold, and follow my fortunes for good or ill. But as I have no personal enemies with the opposite party—and as I have sufficient position in the world to uphold and sanction your choice, whatever it may be, if you think it more prudent to retain your place, tell me so openly, and I think I can contrive that you may do it without loss of character and credit. In that case, confine your ambition merely to rising gradually in your office, without mixing in politics. If, on the other hand, you should prefer to take your chance of my return to office, and so resign your present place ; and, furthermore, should commit yourself to a policy that may then be not only in opposition, but unpopular, I will do my best to introduce you into parliamentary life. I cannot say that I advise the latter."

Randal felt as a man feels after a severe fall—he was literally stunned. At length he faltered out—

"Can you think, sir, that I should ever desert your fortunes—your party—your cause?"

"My dear Leslie," replied the minister, "you are too young to have committed yourself to any men or to any party, except, indeed, in that unlucky pamphlet. This must not be an affair of sentiment, but of sense and reflection. Let us say no more on the point now ; but by considering the *pros* and the *cons*, you can better judge what to do, should the time for option suddenly arrive."

"But I hope that time may not come."

"I hope so too, and most sincerely," said the minister, with deliberate and genuine emphasis.

"What could be so bad for the country?" ejaculated Randal. "It does not seem to me possible, in the nature of things, that you and your party should ever go out !"

"And when we are once out, there will be plenty of wiseacres to say it is out of the nature of things that we should ever come in again. Here we are at the door."

CHAPTER V.

RANDAL passed a sleepless night; but, indeed, he was one of those persons who neither need, nor are accustomed to, much sleep. However, towards morning, when dreams are said to be prophetic, he fell into a most delightful slumber—a slumber peopled by visions fitted to lure on, through labyrinths of law, predestined chancellors, or wreck upon the rocks of glory the inebriate souls of youthful ensigns—dreams from which Rood Hall emerged crowned with the towers of Belvoir or Raby, and looking over subject lands and manors wrested from the nefarious usurpation of Thornhills and Hazeldeans—dreams in which Audley Egerton's gold and power—rooms in Downing Street, and saloons in Grosvenor Square—had passed away to the smiling dreamer, as the empire of Chaldæa passed to Darius the Median. Why visions so belying the gloomy and anxious thoughts that preceded them should visit the pillow of Randal Leslie, surpasses my philosophy to conjecture. He yielded, however, passively to their spell, and was startled to hear the clock strike eleven as he descended the stairs to breakfast. He was vexed at the lateness of the hour, for he had meant to have taken advantage of the unwonted softness of Egerton, and drawn therefrom some promises or proffers to cheer the prospects which the minister had so chillingly expanded before him the preceding night. And it was only at breakfast that he usually found the opportunity of private conference with his busy patron. But Audley Egerton would be sure to have sallied forth— and so he had—only Randal was surprised to hear that he had gone out in his carriage, instead of on foot, as was his habit. Randal soon despatched his solitary meal, and with a new and sudden affection for his office, thitherwards bent his way. As he passed through Piccadilly, he heard behind a voice that had lately become familiar to him, and turning round, saw Baron Levy walking side by side, though not arm-in-arm, with a gentleman almost as smart as himself, but with a jauntier step and a brisker air—a step that, like Diomed's, as described by Shakespeare—

> " Rises on the toe;—that spirit of his
> In aspiration lifts him from the earth."

Indeed, one may judge of the spirits and disposition of a man by his ordinary gait and mien in walking. He who habitually pursues abstract thought, looks down on the ground. He who is accustomed to sudden impulses, or is trying to seize upon some necessary recollection, looks up with a kind of jerk. He who is a steady, cautious, merely practical man, walks on deliberately, his eyes straight before him ; and, even in his most musing moods, observes things around sufficiently to avoid a porter's knot or a butcher's tray. But the man with strong ganglions—of pushing, lively temperament, who, though practical, is yet speculative—the man who is emulous and active, and ever trying to rise in life—sanguine, alert, bold—walks with a spring—looks rather above the heads of his fellow-passengers —but with a quick, easy turn of his own, which is lightly set on his shoulders ; his mouth is a little open—his eye is bright, rather restless, but penetrative—his port has something of defiance—his form is erect, but without stiffness. Such was the appearance of the Baron's companion. And as Randal turned round at Levy's voice, the Baron said to his companion, "A young man in the first circles— you should book him for your fair lady's parties. How d'ye do, Mr. Leslie? Let me introduce you to Mr. Richard Avenel." Then, as he hooked his arm into Randal's, he whispered, "Man of firstrate talent—monstrous rich—has two or three parliamentary seats in his pocket—wife gives parties—her foible."

"Proud to make your acquaintance, sir," said Mr. Avenel, lifting his hat. "Fine day."

"Rather cold too," said Leslie, who, like all thin persons, with weak digestions, was chilly by temperament ; besides, he had enough on his mind to chill his body.

"So much the healthier—braces the nerves," said Mr. Avenel ; "but you young fellows relax the system by hot rooms and late hours. Fond of dancing of course, sir?" Then, without waiting for Randal's negative, Mr. Richard continued rapidly, "Mrs. Avenel has a *soirée dansante* on Thursday—shall be very happy to see you in Eaton Square. Stop, I have a card ;" and he drew out a dozen large invitation cards, from which he selected one, and presented it to Randal. The Baron pressed that young gentleman's arm, and Randal replied courteously that it would give him great pleasure to be introduced to Mrs. Avenel. Then, as he was not desirous to be seen under the wing of Baron Levy, like a pigeon under that of a hawk, he gently extricated himself, and pleading great haste, walked quickly on towards his office.

"That young man will make a figure some day," said the Baron. "I don't know any one of his age with so few prejudices. He is a connection by marriage to Audley Egerton, who—"

"Audley Egerton !" exclaimed Mr. Avenel ; "a d—d haughty, aristocratic, disagreeable, ungrateful fellow ! "

"Why, what do you know of him?"

"He owed his first seat in Parliament to the votes of two near relations of mine, and when I called upon him some time ago, in his office, he absolutely ordered me out of the room. Hang his impertinence; if ever I can pay him off, I guess I shan't fail for want of good will!"

"Ordered you out of the room? That's not like Egerton, who is civil, if formal—at least to most men. You must have offended him in his weak point."

"A man whom the public pays so handsomely should have no weak point. What is Egerton's?"

"Oh, he values himself on being a thorough gentleman—a man of the nicest honour," said Levy, with a sneer. "You must have ruffled his plumes there. How was it?"

"I forget," answered Mr. Avenel, who was far too well versed in the London scale of human dignities since his marriage, not to look back with a blush at his desire of knighthood. "No use bothering our heads now about the plumes of an arrogant popinjay. To return to the subject we were discussing. You must be sure to let me have this money next week."

"Rely on it."

"And you'll not let my bills get into the market; keep them under lock and key."

"So we agreed."

"It is but a temporary difficulty—royal mourning, such nonsense—panic in trade, lest these precious ministers go out. I shall soon float over the troubled waters."

"By the help of a paper boat," said the Baron, laughing; and the two gentlemen shook hands and parted.

CHAPTER VI.

MEANWHILE Audley Egerton's carriage had deposited him at the door of Lord Lansmere's house, at Knightsbridge. He asked for the Countess, and was shown into the drawing-room, which was deserted. Egerton was paler than usual; and as the door opened, he wiped the unwonted moisture from his forehead, and there was a quiver on his firm lip. The Countess too, on entering, showed an emotion almost equally unusual to her self-control. She pressed Audley's hand in silence, and seating herself by his side, seemed to collect her thoughts. At length she said—

"It is rarely indeed that we meet, Mr. Egerton, in spite of your intimacy with Lansmere and Harley. I go so little into your world, and you will not voluntarily come to me."

"Madam," replied Egerton, "I might evade your kind reproach by stating that my hours are not at my disposal ; but I answer you with plain truth,—it must be painful to both of us to meet."

The Countess coloured and sighed, but did not dispute the assertion.

Audley resumed. "And therefore, I presume that, in sending for me, you have something of moment to communicate ? "

"It relates to Harley," said the Countess, as if in apology ; "and I would take your advice."

"To Harley ! Speak on, I beseech you."

"My son has probably told you that he has educated and reared a young girl, with the intention to make her Lady L'Estrange, and hereafter Countess of Lansmere."

"Harley has no secrets from me," said Egerton mournfully.

"This young lady has arrived in England—is here—in this house."

"And Harley too ? "

"No, she came over with Lady N—— and her daughters. Harley was to follow shortly, and I expect him daily. Here is his letter. Observe, he has never yet communicated his intentions to this young person, now intrusted to my care—never spoken to her as the lover."

Egerton took the letter and read it rapidly, though with attention.

"True," said he, as he returned the letter : "and before he does so he wishes you to see Miss Digby and to judge of her yourself—wishes to know if you will approve and sanction his choice."

"It is on this that I would consult you—a girl without rank ;—the father, it is true, a gentleman, though almost equivocally one,—but the mother, I know not what. And Harley, for whom I hoped an alliance with the first houses in England ! " The Countess pressed her hands convulsively together.

EGERTON.—"He is no more a boy. His talents have been wasted—his life a wanderer's. He presents to you a chance of resettling his mind, of re-arousing his native powers, of a home beside your own. Lady Lansmere, you cannot hesitate ! "

LADY LANSMERE.—"I do, I do ! After all that I have hoped, after all that I did to prevent—"

EGERTON (interrupting her).—"You owe him now an atonement ; that is in your power—it is not in mine."

The Countess again pressed Audley's hand, and the tears gushed from her eyes.

"It shall be so. I consent—I consent. I will silence, I will crush back this proud heart. Alas! it well-nigh broke his own! I am glad you speak thus. I like to think he owes my consent to you. In that there is atonement for both."

"You are too generous, madam," said Egerton, evidently moved, though still, as ever, striving to repress emotion. "And now may I see the young lady? This conference pains me; you see even my strong nerves quiver; and at this time I have much to go through— need of all my strength and firmness."

"I hear, indeed, that the Government will probably retire. But it is with honour: it will be soon called back by the voice of the nation."

"Let me see the future wife of Harley L'Estrange," said Egerton, without heed of this consolatory exclamation.

The Countess rose and left the room. In a few minutes she returned with Helen Digby.

Helen was wondrously improved from the pale, delicate child, with the soft smile and intelligent eyes, who had sate by the side of Leonard in his garret. She was about the middle height, still slight, but beautifully formed; that exquisite roundness of proportion which conveys so well the idea of woman, in its undulating pliant grace— formed to embellish life, and soften away its rude angles—formed to embellish, not to protect. Her face might not have satisfied the critical eye of an artist—it was not without defects in regularity; but its expression was eminently gentle and prepossessing; and there were few who would not have exclaimed, "What a lovely countenance!" The mildness of her brow was touched with melancholy—her childhood had left its traces on her youth. Her step was slow, and her manner shy, subdued, and timid.

Audley gazed on her with earnestness as she approached him; and then coming forward, took her hand and kissed it.

"I am your guardian's constant friend," said he, and he drew her gently to a seat beside him, in the recess of a window. With a quick glance of his eye towards the Countess, he seemed to imply the wish to converse with Helen somewhat apart. So the Countess interpreted the glance; and though she remained in the room, she seated herself at a distance, and bent over a book.

It was touching to see how the austere man of business lent himself to draw forth the mind of this quiet, shrinking girl; and if you had listened, you would have comprehended how he came to possess such social influence, and how well, some time or other in the course of his life, he had learned to adapt himself to women.

He spoke first of Harley L'Estrange—spoke with tact and delicacy.

Helen at first answered by monosyllables, and then, by degrees, with grateful and open affection. Audley's brow grew shaded. He then spoke of Italy, and though no man had less of the poet in his nature, yet with the dexterity of one long versed in the world, and who had been accustomed to extract evidences from characters most opposed to his own, he suggested such topics as might serve to arouse poetry in others. Helen's replies betrayed a cultivated taste, and a charming womanly mind ; but they betrayed, also, one accustomed to take its colourings from another's—to appreciate, admire, revere the Lofty and the Beautiful, but humbly and meekly. There was no vivid enthusiasm, no remark of striking originality, no flash of the self-kindling, creative faculty. Lastly, Egerton turned to England —to the critical nature of the times—to the claims which the country possessed upon all who had the ability to serve and guide its troubled destinies. He enlarged warmly on Harley's natural talents, and rejoiced that he had returned to England, perhaps to commence some great career. Helen looked surprised, but her face caught no correspondent glow from Audley's eloquence. He rose, and an expression of disappointment passed over his grave, handsome features, and as quickly vanished.

"Adieu ! my dear Miss Digby ; I fear I have wearied you, especially with my politics. Adieu, Lady Lansmere ; no doubt I shall see Harley as soon as he returns."

Then he hastened from the room, gained his carriage, and ordered the coachman to drive to Downing Street. He drew down the blinds, and leant back. A certain languor became visible in his face, and once or twice he mechanically put his hand to his heart.

"She is good, amiable, docile—will make an excellent wife, no doubt," said he, murmuringly. "But does she love Harley as he has dreamed of love? No ! Has she the power and energy to arouse his faculties, and restore to the world the Harley of old? No ! Meant by Heaven to be the shadow of another's sun—not herself the sun—this child is not the one who can atone for the Past and illume the Future."

CHAPTER VII.

THAT evening Harley L'Estrange arrived at his father's house. The few years that had passed since we saw him last had made no perceptible change in his appearance. He still preserved his elastic youthfulness of form, and singular variety and play of countenance. He seemed unaffectedly rejoiced to greet his parents, and had something of the gaiety and tenderness of a boy returned from school. His manner to Helen bespoke the chivalry that pervaded all the complexities and curves of his character. It was affectionate, but respectful. Hers to him, subdued—but innocently sweet and gently cordial. Harley was the chief talker. The aspect of the times was so critical that he could not avoid questions on politics; and, indeed, he showed an interest in them which he had never evinced before. Lord Lansmere was delighted.

"Why, Harley, you love your country after all?"

"The moment she seems in danger—yes!" replied the Patrician; and the Sybarite seemed to rise into the Athenian.

Then he asked with eagerness about his old friend Audley; and, his curiosity satisfied there, he inquired the last literary news. He had heard much of a book lately published. He named the one ascribed by Parson Dale to Professor Moss; none of his listeners had read it.

Harley pished at this, and accused them all of indolence and stupidity, in his own quaint, metaphorical style. Then he said—"And town gossip?"

"We never hear it," said Lady Lansmere.

"There is a new plough much talked of at Boodles," said Lord Lansmere.

"God speed it. But is not there a new man much talked of at White's?"

"I don't belong to White's."

"Nevertheless, you may have heard of him—a foreigner, a Count di Peschiera."

"Yes," said Lord Lansmere; "he was pointed out to me in the park—a handsome man for a foreigner; wears his hair properly cut; looks gentlemanlike and English."

"Ah, ah! He is here then!" and Harley rubbed his hands.

"Which road did you take? Did you pass the Simplon?"

"No; I came straight from Vienna."

Then, relating with lively vein his adventures by the way, he continued to delight Lord Lansmere by his gaiety till the time came to retire to rest. As soon as Harley was in his own room, his mother joined him.

"Well," said he, "I need not ask if you like Miss Digby? Who would not?"

"Harley, my own son," said the mother, bursting into tears, "be happy your own way; only be happy, that is all I ask."

Harley, much affected, replied gratefully and soothingly to this fond injunction. And then gradually leading his mother on to converse of Helen, asked abruptly—"And of the chance of our happiness—her happiness as well as mine—what is your opinion? Speak frankly."

"Of *her* happiness there can be no doubt," replied the mother proudly. "Of yours, how can you ask me? Have you not decided on that yourself?"

"But still it cheers and encourages one in any experiment, however well considered, to hear the approval of another. Helen has certainly a most gentle temper."

"I should conjecture so. But her mind—"

"Is very well stored."

"She speaks so little—"

"Yes. I wonder why? She's surely a woman."

"Pshaw," said the Countess, smiling, in spite of herself. "But tell me more of the process of your experiment. You took her as a child, and resolved to train her according to your own ideal. Was that easy?"

"It seemed so. I desired to instil habits of truth: she was already by nature truthful as the day; a taste for nature and all things natural—that seemed inborn; perceptions of Art as the interpreter of Nature—those were more difficult to teach. I think they may come. You have heard her play and sing?"

"No."

"She will surprise you. She has less talent for drawing; still, all that teaching could do has been done—in a word, she is accomplished. Temper, heart, mind—these all are excellent." Harley stopped and suppressed a sigh. "Certainly I ought to be very happy," said he; and he began to wind up his watch.

"Of course she must love you," said the Countess, after a pause. "How could she fail?"

"Love me! My dear mother, that is the very question I shall have to ask."

"Ask! Love is discovered by a glance; it has no need of asking."

"I have never discovered it, then, I assure you. The fact is, that before her childhood was passed, I removed her, as you may suppose, from my roof. She resided with an Italian family, near my usual abode. I visited her often, directed her studies, watched her improvement—".

"And fell in love with her?"

"Fall is such a very violent word. No; I don't remember to have had a fall. It was all a smooth inclined plane from the first

step, until at last I said to myself, ‘Harley L’Estrange, thy time
has come. The bud has blossomed into flower. Take it to thy
breast.’ And myself replied to myself, meekly, ‘So be it.’ Then I
found that Lady N——, with her daughters, was coming to England.
I asked her ladyship to take my ward to your house. I wrote to
you, and prayed your assent ; and, that granted, I knew you would
obtain my father’s. I am here—you give me the approval I sought
for. I will speak to Helen to-morrow. Perhaps, after all, she may
reject me.”

“Strange, strange—you speak thus coldly, thus lightly ; you so
capable of ardent love !”

“Mother,” said Harley, earnestly, “be satisfied ! *I* am ! Love,
as of old, I feel, alas ! too well, can visit me never more. But
gentle companionship, tender friendship, the relief and the sunlight
of woman’s smile—hereafter the voices of children—music that,
striking on the hearts of both parents, wakens the most lasting and
the purest of all sympathies : these are my hope. Is the hope so
mean, my fond mother ? ”

Again the Countess wept, and her tears were not dried when she
left the room.

CHAPTER VIII.

H ! Helen, fair Helen—type of the quiet, serene, unnoticed,
deep-felt excellence of woman ! Woman, less as the ideal
that a poet conjures from the air, than as the companion of
a poet on the earth ! Woman, who, with her clear sunny
vision of things actual, and the exquisite fibre of her delicate sense,
supplies the deficiencies of him whose foot stumbles on the soil,
because his eye is too intent upon the stars ! Woman, the provident,
the comforting—angel whose pinions are folded round the heart,
guarding there a divine spring unmarred by the winter of the world !
Helen, soft Helen, is it indeed in thee that the wild and brilliant
“lord of wantonness and ease” is to find the regeneration of his
life—the rebaptism of his soul ? Of what avail thy meek prudent
household virtues to one whom Fortune screens from rough trial ?—
whose sorrows lie remote from thy ken ?—whose spirit, erratic and
perturbed, now rising, now falling, needs a vision more subtle than
thine to pursue, and a strength that can sustain the reason, when it
droops, on the wings of enthusiasm and passion ?

And thou, thyself, O nature, shrinking and humble, that needest to be courted forth from the shelter, and developed under the calm and genial atmosphere of holy, happy love—can such affection as Harley L'Estrange may proffer suffice to thee? Will not the blossoms, yet folded in the petal, wither away beneath the shade that may protect them from the storm, and yet shut them from the sun? Thou who, where thou givest love, seekest, though meekly, for love in return;—to be the soul's sweet necessity, the life's household partner to him who receives all thy faith and devotion—canst thou influence the sources of joy and of sorrow in the heart that does not heave at thy name? Hast thou the charm and the force of the moon, that the tides of that wayward sea shall ebb and flow at thy will? Yet who shall say—who conjecture how near two hearts can become, when no guilt lies between them, and time brings the ties all its own? Rarest of all things on earth is the union in which both, by their contrasts, make harmonious their blending; each supplying the defects of the helpmate, and completing, by fusion, one strong human soul! Happiness enough, where even Peace does but seldom preside, when each can bring to the altar, if not the flame, still the incense. Where man's thoughts are all noble and generous, woman's feelings all gentle and pure, love may follow, if it does not precede;—and if not—, if the roses be missed from the garland, one may sigh for the rose, but one is safe from the thorn.

The morning was mild, yet somewhat overcast by the mist which announces coming winter in London, and Helen walked musingly beneath the trees that surrounded the garden of Lord Lansmere's house. Many leaves were yet left on the boughs; but they were sere and withered. And the birds chirped at times; but their note was mournful and complaining. All within this house, until Harley's arrival, had been strange and saddening to Helen's timid and sub-dued spirits. Lady Lansmere had received her kindly, but with a certain restraint; and the loftiness of manner, common to the Countess with all but Harley, had awed and chilled the diffident orphan. Lady Lansmere's very interest in Harley's choice—her attempts to draw Helen out of her reserve—her watchful eyes when-ever Helen shyly spoke, or shyly moved, frightened the poor child, and made her unjust to herself.

The very servants, though staid, grave, and respectful, as suited a dignified, old-fashioned household, painfully contrasted the bright welcoming smiles and free talk of Italian domestics. Her recol-lections of the happy warm Continental manner, which so sets the bashful at their ease, made the stately and cold precision of all around her doubly awful and dispiriting. Lord Lansmere himself, who did not as yet know the views of Harley, and little dreamed that he was to anticipate a daughter-in-law in the ward, whom he understood Harley, in a freak of generous romance, had adopted, was familiar and courteous, as became a host. But he looked upon Helen as a mere child, and naturally left her to the Countess. The dim sense of her equivocal position—of her comparative humbleness of birth and fortunes, oppressed and pained her; and even her gratitude to Harley was made burthensome by a sentiment of help-lessness. The grateful long to requite. And what could she ever do for him?

Thus musing, she wandered alone through the curving walks; and this sort of mock country landscape—London loud, and even visible, beyond the high gloomy walls, and no escape from the windows of the square formal house—seemed a type of the prison bounds of Rank to one whose soul yearns for simple loving Nature.

Helen's reverie was interrupted by Nero's joyous bark. He had caught sight of her, and came bounding up, and thrust his large head into her hand. As she stooped to caress the dog, happy at his honest greeting, and tears that had been long gathering to the lids fell silently on his face (for I know nothing that more moves us to tears than the hearty kindness of a dog, when something in human beings has pained or chilled us), she heard behind the musical voice of Harley. Hastily she dried or repressed her tears, as her guardian came up, and drew her arm within his own.

"I had so little of your conversation last evening, my dear ward, that I may well monopolize you now, even to the privation of Nero. And so you are once more in your native land?"

Helen sighed softly.

"May I not hope that you return under fairer auspices than those which your childhood knew?"

Helen turned her eyes with ingenuous thankfulness to her guardian, and the memory of all she owed to him rushed upon her heart.

Harley renewed, and with earnest, though melancholy sweetness —"Helen, your eyes thank me; but hear me before your words do. I deserve no thanks. I am about to make to you a strange confession of egotism and selfishness."

"You!—oh, impossible!"

"Judge yourself, and then decide which of us shall have cause to be grateful. Helen, when I was scarcely your age—a boy in years, but more, methinks, a man at heart, with man's strong energies and sublime aspirings, than I have ever since been—I loved, and deeply—"

He paused a moment, in evident struggle. Helen listened in

mute surprise, but his emotion awakened her own; her tender woman's heart yearned to console. Unconsciously her arm rested on his less lightly.

"Deeply, and for sorrow. It is a long tale, that may be told hereafter. The worldly would call my love a madness. I did not reason on it then—I cannot reason on it now. Enough: death smote suddenly, terribly, and to me mysteriously, her whom I loved. The love lived on. Fortunately, perhaps, for me, I had quick distraction, not to grief, but to its inert indulgence. I was a soldier; I joined our armies. Men called me brave. Flattery! I was a coward before the thought of life. I sought death: like sleep, it does not come at our call. Peace ensued. As when the winds fall the sails droop—so when excitement ceased, all seemed to me flat and objectless. Heavy, heavy was my heart. Perhaps grief had been less obstinate, but that I feared I had causes for self-reproach. Since then I have been a wanderer—a self-made exile. My boyhood had been ambitious—all ambition ceased. Flames, when they reach the core of the heart, spread, and leave all in ashes. Let me be brief: I did not mean thus weakly to complain—I to whom Heaven has given so many blessings! I felt, as it were, separated from the common objects and joys of men. I grew startled to see how, year by year, wayward humours possessed me. I resolved again to attach myself to some living heart—it was my sole chance to rekindle my own. But the one I had loved remained as my type of woman, and she was different from all I saw. Therefore I said to myself, 'I will rear from childhood some young fresh life, to grow up into my ideal.' As this thought began to haunt me, I chanced to discover you. Struck with the romance of your early life, touched by your courage, charmed by your affectionate nature, I said to myself, 'Here is what I seek.' Helen, in assuming the guardianship of your life, in all the culture which I have sought to bestow on your docile childhood, I repeat, that I have been but the egotist. And now, when you have reached that age, when it becomes me to speak, and you to listen—now, when you are under the sacred roof of my own mother—now I ask you, can you accept this heart, such as wasted years, and griefs too fondly nursed, have left it? Can you be, at least, my comforter? Can you aid me to regard life as a duty, and recover those aspirations which once soared from the paltry and miserable confines of our frivolous daily being? Helen, here I ask you, can you be all this, and under the name of—Wife?"

It would be in vain to describe the rapid, varying, indefinable emotions that passed through the inexperienced heart of the youthful listener as Harley thus spoke. He so moved all the springs of amaze, compassion, tender respect, sympathy, childlike gratitude, that when he paused and gently took her hand, she remained bewildered, speechless, overpowered. Harley smiled as he gazed upon her blushing, downcast, expressive face. He conjectured at once that the idea of such proposals had never crossed her mind; that she had never contemplated him in the character of wooer; never even sounded her heart as to the nature of such feelings as his image had aroused.

"My Helen," he resumed, with a calm pathos of voice, "there is some disparity of years between us, and perhaps I may not hope henceforth for that love which youth gives to the young. Permit me simply to ask, what you will frankly answer—'Can you have seen in our quiet life abroad, or under the roof of your Italian friends, any one you prefer to me?'"

"No, indeed, no!" murmured Helen. "How could I?—who is like you?" Then, with a sudden effort—for her innate truthfulness took alarm, and her very affection for Harley, childlike and reverent, made her tremble lest she should deceive him—she drew a little aside, and spoke thus:—

"Oh my dear guardian, noblest of all human beings, at least in my eyes, forgive, forgive me, if I seem ungrateful, hesitating; but I cannot, cannot think of myself as worthy of you. I never so lifted my eyes. Your rank, your position—"

"Why should they be eternally my curse? Forget them, and go on."

"It is not only they," said Helen, almost sobbing, "though they are much; but I your type, your ideal!—I?—impossible! Oh, how can I ever be anything even of use, of aid, of comfort to one like you!"

"You can, Helen—you can," cried Harley, charmed by such ingenuous modesty. "May I not keep this hand?"

And Helen left her hand in Harley's, and turned away her face, fairly weeping. A stately step passed under the wintry trees.

"My mother," said Harley L'Estrange, looking up, "I present to you my future wife."

CHAPTER IX.

WITH a slow step and an abstracted air, Harley L'Estrange bent his way towards Egerton's house, after his eventful interview with Helen. He had jus' entered one of the streets leading into Grosvenor Square, when a young man, walking quickly from the opposite direction, came full against him, and drawing back with a brief apology, recognized him, and exclaimed, "What! you in England, Lord L'Estrange! Accept my congratulations on your return. But you seem scarcely to remember me."

"I beg your pardon, Mr. Leslie. I remember you now by your smile; but you are of an age in which it is permitted me to say that you look older than when I saw you last."

"And yet, Lord L'Estrange, it seems to me that you look younger."

Indeed, this reply was so far true that there appeared less difference of years than before between Leslie and L'Estrange; for the wrinkles in the schemer's mind were visible in his visage, while Harley's dreamy worship of Truth and Beauty, seemed to have preserved to the votary the enduring youth of the divinities.

Harley received the compliment with a supreme indifference, which might have been suitable to a Stoic, but which seemed scarcely natural to a gentleman who had just proposed to a lady many years younger than himself.

Leslie renewed—"Perhaps you are on your way to Mr. Egerton's. If so, you will not find him at home; he is at his office."

"Thank you. Then to his office I must re-direct my steps."

"I am going to him myself," said Randal, hesitatingly.

L'Estrange had no prepossessions in favour of Leslie, from the little he had seen of that young gentleman; but Randal's remark was an appeal to his habitual urbanity, and he replied, with well-bred readiness, "Let us be companions so far."

Randal accepted the arm proffered to him; and Lord L'Estrange, as is usual with one long absent f om his native land, bore part as a questioner in the dialogue that ensued.

"Egerton is always the same man, I suppose—too busy for illness, and too firm for sorrow?"

"If he ever feel either, he will never stoop to complain. But, indeed, my dear lord, I should like much to know what you think of his health."

"How! You alarm me!"

"Nay, I did not mean to do that; and pray do not let him know that I went so far. But I have fancied that he looks a little worn and suffering."

"Poor Audley!" said L'Estrange, in a tone of deep affection. "I will sound him, and, be assured, without naming you; for I know well how little he likes to be supposed capable of human infirmity. I am obliged to you for your hint—obliged to you for your interest in one so dear to me."

And Harley's voice was more cordial to Randal than it had ever been before. He then began to inquire what Randal thought of the rumours that had reached himself as to the probable defeat of the Government, and how far Audley's spirits were affected by such risks. But Randal here, seeing that Harley could communicate nothing, was reserved and guarded.

"Loss of office could not, I think, affect a man like Audley," observed Lord L'Estrange. "He would be as great in opposition —perhaps greater; and as to emoluments—"

"The emoluments are good," interposed Randal, with a half sigh.

"Good enough, I suppose, to pay him back about a tenth of what his place costs our magnificent friend—No, I will say one thing for English statesmen, no man amongst them ever yet was the richer for place."

"And Mr. Egerton's private fortune must be large, I take for granted," said Randal, carelessly.

"It ought to be, if he has time to look to it."

Here they passed by the hotel in which lodged the Count di Peschiera.

Randal stopped. "Will you excuse me for an instant? As we are passing this hotel, I will just leave my card here." So saying he gave his card to a waiter lounging by the door. "For the Count di Peschiera," said he aloud.

L'Estrange started; and as Randal again took his arm, said— "So that Italian lodges here? and you know him?"

"I know him but slightly, as one knows any foreigner who makes a sensation."

"He makes a sensation?"

"Naturally: for he is handsome, witty, and said to be very rich —that is, as long as he receives the revenues of his exiled kinsman."

"I see you are well informed, Mr. Leslie. And what is supposed to bring hither the Count di Peschiera?"

"I did hear something, which I did not quite understand, about a bet of his that he would marry his kinsman's daughter ; and so, I conclude, secure to himself all the inheritance ; and that he is therefore here to discover the kinsman and win the heiress. But probably you know the rights of the story, and can tell me what credit to give to such gossip."

"I know this at least, that if he did lay such a wager, I would advise you to take any odds against him that his backers may give," said L'Estrange dryly ; and while his lip quivered with anger, his eye gleamed with arch ironical humour.

"You think, then, that this poor kinsman will not need such an alliance in order to regain his estates?"

"Yes ; for I never yet knew a rogue whom I would not bet against, when he backed his own luck as a rogue against Justice and Providence."

Randal winced, and felt as if an arrow had grazed his heart ; but he soon recovered.

"And indeed there is another vague rumour that the young lady in question is married already—to some Englishman."

This time it was Harley who winced. "Good Heavens! that cannot be true—that would undo all! An Englishman just at this moment! But some Englishman of correspondent rank I trust, or at least one known for opinions opposed to what an Austrian would call Revolutionary doctrines?"

"I know nothing. But it was supposed, merely a private gentleman of good family. Would not that suffice? Can the Austrian Court dictate a marriage to the daughter as a condition for grace to the father?"

"No—not that!" said Harley, greatly disturbed. "But put yourself in the position of any minister to one of the great European monarchies. Suppose a political insurgent, formidable for station and wealth, had been proscribed, much interest made on his behalf, a powerful party striving against it, and just when the minister is disposed to relent, he hears that the heiress to this wealth and this station is married to the native of a country in which sentiments friendly to the very opinions for which the insurgent was proscribed are popularly entertained, and thus that the fortune to be restored may be so employed as to disturb the national security—the existing order of things ;—this, too, at the very time when a popular revolution has just occurred in France,[1] and its effects are felt most in the very land of the exile ;—suppose all this, and then say if anything

---

[1] As there have been so many Revolutions in France, it may be convenient to suggest that, according to the dates of this story, Harley no doubt alludes to that revolution which exiled Charles X. and placed Louis Philippe on the throne.

could be more untoward for the hopes of the banished man, or furnish his adversaries with stronger arguments against the restoration of his fortune? But pshaw—this must be a chimera! If true, I should have known of it."

"I quite agree with your lordship—there can be no truth in such a rumour. Some Englishman, hearing, perhaps, of the probable pardon of the exile, may have counted on an heiress, and spread the report in order to keep off other candidates. By your account, if successful in his suit, he might fail to find an heiress in the bride."

"No doubt of that. Whatever might be arranged, I can't conceive that he would be allowed to get at the fortune, though it might be held in suspense for his children. But indeed it so rarely happens that an Italian girl of high name marries a foreigner, that we must dismiss this notion with a smile at the long face of the hypothetical fortune-hunter. Heaven help him, if he exist!"

"Amen!" echoed Randal, devoutly.

"I hear that Peschiera's sister is returned to England. Do you know her too?"

"A little."

"My dear Mr. Leslie, pardon me if I take a liberty not warranted by our acquaintance. Against the lady I say nothing. Indeed, I have heard some things which appear to entitle her to compassion and respect. But as to Peschiera, all who prize honour suspect him to be a knave—I know him to be one. Now, I think that the longer we preserve that abhorrence for knavery which is the generous instinct of youth, why, the fairer will be our manhood, and the more reverend our age. You agree with me?" And Harley suddenly turning, his eyes fell like a flood of light upon Randal's pale and secret countenance.

"To be sure," murmured the schemer.

Harley, surveying him, mechanically recoiled, and withdrew his arm.

Fortunately for Randal, who somehow or other felt himself slipped into a false position, he scarce knew how or why, he was here seized by the arm; and a clear, open, manly voice cried, "My dear fellow, how are you? I see you are engaged now; but look into my rooms when you can, in the course of the day."

And with a bow of excuse for his interruption, to Lord L'Estrange, the speaker was then turning away, when Harley said—

"No, don't let me take you from your friend, Mr. Leslie. And you need not be in a hurry to see Egerton; for I shall claim the privilege of older friendship for the first interview."

"It is Mr. Egerton's nephew, Frank Hazeldean."

"Pray call him back, and present me to him. He has a face that would have gone far to reconcile Timon to Athens."

Randal obeyed, and after a few kindly words to Frank, Harley insisted on leaving the two young men together, and walked on to Downing Street with a brisker step.

CHAPTER X.

"THAT Lord L'Estrange seems a very good fellow."

"So-so ;—an effeminate humorist—says the most absurd things, and fancies them wise. Never mind him. You wanted to speak to me, Frank ?"

"Yes ; I am so obliged to you for introducing me to Levy. I must tell you how handsomely he has behaved."

"Stop ; allow me to remind you that I did not introduce you to Levy ; you had met him before at Borrowell's, if I recollect right, and he dined with us at the Clarendon—that is all I had to do with bringing you together. Indeed I rather cau ioned you against him than not. Pray don't think I introduced you to a man who, however pleasant and perhaps honest, is still a money-lender. Your father would be justly angry with me if I had done so."

"Oh, pooh ! you are prejudiced against poor Levy. But just hear: I was sitting very ruefully, thinking over those cursed bills, and how the deuce I should renew them, when Levy walked into my rooms ; and, a ter telling me of his long friendship for my Uncle Egerton and his admiration for yourself, and (give me your hand, Randal) saying how touched he felt by your kind sympathy in my troubles, he opened his pocket-book, and showed me the bills safe and sound in his own possession."

"How ?"

"He had bought them up. 'It must be so disagreeable to me,' he said, 'to have them flying about the London money-market, and those Jews would be sure sooner or later to apply to my father. And now,' added Levy, 'I am in no immediate hurry for the money, and we must put the interest upon fairer terms.' In short, nothing could be more liberal than his tone. And he says, 'he is thinking of a way to relieve me altogether, and will call about it in a few days, when his plan is matured.' After all, I must owe this to you, Randal. I dare swear you put it into his head."

"O no, indeed ! On the contrary, I still say, 'Be cautious in all your dealings with Levy.' I don't know, I'm sure, what he means to propose. Have you heard from the Hall lately ?"

"Yes—to-day. Only think—the Riccaboccas have disappeared. My mother writes me word of it—a very odd letter. She seems to suspect that I know where they are, and reproaches me for 'mystery' —quite enigmatical. But there is one sentence in her letter—see, here it is in the postscript—which seems to refer to Beatrice : 'I don't ask you to tell me your secrets, Frank, but Randal will no doubt have assured you that my first consideration will be for your own happiness, in any matter in which your heart is really engaged.'"

"Yes," said Randal, slowly ; "no doubt this refers to Beatrice ; but, as I told you, your mother will not interfere one way or the other—such interference would weaken her influence with the Squire. Besides, as she said, she can't *wish* you to marry a foreigner ; though once married, she would—— But how do you stand now with the Marchesa? Has she consented to accept you?"

"Not quite ; indeed I have not actually proposed. Her manner, though much softened, has not so far emboldened me ; and, besides, before a positive declaration, I certainly must go down to the Hall and speak at least to my mother."

"You must judge for yourself, but don't do anything rash : talk first to me. Here we are at my office. Good-bye ; and—and pray believe that, in whatever you do with Levy, I have no hand in it."

CHAPTER XI.

TOWARDS the evening, Randal was riding fast on the road to Norwood. The arrival of Harley, and the conversation that had passed between the nobleman and Randal, made the latter anxious to ascertain how far Riccabocca was likely to learn L'Estrange's return to England, and to meet with him. For he felt that, should the latter come to know that Riccabocca, in his movements, had gone by Randal's advice, Harley would find that Randal had spoken to him disingenuously ; and, on the other hand, Riccabocca, placed under the friendly protection of Lord L'Estrange, would no longer need Randal Leslie to defend him from the machinations of Peschiera. To a reader happily unaccustomed to dive into the deep and mazy recesses of a schemer's mind, it might seem that Randal's interest in retaining a hold over the exile's confidence would terminate with the assurances that had reached him, from more than one quarter, that Violante might cease to be an heiress if she married himself. "But perhaps," suggests some candid and youthful conjecturer—"perhaps Randal Leslie is in love with this fair creature?" Randal in love!—no! He was too absorbed by harder passions for that blissful folly. Nor, if he could have fallen in love, was Violante the one to attract that sullen, secret heart; her instinctive nobleness, the very stateliness of her beauty, womanlike though it was, awed him. Men of that kind may love some soft slave—they cannot lift their eyes to a queen. They may look down—they cannot look up. But, on the one hand, Randal could not resign altogether the *chance* of securing a fortune that would realize his most dazzling dreams, upon the mere assurance, however probable, which had so dismayed him; and, on the other hand, should he be compelled to relinquish all idea of such alliance, though he did not contemplate the base perfidy of actually assisting Peschiera's avowed designs, still, if Frank's marriage with Beatrice should absolutely depend upon her brother's obtaining the knowledge of Violante's retreat, and that marriage should be as conducive to his interests as he thought he could make it, why,—he did not then push his deductions farther, even to himself—they seemed too black; but he sighed heavily, and that sigh foreboded how weak would be honour and virtue against avarice and ambition. .Therefore, on all accounts, Riccabocca was one of those cards in a sequence, which so calculating a player would not throw out of his hand: it *might* serve for repique—at the worst it might score well in the game. Intimacy with the Italian was still part and parcel in that knowledge which was the synonym of power.

While the young man was thus meditating, on his road to Norwood, Riccabocca and his Jemima were close conferring in their drawing-room. And if you could have there seen them, reader, you would have been seized with equal surprise and curiosity: for some extraordinary communication had certainly passed between them. Riccabocca was evidently much agitated, and with emotions not familiar to him. The tears stood in his eyes at the same time that a smile, the reverse of cynical or sardonic, curved his lips; while his wife was leaning her head on his shoulder, her hand clasped in his, and, by the expression of her face, you might guess that he had paid her some very gratifying compliment, of a nature more genuine and sincere than those which characterized his habitual hollow and dissimulating gallantry. But just at this moment Giacomo entered, and Jemima, with her native English modesty, withdrew in haste from Riccabocca's sheltering side.

"Padrone," said Giacomo, who, whatever his astonishment at the connubial position he had disturbed, was much too discreet to betray it—"Padrone, I see the young Englishman riding towards the house, and I hope when he arrives, you will not forget the alarming information I gave to you this morning."

"Ah—ah!" said Riccabocca, his face falling.

"If the Signorina were but married!"

"My very thought—my constant thought!" exclaimed Riccabocca. "And you really believe the young Englishman loves her?"

"Why else should he come, Excellency?" asked Giacomo, with great *naïveté.*

"Very true; why, indeed?" said Riccabocca. "Jemima, I cannot endure the terrors I suffer on that poor child's account. I will open myself frankly to Randal Leslie. And now, too, that which might have been a serious consideration, in case I return to Italy, will no longer stand in our way, Jemima."

Jemima smiled faintly, and whispered something to Riccabocca, to which he replied—

"Nonsense, *anima mia.* I know it *will* be—have not a doubt of it. I tell you it is as nine to four, according to the nicest calculations. I will speak at once to Randal. He is too young—too timid to speak himself."

"Certainly," interposed Giacomo; "how could he dare to speak, let him love ever so well?"

Jemima shook her head.

"Oh, never fear," said Riccabocca, observing this gesture; "I will give him the trial. If he entertain but mercenary views, I shall soon detect them. I know human nature pretty well, I think, my love; and, Giacomo,—just get me my Machiavelli;—that's right. Now leave me, my dear; I must reflect and prepare myself."

When Randal entered the house, Giacomo, with a smile of peculiar suavity, ushered him into the drawing-room. He found Riccabocca alone, and seated before the fire-place, leaning his face on his hand, with the great folio of Machiavelli lying open on the table.

The Italian received him as courteously as usual; but there was in his manner a certain serious and thoughtful dignity, which was perhaps the more imposing, because but rarely assumed. After a few preliminary observations, Randal remarked that Frank Hazeldean had informed him of the curiosity which the disappearance of the Riccaboccas had excited at the Hall, and inquired carelessly if the Doctor had left instructions as to the forwarding of any letters that might be directed to him at the Casino.

"Letters," said Riccabocca, simply, "I never receive any; or, at least, so rarely, that it was not worth while to take any event so little to be expected into consideration. No; if any letters do reach the Casino, there they will wait."

"Then I can see no possibility of indiscretion; no chance of a clue to your address."

"Nor I either."

Satisfied so far, and knowing that it was not in Riccabocca's habits to read the newspapers, by which he might otherwise have learnt of L'Estrange's arrival in London, Randal then proceeded to inquire, with much seeming interest, into the health of Violante—hoped it did not suffer by confinement, &c. Riccabocca eyed him gravely while he spoke, and then suddenly rising, that air of dignity to which I have before referred became yet more striking.

"My young friend," said he, "hear me attentively, and answer me frankly. I know human nature—" Here a slight smile of proud complacency passed the sage's lips, and his eye glanced toward his Machiavelli.

"I know human nature—at least I have studied it," he renewed more earnestly, and with less evident self-conceit; "and I believe that when a perfect stranger to me exhibits an interest in my affairs, which occasions him no small trouble—an interest (continued the wise man, laying his hand on Randal's shoulder) which scarcely a son could exceed, he must be under the influence of some strong personal motive."

"Oh, sir!" cried Randal, turning a shade more pale, and with a faltering tone. Riccabocca surveyed him with the tenderness of a superior being, and pursued his deductive theories.

"In your case, what is that motive? Not political; for I conclude you share the opinions of your government, and those opinions have not favoured mine. Not that of pecuniary or ambitious calculations; for how can such calculations enlist you on behalf of a ruined exile? What remains? Why, the motive which at your age is ever the most natural and the strongest. I don't blame you. Machiavelli himself allows that such a motive has swayed the wisest minds, and overturned the most solid states. In a word, young man, you are in love, and with my daughter Violante."

Randal was so startled by this direct and unexpected charge upon his own masked batteries, that he did not even attempt his defence. His head drooped on his breast, and he remained speechless.

"I do not doubt," resumed the penetrating judge of human nature, "that you would have been withheld by the laudable and generous scruples which characterize your happy age, from voluntarily disclosing to me the state of your heart. You might suppose that, proud of the position I once held, or sanguine in the hope of regaining my inheritance, I might be over-ambitious in my matrimonial views for Violante ; or that you, anticipating my restoration to honours and fortune, might seem actuated by the last motives which influence love and youth ; and, therefore, my dear young friend, I have departed from the ordinary custom in England, and adopted a very common one in my own country. With us, a suitor seldom presents himself till he is assured of the consent of a father. I have only to say this—if I am right, and you love my daughter, my first object in life is to see her safe and secure ; and, in a word —you understand me."

Now, mightily may it comfort and console us ordinary mortals, who advance no pretence to superior wisdom and ability, to see the huge mistakes made by both these very sagacious personages—Dr. Riccabocca, valuing himself on his profound acquaintance with character, and Randal Leslie, accustomed to grope into every hole and corner of thought and action, wherefrom to extract that knowledge which is power! For whereas the sage, judging not only by his own heart in youth, but by the general influence of the master passion on the young, had ascribed to Randal sentiments wholly foreign to that able diplomatist's nature ; so no sooner had Riccabocca brought his speech to a close, than Randal, judging also by his own heart, and by the general laws which influence men of the mature age and boasted worldly wisdom of the pupil of Machiavelli, instantly decided that Riccabocca presumed upon his youth and inexperience, and meant most nefariously to take him in.

"The poor youth!" thought Riccabocca, "how unprepared he is for the happiness I give him!"

"The cunning old Jesuit!" thought Randal ; "he has certainly learned, since we met last, that he has no chance of regaining his patrimony, and so he wants to impose on me the hand of a girl without a shilling. What other motive can he possibly have! Had his daughter the remotest probability of becoming the greatest heiress in Italy, would he dream of bestowing her on me in this off-hand way? The thing stands to reason."

Actuated by his resentment at the trap thus laid for him, Randal was about to disclaim altogether the disinterested and absurd affection laid to his charge, when it occurred to him that, by so doing, he might mortally offend the Italian—since the cunning never forgive those who refuse to be duped by them—and it might still be conducive to his interest to preserve intimate and familiar terms with Riccabocca ; therefore, subduing his first impulse, he exclaimed,

"O too generous man ! pardon me if I have so long been unable to express my amaze, my gratitude ; but I cannot—no, I cannot, while your prospects remain thus uncertain, avail myself of your—of your inconsiderate magnanimity. Your rare conduct can only redouble my own scruples, if you, as I firmly hope and believe, are restored to your great possessions—you would naturally look so much higher than me. Should these hopes fail, then, indeed, it may be different ; yet even then, what position, what fortune, have I to offer to your daughter worthy of her ?"

"You are well born ! all gentlemen are equals," said Riccabocca, with a sort of easy nobleness. "You have youth, information, talent—sources of certain wealth in this happy country—powerful connections ; and, in fine, if you are satisfied with marrying for love, I shall be contented ;—if not, speak openly. As to the restoration to my possessions, I can scarcely think that probable while my enemy lives. And even in that case, since I saw you last, something has occurred (added Riccabocca, with a strange smile, which seemed to Randal singularly sinister and malignant) that may remove all difficulties. Meanwhile, do not think me so extravagantly magnanimous—do not underrate the satisfaction I must feel at knowing Violante safe from the designs of Peschiera—safe, and for ever, under a husband's roof. I will tell you an Italian proverb— it contains a truth full of wisdom and terror :—

" ' Hai cinquanta Amici ?—non basta.—Hai un Nemico ?—è troppo.' "

"Something has occurred !" echoed Randal, not heeding the conclusion of this speech, and scarcely heeding the proverb which the sage delivered in his most emphatic and tragic tone. "Something has occurred ! My dear friend, be plainer. What has occurred ?" Riccabocca remained silent. "Something that induces you to bestow your daughter on me ?"

Riccabocca nodded, and emitted a low chuckle.

"The very laugh of a fiend," muttered Randal. "Something that makes her not worth bestowing. He betrays himself. Cunning people always do."

"Pardon me," said the Italian at last, "if I don't answer your question ; you will know later ; but, at present, this is a family secret. And now I must turn to another and more alarming cause for my frankness to you." Here Riccabocca's face changed, and assumed an expression of mingled rage and fear. "You must know," he added, sinking his voice, "that Giacomo has seen a strange person loitering about the house, and looking up at the

1 Have you fifty friends ?—it is not enough.—Have you one enemy ?—it is too much.

windows; and he has no doubt—nor have I—that this is some spy or emissary of Peschiera's."

"Impossible; how could he discover you?"

"I know not; but no one else has any interest in doing so. The man kept at a distance, and Giacomo could not see his face."

"It may be but a mere idler. Is this all?"

"No; the old woman who serves us said that she was asked at a shop 'if we were not Italians?'"

"And she answered?"

"'No;' but owned that 'we had a foreign servant, Giacomo.'"

"I will see to this. Rely on it that if Peschiera has discovered you, I will learn it. Nay, I will hasten from you in order to commence inquiry."

"I cannot detain you. May I think that we have now an interest in common?"

"O, indeed yes; but—but—your daughter! how can I dream that one so beautiful, so peerless, will confirm the hope you have extended to me?"

"The daughter of an Italian is brought up to consider that it is a father's right to dispose of her hand."

"But the heart?"

"*Cospetto!*" said the Italian, true to his infamous notions as to the sex, "the heart of a girl is like a convent—the holier the cloister, the more charitable the door."

CHAPTER XII.

RANDAL had scarcely left the house before Mrs. Ricca-bocca, who was affectionately anxious in all that concerned Violante, rejoined her husband.

"I like the young man very well," said the sage—"very well indeed. I find him just what I expected, from my general knowledge of human nature; for as love ordinarily goes with youth, so modesty usually accompanies talent. He is young, *ergo* he is in love; he has talent, *ergo* he is modest—modest and ingenuous."

"And you think not in any way swayed by interest in his affections?"

"Quite ·the contrary; and to prove him the more, I have not said a word as to the worldly advantages which, in any case, would accrue to him from an alliance with my daughter. In any case;

for if I regain my country, her fortune is assured; and if not, I trust (said the poor exile, lifting his brow with stately and becoming pride) that I am too well aware of my child's dignity, as well as my own, to ask any one to marry her to his own worldly injury."

"Eh! I don't quite understand you, Alphonso. To be sure, your dear life is insured for her marriage portion; but—"

"*Pazzie*—stuff!" said Riccabocca, petulantly; "her marriage portion would be as nothing to a young man of Randal's birth and prospects. I think not of that. But listen: I have never consented to profit by Harley L'Estrange's friendship for me; my scruples would not extend to my son-in-law. This noble friend has not only high rank, but considerable influence—influence with the government—influence with Randal's patron—who, between ourselves, does not seem to push the young man as he might do; I judge by what Randal says. I should write, therefore, before anything was settled, to L'Estrange, and I should say to him simply, 'I never asked you to save me from penury, but I do ask you to save a daughter of my house from humiliation. I can give to her no dowry; can her husband owe to my friend that advance in an honourable career—that opening to energy and talent—which is more than a dowry to generous ambition?'"

"Oh, it is in vain you would disguise your rank," cried Jemima, with enthusiasm, "it speaks in all you utter, when your passions are moved."

The Italian did not seem flattered by that eulogy. "Pish," said he, "there you are! rank again!"

But Jemima was right. There was something about her husband that was grandiose and princely, whenever he escaped from his accursed Machiavelli, and gave fair play to his heart.

And he spent the next hour or so in thinking over all that he could do for Randal, and devising for his intended son-in-law the agreeable surprises, which Randal was at that very time racking his yet cleverer brains to disappoint.

These plans conned sufficiently, Riccabocca shut up his Machiavelli, and hunted out of his scanty collection of books Buffon on Man, and various other psychological volumes, in which he soon became deeply absorbed. Why were these works the object of the sage's study? Perhaps he will let us know soon, for it is clearly a secret known to his wife; and though she has hitherto kept one secret, that is precisely the reason why Riccabocca would not wish long to overburthen her discretion with another.

CHAPTER XIII.

RANDAL reached home in time to dress for a late dinner at Baron Levy's.

The Baron's style of living was of that character especially affected both by the most acknowledged exquisites of that day, and, it must be owned, also, by the most egregious *parvenus*. For it is noticeable that it is your *parvenu* who always comes nearest in fashion (so far as externals are concerned) to your genuine exquisite. It is your *parvenu* who is most particular as to the cut of his coat, and the precision of his equipage, and the minutiæ of his *ménage*. Those between the *parvenu* and the exquisite who know their own consequence, and have something solid to rest upon, are slow in following all the caprices of fashion, and obtuse in observation as to those niceties which neither give them another ancestor, nor add another thousand to the account at their banker's ;—as to the last, rather indeed the contrary! There was a decided elegance about the Baron's house and his dinner. If he had been one of the lawful kings of the dandies, you would have cried, " What perfect taste ! "—but such is human nature, that the dandies who dined with him said to each other, " He pretend to imitate D—— ! vulgar dog ! " There was little affectation of your more showy opulence. The furniture in the rooms was apparently simple, but, in truth, costly, from its luxurious comfort—the ornaments and china scattered about the commodes were of curious rarity and great value ; and the pictures on the walls were gems. At dinner, no plate was admitted on the table. The Russian fashion, then uncommon, now more prevalent, was adopted—fruit and flowers in old *Sèvres* dishes of priceless *vertu*, and in sparkling glass of Bohemian fabric. No livery servant was permitted to wait ; behind each guest stood a gentleman dressed so like the guest himself, in fine linen and simple black, that guest and lacquey seemed stereotypes from one plate.

The viands were exquisite ; the wine came from the cellars of deceased archbishops and ambassadors. The company was select ; the party did not exceed eight. Four were the eldest sons of peers, (from a baron to a duke ;) one was a professed wit, never to be got without a month's notice, and, where a *parvenu* was host, a certainty of green peas and peaches—out of season ; the sixth, to Randal's astonishment, was Mr. Richard Avenel ; himself and the Baron made up the complement.

The eldest sons recognized each other with a meaning smile ; the most juvenile of them, indeed, (it was his first year in London,) had the grace to blush and look sheepish. The others were more hardened ; but they all united in regarding with surprise both Randal and Dick Avenel. The former was known to most of them personally, and to all, by repute, as a grave, clever, promising young man, rather prudent than lavish, and never suspected to have got into a scrape. What the deuce did he do there ? Mr. Avenel puzzled them yet more. A middle-aged man, said to be in business, whom they had observed "about town" (for he had a noticeable face and figure)—that is, seen riding in the park, or lounging in the pit at the opera, but never set eyes on at a recognized club, or in the coteries of their "set ;" a man whose wife gave horrid third-rate parties, that took up half a column in the *Morning Post* with a list of "The Company Present," in which a sprinkling of dowagers fading out of fashion, and a foreign title or two, made the darkness of the obscurer names doubly dark. Why this man should be asked to meet *them*, by Baron Levy, too—a decided tuft-hunt and would-be exclusive—called all their faculties into exercise. The wit, who, being the son of a small tradesman, but in the very best society, gave himself far greater airs than the young lords, impertinently solved the mystery.—"Depend on it," whispered he to Spendquick—" depend on it the man is the X.Y. of the *Times* who offers to lend any sum of money from £10 to half-a-million. He's the man who has all your bills ; Levy is only his jackal."

" 'Pon my soul," said Spendquick, rather alarmed, "if that's the case, one may as well be civil to him."

" *You*, certainly," said the wit. "But I never have found an X.Y. who would advance me the L. s.; and therefore, I shall not be more respectful to X.Y. than to any other unknown quantity."

By degrees, as the wine circulated, the party grew gay and sociable. Levy was really an entertaining fellow ; had all the gossip of the town at his fingers' ends ; and possessed, moreover, that pleasant art of saying ill-natured things of the absent, which those present always enjoy. By degrees, too, Mr. Richard Avenel came out ; and, as the whisper had circulated round the table that he was X.Y., he was listened to with a profound respect, which greatly elevated his spirits. Nay, when the wit tried once to show him up or mystify him, Dick answered with a bluff spirit, that, though very coarse, was found so humorous by Lord Spendquick and other gentlemen similarly situated in the money-market, that they turned the laugh against the wit, and silenced him for the rest of the night—a circumstance which made the party go off much more pleasantly. After dinner, the conversation, quite that of single men, easy and *débonnaire*, glanced from the turf, and the ballet, and the last scandal, towards politics ; for the times were such that politics were discussed everywhere, and three of the young lords were county members.

Randal said little, but, as was his wont, listened attentively ; and he was aghast to find how general was the belief that the Government was doomed. Out of regard to him, and with that delicacy of breeding which belongs to a certain society, nothing personal to Egerton was said, except by Avenel, who, however, on blurting out some rude expressions respecting that minister, was instantly checked by the Baron.

"Spare my friend, and Mr. Leslie's near connection," said he, with a polite but grave smile.

"Oh," said Avenel, "public men, whom we pay, are public property—aren't they, my lord ? " appealing to Spendquick.

"Certainly," said Spendquick, with great spirit—"public property, or why should we pay them ? There must be a very strong motive to induce us to do that ! I hate paying people. In fact," he subjoined in an aside, " I never do."

"However," resumed Mr. Avenel, graciously, "I don't want to hurt your feelings, Mr. Leslie. As to the feelings of our host, the Baron, I calculate that they have got tolerably tough by the exercise they have gone through."

"Nevertheless," said the Baron, joining in the laugh which any lively saying by the supposed X.Y. was sure to excite—"nevertheless, 'love me, love my dog,' love me, love my Egerton."

Randal started, for his quick ear and subtle intelligence caught something sinister and hostile in the tone with which Levy uttered this equivocal comparison, and his eye darted towards the Baron. But the Baron had bent down his face, and was regaling himself upon an olive.

By and by the party rose from table. The four young noblemen had their engagements elsewhere, and proposed to separate without re-entering the drawing-room. As, in Goethe's theory, monads which have affinities with each other are irresistibly drawn together, so these gay children of pleasure had, by a common impulse, on rising from table, moved each to each, and formed a group round the fire-place. Randal stood a little apart, musing ; the wit examined the pictures through his eye-glass ; and Mr. Avenel drew the Baron towards the sideboard, and there held him in whispered conference. This colloquy did not escape the young gentlemen round the fire-place : they glanced towards each other.

"Settling the percentage on renewal," said one, *sotto voce.*

"X.Y. does not seem such a very bad fellow," said another.

"He looks rich, and talks rich," said a third.

"A decided independent way of expressing his sentiments; those moneyed men generally have."

"Good heavens!" ejaculated Spendquick, who had been keeping his eye anxiously fixed on the pair, "do look; X.Y. is actually taking out his pocket-book; he is coming this way. Depend on it he has got our bills—mine is due to-morrow!"

"And mine too," said another, edging off. "Why, it is a perfect *guet-apens.*"

Meanwhile, breaking away from the Baron, who appeared anxious to detain him, and failing in that attempt, turned aside, as if not to see Dick's movements—a circumstance which did not escape the notice of the group, and confirmed all their suspicions, Mr. Avenel, with a serious, thoughtful face, and a slow step, approached the group. Nor did the great Roman general more nervously "flutter the dove-cots in Corioli," than did the advance of the supposed X.Y. agitate the bosoms of Lord Spendquick and his sympathizing friends. Pocket-book in hand, and apparently feeling for something formidable within its mystic recesses, step by step came Dick Avenel towards the fire-place. The group stood still, fascinated by horror.

"Hum," said Mr. Avenel, clearing his throat.

"I don't like that hum at all," muttered Spendquick.

"Proud to have made your acquaintance, gentlemen," said Dick, bowing.

The gentlemen, thus addressed, bowed low in return.

"My friend the Baron thought this not exactly the time to—" Dick stopped a moment; you might have knocked down those four young gentlemen, though four finer specimens of humanity no aristocracy in Europe could produce—you might have knocked them down with a feather! "But," renewed Avenel, not finishing his sentence, "I have made it a rule in life never to lose securing a good opportunity; in short, to make the most of the present moment. And," added he, with a smile which froze the blood in Lord Spendquick's veins, "the rule has made me a very warm man! Therefore, gentlemen, allow me to present you each with one of these"—every hand retreated behind the back of its well-born owner—when, to the inexpressible relief of all, Dick concluded with —"a little *soirée dansante,*" and extended four cards of invitation.

"Most happy!" exclaimed Spendquick. "I don't dance in general; but to oblige X—— I mean to have a better acquaintance, sir, with *you*—I would dance on the tight-rope."

There was a good-humoured, pleasant laugh at Spendquick's enthusiasm, and a general shaking of hands and pocketing of the invitation cards.

"You don't look like a dancing man," said Avenel, turning to the wit, who was plump and somewhat gouty—as wits who dine out five days in the week generally are ; "but we shall have supper at one o'clock."

Infinitely offended and disgusted, the wit replied, dryly, "that every hour of his time was engaged for the rest of the season," and, with a stiff salutation to the Baron, took his departure. The rest, in good spirits, hurried away to their respective cabriolets; and Leslie was following them into the hall, when the Baron, catching hold of him, said, "Stay, I want to talk to you."

CHAPTER XIV.

THE Baron turned into his drawing-room, and Leslie followed.

"Pleasant young men, those," said Levy, with a slight sneer, as he threw himself into an easy chair and stirred the fire. "And not at all proud ; but, to be sure, they are—under great obligations to me. Yes ; they owe me a great deal. *Apropos*, I have had a long talk with Frank Hazeldean—fine young man— remarkable capacities for business. I can arrange his affairs for him. I find, on reference to the Will Office, that you were quite right ; the Casino property is entailed on Frank. He will have the fee simple. He can dispose of the reversion entirely. So that there will be no difficulty in our arrangements."

"But I told you also that Frank had scruples about borrowing on the event of his father's death."

"Ah—you did so. Filial affection! I never take that into account in matters of business. Such little scruples, though they are highly honourable to human nature, soon vanish before the prospect of the King's Bench. And, too, as you so judiciously remarked, our clever young friend is in love with Madame di Negra."

"Did he tell you that ?"

"No ; but Madame di Negra did ! "

"You know her ?"

"I know most people in good society, who now and then require friend in the management of their affairs. And having made sure of the fact you stated, as to Hazeldean's contingent property (excuse my prudence), I have accommodated Madame di Negra, and bought up her debts."

"You have—you surprise me!"

"The surprise will vanish on reflection. But you are very new to the world yet, my dear Leslie. By the way, I have had an interview with Peschiera—"

"About his sister's debts?"

"Partly. A man of the nicest honour is Peschiera."

Aware of Levy's habit of praising people for the qualities in which, according to the judgment of less penetrating mortals, they were most deficient, Randal only smiled at this eulogy, and waited for Levy to resume. But the Baron sate silent and thoughtful for a minute or two, and then wholly changed the subject.

"I think your father has some property in ——shire, and you probably can give me a little information as to certain estates of a Mr. Thornhill, estates which, on examination of the title-deeds, I find once, indeed, belonged to your family." The Baron glanced at a very elegant memorandum-book.—"The manors of Rood and Dulmansberry, with sundry farms thereon. Mr. Thornhill wants to sell them—an old client of mine, Thornhill. He has applied to me on the matter. Do you think it an improvable property?"

Randal listened with a livid cheek and a throbbing heart. We have seen that, if there was one ambitious scheme in his calculation which, though not absolutely generous and heroic, still might win its way to a certain sympathy in the undebased human mind, it was the hope to restore the fallen fortunes of his ancient house, and re-possess himself of the long alienated lands that surrounded the dismal wastes of the mouldering Hall. And now to hear that those lands were getting into the inexorable gripe of Levy—tears of bitterness stood in his eyes.

"Thornhill," continued Levy, who watched the young man's countenance—"Thornhill tells me that that part of his property—the old Leslie lands—produces £2000 a-year, and that the rental could be raised. He would take £50,000 for it—£20,000 down, and suffer the remaining £30,000 to lie on mortgage at four per cent. It seems a very good purchase. What do you say?"

"Don't ask me," said Randal, stung into rare honesty; "for I had hoped I might live to repossess myself of that property."

"Ah! indeed. It would be a very great addition to your consequence in the world—not from the mere size of the estate, but from its hereditary associations. And if you have any idea of the purchase—believe me, I'll not stand in your way."

"How can I have any idea of it?"

"But I thought you said you had."

"I understood that these lands could not be sold till Mr. Thornhill's son came of age, and joined in getting rid of the entail."

"Yes, so Thornhill himself supposed, till, on examining the title-deeds, I found he was under a mistake. These lands are not comprised in the settlement made by old Jasper Thornhill, which ties up the rest of the property. The title will be perfect. Thornhill wants to settle the matter at once—losses on the turf, you understand; an immediate purchaser would get still better terms. A Sir John Spratt would give the money;—but the addition of these lands would make the Spratt property of more consequence in the county than the Thornhill. So my client would rather take a few thousands less from a man who don't set up to be his rival. Balance of power in counties as well as nations."

Randal was silent.

"Well," said Levy, with great kindness of manner, "I see I pain you; and though I am what my very pleasant guests would call a *parvenu*, I comprehend your natural feelings as a gentleman of ancient birth. *Parvenu!* Ah! is it not strange, Leslie, that no wealth, no fashion, no fame can wipe out that blot. They call me a *parvenu*, and borrow my money. They call our friend the wit, a *parvenu*, and submit to all his insolence—if they condescend to regard his birth at all—provided they can but get him to dinner. They call the best debater in the Parliament of England a *parvenu*, and will entreat him, some day or other, to be prime minister, and ask him for stars and garters. A droll world, and no wonder the *parvenus* want to upset it.

Randal had hitherto supposed that this notorious tuft-hunter—this dandy capitalist—this money-lender, whose whole fortune had been wrung from the wants and follies of an aristocracy, was naturally a firm supporter of things as they are—how could things be better for men like Baron Levy? But the usurer's burst of democratic spleen did not surprise his precocious and acute faculty of observation. He had before remarked, that it is the persons who fawn most upon an aristocracy, and profit the most by the fawning, who are ever at heart its bitterest disparagers. Why is this? Because one full half of democratic opinion is made up of envy; and we can only envy what is brought before our eyes, and what, while very near to us, is still unattainable. No man envies an archangel.

"But," said Levy, throwing himself back in his chair, "a new order of things is commencing; we shall see. Leslie, it is lucky for you that you did not enter parliament under the government; it would be your political ruin for life."

"You think, then, that the ministry really cannot last?"

"Of course I do; and what is more, I think that a ministry of the same principles cannot be restored. You are a young man of talent and spirit; your birth is nothing compared to the rank of the reigning party; it would tell, to a certain degree, in a democratic one. I say, you should be more civil to Avenel; he could return you to parliament at the next election."

"The next election! In six years! We have just had a general election."

"There will be another before this year, or half of it, or perhaps a quarter of it, is out."

"What makes you think so?"

"Leslie, let there be confidence between us; we can help each other. Shall we be friends?"

"With all my heart. But though you may help me, how can I help you?"

"You have helped me already to Frank Hazeldean and the Casino estate. All clever men can help me. Come, then, we are friends; and what I say is secret. You ask me why I think there will be a general election so soon? I will answer you frankly. Of all the public men I ever met with, there is no one who had so clear a vision of things immediately before him as Audley Egerton."

"He has that character. Not *far*-seeing, but *clear*-sighted to a certain limit."

"Exactly so. No one better, therefore, knows public opinion, and its immediate ebb and flow."

"Granted."

"Egerton, then, counts on a general election within three months; and I have lent him the money for it."

"Lent him the money! Egerton borrow money of you—the rich Audley Egerton!"

"Rich!" repeated Levy in a tone impossible to describe, and accompanying the word with that movement of the middle finger and thumb, commonly called a "snap," which indicates profound contempt.

He said no more. Randal sate stupefied. At length the latter muttered, "But if Egerton is really not rich—if he lose office, and without the hope of return to it——"

"If so, he is ruined!" said Levy, coldly; "and therefore, from regard to you, and feeling interest in your future fate, I say—Rest no hopes of fortune or career upon Audley Egerton. Keep your place for the present, but be prepared at the next election to stand upon popular principles. Avenel shall return you to parliament; and the rest is with luck and energy. And now, I'll not detain you longer," said Levy, rising and ringing the bell. The servant entered.

"Is my carriage here?"

"Yes, Baron."

"Can I set you down anywhere?"

"No, thank you, I prefer walking."

"Adieu, then. And mind you remember the *soirée dansante* at Mrs. Avenel's." Randal mechanically shook the hand extended to him, and went down the stairs.

The fresh frosty air roused his intellectual faculties, which Levy's ominous words had almost paralyzed.

And the first thing the clever schemer said to himself was this—

"But what can be the man's motive in what he said to me?"

The next was—

"Egerton ruined! What am I, then?"

And the third was—

"And that fair remnant of the old Leslie property! £20,000 down—how to get the sum? Why should Levy have spoken to me of this?"

And lastly, the soliloquy rounded back—"The man's motives! His motives?"

Meanwhile, the Baron threw himself into his chariot—the most comfortable easy chariot you can possibly conceive—single man's chariot—perfect taste—no married man ever had such a chariot; and in a few minutes he was at ——'s hotel, and in the presence of Giulio Franzini, Count di Peschiera.

"*Mon cher*," said the Baron, in very good French, and in a tone of the most familiar equality with the descendant of the princes and heroes of grand mediæval Italy—"*Mon cher*, give me one of your excellent cigars. I think I have put all matters in train."

"You have found out—"

"No; not so fast yet," said the Baron, lighting the cigar extended to him. "But you said that you should be perfectly contented if it only cost you £20,000 to marry off your sister, (to whom that sum is legally due,) and to marry yourself to the heiress."

"I did, indeed."

"Then I have no doubt I shall manage both objects for that sum, if Randal Leslie really knows where the young lady is, and can assist you. Most promising able man is Randal Leslie—but innocent as a babe just born."

"Ha, ha! Innocent? *Que diable!*"

"Innocent as this cigar, *mon cher*—strong certainly, but smoked very easily. *Soyez tranquille!*"

CHAPTER XV.

WHO has not seen, who not admired, that noble picture by Daniel Maclise, which refreshes the immortal name of my ancestor Caxton! For myself, while with national pride I heard the admiring murmurs of the foreigners who grouped around it (nothing, indeed, of which our nation may be more proud had they seen in the Crystal Palace)—heard, with no less a pride in the generous nature of fellow-artists, the warm applause of living and deathless masters, sanctioning the enthusiasm of the popular crowd ;—what struck me more than the precision of drawing, for which the artist has been always renowned, and the just, though gorgeous affluence of colour which he has more recently acquired, was the profound depth of conception, out of which this great work had so elaborately arisen. That monk, with his scowl towards the printer and his back on the Bible over which *his form casts a shadow*—the whole transition between the mediæval Christianity of cell and cloister, and the modern Christianity that rejoices in the daylight, is depicted there, in the shadow that obscures the Book—in the scowl that is fixed upon the Book-diffuser ;—that sombre, musing face of Richard, Duke of Gloucester, with the beauty of Napoleon, darkened to the expression of a Fiend, looking far and anxiously into futurity as if foreseeing there what antagonism was about to be created to the schemes of secret crime and un-relenting force ;—the chivalrous head of the accomplished Rivers, seen but in profile, under his helmet, as if the age when Chivalry must defend its noble attributes, in steel, was already half passed away : and, not least grand of all, the rude thews and sinews of the artisan forced into service on the type, and the ray of intellect, fierce, and menacing revolutions yet to be, struggling through his rugged features, and across his low knitted brow ;—all this, which showed how deeply the idea of the discovery in its good and its evil, its saving light and its perilous storms, had sunk into the artist's soul, charmed me as affecting the exact union between sentiment and execution, which is the true and rare consummation of the Ideal in Art. But observe, while in these personages of the group are depicted the deeper and graver agencies implicated in the bright but terrible invention—observe how little the light epicures of the hour heed the scowl of the monk, or the restless gesture of Richard, or the troubled gleam in the eyes of the artisan—King Edward, handsome *Poco curante*, delighted in the surprise of a child, with a new toy; and Clarence, with his curious, yet careless, glance—all the while Caxton himself, calm, serene, untroubled, intent solely upon the manifestation of his discovery, and no doubt supremely indifferent whether the first proofs of it shall be dedicated to a Rivers or an Edward, a Richard or a Henry, Plantagenet or Tudor—'tis all the same to that comely, gentle-looking man. So is it ever with your Abstract Science!—not a jot cares its passionless logic for the woe or weal of a generation or two. The stream, once emerged from its source, passes on into the great Intellectual Sea, smiling over the wretch that it drowns, or under the keel of the ship which it serves as a slave.

Now, when about to commence the present chapter on the Varieties of Life, this masterpiece of thoughtful art forced itself on my re-collection, and illustrated what I designed to convey. In the surface of every age, it is often that which but amuses, for the moment, the ordinary children of pleasant existence, the Edwards and the Clarences (be they kings and dukes, or simplest of simple subjects), which afterwards towers out as the great serious epoch of the time. When we look back upon human records, how the eye settles upon Writers as the main land-marks of the past! We talk of the age of Augustus, of Elizabeth, of Louis XIV., of Anne, as the notable eras of the world. Why? Because it is their writers who have made them so. Intervals between one age of authors and another lie unnoticed, as the flats and common lands of uncultured history. And yet, strange to say, when these authors are living amongst us, they occupy a very small portion of our thoughts, and fill up but desultory interstices in the bitumen and tufo wherefrom we build up the Babylon of our lives! So it is, and perhaps so it should be, whether it pleases the conceit of penmen or not. Life is meant to be active; and books, though they give the action to future gene-rations, administer but to the holiday of the present.

And so, with this long preface, I turn suddenly from the Randals and the Egertons, and the Levys, Avenels, and Peschieras—from the plots and passions of practical life, and drop the reader suddenly into one of those obscure retreats wherein Thought weaves, from unnoticed moments, a new link to the chain that unites the ages.

Within a small room, the single window of which opened on a fanciful and fairy-like garden, that has been before described, sate a young man alone. He had been writing; the ink was not dry on his manuscript, but his thoughts had been suddenly interrupted from his work, and his eyes, now lifted from the letter which had occa-sioned that interruption, sparkled with delight. "He will come," exclaimed the young man; "come here—to the home which I owe to him. I have not been unworthy of his friendship. And she "—

his breast heaved, but the joy faded from his face. "Oh, strange, strange, that I feel sad at the thought to see her again. See *her*—Ah no! my own comforting Helen—my own Child-angel! *Her* I can never see again! The grown woman—that is not my Helen. And yet—and yet" (he resumed after a pause), "if ever she read the pages in which thought flowed and trembled under her distant starry light—if ever she see how her image has rested with me, and feel that, while others believe that I invent, I have but remembered—will she not, for a moment, be my own Helen again! Again, in heart and in fancy, stand by my side on the desolate bridge—hand in hand—orphans both, as we stood in the days so sorrowful, yet, as I recall them, so sweet.—Helen in England, it is a dream!"

He rose, half-consciously, and went to the window. The fountain played merrily before his eyes, and the birds in the aviary carolled loud to his ear. "And in this house," he murmured. "I saw her last! And there, where the fountain now throws its spray on high—there her benefactor and mine told me that I was to lose *her*, that I might win—fame. Alas!"

At this time a woman, whose dress was somewhat above her mien and air, which, though not without a certain respectability, were very homely, entered the room; and, seeing the young man standing thus thoughtful by the window, paused. She was used to his habits; and since his success in life, had learned to respect them. So she did not disturb his reverie, but began softly to arrange the room—dusting, with the corner of her apron, the various articles of furniture, putting a stray chair or two in its right place, but not touching a single paper. Virtuous woman, and rare as virtuous!

The young man turned at last, with a deep, yet not altogether painful sigh—

"My dear mother, good day to you. Ah, you do well to make the room look its best. Happy news! I expect a visitor!"

"Dear me, Leonard, will he want lunch—or what?"

"Nay, I think not, mother. It is he to whom we owe all—'*Hæc otia fecit.*' Pardon my Latin; it is Lord L'Estrange."

The face of Mrs. Fairfield (the reader has long since divined the name) changed instantly, and betrayed a nervous twitch of all the muscles, which gave her a family likeness to old Mrs. Avenel.

"Do not be alarmed, mother. He is the kindest—"

"Don't talk so; I can't bear it!" cried Mrs. Fairfield.

"No wonder you are affected by the recollection of all his benefits. But when once you have seen him, you will find yourself ever after at your ease. And so, pray smile and look as good as you are; for I am proud of your open honest look when you are pleased, mother. And he must see your heart in your face as I do."

With this, Leonard put his arm round the widow's neck and kissed her. She clung to him fondly for a moment, and he felt her tremble from head to foot. Then she broke from his embrace, and hurried out of the room. Leonard thought perhaps she had gone to improve her dress, or to carry her housewife energies to the decoration of the other rooms; for "the house" was Mrs. Fairfield's hobby and passion; and now that she worked no more, save for her amusement, it was her main occupation. The hours she contrived to spend daily in bustling about those little rooms, and leaving everything therein to all appearance precisely the same, were among the marvels in life which the genius of Leonard had never comprehended. But she was always so delighted when Mr. Norreys or some rare visitor came; and said, (Mr. Norreys never failed to do so,) "How neatly all is kept here. What could Leonard do without you, Mrs. Fairfield?"

And, to Norreys' infinite amusement, Mrs. Fairfield always returned the same answer. "'Deed, sir, and thank you kindly, but 'tis my belief that the drawin'-room would be awful dusty."

Once more left alone, Leonard's mind returned to the state of reverie, and his face assumed the expression that had now become to it habitual. Thus seen, he was changed much since we last beheld him. His cheek was more pale and thin, his lips more firmly compressed, his eye more fixed and abstract. You could detect, if I may borrow a touching French expression, that "sorrow had passed by there." But the melancholy on his countenance was ineffably sweet and serene, and on his ample forehead there was that power, so rarely seen in early youth—the power that has conquered, and betrays its conquests but in calm. The period of doubt, of struggle, of defiance, was gone perhaps for ever; genius and soul were reconciled to human life. It was a face most lovable; so gentle and peaceful in its character. No want of fire : on the contrary, the fire was so clear and so steadfast, that it conveyed but the impression of light. The candour of boyhood; the simplicity of the villager were still there—refined by intelligence, but intelligence that seemed to have traversed through knowledge—not with the footstep, but the wing—unsullied by the mire—tending towards the star—seeking through the various grades of Being but the lovelier forms of truth and goodness; at home as should be the Art that consummates the Beautiful—

> "In den heitern Regionen
> Wo die reinen Formen wohnen." [1]

---

[1] At home—" In the serene regions
     Where dwell the pure forms."

From this reverie Leonard did not seek to rouse himself till
the bell at the garden gate rang loud and shrill; and then
starting up and hurrying into the hall, his hand was grasped in
Harley's.

CHAPTER XVI.

FULL and happy hour passed away in Harley's
questions and Leonard's answers; the dialogue that
naturally ensued between the two, on the first interview after an absence of years so eventful to the
younger man.

The history of Leonard during this interval was almost solely
internal, the struggle of intellect with its own difficulties, the
wanderings of imagination through its own adventurous worlds.

The first aim of Norreys, in preparing the mind of his pupil for
its vocation, had been to establish the equilibrium of its powers,
to calm into harmony the elements rudely shaken by the trials and
passions of the old hard outer life.

The theory of Norreys was briefly this. The education of a
superior human being is but the development of ideas in one for the
benefit of others. To this end, attention should be directed—1st,
To the value of the ideas collected; 2ndly, To their discipline;
3rdly, To their expression. For the first, acquirement is necessary;
for the second, discipline; for the third, art. The first compre-
hends knowledge, purely intellectual, whether derived from observation, memory, reflection, books or men, Aristotle or Fleet Street.
The second demands *training*, not only intellectual, but moral; the
purifying and exaltation of motives; the formation of habits; in
which method is but a part of a divine and harmonious symmetry—
an union of intellect and conscience. Ideas of value, stored by the
first process; marshalled into force, and placed under guidance, by
the second; it is the result of the third, to place them before the
world in the most attractive or commanding form. This may be
done by actions no less than words; but the adaptation of means to
end, the passage of ideas from the brain of one man into the lives
and souls of all, no less in action than in books, requires study.
Action has its art as well as literature. Here Norreys had but to
deal with the calling of the scholar, the formation of the writer, and
so to guide the perceptions towards those varieties in the sublime
and beautiful, the just combination of which is at once CREATION.

Man himself is but a combination of elements. He who combines in nature, creates in art.

Such, very succinctly and inadequately expressed, was the system upon which Norreys proceeded to regulate and perfect the great native powers of his pupil; and though the reader may perhaps say that no system laid down by another can either form genius or dictate to its results, yet probably nine-tenths at least of those in whom we recognize the luminaries of our race, have passed, unconsciously to themselves (for self-education is rarely conscious of its phases), through each of these processes. And no one who pauses to reflect will deny, that, according to this theory, illustrated by a man of vast experience, profound knowledge, and exquisite taste, the struggles of genius would be infinitely lessened; its vision cleared and strengthened, and the distance between effort and success notably abridged.

Norreys, however, was far too deep a reasoner to fall into the error of modern teachers, who suppose that education can dispense with labour. No mind becomes muscular without rude and early exercise. Labour should be strenuous, but in right directions. All that we can do for it is to save the waste of time in blundering into needless toils.

The master had thus first employed his neophyte in arranging and compiling materials for a great critical work in which Norreys himself was engaged. In this stage of scholastic preparation, Leonard was necessarily led to the acquisition of languages, for which he had great aptitude—the foundations of a large and comprehensive erudition were solidly constructed. He traced by the ploughshare the walls of the destined city. Habits of accuracy and of generalization became formed insensibly; and that precious faculty which seizes, amidst accumulated materials, those that serve the object for which they are explored,—(that faculty which quadruples all force, by concentrating it on one point)—once roused into action, gave purpose to every toil and quickness to each perception. But Norreys did not confine his pupil solely to the mute world of a library; he introduced him to some of the first minds in arts, science, and letters—and active life. "These," said he, "are the living ideas of the present, out of which books for the future will be written: study them; and here, as in the volumes of the past, diligently amass and deliberately compile."

By degrees Norreys led on that young, ardent mind from the selection of ideas to their æsthetic analysis—from compilation to criticism; but criticism severe, close, and logical—a reason for each word of praise or of blame. Led in this stage of his career to examine into the laws of beauty, a new light broke upon his mind;

from amidst the masses of marble he had piled around him, rose the vision of the statue.

And so, suddenly one day Norreys said to him, "I need a compiler no longer—maintain yourself by your own creations." And Leonard wrote, and a work flowered up from the seed deep buried, and the soil well cleared to the rays of the sun and the healthful influence of expanded air.

That first work did not penetrate to a very wide circle of readers, not from any perceptible fault of its own—there is luck in these things; the first anonymous work of an original genius is rarely at once eminently successful. But the more experienced recognized the promise of the book. Publishers, who have an instinct in the discovery of available talent, which often forestalls the appreciation of the public, volunteered liberal offers. "Be fully successful this time," said Norreys; "think not of models nor of style. Strike at once at the common human heart—throw away the corks—swim out boldly. One word more—never write a page till you have walked from your room to Temple Bar, and, mingling with men, and reading the human face, learn why great poets have mostly passed their lives in cities."

Thus Leonard wrote again, and woke one morning to find himself famous. So far as the chances of all professions dependent on health will permit, present independence, and, with foresight and economy, the prospects of future competence were secured.

"And, indeed," said Leonard, concluding a longer but a simpler narrative than is here told—"indeed, there is some chance that I may obtain at once a sum that will leave me free for the rest of my life to select my own subjects and write without care for remuneration. This is what I call the true (and, perhaps, alas! the rare) independence of him who devotes himself to letters. Norreys, having seen my boyish plan for the improvement of certain machinery in the steam-engine, insisted on my giving much time to mechanics. The study that once pleased me so greatly, now seemed dull, but I went into it with good heart; and the result is, that I have improved so far on my original idea, that my scheme has met the approbation of one of our most scientific engineers: and I am assured that the patent for it will be purchased of me upon terms which I am ashamed to name to you, so disproportioned do they seem to the value of so simple a discovery. Meanwhile, I am already rich enough to have realized the two dreams of my heart—to make a home in the cottage where I had last seen you and Helen—I mean Miss Digby; and to invite to that home her who had sheltered my infancy."

"Your mother, where is she? Let me see her."

Leonard ran out to call the widow, but to his surprise and vexation, learned that she had quitted the house before L'Estrange arrived.

He came back perplexed how to explain what seemed ungracious and ungrateful, and spoke with hesitating lip and flushed cheek of the widow's natural timidity and sense of her own homely station. "And so overpowered is she," added Leonard, "by the recollection of all that we owe to you, that she never hears your name without agitation or tears, and trembled like a leaf at the thought of seeing you."

"Ha!" said Harley, with visible emotion. "Is it so?" And he bent down, shading his face with his hand. "And," he renewed, after a pause, but not looking up—"and you ascribe this fear of seeing me, this agitation at my name, solely to an exaggerated sense of—of the circumstances attending my acquaintance with yourself?"

"And, perhaps to a sort of shame that the mother of one you have made her proud of is but a peasant."

"That is all," said Harley, earnestly, now looking up and fixing eyes in which stood tears upon Leonard's ingenuous brow.

"Oh, my dear Lord, what else can it be? Do not judge her harshly."

L'Estrange arose abruptly, pressed Leonard's hand, muttered something not audible, and then drawing his young friend's arm in his, led him into the garden, and turned the conversation back to its former topics.

Leonard's heart yearned to ask after Helen, and yet something withheld him from doing so, till, seeing Harley did not volunteer to speak of her, he could not resist his impulse. "And Helen—Miss Digby—is she much changed?"

"Changed, no—yes; very much."

"Very much!" Leonard sighed.

"I shall see her again?"

"Certainly," said Harley, in a tone of surprise. "How can you doubt it? And I reserve to you the pleasure of saying that you are renowned. You blush; well, I will say that for you. But you shall give her your books."

"She has not yet read them, then?—not the last? The first was not worthy of her attention," said Leonard, disappointed.

"She has only just arrived in England; and, though your books reached me in Germany, she was not then with me. When I have settled some business that will take me from town, I shall present you to her and my mother." There was a certain embarrassment in Harley's voice as he spoke; and, turning round abruptly, he exclaimed, "But you have shown poetry even here. I could not have conceived that so much beauty could be drawn from what appeared to me the most commonplace of all suburban gardens. Why, surely, where that charming fountain now plays stood the rude bench in which I read your verses."

" It is true ; I wished to unite all together my happiest associations. I think I told you, my Lord, in one of my letters, that I had owed a very happy, yet very struggling time in my boyhood to the singular kindness and generous instructions of a foreigner whom I served. This fountain is copied from one that I made in his garden, and by the margin of which many a summer day I have sat and dreamt of fame and knowledge."

"True, you told me of that ; and your foreigner will be pleased to hear of your success, and no less so of your grateful recollections. By the way, you did not mention his name."

" Riccabocca."

" Riccabocca ! My own dear and noble friend !—is it possible ? One of my reasons for returning to England is connected with him. You shall go down with me and see him. I meant to start this evening."

"My dear Lord," said Leonard, "I think that you may spare yourself so long a journey. I have reason to suspect that Signor Riccabocca is my nearest neighbour. Two days ago I was in the garden, when suddenly lifting my eyes to yon hillock I perceived the form of a man seated amongst the brushwood ; and, though I could not see his features, there was something in the very outline of his figure and his peculiar posture, that irresistibly reminded me of Riccabocca. I hastened out of the garden and ascended the hill, but he was gone. My suspicions were so strong that I caused inquiry to be made at the different shops scattered about, and learned that a family consisting of a gentleman, his wife, and daughter, had lately come to live in a house that you must have passed in your way hither, standing a little back from the road, surrounded by high walls ; and though they were said to be English, yet from the description given to me of the gentleman's person by one who had noticed it, by the fact of a foreign servant in their employ, and by the very name 'Richmouth,' assigned to the new comers, I can scarcely doubt that it is the family you seek."

" And you have not called to ascertain ?"

"Pardon me, but the family so evidently shunning observation, (no one but the master himself ever seen without the walls,) the adoption of another name too—led me to infer that Signor Riccabocca has some strong motive for concealment ; and now, with my improved knowledge of life, and recalling all the past, I cannot but suppose that Riccabocca was not what he appeared. Hence, I have hesitated on formally obtruding myself upon his secrets, whatever they be, and have rather watched for some chance occasion to meet him in his walks."

"You did right, my dear Leonard ; but my reasons for seeing my old friend forbid all scruples of delicacy, and I will go at once to his house."

"You will tell me, my Lord, if I am right."

"I hope to be allowed to do so. Pray, stay at home till I return. And now, ere I go, one question more : You indulge conjectures as to Riccabocca, because he has changed his name—why have you dropped your own ?"

"I wished to have no name," said Leonard, colouring deeply, "but that which I could make myself."

"Proud poet, this I can comprehend. But from what reason did you assume the strange and fantastic name of Oran ?"

The flush on Leonard's face became deeper. "My Lord," said he in a low voice, "it is a childish fancy of mine ; it is an anagram."

"Ah !"

"At a time when my cravings after knowledge were likely much to mislead, and perhaps undo me, I chanced on some poems that suddenly affected my whole mind, and led me up into purer air ; and I was told that these poems were written in youth, by one who had beauty and genius—one who was in her grave—a relation of my own, and her familiar name was Nora—"

"Ah !" again ejaculated Lord L'Estrange, and his arm pressed heavily upon Leonard's.

"So, somehow or other," continued the young author, falteringly, "I wished that if ever I won to a poet's fame, it might be to my own heart, at least, associated with this name of Nora—with her whom death had robbed of the fame that she might otherwise have won—with her who—"

He paused, greatly agitated.

Harley was no less so. But, as if by a sudden impulse, the soldier bent down his manly head and kissed the poet's brow ; then he hastened to the gate, flung himself on his horse, and rode away.

CHAPTER XVII.

LORD L'ESTRANGE did not proceed at once to Riccabocca's house. He was under the influence of a remembrance too deep and too strong to yield easily to the lukewarm claim of friendship. He rode fast and far ; and impossible it would be to define the feelings that passed through a mind so acutely sensitive, and so rootedly tenacious of all affections.

When recalling his duty to the Italian, he once more struck into the road to Norwood, the slow pace of his horse was significant of his own exhausted spirits; a deep dejection had succeeded to feverish excitement. "Vain task," he murmured, "to wean myself from the dead! Yet I am now betrothed to another; and she, with all her virtues, is not the one to—" He stopped short in generous self-rebuke. "Too late to think of that! Now, all that should remain to me is to insure the happiness of the life to which I have pledged my own. But—" He sighed as he so murmured. On reaching the vicinity of Riccabocca's house, he put up his horse at a little inn, and proceeded on foot across the heathland towards the dull square building, which Leonard's description had sufficed to indicate as the exile's new home. It was long before any one answered his summons at the gate. Not till he had thrice rung did he hear a heavy step on the gravel walk within; then the wicket within the gate was partially drawn aside, a dark eye gleamed out, and a voice in imperfect English asked who was there.

"Lord L'Estrange; and if I am right as to the person I seek, that name will at once admit me."

The door flew open as did that of the mystic cavern at the sound of "Open, Sesame;" and Giacomo, almost weeping with joyous emotion, exclaimed, in Italian, "The good Lord! Holy San Giacomo! thou hast heard me at last! We are safe now." And dropping the blunderbuss with which he had taken the precaution to arm himself, he lifted Harley's hand to his lips, in the affectionate greeting familiar to his countrymen.

"And the Padrone?" asked Harley, as he entered the jealous precincts.

"Oh, he is just gone out; but he will not be long. You will wait for him?"

"Certainly. What lady is that I see at the far end of the garden?"

"Bless her, it is our Signorina. I will run and tell her you are come."

"That I am come; but she cannot know me even by name."

"Ah, Excellency, can you think so? Many and many a time has she talked to me of you, and I have heard her pray to the holy Madonna to bless you, and in a voice so sweet—"

"Stay, I will present myself to her. Go into the house, and we will wait without for the Padrone. Nay, I need the air, my friend." Harley, as he said this, broke from Giacomo, and approached Violante.

The poor child, in her solitary walk in the obscurer parts of the dull garden, had escaped the eye of Giacomo when he had gone forth to answer the bell; and she, unconscious of the fears of which she was the object, had felt something of youthful curiosity at the summons at the gate, and the sight of a stranger in close and friendly conference with the unsocial Giacomo.

As Harley now neared her with that singular grace of movement which belonged to him, a thrill shot through her heart—she knew not why. She did not recognize his likeness to the sketch taken by her father from his recollections of Harley's early youth. She did not guess who he was; and yet she felt herself colour, and, naturally fearless though she was, turned away with a vague alarm.

"Pardon my want of ceremony, Signorina," said Harley, in Italian; "but I am so old a friend of your father's that I cannot feel as a stranger to yourself."

Then Violante lifted to him her dark eyes so intelligent and so innocent—eyes full of surprise, but not displeased surprise. And Harley himself stood amazed, and almost abashed, by the rich and marvellous beauty that beamed upon him. "My father's friend," she said, hesitatingly, "and I never to have seen you!"

"Ah, Signorina," said Harley, (and something of its native humour, half arch, half sad, played round his lip,) "you are mistaken there; you have seen me before, and you received me much more kindly then—"

"Signor!" said Violante, more and more surprised, and with a yet richer colour on her cheeks.

Harley, who had now recovered from the first effect of her beauty, and who regarded her as men of his years and character are apt to regard ladies in their teens, as more child than woman, suffered himself to be amused by her perplexity; for it was in his nature, that the graver and more mournful he felt at heart, the more he sought to give play and whim to his spirits.

"Indeed, Signorina," said he, demurely, "you insisted then on placing one of those fair hands in mine; the other (forgive me the fidelity of my recollections) was affectionately thrown around my neck."

"Signor!" again exclaimed Violante; but this time there was anger in her voice as well as surprise, and nothing could be more charming than her look of pride and resentment.

Harley smiled again, but with so much kindly sweetness, that the anger vanished at once, or rather Violante felt angry with herself that she was no longer angry with him. But she had looked so beautiful in her anger, that Harley wished, perhaps, to see her angry again. So, composing his lips from their propitiatory smile, he resumed, gravely—

"Your flatterers will tell you, Signorina, that you are much improved since then, but I liked you better as you were; not but what I hope to return some day what you then so generously pressed upon me."

"Pressed upon you!—I? Signor, you are under some strange mistake."

"Alas! no; but the female heart is so capricious and fickle! You pressed it upon me, I assure you. I own that I was not loath to accept it."

"Pressed it! Pressed what?"

"Your kiss, my child," said Harley; and then added, with a serious tenderness, "And I again say that I hope to return it some day—when I see you, by the side of father and of husband, in your native land—the fairest bride on whom the skies of Italy ever smiled! And now, pardon a hermit and a soldier for his rude jests, and give your hand, in token of that pardon,—to Harley L'Estrange."

Violante, who at the first words of his address had recoiled, with a vague belief that the stranger was out of his mind, sprang forward as it closed, and, in all the vivid enthusiasm of her nature, pressed the hand held out to her, with both her own. "Harley L'Estrange—the preserver of my father's life!" she cried; and her eyes were fixed on his with such evident gratitude and reverence, that Harley felt at once confused and delighted. She did not think at that instant of the hero of her dreams—she thought but of him who had saved her father. But, as his eyes sank before her own, and his head uncovered, bowed over the hand he held, she recognized the likeness to the features on which she had so often gazed. The first bloom of youth was gone, but enough of youth still remained to soften the lapse of years, and to leave to manhood the attractions which charm the eye. Instinctively she withdrew her hands from his clasp, and, in her turn, looked down.

In this pause of embarrassment to both, Riccabocca let himself into the garden by his own latch-key, and, startled to see a man by the side of Violante, sprang forward with an abrupt and angry cry. Harley heard, and turned.

As if restored to courage and self-possession by the sense of her father's presence, Violante again took the hand of the visitor. "Father," she said, simply, "it is he—*he* is come at last." And then, retiring a few steps, she contemplated them both; and her face was radiant with happiness—as if something, long silently missed and looked for, was as silently found, and life had no more a want, nor the heart a void.

BOOK TENTH.

INITIAL CHAPTER.

UPON THIS FACT—THAT THE WORLD IS STILL MUCH THE SAME AS IT ALWAYS HAS BEEN.

IT is observed by a very pleasant writer—read now-a-days only by the brave pertinacious few who still struggle hard to rescue from the House of Pluto the souls of departed authors, jostled and chased as those souls are by the noisy footsteps of the living—it is observed by the admirable Charron, that "judgment and wisdom is not only the best, but the happiest portion God Almighty hath distributed among men ; for though this distribution be made with a very uneven hand, yet nobody thinks himself stinted or ill-dealt with, but he that hath never so little is contented in *this* respect." [1]

And, certainly, the present narrative may serve in notable illustration of the remark so dryly made by the witty and wise preacher. For whether our friend Riccabocca deduce theories for daily life from the great folio of Machiavelli ; or that promising young gentleman, Mr. Randal Leslie, interpret the power of knowledge into the art of being too knowing for dull honest folks to cope with him ; or acute Dick Avenel push his way up the social ascent with a blow for those before, and a kick for those behind him, after the approved fashion of your strong New Man ; or Baron Levy—that cynical impersonation of Gold—compare himself to the Magnetic Rock in the Arabian tale, to which the nails in every ship that approaches the influence of the loadstone fly from the planks, and a shipwreck per day adds its waifs to the Rock ; questionless, at least, it is, that each of those personages believes that Providence has bestowed on him an elder son's inheritance of wisdom.   Nor, were we to glance towards the obscurer paths of life, should we find good Parson Dale deem himself worse off than the rest of the world in this precious

---

[1] Translation of *Charron on Wisdom.* By G. STANHOPE, D.D., late Dean of Canterbury (1729). A translation remarkable for ease, vigour, and (despite that contempt for the strict rules of grammar, which was common enough amongst writers at the commencement of the last century) for the idiomatic raciness of its English.

commodity—as, indeed, he has signally evinced of late in that shrewd guess of his touching Professor Moss;—even plain Squire Hazeldean takes it for granted that he could teach Audley Egerton a thing or two worth knowing in politics; Mr. Stirn thinks that there is no branch of useful lore on which he could not instruct the Squire; while Sprott, the tinker, with his bag full of tracts and lucifer matches, regards the whole framework of modern society, from a rick to a constitution, with the profound disdain of a revolutionary philosopher. Considering that every individual thus brings into the stock of the world so vast a share of intelligence, it cannot but excite our wonder to find that Oxenstiern is popularly held to be right when he said, "See, my son, how little wisdom it requires to govern States;"—that is, Men! That so many millions of persons, each with a profound assurance that he is possessed of an exalted sagacity, should concur in the ascendancy of a few inferior intellects, according to a few stupid, prosy, matter-of-fact rules as old as the hills, is a phenomenon very discreditable to the spirit and energy of the aggregate human species! It creates no surprise that one sensible watch-dog should control the movements of a flock of silly grass-eating sheep; but that two or three silly grass-eating sheep should give the law to whole flocks of such mighty sensible watch dogs—*Diavolo!* Dr. Riccabocca, explain *that*, if you can! And wonderfully strange it is, that notwithstanding all the march of enlightenment, notwithstanding our progressive discoveries in the laws of nature—our railways, steam-engines, animal magnetism, and electro-biology—we have never made any improvement that is generally acknowledged, since men ceased to be troglodytes and nomads, in the old-fashioned gamut of flats and sharps, which attunes into irregular social jog-trot all the generations that pass from the cradle to the grave; still, "*the desire for something we have not*" impels all the energies that keep us in movement, for good or for ill, according to the checks or the directions of each favourite desire.

A friend of mine once said to a *millionaire*, whom he saw for ever engaged in making money which he never seemed to have any pleasure in spending, "Pray, Mr. ——, will you answer me one question: You are said to have two millions, and you spend £600 a-year. In order to rest and enjoy, what will content you?"

"A little more," answered the *millionaire*. That "little more" is the mainspring of civilization. Nobody ever gets it!

"Philus," saith a Latin writer, "was not so rich as Lælius; Lælius was not so rich as Scipio; Scipio was not so rich as Crassus; and Crassus was not so rich—as he wished to be!" If John Bull were once contented, Manchester might shut up its mills. It is the "little more" that makes a mere trifle of the National Debt !—Long life to it !

Still, mend our law-books as we will, one is forced to confess that knaves are often seen in fine linen, and honest men in the most shabby old rags ; and still, notwithstanding the exceptions, knavery is a very hazardous game ; and honesty, on the whole, by far the best policy. Still, most of the Ten Commandments remain at the core of all the Pandects and Institutes that keep our hands off our neighbours' throats, wives, and pockets ; still, every year shows that the Parson's maxim—*non quieta movere*—is as prudent for the health of communities as when Apollo recommended his votaries not to rake up a fever by stirring the Lake Camarina ; still people, thank Heaven, decline to reside in parallelograms, and the surest token that we live under a free government is, when we are governed by persons whom we have a full right to imply, by our censure and ridicule, are blockheads compared to ourselves ! Stop that delightful privilege, and, by Jove ! sir, there is neither pleasure nor honour in being governed at all ! You might as well be—a Frenchman !

CHAPTER II.

THE Italian and his friend are closeted together.

"And why have you left your home in ——shire ? and why this new change of name ? "

"Peschiera is in England."

"I know it."

."And bent on discovering me ; and, it is said, of stealing from me my child."

"He has had the assurance to lay wagers that he will win the hand of your heiress. I know that too ; and therefore I have come to England—first to baffle his design—for I do not think your fears altogether exaggerated—and next to learn from you how to follow up a clue which, unless I am too sanguine, may lead to his ruin, and your unconditional restoration. Listen to me. You are aware that, after the skirmish with Peschiera's armed hirelings sent in search of you, I received a polite message from the Austrian government, requesting me to leave its Italian domains. Now, as I hold it the obvious duty of any foreigner, admitted to the hospitality of a state, to refrain from all participation in its civil disturbances, so I thought my honour assailed at this intimation, and went at once to Vienna to explain to the Minister there (to whom I was personally known), that though I had, as became man to man, aided to protect a refugee, who had taken shelter under my roof, from the infuriated soldiers at the command of his private foe, I had not only not shared in any attempt at revolt, but dissuaded, as far as I could, my Italian friends from their enterprise; and that, because, without discussing its merits, I believed, as a military man and a cool spectator, the enterprise could only terminate in fruitless bloodshed. I was enabled to establish my explanation by satisfactory proof; and my acquaintance with the Minister assumed something of the character of friendship. I was then in a position to advocate your cause, and to state your original reluctance to enter into the plots of the in-surgents. I admitted freely that you had such natural desire for the independence of your native land, that, had the standard of Italy been boldly hoisted by its legitimate chiefs, or at the common up-rising of its whole people, you would have been found in the van, amidst the ranks of your countrymen; but I maintained that you would never have shared in a conspiracy frantic in itself, and defiled by the lawless schemes and sordid ambition of its main projectors, had you not been betrayed and decoyed into it by the misrepre-sentations and domestic treachery of your kinsman—the very man who denounced you. Unfortunately, of this statement I had no proof but your own word. I made, however, so far an impression in your favour, and, it may be, against the traitor, that your property was not confiscated to the State, nor handed over, upon the plea of your civil death, to your kinsman."

"How!—I do not understand. Peschiera has the property?"

"He holds the revenues but of one half upon pleasure, and they would be withdrawn, could I succeed in establishing the case that exists against him. I was forbidden before to mention this to you; the Minister, not inexcusably, submitted you to the probation of unconditional exile. Your grace might depend upon your own forbearance from further conspiracies—forgive the word. I need not say I was permitted to return to Lombardy. I found, on my arrival, that—that your unhappy wife had been to my house, and exhibited great despair at hearing of my departure."

Riccabocca knit his dark brows, and breathed hard.

"I did not judge it necessary to acquaint you with this circum-stance, nor did it much affect me. I believed in her guilt—and what could now avail her remorse, if remorse she felt? Shortly afterwards, I heard that she was no more."

"Yes," muttered Riccabocca, "she died in the same year that I left Italy.   It must be a strong reason that can excuse a friend for reminding me even that she once lived!"

"I come at once to that reason," said L'Estrange, gently.   "This autumn I was roaming through Switzerland, and, in one of my pedestrian excursions amidst the mountains, I met with an accident, which confined me for some days to a sofa at a little inn in an obscure village.   My hostess was an Italian; and, as I had left my servant at a town at some distance, I required her attention till I could write to him to come to me.   I was thankful for her cares, and amused by her Italian babble.   We became very good friends. She told me she had been servant to a lady of great rank, who had died in Switzerland; and that, being enriched by the generosity of her mistress, she had married a Swiss innkeeper, and his people had become hers.   My servant arrived, and my hostess learned my name, which she did not know before.   She came into my room greatly agitated.   In brief, this woman had been servant to your wife.   She had accompanied her to my villa, and known of her anxiety to see me, as your friend.   The government had assigned to your wife your palace at Milan, with a competent income.   She had refused to accept of either.   Failing to see me, she had set off towards England, resolved upon seeing yourself; for the journals had stated that to England you had escaped."

"She dared!—shameless!   And see, but a moment before, I had forgotten all but her grave in a foreign soil—and these tears had forgiven her," murmured the Italian.

"Let them forgive her still," said Harley, with all his exquisite sweetness of look and tone.   "I resume.   On entering Switzerland your wife's health, which you know was always delicate, gave way. To fatigue and anxiety succeeded fever, and delirium ensued.   She had taken with her but this one female attendant—the sole one she could trust—on leaving home.   She suspected Peschiera to have bribed her household.   In the presence of this woman she raved of her innocence—in accents of terror and aversion, denounced your kinsman—and called on you to vindicate her name and your own."

"Ravings indeed!   Poor Paulina!" groaned Riccabocca, covering his face with both hands.

"But in her delirium there were lucid intervals.   In one of these she rose, in spite of all her servant could do to restrain her, took from her desk several letters, and reading them over, exclaimed piteously, 'But how to get them to him?—whom to trust?   And his friend is gone!'   Then an idea seemed suddenly to flash upon her, for she uttered a joyous exclamation, sate down, and wrote long and rapidly, enclosed what she wrote with all the letters, in one packet, which she sealed carefully, and bade her servant carry to the post, with many injunctions to take it with her own hand, and pay the charge on it. 'For oh!' said she (I repeat the words as my informant told them to me)—'for, oh! this is my sole chance to prove to my husband that, though I have erred, I am not the guilty thing he believes me; the sole chance, too, to redeem my error, and restore, perhaps, to my husband his country, to my child her heritage.' The servant took the letter to the post; and when she returned, her lady was asleep, with a smile upon her face. But from that sleep, she woke again delirious, and before the next morning her soul had fled." Here Riccabocca lifted one hand from his face and grasped Harley's arm, as if mutely beseeching him to pause. The heart of the man struggled hard with his pride and his philosophy; and it was long before Harley could lead him to regard the worldly prospects which this last communication from his wife might open to his ruined fortunes. Not, indeed, till Riccabocca had persuaded himself, and half persuaded Harley (for strong indeed was all presumption of guilt against the dead), that his wife's protestations of innocence from all but error had been but ravings.

"Be this as it may," said Harley, "there seems every reason to suppose that the letters enclosed were Peschiera's correspondence, and that, if so, these would establish the proof of his influence over your wife, and of his perfidious machinations against yourself. I resolved, before coming hither, to go round by Vienna. There I heard, with dismay, that Peschiera had not only obtained the imperial sanction to demand your daughter's hand, but had boasted to his profligate circle that he should succeed; and he was actually on his road to England. I saw at once that could this design, by any fraud or artifice, be successful with Violante, (for of your consent, I need not say, I did not dream,) the discovery of the packet, whatever its contents, would be useless: Peschiera's end would be secured. I saw also that his success would suffice for ever to clear his name; for his success must imply your consent (it would be to disgrace your daughter, to assert that she had married without it), and your consent would be his acquittal. I saw, too, with alarm, that to all means for the accomplishment of his project he would be urged by despair; for his debts are great, and his character nothing but new wealth can support. I knew that he was able, bold, determined, and that he had taken with him a large supply of money borrowed upon usury;—in a word, I trembled for you both. I have now seen your daughter, and I tremble no more. Accomplished seducer as Peschiera boasts himself, the first look upon her face so sweet, yet so noble, convinced me that she is proof against a legion of Peschieras. Now, then, return we to this all-important subject—to this packet. It never reached you. Long years have passed since then. Does it exist still? Into whose hands would it have fallen? Try to summon up all your recollections. The servant could not remember the name of the person to whom it was addressed; she only insisted that the name began with a B, that it was directed to England, and that to England she accordingly paid the postage. Whom then, with a name that begins with B, or (in case the servant's memory here mislead her) whom did you or your wife know, during your visit to England, with sufficient intimacy to make it probable that she would select such a person for her confidant?"

"I cannot conceive," said Riccabocca, shaking his head. "We came to England shortly after our marriage. Paulina was affected by the climate. She spoke not a word of English, and indeed not even French, as might have been expected from her birth, for her father was poor, and thoroughly Italian. She refused all society. I went, it is true, somewhat into the London world—enough to induce me to shrink from the contrast that my second visit as a beggared refugee would have made to the reception I met with on my first—but I formed no intimate friendships. I recall no one whom she could have written to as intimate with me."

"But," persisted Harley, "think again. Was there no lady well acquainted with Italian, and with whom, perhaps, for that very reason, your wife became familiar?"

"Ah, it is true. There was one old lady of retired habits, but who had been much in Italy. Lady—Lady—I remember—Lady Jane Horton."

"Horton—Lady Jane!" exclaimed Harley; "again! thrice in one day—is this wound never to scar over?" Then, noting Riccabocca's look of surprise, he said, "Excuse me, my friend; I listen to you with renewed interest. Lady Jane was a distant relation of my own; she judged me, perhaps, harshly—and I have some painful associations with her name; but she was a woman of many virtues. Your wife knew her?"

"Not, however, intimately—still, better than any one else in London. But Paulina would not have written to her; she knew that Lady Jane had died shortly after her own departure from England. I myself was summoned back to Italy on pressing business; she was too unwell to journey with me as rapidly as I was obliged to travel; indeed, illness detained her several weeks in England. In this interval she might have made acquaintances. Ah, now I see; I guess. You say the name began with B. Paulina, in my absence, engaged a companion—a Mrs. Bertram. This lady accompanied her abroad. Paulina became excessively attached to her, she knew Italian so well. Mrs. Bertram left her on the road, and returned to England, for some private affairs of her own. I forget why or wherefore; if, indeed, I ever asked or learned. Paulina missed her sadly, often talked of her, wondered why she never heard from her. No doubt it was to this Mrs. Bertram that she wrote!"

"And you don't know the lady's friends, or address?

"No."

"Nor who recommended her to your wife?"

"No."

"Probably Lady Jane Horton?"

"It may be so. Very likely."

"I will follow up this track, slight as it is."

"But if Mrs. Bertram received the communication, how comes it that it never reached myself—O, fool that I am, how should it! I, who guarded so carefully my incognito!"

"True. This your wife could not foresee; she would naturally imagine that your residence in England would be easily discovered. But many years must have passed since your wife lost sight of this Mrs. Bertram, if their acquaintance was made so soon after your marriage; and now it is a long time to retrace—before even your Violante was born."

"Alas! yes. I lost two fair sons in the interval. Violante was born to me as the child of sorrow."

"And to make sorrow lovely! how beautiful she is!"

The father smiled proudly.

"Where, in the loftiest houses of Europe, find a husband worthy of such a prize?"

"You forget that I am still an exile—she still dowerless. You forget that I am pursued by Peschiera; that I would rather see her a beggar's wife—than—Pah, the very thought maddens me, it is so foul. *Corpo di Bacco!* I have been glad to find her a husband already."

"Already! Then that young man spoke truly?"

"What young man?"

"Randal Leslie. How! You know him?" Here a brief explanation followed. Harley heard with attentive ear, and marked vexation, the particulars of Riccabocca's connection and implied engagement with Leslie.

"There is something very suspicious to me in all this," said he. "Why should this young man have so sounded me as to Violante's chance of losing fortune if she married an Englishman?"

"Did he? O, pooh! Excuse him. It was but his natural wish to seem ignorant of all about me. He did not know enough of my intimacy with you to betray my secret."

"But he knew enough of it—must have known enough to have made it right that he should tell you I was in England. He does not seem to have done so."

"No—*that* is strange—yet scarcely strange; for, when we last met, his head was full of other things—love and marriage. *Basta!* youth will be youth."

"He has no youth left in him!" exclaimed Harley, passionately. "I doubt if he ever had any. He is one of those men who come into the world with the pulse of a centenarian. You and I never shall be as old—as he was in long clothes. Ah, you may laugh; but I am never wrong in my instincts. I disliked him at the first— his eye, his smile, his voice, his very footstep. It is madness in you to countenance such a marriage; it may destroy all chance of your restoration."

"Better that than infringe my word once passed."

"No, no," exclaimed Harley; "your word is not passed—it shall not be passed. Nay, never look so piteously at me. At all events, pause till we know more of this young man. If he be worthy of her without a dower, why, then, let him lose you your heritage. I should have no more to say."

"But why lose me my heritage? There is no law in Austria which can dictate to a father what husband to choose for his daughter."

"Certainly not. But you are out of the pale of law itself just at present; and it would surely be a reason for state policy to withhold your pardon, and it would be to the loss of that favour with your own countrymen, which would now make that pardon so popular, if it were known that the representative of your name were debased by your daughter's alliance with an English adventurer—a clerk in a public office! O, sage in theory, why are you such a simpleton in action?"

Nothing moved by this taunt, Riccabocca rubbed his hands, and then stretched them comfortably over the fire.

"My friend," said he, "the representation of my name would pass to my son."

"But you have no son?"

"Hush! I am going to have one; my Jemima informed me of it yesterday morning; and it was upon that information that I resolved to speak to Leslie. Am I a simpleton now?"

"Going to have a son," repeated Harley, looking very bewildered; "how do you know it is to be a son?"

"Physiologists are agreed," said the sage, positively, "that where the husband is much older than the wife, and there has been a long interval without children before she condescends to increase the population of the world—she (that is, it is at least as nine to four)—she brings into the world a male. I consider that point, therefore, as settled, according to the calculations of statisticians and the researches of naturalists."

Harley could not help laughing, though he was still angry and disturbed.

"The same man as ever; always the fool of philosophy."

"*Cospetto!*" said Riccabocca. "I am rather the philosopher of fools. And talking of that, shall I present you to my Jemima?"

"Yes; but in turn I must present you to one who remembers with gratitude your kindness, and whom your philosophy, for a wonder, has not ruined. Some time or other you must explain that to me. Excuse me for a moment; I will go for him."

"For him;—for whom? In my position I must be cautious; and—"

"I will answer for his faith and discretion. Meanwhile order dinner, and let me and my friend stay to share it."

"Dinner? *Corpo di Bacco!*—not that Bacchus can help us here. What will Jemima say?"

"Henpecked man, settle that with your connubial tyrant. But dinner it must be."

I leave the reader to imagine the delight of Leonard at seeing once more Riccabocca unchanged and Violante so improved; and the kind Jemima too. And their wonder at him and his history, his books and his fame. He narrated his struggles and adventures with a simplicity that removed from a story so personal the character of egotism. But when he came to speak of Helen, he was brief and reserved.

Violante would have questioned more closely; but, to Leonard's relief, Harley interposed.

"You shall see her whom he speaks of before long, and question her yourself."

With these words, Harley turned the young man's narrative into new directions; and Leonard's words again flowed freely. Thus the evening passed away happily to all save Riccabocca. For the thought of his dead wife rose ever and anon before the exile; but when it did, and became too painful, he crept nearer to Jemima, and looked in her simple face, and pressed her cordial hand. And yet the monster had implied to Harley that his comforter was a fool— so she was, to love so contemptible a slanderer of herself, and her sex.

Violante was in a state of blissful excitement; she could not analyze her own joy. But her conversation was chiefly with Leonard; and the most silent of all was Harley. He sate listening to Leonard's warm, yet unpretending eloquence—that eloquence which flows so naturally from genius, when thoroughly at its ease, and not chilled back on itself by hard, unsympathizing hearers—listened, yet more charmed, to the sentiments less profound, yet no less earnest—sentiments so feminine, yet so noble, with which Violante's fresh virgin heart responded to the poet's kindling soul. Those sentiments of hers were so unlike all he heard in the common world —so akin to himself in his gone youth! Occasionally—at some high thought of her own, or some lofty line from Italian song, that she cited with lighted eyes, and in melodious accents—occasionally he reared his knightly head, and his lip quivered, as if he had heard the sound of a trumpet. The inertness of long years was shaken. The Heroic, that lay deep beneath all the humours of his temperament, was reached, appealed to; and stirred within him, rousing up all the bright associations connected with it, and long dormant. When he arose to take leave, surprised at the lateness of the hour, Harley said, in a tone that bespoke the sincerity of the compliment, "I thank you for the happiest hours I have known for years." His eye dwelt on Violante as he spoke. But timidity returned to her with his words—at his look; and it was no longer the inspired muse, but the bashful girl that stood before him.

· "And when shall I see you again?" asked Riccabocca, disconsolately, following his guest to the door.

"When? Why, of course, to-morrow. Adieu! my friend. No wonder you have borne your exile so patiently,—with such a child!"

He took Leonard's arm, and walked with him to the inn where he had left his horse. Leonard spoke of Violante with enthusiasm. Harley was silent.

CHAPTER III.

THE next day a somewhat old-fashioned, but exceedingly patrician, equipage stopped at Riccabocca's garden-gate. Giacomo, who, from a bed-room window, had caught sight of its winding towards the house, was seized with indefinable terror when he beheld it pause before their walls, and heard the shrill summons at the portal. He rushed into his master's presence, and implored him not to stir—not to allow any one to give ingress to the enemies the machine might disgorge. "I have heard," said he, "how a town in Italy—I think it was Bologna—was once taken and given to the sword, by incautiously admitting a wooden horse, full of the troops of Barbarossa, and all manner of bombs and Congreve rockets."

"The story is differently told in Virgil," quoth Riccabocca, peeping out of the window. "Nevertheless, the machine looks very large and suspicious; unloose Pompey."

"Father," said Violante, colouring, "it is your friend, Lord L'Estrange; I hear his voice."

"Are you sure?"

"Quite. How can I be mistaken?"

"Go, then, Giacomo; but take Pompey with thee—and give the alarm, if we are deceived."

But Violante was right, and in a few moments Lord L'Estrange was seen walking up the garden, and giving the arm to two ladies.

"Ah," said Riccabocca, composing his dressing-robe round him, "go, my child, and summon Jemima. Man to man; but, for Heaven's sake, woman to woman."

Harley had brought his mother and Helen, in compliment to the ladies of his friend's household.

The proud Countess knew that she was in the presence of Adversity, and her salute to Riccabocca was only less respectful than that with which she would have rendered homage to her sovereign. But Riccabocca, always gallant to the sex that he pretended to despise, was not to be outdone in ceremony; and the bow which replied to the curtsey would have edified the rising generation, and delighted such surviving relics of the old Court breeding as may linger yet amidst the gloomy pomp of the Faubourg St. Germain. These dues paid to etiquette, the Countess briefly introduced Helen, as Miss Digby, and seated herself near the exile. In a few moments the two elder personages became quite at home with each other; and, really, perhaps Riccabocca had never, since we have known him, showed to such advantage as by the side of his polished, but somewhat formal visitor. Both had lived so little with our modern, ill-bred age! They took out their manners of a former race, with a sort of pride in airing once more such fine lace and superb brocade. Riccabocca gave truce to the shrewd but homely wisdom of his proverbs—perhaps he remembered that Lord Chesterfield denounces proverbs as vulgar;—and gaunt though his figure, and far from elegant though his dressing-robe, there was that about him which spoke undeniably of the *grand seigneur*—of one to whom a Marquis de Dangeau would have offered a *fauteuil* by the side of the Rohans and Montmorencies.

Meanwhile Helen and Harley seated themselves a little apart, and were both silent—the first, from timidity; the second, from abstraction.   At length the door opened, and Harley suddenly sprang to his feet—Violante and Jemima entered.   Lady Lansmere's eyes first rested on the daughter, and she could scarcely refrain from an exclamation of admiring surprise; but then, when she caught sight of Mrs. Riccabocca's somewhat humble, yet not obsequious mien—looking a little shy, a little homely, yet still thoroughly a gentlewoman (though of your plain, rural kind of that genus)—she turned from the daughter, and with the *savoir vivre* of the fine old school, paid her first respects to the wife; respects literally, for her manner implied respect,—but it was more kind, simple, and cordial than the respect she had shown to Riccabocca; —as the sage himself had said, here " it was Woman to Woman." And then she took Violante's hand in both hers, and gazed on her as if she could not resist the pleasure of contemplating so much beauty.   " My son," she said, softly, and with a half sigh—" my son in vain told me not to be surprised.   This is the first time I have ever known reality exceed description ! "

Violante's blush here made her still more beautiful; and as the Countess returned to Riccabocca, she stole gently to Helen's side.

"Miss Digby, my ward," said Harley, pointedly, observing that his mother had neglected her duty of presenting Helen to the ladies. He then reseated himself, and conversed with Mrs. Riccabocca; but his bright, quick eye glanced over at the two girls. , They were about the same age—and youth was all that, to the superficial eye, they seemed to have in common.   A greater contrast could not well be conceived; and, what is strange, both gained by it.   Violante's brilliant loveliness seemed yet more dazzling, and Helen's fair, gentle face yet more winning.   Neither had mixed much with girls of her own age ; each took to the other at first sight.   Violante, as the less shy, began the conversation.

" You are his ward—Lord L'Estrange's ? "

" Yes."

" Perhaps you came with him from Italy?"

"No, not exactly.   But I have been in Italy for some years."

"Ah ! you regret—nay, I am foolish—you return to your native land.   But the skies in Italy are so blue—here it seems as if nature wanted colours."

"Lord L'Estrange says that you were very young when you left Italy ; you remember it well.   He, too, prefers Italy to England."

"He !   Impossible ! "

"Why impossible, fair sceptic?" cried Harley, interrupting himself in the midst of a speech to Jemima.

Violante had not dreamed that she could be overheard—she was speaking low; but, though visibly embarrassed, she answered distinctly—

"Because in England there is the noblest career for noble minds."

Harley was startled, and replied, with a slight sigh, "At your age I should have said as you do. But this England of ours is so crowded with noble minds, that they only jostle each other, and the career is one cloud of dust."

"So, I have read, seems a battle to a common soldier, but not to the chief."

"You have read good descriptions of battles, I see."

Mrs. Riccabocca, who thought this remark a taunt upon her step-daughter's studies, hastened to Violante's relief.

"Her papa made her read the history of Italy, and I believe that is full of battles."

Harley.—"All history is, and all women are fond of war and of warriors. I wonder why?"

Violante (turning to Helen, and in a very low voice, resolved that Harley should not hear this time).—"We can guess why—can we not?"

Harley (hearing every word as if it had been spoken in St. Paul's Whispering Gallery).—"If you can guess, Helen, pray tell me."

Helen (shaking her pretty head, and answering, with a livelier smile than usual).—"But I am not fond of war and warriors."

Harley to Violante.—"Then I must appeal at once to you, self-convicted Bellona that you are. Is it from the cruelty natural to the female disposition?"

Violante (with a sweet musical laugh).—"From two propensities still more natural to it."

Harley.—"You puzzle me: what can they be?"

Violante.—"Pity and admiration; we pity the weak and admire the brave."

Harley inclined his head, and was silent.

Lady Lansmere had suspended her conversation with Riccabocca to listen to this dialogue. "Charming!" she cried. "You have explained what has often perplexed me. Ah, Harley, I am glad to see that your satire is foiled: you have no reply to that."

"No; I willingly own myself defeated, too glad to claim the Signorina's pity, since my cavalry sword hangs on the wall, and I can have no longer a professional pretence to her admiration."

He then rose, and glanced towards the window. "But I see a more formidable disputant for my conqueror to encounter is coming into the field—one whose profession it is to substitute some other romance for that of camp and siege."

"Our friend Leonard," said Riccabocca, turning his eye also towards the window. "True; as Quevedo says, wittily, 'Ever since there has been so great a demand for type, there has been much less lead to spare for cannon-balls.'"

Here Leonard entered. Harley had sent Lady Lansmere's footman to him with a note, that prepared him to meet Helen. As he came into the room, Harley took him by the hand and led him to Lady Lansmere.

"The friend of whom I spoke. Welcome him now for my sake, ever after for his own;" and then, scarcely allowing time for the Countess's elegant and gracious response, he drew Leonard towards Helen. "Children," said he, with a touching voice, that thrilled through the hearts of both, "go and seat yourselves yonder, and talk together of the past. Signorina, I invite you to renewed discussion upon the abstruse metaphysical subject you have started; let us see if we cannot find gentler sources for pity and admiration than war and warriors." He took Violante aside to the window. "You remember that Leonard, in telling you his history last night, spoke, you thought, rather too briefly of the little girl who had been his companion in the rudest time of his trials. When you would have questioned more, I interrupted you, and said, 'You should see her shortly, and question her yourself.' And now what think you of Helen Digby? Hush, speak low. But her ears are not so sharp as mine."

VIOLANTE.—"Ah! that is the fair creature whom Leonard called his child-angel? What a lovely innocent face!—the angel is there still."

HARLEY (pleased both at the praise and with her who gave it).— "You think so; and you are right. Helen is not communicative. But fine natures are like fine poems—a glance at the first two lines suffices for a guess into the beauty that waits you if you read on."

Violante gazed on Leonard and Helen as they sat apart. Leonard was the speaker, Helen the listener; and though the former had, in his narrative the night before, been indeed brief as to the episode in his life connected with the orphan, enough had been said to interest Violante in the pathos of their former position towards each other, and in the happiness they must feel in their meeting again— separated for years on the wide sea of life, now both saved from the storm and shipwreck. The tears came into her eyes. "True," she said, very softly, "There is more here to move pity and admiration than in—" She paused.

HARLEY.—"Complete the sentence. Are you ashamed to retract? Fie on your pride and obstinacy."

VIOLANTE.—"No; but even here there have been war and heroism—the war of genius with adversity, and heroism in the comforter who shared it and consoled. Ah! wherever pity and admiration are both felt, something nobler than mere sorrow must have gone before: the heroic must exist."

"Helen does not know what the word heroic means," said Harley, rather sadly; "you must teach her."

"Is it possible," thought he as he spoke, "that a Randal Leslie could have charmed this grand creature? No 'Heroic' surely, in that sleek young placeman." "Your father," he said aloud, and fixing his eyes on her face, "sees much, he tells me, of a young man about Leonard's age, as to date; but I never estimate the age of men by the parish register; and I should speak of that so-called young man as a contemporary of my great-grandfather;—I mean Mr. Randal Leslie. Do you like him?"

"Like him?" said Violante, slowly, and as if sounding her own mind.—"Like him—yes."

"Why?" asked Harley, with dry and curt indignation.

"His visits seem to please my dear father. Certainly I like him."

"Hum. He professes to like you, I suppose?"

Violante laughed unsuspiciously. She had half a mind to reply, "Is that so strange?" But her respect for Harley stopped her. The words would have seemed to her pert.

"I am told he is clever," resumed Harley.

"O, certainly."

"And he is rather handsome. But I like Leonard's face better."

"Better—that is not the word. Leonard's face is as that of one who has gazed so often upon Heaven; and Mr. Leslie's—there is neither sunlight nor starlight reflected there."

"My dear Violante!" exclaimed Harley, overjoyed; and he pressed her hand.

The blood rushed over the girl's cheek and brow; her hand trembled in his. But Harley's familiar exclamation might have come from a father's lips.

At this moment Helen softly approached them, and looking timidly into her guardian's face, said, "Leonard's mother is with him: he asks me to call and see her. May I?"

"May you! A pretty notion the Signorina must form of your

enslaved state of pupilage, when she hears you ask that question. Of course you may."

"Will you come with us?"

Harley looked embarrassed. He thought of the widow's agitation at his name ; of that desire to shun him, which Leonard had confessed, and of which he thought he divined the cause. And so divining, he too shrank from such a meeting.

"Another time, then," said he, after a pause.

Helen looked disappointed, but said no more.

Violante was surprised at this ungracious answer. She would have blamed it as unfeeling in another. But all that Harley did was right in her eyes.

"Cannot I go with Miss Digby?" said she, "and my mother will go too, We both know Mrs. Fairfield. We shall be so pleased to see her again."

"So be it," said Harley ; " I will wait here with your father till you come back. O, as to my mother, she will excuse the—excuse Madame Riccabocca, and you too. See how charmed she is with *your* father, I must stay to watch over the conjugal interests of *mine.*"

But Mrs. Riccabocca had too much good old country breeding to leave the Countess ; and Harley was forced himself to appeal to Lady Lansmere. When he had explained the case in point, the Countess rose and said—

"But I will call myself, with Miss Digby."

"No," said Harley, gravely, but in a whisper. "No—I would rather not. I will explain later."

"Then," said the Countess aloud, after a glance of surprise at her son, "I must insist on your performing this visit, my dear madam, and you Signorina, In truth, I have something to say confidentially to—"

"To me," interrupted Riccabocca. "Ah, Madame la Comtesse, you restore me to five-and-twenty. Go, quick—O jealous and injured wife ; go, both of you, quick ; and you, too, Harley."

"Nay," said Lady Lansmere, in the same tone, " Harley must stay, for my design is not at present upon destroying your matrimonial happiness, whatever it may be later. It is a design so innocent that my son will be a partner in it."

Here the Countess put her lips to Harley's ear, and whispered. He received her communication in attentive silence ; but when she had done, pressed her hand, and bowed his head, as if in assent to a proposal.

In a few minutes the three ladies and Leonard were on their road to the neighbouring cottage.

Violante, with her usual delicate intuition, thought that Leonard and Helen must have much to say to each other; and (ignorant, as Leonard himself was, of Helen's engagement to Harley) began already, in the romance natural to her age, to predict for them happy and united days in the future. So she took her stepmother's arm, and left Helen and Leonard to follow.

"I wonder," she said, musingly, "how Miss Digby became Lord L'Estrange's ward. I hope she is not very rich, nor very high-born."

"La, my love," said the good Jemima, "that is not like you; you are not envious of her, poor girl?"

"Envious! Dear mamma, what a word! But don't you think Leonard and Miss Digby seem born for each other? And then the recollections of their childhood—the thoughts of childhood are so deep, and its memories so strangely soft!" The long lashes drooped over Violante's musing eyes as she spoke. "And therefore," she said, after a pause—"therefore I hoped that Miss Digby might not be very rich nor very high-born."

"I understand you now, Violante," exclaimed Jemima, her own early passion for match-making instantly returning to her; "for as Leonard, however clever and distinguished, is still the son of Mark Fairfield, the carpenter, it would spoil all if Miss Digby was, as you say, rich and high-born. I agree with you—a very pretty match— a very pretty match, indeed. I wish dear Mrs. Dale were here now —she is so clever in settling such matters."

Meanwhile Leonard and Helen walked side by side a few paces in the rear. He had not offered her his arm. They had been silent hitherto since they left Riccabocca's house.

Helen now spoke first, In similar cases it is generally the woman, be she ever so timid, who does speak first. And here Helen was the bolder; for Leonard did not disguise from himself the nature of his feelings, and Helen was engaged to another; and her pure heart was fortified by the trust reposed in it.

"And have you ever heard more of the good Dr. Morgan, who had powders against sorrow, and who meant to be so kind to us— though," she added, colouring, "we did not think so then?"

"He took my child-angel from me," said Leonard, with visible emotion; "and if she had not returned, where and what should I be now? But I have forgiven him. No, I have never met him since."

"And that terrible Mr. Burley?"

"Poor, poor Burley! He, too, is vanished out of my present life. I have made many inquiries after him; all I can hear is that he went abroad, supposed as a correspondent to some journal. I should like so much to see him again, now that perhaps I could help him as he helped me."

"*Helped* you—ah!"

Leonard smiled with a beating heart, as he saw again the dear prudent, warning look, and involuntarily drew closer to Helen. She seemed more restored to him and to her former self.

"Helped me much by his instructions; more, perhaps, by his very faults. You cannot guess, Helen,—I beg pardon, Miss Digby —but I forgot that we are no longer children: you cannot guess how much we men, and more than all, perhaps, we writers whose task it is to unravel the web of human actions, owe even to our own past errors; and if we learned nothing by the errors of others, we should be dull indeed. We must know where the roads divide, and have marked where they lead to, before we can erect our sign-post; and books are the sign-posts in human life."

"Books! and I have not yet read yours. And Lord L'Estrange tells me you are famous now. Yet you remember me still—the poor orphan child, whom you first saw weeping at her father's grave, and with whom you burdened your own young life, over-burdened already. No, still call me Helen—you must always be to me—a brother! Lord L'Estrange feels *that;* he said so to me when he told me that we were to meet again. He is so generous, so noble. Brother!" cried Helen, suddenly, and extending her hand, with a sweet but sublime look in her gentle face—"brother, we will never forfeit his esteem; we will both do our best to repay him! Will we not?—say so!"

Leonard felt overpowered by contending and unanalyzed emotions. Touched almost to tears by the affectionate address—thrilled by the hand that pressed his own—and yet with a vague fear, a consciousness that something more than the words themselves was implied— something that checked all hope. And this word "brother," once so precious and so dear, why did he shrink from it now?—why could he not too say the sweet word "sister?"

"She is above me now and evermore!" he thought, mournfully; and the tones of his voice, when he spoke again, were changed. The appeal to renewed intimacy but made him more distant; and to that appeal itself he made no direct answer; for Mrs. Riccabocca, now turning round, and pointing to the cottage which came in view, with its picturesque gable-ends, cried out—

"But is that your house, Leonard? I never saw anything so pretty."

"You do not remember it then," said Leonard to Helen, in

accents of melancholy reproach—"there where I saw you last! I doubted whether to keep it exactly as it was, and I said, 'No! the association is not changed because we try to surround it with whatever beauty we can create; the dearer the association, the more the Beautiful becomes to it natural.' Perhaps you don't understand this —perhaps it is only we poor poets who do."

"I understand it," said Helen, gently. She looked wistfully at the cottage.

" So changed—I have so often pictured it to myself—never, never like this; yet I loved it, commonplace as it was to my recollection; and the garret, and the tree in the carpenter's yard."

She did not give these thoughts utterance. And they now entered the garden.

CHAPTER IV.

MRS. FAIRFIELD was a proud woman when she received Mrs. Riccabocca and Violante in her grand house; for a grand house to her was that cottage to which her boy Lenny had brought her home. Proud, indeed, ever was Widow Fairfield; but she thought then in her secret heart, that if ever she could receive in the drawing-room of that grand house the great Mrs. Hazeldean, who had so lectured her for refusing to live any longer in the humble tenement rented of the Squire, the cup of human bliss would be filled, and she could contentedly die of the pride of it. She did not much notice Helen—her attention was too absorbed by the ladies who renewed their old acquaintance with her, and she carried them all over the house, yea, into the very kitchen; and so, somehow or other, there was a short time when Helen and Leonard found themselves alone. It was in the study. Helen had unconsciously seated herself in Leonard's own chair, and she was gazing with anxious and wistful interest on the scattered papers, looking so disorderly (though, in truth, in that disorder there was method, but method only known to the owner), and at the venerable well-worn books, in all languages, lying on the floor, on the chairs —anywhere. I must confess that Helen's first tidy womanlike idea was a great desire to arrange the litter. "Poor Leonard," she thought to herself—"the rest of the house so neat, but no one to take care of his own room and of him!"

As if he divined her thought, Leonard smiled and said, "It would be a cruel kindness to the spider, if the gentlest hand in the world tried to set its cobweb to rights."

HELEN.—"You were not quite so bad in the old days."

LEONARD.—"Yet even then, you were obliged to take care of the money. I have more books now, and more money. My present housekeeper lets me take care of the books, but she is less indulgent as to the money."

HELEN (archly).—"Are you as absent as ever?"

LEONARD.—"Much more so, I fear. The habit is incorrigible. Miss Digby—"

HELEN.—"Not Miss Digby—sister, if you like."

LEONARD (evading the word that implied so forbidden an affinity). —"Helen, will you grant me a favour? Your eyes and your smile say, 'yes.' Will you lay aside, for one minute, your shawl and bonnet? What! can you be surprised that I ask it? Can you not understand that I wish for one minute to think that you are at home again under this roof?"

Helen cast down her eyes, and seemed troubled; then she raised them, with a soft angelic candour in their dovelike blue, and, as if in shelter from all thoughts of more warm affection, again murmured "*brother*," and did as he asked her.

So there she sate, amongst the dull books, by his table, near the open window—her fair hair parted on her forehead—looking so good, so calm, so happy! Leonard wondered at his own self-command. His heart yearned to her with such inexpressible love— his lips so longed to murmur—"Ah, as now so could it be for ever! Is the home too mean?" But that word "brother" was as a talis-man between her and him.

Yet she looked so at home—perhaps so at home she felt!—more certainly than she had yet learned to do in that stiff stately house in which she was soon to have a daughter's rights. Was she suddenly made aware of this—that she so suddenly arose—and with a look of alarm and distress on her face—

"But—we are keeping Lady Lansmere too long," she said, falter-ingly. "We must go now," and she hastily took up her shawl and bonnet.

Just then Mrs. Fairfield entered with the visitors, and began making excuses for inattention to Miss Digby, whose identity with Leonard's child-angel she had not yet learned.

Helen received these apologies with her usual sweetness. "Nay," she said, "your son and I are such old friends, how could you stand on ceremony with me?"

"Old friends!" Mrs. Fairfield stared amazed, and then sur-veyed the fair speaker more curiously than she had yet done. "Pretty nice spoken thing," thought the widow; "as nice spoken as Miss Violante, and humbler-looking like,—though, as to dress, I never see anything so elegant out of a picter."

Helen now appropriated Mrs. Riccabocca's arm ; and, after a kind leave-taking with the widow, the ladies returned towards Riccabocca's house.

Mrs. Fairfield, however, ran after them with Leonard's hat and gloves, which he had forgotten.

"'Deed, boy," she said kindly, yet scoldingly, "but there'd be no more fine books, if the Lord had not fixed your head on your shoulders. You would not think it, marm," she added to Mrs. Riccabocca, "but sin' he has left you, he's not the 'cute lad he was ; very helpless at times, marm ! "

Helen could not resist turning round, and looking at Leonard, with a sly smile.

The widow saw the smile, and catching Leonard by the arm, whispered, "But, where before have you seen that pretty young lady ? Old friends ! "

" Ah, mother," said Leonard sadly, " it is a long tale ; you have heard the beginning—who can guess the end ?"—and he escaped. But Helen still leant on the arm of Mrs. Riccabocca, and, in the walk back, it seemed to Leonard as if the winter had resettled in the sky.

Yet he was by the side of Violante, and she spoke to him with such praise of Helen ! Alas ! it is not always so sweet as folks say, to hear the praises of one we love. Sometimes those praises seem to ask ironically, " And what right hast thou to hope because thou lovest ? *All* love *her*."

CHAPTER V.

NO sooner had Lady Lansmere found herself alone with Riccabocca and Harley, than she laid her hand on the exile's arm, and, addressing him by a title she had not before given him, and from which he appeared to shrink nervously, said—"Harley, in bringing me to visit you, was forced to reveal to me your incognito, for I should have discovered it. You may not remember me, in spite of your gallantry. But I mixed more in the world than I do now, during your first visit to England, and once sate next to you at dinner at Carlton House. Nay, no compliments, but listen to me. Harley tells me you have cause for some alarm respecting the designs of an audacious and unprincipled adventurer, I may call him; for adventurers are of all ranks. Suffer your daughter to come to me, on a visit, as long as you please. With me, at least, she will be safe; and if you too, and the—"

"Stop, my dear madam," interrupted Riccabocca, with great vivacity, "your kindness overpowers me. I thank you most gratefully for your invitation to my child; but—"

"Nay," in his turn interrupted Harley, "no buts. I was not aware of my mother's intention when she entered this room. But since she whispered it to me, I have reflected on it, and am convinced that it is but a prudent precaution. Your retreat is known to Mr. Leslie—he is known to Peschiera. Grant that no indiscretion of Mr. Leslie's betray the secret; still I have reason to believe that the Count guesses Randal's acquaintance with you. Audley Egerton this morning told me he had gathered that, not from the young man himself, but from questions put to himself by Madame di Negra; and Peschiera might, and would set spies to track Leslie to every house that he visits—might and would, still more naturally, set spies to track myself. Were this man an Englishman, I should laugh at his machinations; but he is an Italian, and has been a conspirator. What he could do I know not; but an assassin can penetrate into a camp, and a traitor can creep through closed walls to one's hearth. With my mother, Violante must be safe; that you cannot oppose. And why not come yourself?"

Riccabocca had no reply to these arguments, so far as they affected Violante; indeed, they awakened the almost superstitious terror with which he regarded his enemy, and he consented at once that Violante should accept the invitation proffered. But he refused it for himself and Jemima.

"To say truth," said he, simply, "I made a secret vow, on re-entering England, that I would associate with none who knew the rank I had formerly held in my own land. I felt that all my philosophy was needed, to reconcile and habituate myself to my altered circumstances. In order to find in my present existence, however humble, those blessings which make all life noble—dignity and peace—it was necessary for poor, weak human nature, wholly to dismiss the past. It would unsettle me sadly, could I come to your house, renew awhile, in your kindness and respect—nay, in the very atmosphere of your society—the sense of what I have been; and then (should the more than doubtful chance of recall from my exile fail me) to awake, and find myself for the rest of life what I am. And though, were I alone, I might trust myself perhaps to the danger—yet my wife: she is happy and contented now; would she be so, if you had once spoiled her for the simple position of Dr. Riccabocca's wife? Should I not have to listen to regrets, and hopes, and fears that would prick sharp through my thin cloak of philosophy? Even as it is, since in a moment of weakness I confided my secret to her, I have had 'my rank' thrown at me—with a careless hand, it is true—but it hits hard nevertheless. No stone hurts like one taken from the ruins of one's own home; and the grander the home, why, the heavier the stone! Protect, dear madam—protect my daughter, since her father doubts his own power to do so. But—ask no more."

Riccabocca was immovable here. And the matter was settled as he decided, it being agreed that Violante should be still styled but the daughter of Dr. Riccabocca.

"And now, one word more," said Harley. "Do not confide to Mr. Leslie these arrangements; do not let him know where Violante is placed—at least, until I authorize such confidence in him. It is sufficient excuse, that it is no use to know unless he called to see her, and his movements, as I said before, may be watched. You can give the same reason to suspend his visits to yourself. Suffer me, meanwhile, to mature my judgment on this young man. In the meanwhile, also, I think that I shall have means of ascertaining the real nature of Peschiera's schemes. His sister has sought to know me; I will give her the occasion. I have heard some things of her in my last residence abroad, which make me believe that she cannot be wholly the Count's tool in any schemes nakedly villainous; that she has some finer qualities in her than I once supposed; and that she can be won from his influence. It is a state of war; we will carry it into the enemy's camp. You will promise me, then, to refrain from all further confidence in Mr. Leslie."

"For the present, yes," said Riccabocca, reluctantly.

"Do not even say that you have seen me, unless he first tell you that I am in England, and wish to learn your residence. I will give him full occasion to do so. Pish! don't hesitate; you know your own proverb—

'Boccha chiusa, ed occhio aperto
Non fece mai nissun deserto.'

'The closed mouth and the open eye,' &c."

"That's very true," said the Doctor, much struck. "Very true. '*In boccha chiusa non c'entrano mosche.*' One can't swallow flies if one keeps one's mouth shut. *Corpo di Bacco!* that's very true indeed."

CHAPTER VI.

VIOLANTE and Jemima were both greatly surprised, as the reader may suppose, when they heard, on their return, the arrangements already made for the former. The Countess insisted on taking her at once, and Riccabocca briefly said, "Certainly, the sooner the better." Violante was stunned and bewildered. Jemima hastened to make up a little bundle of things necessary, with many a woman's sigh that the poor wardrobe contained so few things befitting. But among the clothes she slipped a purse, containing the savings of months, perhaps of years, and with it a few affectionate lines, begging Violante to ask the Countess to buy her all that was proper for her father's child. There is always something hurried and uncomfortable in the abrupt and unexpected withdrawal of any member from a quiet household. The small party broke into still smaller knots. Violante hung on her father, and listened vaguely to his not very lucid explanations. The Countess approached Leonard, and, according to the usual mode with persons of quality addressing young authors, complimented him highly on the books she had not read, but which her son assured her were so remarkable. She was a little anxious to know where Harley had first met with Mr. Oran, whom he called his friend ; but she was too high-bred to inquire, or to express any wonder that rank should be friends with genius. She took it for granted that they had formed their acquaintance abroad.

Harley conversed with Helen.—"You are not sorry that Violante is coming to us ? She will be just such a companion for you as I could desire ; of your own years too."

HELEN (ingenuously).—"It is hard to think I am not younger than she is."

HARLEY.—"Why, my dear Helen ?"

HELEN.—"She is so brilliant. She talks so beautifully. And I—"

HARLEY.—"And you want but the habit of talking, to do justice to your own beautiful thoughts."

Helen looked at him gratefully, but shook her head. It was a common trick of hers, and always when she was praised.

At last the preparations were made—the farewell was said. Violante was in the carriage by Lady Lansmere's side. Slowly moved on the stately equipage with its four horses and trim postilions, heraldic badges on their shoulders, in the style rarely seen in the neighbourhood of the metropolis, and now fast vanishing even amidst distant counties.

Riccabocca, Jemima, and Jackeymo continued to gaze after it from the gate.

"She is gone," said Jackeymo, brushing his eyes with his coat-sleeve. "But it is a load off one's mind."

"And another load on one's heart," murmured Riccabocca. "Don't cry, Jemima; it may be bad for you, and bad for *him* that is to come. It is astonishing how the humours of the mother may affect the unborn. I should not like to have a son who has a more than usual propensity to tears."

The poor philosopher tried to smile; but it was a bad attempt. He went slowly in, and shut himself with his books. But he could not read. His whole mind was unsettled. And though, like all parents, he had been anxious to rid himself of a beloved daughter for life, now that she was gone but for a while, a string seemed broken in the Music of Home.

CHAPTER VII.

THE evening of the same day, as Egerton, who was to entertain a large party at dinner, was changing his dress, Harley walked into his room.

Egerton dismissed his valet by a sign, and continued his toilet.

"Excuse me, my dear Harley, I have only ten minutes to give you. I expect one of the royal dukes, and punctuality is the stern virtue of men of business, and the graceful courtesy of princes."

Harley had usually a jest for his friend's aphorisms; but he had none now. He laid his hand kindly on Egerton's shoulder—"Before I speak of my business, tell me how you are—better?"

"Better—nay, I am always well. Pooh! I may look a little tired—years of toil will tell on the countenance. But that matters little : the period of life has passed with me when one cares how one looks in the glass."

As he spoke, Egerton completed his dress, and came to the hearth, standing there, erect and dignified as usual, still far hand-somer than many a younger man, and with a form that seemed to have ample vigour to support for many a year the sad and glorious burthen of power.

"So now to your business, Harley."

"In the first place, I want you to present me, at the earliest opportunity, to Madame di Negra. You say she wished to know me."

"Are you serious?"

"Yes."

"Well, then, she receives this evening. I did not mean to go; but when my party breaks up—"

"You can call for me at 'The Travellers.' Do!"

"Next—you knew Lady Jane Horton better even than I did, at least in the last year of her life." Harley sighed, and Egerton turned and stirred the fire.

"Pray, did you ever see at her house, or hear her speak of, a Mrs. Bertram?"

"Of whom?" said Egerton, in a hollow voice, his face still turned towards the fire.

"A Mrs. Bertram; but Heavens! my dear fellow, what is the matter? Are you ill?"

"A spasm at the heart, that is all—don't ring—I shall be better presently—go on talking. Mrs. —— why do you ask"?

"Why? I have hardly time to explain; but I am, as I told you, resolved on righting my old Italian friend, if Heaven will help me, as it ever does help the just when they bestir themselves; and this Mrs. Bertram is mixed up in my friend's affairs."

"His! How is that possible?"

Harley rapidly and succinctly explained. Audley listened attentively, with his eyes fixed on the floor, and still seeming to labour under great difficulty of breathing.

As last he answered, "I remember something of this Mrs.—Mrs. —Bertram. But your inquiries after her would be useless. I think I have heard that she is long since dead; nay, I am sure of it."

"Dead!—that is most unfortunate. But do you know any of her relations or friends? Can you suggest any mode of tracing this packet, if it came to her hands?"

"No."

"And Lady Jane had scarcely any friend that I remember, except my mother, and she knows nothing of this Mrs. Bertram. How unlucky! I think I shall advertise. Yet, no. I could only distinguish this Mrs. Bertram from any other of the same name, by stating with whom she had gone abroad, and that would catch the attention of Peschiera, and set him to counterwork us."

"And what avails it?" said Egerton. "She whom you seek is no more—no more!" He paused, and went on rapidly—"The packet did not arrive in England till years after her death—was no doubt returned to the post-office—is destroyed long ago."

Harley looked very much disappointed. Egerton went on in a sort of set mechanical voice, as if not thinking of what he said, but speaking from the dry practical mode of reasoning which was habitual to him, and by which the man of the world destroys the hopes of an enthusiast. Then starting up at the sound of the first thundering knock at the street door, he said, "Hark! you must excuse me."

"I leave you, my dear Audley. But I must again ask—Are you better now?"

"Much, much—quite well. I will call for you—probably between eleven and twelve."

CHAPTER VIII.

IF any one could be more surprised at seeing Lord L'Estrange at the house of Madame di Negra that evening than the fair hostess herself, it was Randal Leslie. Something instinctively told him that this visit threatened interference with whatever might be his ultimate projects in regard to Riccabocca and Violante. But Randal Leslie was not one of those who shrink from an intellectual combat. On the contrary, he was too confident of his powers of intrigue, not to take a delight in their exercise. He could not conceive that the indolent Harley could be a match for his own restless activity and dogged perseverance. But in a very few moments fear crept on him. No man of his day could produce a more brilliant effect than Lord L'Estrange, when he deigned to desire it. Without much pretence to that personal beauty which strikes at first sight, he still retained all the charm of countenance, and all the grace of manner, which had made him in boyhood the spoiled darling of society. Madame di Negra had collected but a small circle round her, still it was of the *élite* of the great world; not, indeed, those more precise and reserved *dames de chateau*, whom the lighter and easier of the fair dispensers of fashion ridicule as prudes; but nevertheless, ladies were there, as unblemished in reputation, as high in rank; flirts and coquettes, perhaps—nothing more; in short, "charming women" —the gay butterflies that hover over the stiff parterre. And there were ambassadors and ministers, and wits and brilliant debaters, and first-rate dandies (dandies, when first-rate, are generally very agreeable men). Amongst all these various persons, Harley, so long a stranger to the London world, seemed to make himself at home with the ease of an Alcibiades. Many of the less juvenile ladies remembered him, and rushed to claim his acquaintance, with nods and becks, and wreathed smiles. He had ready compliment for each. And few indeed were there, men or women, for whom Harley L'Estrange had not appropriate attraction. Distinguished reputation as soldier and scholar for the grave; whim and pleasantry for the gay; novelty for the sated; and for the more vulgar natures was he not Lord L'Estrange, unmarried, possessed already of a large independence, and heir to an ancient earldom, and some fifty thousands a-year?

Not till he had succeeded in the general effect—which, it must be owned, he did his best to create—did Harley seriously and especially devote himself to his hostess. And then he seated himself by her side; and, as if in compliment to both, less pressing admirers insensibly slipped away and edged off.

Frank Hazeldean was the last to quit his ground behind Madame di Negra's chair; but when he found that the two began to talk in Italian, and he could not understand a word they said, he too—fancying, poor fellow, that he looked foolish, and cursing his Eton education that had neglected, for languages spoken by the dead, of which he had learned little, those still in use among the living, of which he had learned nought—retreated towards Randal, and asked wistfully, "Pray, what age should you say L'Estrange was? He must be devilish old, in spite of his looks. Why, he was at Waterloo!"

"He is young enough to be a terrible rival," answered Randal, with artful truth.

Frank turned pale, and began to meditate dreadful bloodthirsty thoughts, of which hair-triggers and Lord's Cricket-ground formed the staple.

Certainly there was apparent ground for a lover's jealousy. For Harley and Beatrice now conversed in a low tone, and Beatrice seemed agitated, and Harley earnest. Randal himself grew more and more perplexed. Was Lord L'Estrange really enamoured of the Marchesa? If so, farewell to all hopes of Frank's marriage with her! Or was he merely playing a part in Riccabocca's interest; pretending to be the lover, in order to obtain an influence over her mind, rule her through her ambition, and secure an ally against her brother? Was this *finesse* compatible with Randal's notions of Harley's character? Was it consistent with that chivalric and soldierly spirit of honour which the frank nobleman affected, to make love to a woman in mere *ruse de guerre?* Could mere friend-ship for Riccabocca be a sufficient inducement to a man, who, whatever his weaknesses or his errors, seemed to wear on his very forehead a soul above deceit, to stoop to paltry means, even for a worthy end? At this question, a new thought flashed upon Randal —might not Lord L'Estrange have speculated himself upon winning Violante?—would not that account for all the exertions he had made on behalf of her inheritance at the court of Vienna—exertions of which Peschiera and Beatrice had both complained? Those objections which the Austrian government might take to Violante's marriage with some obscure Englishman would probably not exist against a man like Harley L'Estrange, whose family not only belonged to the highest aristocracy of England, but had always supported opinions in vogue amongst the leading governments of Europe. Harley himself, it is true, had never taken part in politics, but his notions were, no doubt, those of a high-born soldier, who had fought, in alliance with Austria, for the restoration of the Bourbons. And this immense wealth—which Violante might lose, if she married one like Randal himself—her marriage with the heir of the Lansmeres might actually tend only to secure. Could Harley, with all his own expectations, be indifferent to such a prize?—and no doubt he had learned Violante's rare beauty in his correspondence with Riccabocca.

Thus considered, it seemed natural to Randal's estimate of human nature, that Harley's more prudish scruples of honour, as regards what is due to women, could not resist a temptation so strong. Mere friendship was not a motive powerful enough to shake them, but ambition was.

While Randal was thus cogitating, Frank thus suffering, and many a whisper, in comment on the evident flirtation between the beautiful hostess and the accomplished guest, reached the ears both of the brooding schemer and the jealous lover, the conversation between the two objects of remark and gossip had taken a new turn. Indeed, Beatrice had made an effort to change it.

"It is long, my lord," said she, still speaking Italian, "since I have heard sentiments like those you address to me; and if I do not feel myself wholly unworthy of them, it is from the pleasure I have felt in reading sentiments equally foreign to the language of the world in which I live." She took a book from the table as she spoke: "Have you seen this work?"

Harley glanced at the title-page. "To be sure I have, and I know the author."

"I envy you that honour. I should so like also to know one who has discovered to me deeps in my own heart which I had never explored."

"Charming Marchesa, if the book has done this, believe me that I have paid you no false compliment—formed no overflattering estimate of your nature; for the charm of the work is but in its simple appeal to good and generous emotions, and it can charm none in whom those emotions exist not!"

"Nay, that cannot be true, or why is it so popular?"

"Because good and generous emotions are more common to the human heart than we are aware of till the appeal comes."

"Don't ask me to think that! I have found the world so base."

"Pardon me a rude question; but what do you know of the world?"

Beatrice looked first in surprise at Harley, then glanced round the room with significant irony.

"As I thought; you call this little room 'the world.' Be it so. I will venture to say, that if the people in this room were suddenly converted into an audience before a stage, and you were as consummate in the actor's art as you are in all others that please and command—"

"Well?"

"And were to deliver a speech full of sordid and base sentiments, you would be hissed. But let any other woman, with half your powers, arise and utter sentiments sweet and womanly, or honest and lofty—and applause would flow from every lip, and tears rush to many a worldly eye. The true proof of the inherent nobleness of our common nature is in the sympathy it betrays with what is noble wherever crowds are collected. Never believe the world is base;—if it were so, no society could hold together for a day. But you would know the author of this book? I will bring him to you."

"Do."

"And now," said Harley, rising, and with his candid, winning smile, "do you think we shall ever be friends?"

"You have startled me so, that I can scarcely answer. But why would you be friends with me?"

"Because you need a friend. You have none?"

"Strange flatterer!" said Beatrice, smiling, though very sadly; and looking up, her eye caught Randal's.

"Pooh!" said Harley, "you are too penetrating to believe that you inspire friendship *there*. Ah, do you suppose that, all the while I have been conversing with you, I have not noticed the watchful gaze of Mr. Randal Leslie? What tie can possibly connect you together I know not yet; but I soon shall."

"Indeed! you talk like one of the old Council of Venice. You try hard to make me fear you," said Beatrice, seeking to escape from the graver kind of impression Harley had made on her, by the affectation, partly of coquetry, partly of levity.

"And I," said L'Estrange, calmly, "tell you already, that I fear you no more." He bowed, and passed through the crowd to rejoin Audley, who was seated in a corner whispering with some of his political colleagues. Before Harley reached the minister, he found himself close to Randal and young Hazeldean.

He bowed to the first, and extended his hand to the last. Randal felt the distinction, and his sullen, bitter pride was deeply galled— a feeling of hate towards Harley passed into his mind. He was pleased to see the cold hesitation with which Frank just touched the hand offered to him. But Randal had not been the only person whose watch upon Beatrice the keen-eyed Harley had noticed. Harley had seen the angry looks of Frank Hazeldean, and divined the cause. So he smiled forgivingly at the slight he had received.

"You are like me, Mr. Hazeldean," said he. "You think something of the heart should go with all courtesy that bespeaks friendship—

'The hand of Douglas is his own.'"

Here Harley drew aside Randal. "Mr. Leslie, a word with you. If I wished to know the retreat of Dr. Riccabocca, in order to render him a great service, would you confide to me that secret?"

"That woman has let out her suspicions that I know the exile's retreat," thought Randal; and with quick presence of mind, he replied at once—

"My Lord, yonder stands a connection of Dr. Riccabocca's. Mr. Hazeldean is surely the person to whom you should address this inquiry."

"Not so, Mr. Leslie; for I suspect that he cannot answer it, and that you can. Well, I will ask something that it seems to me you may grant without hesitation. Should you see Dr. Riccabocca, tell him that I am in England, and so leave it to him to communicate with me or not; but perhaps you have already done so?"

"Lord L'Estrange," said Randal, bowing low, with pointed formality, "excuse me if I decline either to disclaim or acquiesce in the knowledge you impute to me. If I am acquainted with any secret intrusted to me by Dr. Riccabocca, it is for me to use my own discretion how best to guard it. And for the rest, after the Scotch earl, whose words your lordship has quoted, refused to touch the hand of Marmion, Douglas could scarcely have called Marmion back in order to give him—a message!"

Harley was not prepared for this tone in Mr. Egerton's *protégé,* and his own gallant nature was rather pleased than irritated by a haughtiness that at least seemed to bespeak independence of spirit. Nevertheless, L'Estrange's suspicions of Randal were too strong to be easily set aside, and therefore he replied, civilly, but with covert taunt—

"I submit to your rebuke, Mr. Leslie, though I meant not the offence you would ascribe to me. I regret my unlucky quotation yet the more, since the wit of your retort has obliged you to identify yourself with Marmion, who, though a clever and brave fellow, was an uncommonly—tricky one." And so Harley, certainly having the best of it, moved on, and joining Egerton, in a few minutes more both left the room.

"What was L'Estrange saying to you?" asked Frank. "Something about Beatrice I am sure."

"No; only quoting poetry."

"Then what made you look so angry, my dear fellow? I know it was your kind feeling for me. As you say, he is a formidable rival. But that can't be his own hair. Do you think he wears a *toupet?* I am sure he was praising Beatrice. He is evidently very much smitten with her. But I don't think she is a woman to be caught by *mere* rank and fortune! Do you? Why can't you speak?"

"If you do not get her consent soon, I think she is lost to you," said Randal, slowly; and before Frank could recover his dismay, glided from the house.

CHAPTER IX.

IOLANTE'S first evening at the Lansmeres had passed more happily to her than the first evening under the same roof had done to Helen. True that she missed her father much—Jemima somewhat; but she so identified her father's cause with Harley, that she had a sort of vague feeling that it was to promote that cause that she was on this visit to Harley's parents. And the Countess, it must be owned, was more emphatic-ally cordial to her than she had ever yet been, to Captain Digby's orphan. But perhaps the real difference in the heart of either girl was this, that Helen felt awe of Lady Lansmere, and Violante felt only love for Lord L'Estrange's mother. Violante, too, was one of those persons whom a reserved and formal person, like the Countess, "can get on with," as the phrase goes. Not so poor little Helen—so shy herself, and so hard to coax into more than gentle monosyllables. And Lady Lansmere's favourite talk was always of Harley. Helen had listened to such talk with respect and interest. Violante listened to it with inquisitive eagerness—with blushing delight. The mother's heart noticed the distinction between the two, and no wonder that that heart moved more to Violante than to Helen. Lord Lansmere, too, like most gentlemen of his age, clumped all young ladies together, as a harmless, amiable, but singularly stupid class of the genus-Petticoat, meant to look pretty, play the piano, and talk to each other about frocks and sweethearts. Therefore this animated dazzling creature, with her infinite variety of look and play of mind, took him by surprise, charmed him into attention, and warmed him into gallantry. Helen sate in her quiet corner, at her work, sometimes listening with almost mournful, though certainly unenvious, admiration at Violante's vivid, yet ever unconscious, eloquence of word and thought—sometimes plunged deep into her own secret meditations. And all the while the work went on the same, under the small, noiseless fingers. This was one of Helen's habits that irritated the nerves of Lady Lansmere. She despised young ladies who were fond of work. She did not comprehend how often it is the resource of the sweet womanly mind, not from want of thought, but from the silence and the depth of it. Violante was surprised, and perhaps disappointed, that Harley had left the house before dinner, and did not return all the evening. But Lady Lansmere, in making excuse for his absence, on the plea of engagements, found so good an opportunity to talk of his ways in general—of his rare promise in boyhood—of her regret at the inaction of his maturity—of her hope to see him yet do justice to his natural powers, that Violante almost ceased to miss him.

And when Lady Lansmere conducted her to her room, and, kissing her cheek tenderly, said, "But you are just the person Harley admires—just the person to rouse him from melancholy dreams, of which his wild humours are now but the vain disguise" —Violante crossed her arms on her bosom, and her bright eyes, deepened into tenderness, seemed to ask, "He melancholy—and why?"

On leaving Violante's room, Lady Lansmere paused before the door of Helen's; and, after musing a little while, entered softly.

Helen had dismissed her maid ; and, at the moment Lady Lansmere entered, she was kneeling at the foot of the bed, her hands clasped before her face.

Her form, thus seen, looked so youthful and childlike—the

attitude itself was so holy and so touching, that the proud and cold expression on Lady Lansmere's face changed. She shaded the light involuntarily, and seated herself in silence that she might not disturb the act of prayer.

When Helen rose, she was startled to see the Countess seated by the fire ; and hastily drew her hand across her eyes. She had been weeping.

Lady Lansmere did not, however, turn to observe those traces of tears, which Helen feared were too visible. The Countess was too absorbed in her own thoughts ; and as Helen timidly approached, she said—still with her eyes on the clear low fire—"I beg your pardon, Miss Digby, for my intrusion ; but my son has left it to me to prepare Lord Lansmere to learn the offer you have done Harley the honour to accept. I have not yet spoken to my lord ; it may be days before I find a fitting occasion to do so ; meanwhile I feel assured that your sense of propriety will make you agree with me that it is due to Lord L'Estrange's father, that strangers should not learn arrangements of such moment in his family, before his own consent be obtained."

Here the Countess came to a full pause ; and poor Helen, finding herself called upon for some reply to this chilling speech, stammered out, scarce audibly—

"Certainly, madam, I never dreamed of—"

"That is right, my dear," interrupted Lady Lansmere, rising suddenly, and as if greatly relieved. "I could not doubt your superiority to ordinary girls of your age, with whom these matters are never secret for a moment. Therefore, of course, you will not mention, at present, what has passed between you and Harley, to any of the friends with whom you may correspond."

"I have no correspondents—no friends, Lady Lansmere," said Helen, deprecatingly, and trying hard not to cry.

"I am very glad to hear it, my dear ; young ladies never should have. Friends, especially friends who correspond, are the worst enemies they can have. Good night, Miss Digby. I need not add, by the way, that though we are bound to show all kindness to this young Italian lady, still she is wholly unconnected with our family ; and you will be as prudent with her as you would have been with your correspondents—had you had the misfortune to have any."

Lady Lansmere said the last words with a smile, and left an ungenial kiss (the stepmother's kiss) on Helen's bended brow. She then left the room, and Helen sate on the seat vacated by the stately unloving form, and again covered her face with her hands, and again wept. But when she rose at last, and the light fell upon her face, that soft face was sad indeed, but serene—serene, as if with some inward sense of duty—sad, as with the resignation which accepts patience instead of hope.

CHAPTER X.

THE next morning Harley appeared at breakfast.   He was in gay spirits, and conversed more freely with Violante than he had yet done.   He seemed to amuse himself by attacking all she said, and provoking her to argument. Violante was naturally a very earnest person ; whether grave or gay, she spoke with her heart on her lips, and her soul in her eyes.   She did not yet comprehend the light vein of Harley's irony, so she grew piqued and chafed ; and she was so lovely in anger ; it so bright-ened her beauty and animated her words, that no wonder Harley thus maliciously teased her.   But what, perhaps, she liked still less than the teasing—though she could not tell why—was the kind of familiarity that Harley assumed with her—a familiarity as if he had known her all her life—that of a good-humoured elder brother, or a bachelor uncle.   To Helen, on the contrary, when he did not address her apart, his manner was more respectful.   He did not call *her* by her Christian name, as he did Violante, but " Miss Digby," and softened his tone and inclined his head when he spoke to her. Nor did he presume to jest at the very few and brief sentences he drew from Helen, but rather listened to them with deference, and invariably honoured them with approval.   After breakfast he asked Violante to play or sing ; and when she frankly owned how little she had cultivated those accomplishments, he persuaded Helen to sit down to the piano, and stood by her side while she did so, turn-ing over the leaves of her music-book with the ready devotion of an admiring amateur.   Helen always played well, but less well than usual that day, for her generous nature felt abashed.   It was as if she were showing off to mortify Violante.   But Violante, on the other hand, was so passionately fond of music, that she had no feeling left for the sense of her own inferiority.   Yet she sighed when Helen rose, and Harley thanked Miss Digby for the delight she had given him.

The day was fine.   Lady Lansmere proposed to walk in the garden.   While the ladies went up-stairs for their shawls and bonnets, Harley lighted his cigar, and stepped from the window upon the lawn.   Lady Lansmere joined him before the girls came out.

"Harley," said she, taking his arm, "what a charming companion you have introduced to us! I never met with any that both pleased and delighted me like this dear Violante. Most girls who possess some power of conversation, and who have dared to think for themselves, are so pedantic, or so masculine; but *she* is always so simple, and always still the girl. Ah, Harley!"

"Why that sigh, my dear mother?"

"I was thinking how exactly she would have suited you—how proud I should have been of such a daughter-in-law—and how happy you would have been with such a wife."

Harley started. "Tut," said he, peevishly, "she is a mere child; you forget my years."

"Why," said Lady Lansmere, surprised, "Helen is quite as young as Violante."

"In dates—yes. But Helen's character is so staid;—what it is now it will be ever; and Helen, from gratitude, respect, or pity, condescends to accept the ruins of my heart;—while this bright Italian has the soul of a Juliet, and would expect in a husband all the passion of a Romeo. Nay, mother, hush. Do you forget that I am engaged—and of my own free will and choice? Poor dear Helen! Apropos, have you spoken to my father, as you undertook to do?"

"Not yet. I must seize the right moment. You know that my lord requires management."

"My dear mother, that female notion of managing us, men, costs you, ladies, a great waste of time, and occasions us a great deal of sorrow. Men are easily managed by plain truth. *We* are brought up to respect it, strange as it may seem to you!"

Lady Lansmere smiled with the air of superior wisdom, and the experience of an accomplished wife. "Leave it to me, Harley, and rely on my Lord's consent."

Harley knew that Lady Lansmere always succeeded in obtaining her way with his father; and he felt that the Earl might naturally be disappointed in such an alliance, and, without due propitiation, evince that disappointment in his manner to Helen. Harley was bound to save her from all chance of such humiliation. He did not wish her to think that she was not welcomed into his family; therefore he said, "I resign myself to your promise and your diplomacy. Meanwhile, as you love me, be kind to my betrothed."

"Am I not so?"

"Hem. Are you as kind as if she were the great heiress you believe Violante to be?"

"Is it," answered Lady Lansmere, evading the question—"is it because one is an heiress and the other is not that you make so marked a difference in your own manner to the two; treating Violante as a spoilt child, and Miss Digby as—"

"The destined wife of Lord L'Estrange, and the daughter-in-law of Lady Lansmere—yes."

The Countess suppressed an impatient exclamation that rose to her lips, for Harley's brow wore that serious aspect which it rarely assumed save when he was in those moods in which men must be soothed, not resisted. And after a pause he went on—"I am going to leave you to-day. I have engaged apartments at the Clarendon. I intend to gratify your wish, so often expressed, that I should enjoy what are called the pleasures of my rank, and the privileges of single-blessedness—celebrate my adieu to celibacy, and blaze once more, with the splendour of a setting sun, upon Hyde Park and May Fair."

"You are a positive enigma. Leave our house, just when you are betrothed to its inmate! Is that the natural conduct of a lover?"

"How can your woman eyes be so dull, and your woman heart so obtuse?" answered Harley, half-laughing, half-scolding. "Can you not guess that I wish that Helen and myself should both lose the association of mere ward and guardian; that the very familiarity of our intercourse under the same roof almost forbids us to be lovers; that we lose the joy to meet, and the pang to part. Don't you remember the story of the Frenchman, who for twenty years loved a lady, and never missed passing his evenings at her house. She became a widow. 'I wish you joy,' cried his friend; 'you may now marry the woman you have so long adored.' 'Alas,' said the poor Frenchman, profoundly dejected; 'and if so, where shall I spend my evenings?'"

Here Violante and Helen were seen in the garden, walking affectionately arm in arm.

"I don't perceive the point of your witty, heartless anecdote," said Lady Lansmere, obstinately. "Settle that, however, with Miss Digby. But, to leave the very day after your friend's daughter comes as a guest!—what will *she* think of it?"

Lord L'Estrange looked steadfastly at his mother. "Does it matter much what she thinks of me?—of a man engaged to another; and old enough to be—"

"I wish to Heaven you would not talk of your age, Harley; it is a reflection upon mine; and I never saw you look so well nor so handsome." With that she drew him on towards the young ladies; and, taking Helen's arm, asked her, aside, "If she knew that Lord

L'Estrange had engaged rooms at the Clarendon ; and if she understood why?" As, while she said this, she moved on, Harley was
left by Violante's side.

"You will be very dull here, I fear, my poor child," said he.

"Dull ! But why *will* you call me child? Am I so very—very
child-like?"

"Certainly, you are to me—a mere infant. Have I not seen you
one ; have I not held you in my arms?"

VIOLANTE.—"But that was a long time ago !"

HARLEY.—"True. But if years have not stood still for you,
they have not been stationary for me. There is the same difference
between us now that there was then. And, therefore, permit me
still to call you child, and as child to treat you !"

VIOLANTE.—"I will do no such thing. Do you know that I
always thought I was good-tempered till this morning."

HARLEY.—"And what undeceived you? Did you break your
doll ?"

VIOLANTE (with an indignant flash from her dark eyes).—"There !
—again !—you delight in provoking me !"

HARLEY.—"It *was* the doll, then. Don't cry ; I will get you
another."

Violante plucked her arm from him, and walked away towards
the Countess in speechless scorn. Harley's brow contracted, in
thought and in gloom. He stood still for a moment or so, and then
joined the ladies.

"I am trespassing sadly on your morning; but I wait for a visitor
whom I sent to before you were up. He is to be here at twelve.
With your permission, I will dine with you to-morrow, and you will
invite him to meet me."

"Certainly. And who is your friend? I guess—the young
author ?"

"Leonard Fairfield," cried Violante, who had conquered, or felt
ashamed, of her short-lived anger.

"Fairfield !" repeated Lady Lansmere. "I thought, Harley,
you said the name was Oran."

"He has assumed the latter name. He is the son of Mark Fairfield, who married an Avenel. Did you recognize no family
likeness?—none in those eyes—mother?" said Harley, sinking his
voice into a whisper.

"No," answered the Countess, falteringly.

Harley, observing that Violante was now speaking to Helen
about Leonard, and that neither was listening to him, resumed in
the same low tone, "And his mother—Nora's sister,—shrank from

seeing me ! That is the reason why I wished you not to call. She has not told the young man *why* she shrank from seeing me ; nor have I explained it to him as yet. Perhaps I never shall."

"Indeed, dearest Harley," said the Countess, with great gentleness, "I wish you too much to forget the folly—well, I will not say that word—the sorrows of your boyhood, not to hope that you will rather strive against such painful memories than renew them by unnecessary confidence to any one ; least of all to the relation of—"

"Enough !—don't name her ; the very name pains me. And as to confidence, there are but two persons in the world to whom I ever bare the old wounds—yourself and Egerton. Let this pass. Ha !—a ring at the bell—that is he ! "

CHAPTER XI.

LEONARD entered on the scene, and joined the party in the garden. The Countess, perhaps to please her son, was more than civil—she was markedly kind to him. She noticed him more attentively than she had hitherto done ; and, with all her prejudices of birth, was struck to find the son of Mark Fairfield the carpenter so thoroughly the gentleman. He might not have the exact tone and phrase by which Convention stereotypes those born and schooled in a certain world ; but the aristocrats of Nature can dispense with such trite minutiæ. And Leonard had lived, of late at least, in the best society that exists, for the polish of language and the refinement of manners,—the society in which the most graceful ideas are clothed in the most graceful forms—the society which really, though indirectly, gives the law to courts—the society of the most classic authors, in the various ages in which literature has flowered forth from civilization. And if there was something in the exquisite sweetness of Leonard's voice, look, and manner, which the Countess acknowledged to attain that perfection in high breeding, which, under the name of "suavity," steals its way into the heart, so her interest in him was aroused by a certain subdued melancholy which is rarely without distinction, and never without charm. He and Helen exchanged but few words. There was but one occasion in which they could have spoken apart, and Helen herself contrived to elude it. His face brightened at Lady Lansmere's cordial invitation, and he glanced at Helen as he accepted it ; but her eye did not meet his own.

"And now," said Harley, whistling to Nero, whom his ward was silently caressing, "I must take Leonard away. Adieu! all of you, till to-morrow at dinner. Miss Violante, is the doll to have blue eyes or black?"

Violante turned her own black eyes in mute appeal to Lady Lansmere, and nestled to that lady's side as if in refuge from unworthy insult.

CHAPTER XII.

"LET the carriage go to the Clarendon," said Harley to his servant; "I and Mr. Oran will walk to town. Leonard, I think you would rejoice at an occasion to serve your old friends, Dr. Riccabocca and his daughter?"

"Serve them! O yes." And there instantly returned to Leonard the recollection of Violante's words when, on leaving his quiet village, he had sighed to part from all those he loved; and the little dark-eyed girl had said, proudly, yet consolingly, "But to SERVE those you love!" He turned to L'Estrange, with beaming, inquisitive eyes.

"I said to our friend," resumed Harley, "that I would vouch for your honour as my own. I am about to prove my words, and to confide the secrets which your penetration has indeed divined;—our friend is not what he seems." Harley then briefly related to Leonard the particulars of the exile's history, the rank he had held in his native land, the manner in which, partly through the misrepresentations of a kinsman he had trusted, partly through the influence of a wife he had loved, he had been drawn into schemes which he believed bounded to the emancipation of Italy from a foreign yoke by the united exertions of her best and bravest sons.

"A noble ambition," interrupted Leonard, manfully. "And pardon me, my Lord, I should not have thought that you would speak of it in a tone that implies blame."

"The ambition in itself was noble," answered Harley. "But the cause to which it was devoted became defiled in its dark channel through Secret Societies. It is the misfortune of all miscellaneous political combinations, that with the purest motives of their more generous members are ever mixed the most sordid interests, and the fiercest passions of mean confederates. When those combinations act openly, and in day-light, under the eye of Public Opinion, the healthier elements usually prevail; where they are shrouded in mystery—where they are subjected to no censor in the discussion of the impartial and dispassionate—where chiefs working in the dark exact blind obedience, and every man who is at war with law is at once admitted as a friend of freedom—the history of the world tells us that patriotism soon passes away. Where all is in public, public virtue, by the natural sympathies of the common mind, and by the wholesome control of shame, is likely to obtain ascendancy; where all is in private, and shame is but for him who refuses the abnegation of his conscience, each man seeks the indulgence of his private vice. And hence, in Secret Societies (from which may yet proceed great danger to all Europe), we find but foul and hateful Eleusinia, affording pretexts to the ambition of the great, to the licence of the penniless, to the passions of the revengeful, to the anarchy of the ignorant. In a word, the societies of these Italian Carbonari did but engender schemes in which the abler chiefs disguised new forms of despotism, and in which the revolutionary many looked forward to the overthrow of all the institutions that stand between Law and Chaos. Naturally, therefore" (added L'Estrange, dryly), "when their schemes were detected, and the conspiracy foiled, it was for the silly, honest men entrapped into the league to suffer—the leaders turned king's evidence, and the common mercenaries became—banditti." Harley then proceeded to state that it was just when the *soi-disant* Riccabocca had discovered the true nature and ulterior views of the conspirators he had joined, and actually withdrawn from their councils, that he was denounced by the kinsman who had duped him into the enterprise, and who now profited by his treason. Harley next spoke of the packet despatched by Riccabocca's dying wife, as it was supposed, to Mrs. Bertram, and of the hopes he founded on the contents of that packet, if discovered. He then referred to the design which had brought Peschiera to England—a design which that personage had avowed with such effrontery to his companions at Vienna, that he had publicly laid wagers on his success.

"But these men can know nothing of England—of the safety of English laws," said Leonard, naturally. "We take it for granted that Riccabocca, if I am still so to call him, refuses his consent to the marriage between his daughter and his foe. Where, then, the danger? This Count, even if Violante were not under your mother's roof, could not get an opportunity to see her. He could not attack the house and carry her off like a feudal baron in the middle ages."

"All this is very true," answered Harley. "Yet I have found through life that we cannot estimate danger by external circumstances, but by the character of those from whom it is threatened. This Count is a man of singular audacity, of no mean natural talents—

talents practised in every art of duplicity and intrigue ; one of those
men whose boast it is that they succeed in whatever they undertake ;
and he is, here, urged on the one hand by all that can whet the
avarice, and on the other, by all that can give invention to despair.
Therefore, though I cannot guess what plan he may possibly adopt,
I never doubt that some plan, formed with cunning and pursued
with daring, will be embraced the moment he discovers Violante's
retreat, unless, indeed, we can forestall all peril by the restoration
of her father, and the detection of the fraud and falsehood to which
Peschiera owes the fortune he appropriates.　Thus, while we must
prosecute to the utmost our inquiries for the missing documents, so
it should be our care to possess ourselves, if possible, of such knowledge of the Count's machinations as may enable us to defeat them.
Now, it was with satisfaction that I learned in Germany that Peschiera's sister was in London.　I knew enough both of his disposition
and of the intimacy between himself and this lady, to make me
think it probable he will seek to make her his instrument and accom-
plice, should he require one.　Peschiera (as you may suppose by
his audacious wager) is not one of those secret villains who would
cut off their right hand if it could betray the knowledge of what
was done by the left—rather one of those self-confident vaunting
knaves of high animal spirits, and conscience so obtuse that it clouds
their intellect—who must have some one to whom they can boast of
their abilities and confide their projects.　And Peschiera has done
all he can to render this poor woman so wholly dependent on him,
as to be his slave and his tool.　But I have learned certain traits in
her character that show it to be impressionable to good, and with
tendencies to honour.　Peschiera had taken advantage of the admiration she excited, some years ago, in a rich young Englishman, to
entice this admirer into gambling, and sought to make his sister
both a decoy and an instrument in his designs of plunder.　She did
not encourage the addresses of our countryman, but she warned him
of the snare laid for him, and entreated him to leave the place lest
her brother should discover and punish her honesty.　The Englishman told me this himself.　In fine, my hope of detaching this lady
from Peschiera's interests, and inducing her to forewarn us of his
purpose, consists but in the innocent, and, I hope, laudable artifice,
of redeeming herself—of appealing to, and calling into disused
exercise, the better springs of her nature."

Leonard listened with admiration and some surprise to the singularly subtle and sagacious insight into character which Harley evinced
in the brief clear strokes by which he had thus depicted Peschiera
and Beatrice, and was struck by the boldness with which Harley

rested a whole system of action upon a few deductions drawn from his reasonings on human motive and characteristic bias. Leonard had not expected to find so much practical acuteness in a man who, however accomplished, usually seemed indifferent, dreamy, and abstracted to the ordinary things of life. But Harley L'Estrange was one of those whose powers lie dormant till circumstance supplies to them all they need for activity—the stimulant of a motive.

Harley resumed—" After a conversation I had with the lady last night, it occurred to me that in this part of our diplomacy you could render us essential service. Madame di Negra—such is the sister's name—has conceived an admiration for your genius, and a strong desire to know you personally. I have promised to present you to her ; and I shall do so after a preliminary caution. The lady is very handsome, and very fascinating. It is possible that your heart and your senses may not be proof against her attractions."

" O, do not fear that !" exclaimed Leonard, with a tone of conviction so earnest that Harley smiled.

" Forewarned is not always forearmed against the might of beauty, my dear Leonard ; so I cannot at once accept your assurance. But listen to me ! Watch yourself narrowly, and if you find that you are likely to be captivated, promise, on your honour, to retreat at once from the field. I have no right, for the sake of another, to expose you to danger ; and Madame di Negra, whatever may be her good qualities, is the last person I should wish to see you in love with."

" In love with her ! Impossible !"

" Impossible is a strong word," returned Harley ; " still, I own fairly (and this belief alone warrants me in trusting you to her fascinations) that I do think, as far as one man can judge of another, that she is not the woman to attract you ; and, if filled by one pure and generous object in your intercourse with her, you will see her with purged eyes. Still I claim your promise as one of honour."

" I give it," said Leonard, positively. " But how can I serve Riccabocca ? How aid in—"

" Thus," interrupted Harley.—" The spell of your writings is, that, unconsciously to ourselves, they make us better and nobler. And your writings are but the impressions struck off from your mind. Your conversation, when you are roused, has the same effect. And as you grow more familiar with Madame di Negra, I wish you to speak of your boyhood, your youth. Describe the exile as you have seen him—so touching amidst his foibles, so grand amidst the petty privations of his fallen fortunes, so benevolent while poring over his hateful Machiavelli, so stingless in his wisdom of the serpent, so playfully astute in his innocence of the dove—I leave the picture to your knowledge of humour and pathos. Describe Violante brooding over her Italian Poets, and filled with dreams of her fatherland ; describe her with all the flashes of her princely nature, shining forth through humble circumstance and obscure position ; waken in your listener compassion, respect, admiration for her kindred exiles ;—and I think our work is done. She will recognize evidently those whom her brother seeks. She will question you closely where you met with them—where they now are. Protect that secret ; say at once that it is not your own. Against your descriptions and the feelings they excite, she will not be guarded as against mine. And there are other reasons why your influence over this woman of mixed nature may be more direct and effectual than my own."

"Nay, I cannot conceive that."

"Believe it, without asking me to explain," answered Harley.

For he did not judge it necessary to say to Leonard, "I am high-born and wealthy—you a peasant's son, and living by your exertions. This woman is ambitious and distressed. She might have projects on me that would counteract mine on her. You she would but listen to, and receive, through the sentiments of good or of poetical that are in her—you she would have no interest to subjugate, no motive to ensnare."

"And now," said Harley, turning the subject, "I have another object in view. This foolish sage friend of ours, in his bewilderment and fears, has sought to save Violante from one rogue by promising her hand to a man who, unless my instincts deceive me, I suspect much disposed to be another. Sacrifice such exuberance of life and spirit to that bloodless heart, to that cold and earthward intellect ! By Heaven, it shall not be !"

"But whom can the exile possibly have seen of birth and fortunes to render him a fitting spouse for his daughter ? Whom, my lord, except yourself ?"

"Me !" exclaimed Harley, angrily, and changing colour. "I worthy of such a creature ? I—with my habits ! I—silken egotist that I am ! And you, a poet, to form such an estimate of one who might be the queen of a poet's dream !"

"My Lord, when we sate the other night round Riccabocca's hearth—when I heard her speak, and observed you listen, I said to myself, from such knowledge of human nature as comes, we know not how, to us poets—I said, 'Harley L'Estrange has looked long and wistfully on the heavens, and he now hears the murmur of the wings that can waft him towards them.' And then I sighed, for I thought how the world rules us all in spite of ourselves, and I said, 'What pity for both, that the exile's daughter is not the worldly equal of the peer's son!' And you too sighed, as I thus thought; and I fancied that, while you listened to the music of the wing, you felt the iron of the chain. But the exile's daughter *is* your equal in birth, and you are her equal in heart and soul."

"My poor Leonard, you rave," answered Harley, calmly. "And if Violante is not to be some young prince's bride, she should be some young poet's."

"Poet's! O, no!" said Leonard, with a gentle laugh. "Poets need repose where *they* love!"

Harley was struck by the answer, and mused over it in silence. "I comprehend," thought he; "it is a new light that dawns on me. What is needed by the man whose whole life is one strain after glory—whose soul sinks, in fatigue, to the companionship of earth—is not the love of a nature like his own. He is right—it is repose! While I!—it is true—boy that he is, his intuitions are wiser than all my experience! It *is* excitement—energy—elevation, that Love should bestow on me. But I have chosen; and, at least, with Helen, my life will be calm, and my hearth sacred. Let the rest sleep in the same grave as my youth."

"But," said Leonard, wishing kindly to arouse his noble friend from a reverie which he felt was mournful, though he did not divine its true cause—"but you have not yet told me the name of the Signora's suitor. May I know?"

"Probably one you never heard of. Randal Leslie—a placeman. You refused a place;—you were right."

"Randal Leslie? Heaven forbid!" cried Leonard, revealing his surprise at the name.

"Amen! But what do you know of him?"

Leonard related the story of Burley's pamphlet.

Harley seemed delighted to hear his suspicions of Randal confirmed. "The paltry pretender!—and yet I fancied that he might be formidable! However, we must dismiss him for the present;—we are approaching Madame di Negra's house. Prepare yourself, and remember your promise."

CHAPTER XIII.

SOME days have passed by. Leonard and Beatrice di Negra have already made friends. Harley is satisfied with his young friend's report. He himself has been actively occupied. He has sought, but hitherto in vain, all trace of Mrs. Bertram; he has put that investigation into the hands of his lawyer, and his lawyer has not been more fortunate than himself. Moreover, Harley has blazed forth again in the London world, and promises again *de faire fureur;* but he has always found time to spend some hours in the twenty-four at his father's house. He has continued much the same tone with Violante, and she begins to accustom herself to it, and reply saucily. His calm courtship to Helen flows on in silence. Leonard, too, has been a frequent guest at the Lansmeres: all welcome and like him there. Peschiera has not evinced any sign of the deadly machinations ascribed to him. He goes less into the drawing-room world; for in that world he meets Lord L'Estrange; and brilliant and handsome though Peschiera be, Lord L'Estrange, like Rob Roy Macgregor, is "on his native heath," and has the decided advantage over the foreigner. Peschiera, however, shines in the clubs, and plays high. Still scarcely an evening passes in which he and Baron Levy do not meet.

Audley Egerton has been intensely occupied with affairs. Only seen once by Harley. Harley then was about to deliver himself of his sentiments respecting Randal Leslie, and to communicate the story of Burley and the pamphlet. Egerton stopped him short.

"My dear Harley, don't try to set me against this young man. I wish to hear nothing in his disfavour. In the first place, it would not alter the line of conduct I mean to adopt with regard to him. He is my wife's kinsman; I charged myself with his career, as a wish of hers, and therefore as a duty to myself. In attaching him so young to my own fate, I drew him necessarily away from the professions in which his industry and talents (for he has both in no common degree) would have secured his fortunes; therefore, be he bad, be he good, I shall try to provide for him as I best can; and, moreover, cold as I am to him, and worldly though perhaps he be, I have somehow or other conceived an interest in him—a liking to him. He has been under my roof, he is dependent on me; he has been docile and prudent, and I am a lone childless man; therefore, spare him, since in so doing you spare me; and ah, Harley, I have so many cares on me *now,* that—"

"O, say no more, my dear, dear Audley," cried the generous friend; "how little people know you!"

Audley's hand trembled. Certainly his nerves began to show wear and tear.

Meanwhile, the object of this dialogue—the type of perverted intellect—of mind without heart—of knowledge which had no aim but power—was in a state of anxious perturbed gloom. He did not know whether wholly to believe Levy's assurance of his patron's ruin. He could not believe it when he saw that great house in Grosvenor Square, its hall crowded with lacqueys, its sideboard blazing with plate; when no dun was ever seen in the antechamber; when not a tradesman was ever known to call twice for a bill. He hinted to Levy the doubts all these phenomena suggested to him; but the Baron only smiled ominously, and said,—

"True, the tradesmen are always paid; but the *how* is the question! Randal, *mon cher*, you are too innocent. I have but two pieces of advice to suggest, in the shape of two proverbs— 'Wise rats run from a falling house,' and, 'Make hay while the sun shines.' Apropos, Mr. Avenel likes you greatly, and has been talking of the borough of Lansmere for you. He has contrived to get together a great interest there. Make much of him."

Randal had indeed been to Mrs. Avenel's *soirée dansante*, and called twice and found her at home, and been very bland and civil, and admired the children. She had two, a boy and a girl, very like their father, with open faces as bold as brass. And as all this had won Mrs. Avenel's good graces, so it had propitiated her husband's. Avenel was shrewd enough to see how clever Randal was. He called him "smart," and said "he would have got on in America," which was the highest praise Dick Avenel ever accorded to any man. But Dick himself looked a little careworn; and this was the first year in which he had murmured at the bills of his wife's dressmaker, and said with an oath, that "there was such a thing as going *too* much ahead."

Randal had visited Dr. Riccabocca, and found Violante flown. True to his promise to Harley, the Italian refused to say where, and suggested, as was agreed, that for the present it would be more prudent if Randal suspended his visits to himself. Leslie, not liking this proposition, attempted to make himself still necessary, by working on Riccabocca's fears as to that espionage on his retreat, which had been among the reasons that had hurried the sage into offering Randal Violante's hand. But Riccabocca had already learned that the fancied spy was but his neighbour Leonard; and, without so saying, he cleverly contrived to make the supposition of such espionage an additional reason for the cessation of Leslie's visits. Randal then, in his own artful, quiet, roundabout way, had sought to find out if any communication had passed between L'Estrange and Riccabocca. Brooding over Harley's words to him, he suspected there had been such communication, with his usual penetrating astuteness. Riccabocca, here, was less on his guard, and rather parried the sidelong questions than denied their inferences.

Randal began already to surmise the truth. Where was it likely Violante should go but to the Lansmeres? This confirmed his idea of Harley's pretensions to her hand. With such a rival what chance had he? Randal never doubted for a moment that the pupil of Machiavelli would "throw him over," if such an alliance to his daughter really presented itself. The schemer at once discarded from his projects all further aim on Violante; either she would be poor, and he would not have her; or she would be rich, and her father would give her to another. As his heart had never been touched by the fair Italian, so the moment her inheritance became more doubtful, it gave him no pang to lose her; but he did feel very sore and resentful at the thought of being supplanted by Lord L'Estrange,—the man who had insulted him.

Neither, as yet, had Randal made any way in his designs on Frank. For several days Madame di Negra had not been at home either to himself or young Hazeldean; and Frank, though very unhappy, was piqued and angry; and Randal suspected, and suspected, and suspected, he knew not exactly what, but that the devil was not so kind to him there as that father of lies ought to have been to a son so dutiful. Yet, with all these discouragements, there was in Randal Leslie so dogged and determined a conviction of his own success—there was so great a tenacity of purpose under obstacles, and so vigilant an eye upon all chances that could be turned to his favour, that he never once abandoned hope, nor did more than change the details in his main schemes. Out of calculations apparently the most far-fetched and improbable, he had constructed a patient policy, to which he obstinately clung. How far his reasonings and patience served to his ends, remains yet to be seen. But could our contempt for the baseness of Randal himself be separated from the faculties which he elaborately degraded to the service of that baseness, one might allow that there was something one could scarcely despise in this still self-reliance, this inflexible resolve. Had such qualities, aided as they were by abilities of no ordinary acuteness, been applied to objects commonly honest, one would have backed Randal Leslie against any fifty picked prize-men from the colleges. But there are judges of weight and metal

who do that now, especially Baron Levy, who says to himself as he
eyes that pale face all intellect, and that spare form all nerve, "This
is a man who must make way in life ; he is worth helping."

By the words "worth helping," Baron Levy meant "worth
getting into my power, that he may help me."

CHAPTER XIV.

BUT Parliament had met. Events that belong to history
had contributed yet more to weaken the administration.
Randal Leslie's interest became absorbed in politics ; for
the stake to him was his whole political career. Should
Audley lose office, and for good, Audley could aid him no more ;
but to abandon his patron, as Levy recommended, and pin himself,
in the hope of a seat in Parliament, to a stranger—an obscure
stranger, like Dick Avenel—that was a policy not to be adopted at
a breath. Meanwhile, almost every night, when the House met,
that pale face and spare form, which Levy so identified with shrewdness and energy, might be seen amongst the benches appropriated
to those more select strangers who obtain the Speaker's order of
admission. There, Randal heard the great men of that day, and
with the half-contemptuous surprise at their fame, which is common
enough amongst clever, well-educated young men, who know not
what it is to speak in the House of Commons. He heard much
slovenly English, much trite reasoning, some eloquent thoughts, and
close argument, often delivered in a jerking tone of voice (popularly
called the Parliamentary *twang*), and often accompanied by gesticula-
tions that would have shocked the manager of a provincial theatre.
He thought how much better than these great dons (with but one
or two exceptions) he himself could speak—with what more refined
logic—with what more polished periods—how much more like
Cicero and Burke ! Very probably he might have so spoken, and
for that very reason have made that deadest of all dead failures—a
pretentious imitation of Burke and Cicero. One thing, however,
he was obliged to own, viz., that in a popular representative assembly it is not precisely knowledge which is power, or if knowledge,
it is but the knowledge of that particular assembly, and what will
best take with it ;—passion, invective, sarcasm, bold declamation,
shrewd common sense, the readiness so rarely found in a very profound mind—he owned that all these were the qualities that told ;
when a man who exhibited nothing but "knowledge," in the

ordinary sense of the word, stood an imminent chance of being coughed down.

There at his left—last but one in the row of the ministerial chiefs —Randal watched Audley Egerton, his arms folded on his breast, his hat drawn over his brows, his eyes fixed with steady courage on whatever speaker in the Opposition held possession of the floor. And twice Randal heard Egerton speak, and marvelled much at the effect that minister produced. For of those qualities enumerated above, and which Randal had observed to be most sure of success, Audley Egerton only exhibited to a marked degree—the common sense and the readiness. And yet, though but little applauded by noisy cheers, no speaker seemed more to satisfy friends, and command respect from foes. The true secret was this, which Randal might well not divine, since that young person, despite his ancient birth, his Eton rearing, and his refined air, was not one of Nature's gentlemen;—the true secret was, that Audley Egerton moved, looked, and spoke like a thorough gentleman of England. A gentleman of more than average talents and of long experience, speaking his sincere opinions—not a rhetorician aiming at effect. Moreover, Egerton was a consummate man of the world. He said, with nervous simplicity, what his party desired to be said, and put what his opponents felt to be the strong points of the case. Calm and decorous, yet spirited and energetic, with little variety of tone, and action subdued and rare, but yet signalized by earnest vigour, Audley Egerton impressed the understanding of the dullest, and pleased the taste of the most fastidious.

But once, when allusions were made to a certain popular question, on which the premier had announced his resolution to refuse all concession, and on the expediency of which it was announced that the cabinet was nevertheless divided—and when such allusions were coupled with direct appeals to Mr. Egerton, as "the enlightened member of a great commercial constituency," and with a flattering doubt that "that Right Honourable gentleman, member for that great city, identified with the cause of the Burgher class, could be so far behind the spirit of the age as his official chief,"—Randal observed that Egerton drew his hat still more closely over his brows, and turned to whisper with one of his colleagues. He could not be *got up* to speak.

That evening Randal walked home with Egerton, and intimated his surprise that the minister had declined what seemed to him a good occasion for one of those brief, weighty replies by which Audley was chiefly distinguished—an occasion to which he had been loudly invited by the "hears" of the House.

"Leslie," answered the statesman, briefly, "I owe all my success in Parliament to this rule—I have never spoken against my convictions. I intend to abide by it to the last."

"But if the question at issue comes before the House, you will vote against it?"

"Certainly, I vote as a member of the cabinet. But since I am not leader and mouthpiece of the party, I retain as an individual the privilege to speak or keep silence."

"Ah, my dear Mr. Egerton," exclaimed Randal, "forgive me. But this question, right or wrong, has got such hold of the public mind. So little, if conceded in time, would give content; and it is so clear (if I may judge by the talk I hear everywhere I go) that by refusing all concessions, the Government must fall, that I wish—"

"So do I wish," interrupted Egerton, with a gloomy, impatient sigh—"so do I wish! But what avails it? If my advice had been taken but three weeks ago—now it is too late—we could have doubled the rock; we refused, we must split upon it."

This speech was so unlike the discreet and reserved minister, that Randal gathered courage to proceed with an idea that had occurred to his own sagacity. And before I state it, I must add that Egerton had of late shown much more personal kindness to his *protégé;* whether his spirits were broken, or that at last, close and compact as his nature of bronze was, he felt the imperious want to groan aloud in some loving ear, the stern Audley seemed tamed and softened. So Randal went on.

"May I say what I have heard expressed with regard to you and your position—in the streets—in the clubs?"

"Yes, it is in the streets and the clubs that statesmen should go to school. Say on."

"Well, then, I have heard it made a matter of wonder why you, and one or two others I will not name, do not at once retire from the ministry, and on the avowed ground that you side with the public feeling on this irresistible question."

"Eh!"

"It is clear that in so doing you would become the most popular man in the country—clear that you would be summoned back to power on the shoulders of the people. No new cabinet could be formed without you, and your station in it would perhaps be higher, for life, than that which you may now retain but for a few weeks longer. Has not this ever occurred to you?"

"Never," said Audley, with dry composure.

Amazed at such obtuseness, Randal exclaimed, "Is it possible!

And, yet, forgive me if I say I think you are ambitious, and love power."

"No man more ambitious; and if by power you mean office, it has grown the habit of my life, and I shall not know what to do without it."

"And how, then, has what seems to me so obvious never occurred to you?"

"Because you are young, and therefore I forgive you; but not the gossips who could wonder why Audley Egerton refused to betray the friends of his whole career, and to profit by the treason."

"But one should love one's country before a party."

"No doubt of that; and the first interest of a country is the honour of its public men."

"But men may leave their party without dishonour!"

"Who doubts that? Do you suppose that if I were an ordinary independent member of Parliament, loaded with no obligations, charged with no trust, I could hesitate for a moment what course to pursue? Oh, that I were but the member for * * *! Oh, that I had the full right to be a free agent! But if a member of a cabinet, a chief in whom thousands confide, because he is outvoted in a council of his colleagues, suddenly retires, and by so doing breaks up the whole party whose confidence he has enjoyed, whose rewards he has reaped, to whom he owes the very position which he employs to their ruin—own that though his choice may be honest, it is one which requires all the consolations of conscience."

"But you will have those consolations. And," added Randal, energetically, "the gain to your career will be so immense!"

"That is precisely what it cannot be," answered Egerton, gloomily. "I grant that I may, if I choose, resign office with the present Government, and so at once destroy that Government; for my resignation on such ground would suffice to do it. I grant this; but for that very reason I could not the next day take office with another administration. I could not accept wages for desertion. No gentleman could! and therefore—" Audley stopped short, and buttoned his coat over his broad breast. The action was insignificant; it said that the man's mind was made up.

In fact, whether Audley Egerton was right or wrong in his theory depends upon much subtler, and perhaps loftier views in the casuistry of political duties, than it was in his character to take. And I guard myself from saying anything in praise or disfavour of his notions, or implying that he is a fit or unfit example in a parallel case. I am but describing the man as he was, and as a man like him would inevitably be, under the influences in which he lived, and in that peculiar world of which he was so emphatically a member. "*Ce n'est pas moi qui parle, c'est Marc Aurèle.*"

He speaks, not I.

Randal had no time for further discussion. They now reached Egerton's house, and the minister, taking the chamber candlestick from his servant's hand, nodded a silent good-night to Leslie, and with a jaded look retired to his room.

CHAPTER XV.

BUT not on the threatened question was that eventful campaign of Party decided. The Government fell less in battle than skirmish. It was one fatal Monday—a dull question of finance and figures. Prosy and few were the speakers. All the Government silent, save the Chancellor of the Exchequer, and another business-like personage connected with the Board of Trade, whom the House would hardly condescend to hear. The House was in no mood to think of facts and figures. Early in the evening, between nine and ten, the Speaker's sonorous voice sounded, "Strangers must withdraw!" And Randal, anxious and foreboding, descended from his seat and went out of the fatal doors. He turned to take a last glance at Audley Egerton. The whipper-in was whispering to Audley; and the minister pushed back his hat from his brows, and glanced round the House, and up into the galleries, as if to calculate rapidly the relative numbers of the two armies in the field; then he smiled bitterly, and threw himself back into his seat. That smile long haunted Leslie.

Amongst the strangers thus banished with Randal, while the division was being taken, were many young men, like himself, connected with the administration—some by blood, some by place. Hearts beat loud in the swarming lobbies. Ominous mournful whispers were exchanged. "They say the Government will have a majority of ten." "No; I hear they will certainly be beaten." "H—— says by fifty." "I don't believe it," said a Lord of the Bedchamber; "it is impossible. I left five Government members dining at the 'Travellers.'" "No one thought the division would be so early." "A trick of the Whigs—shameful." "Wonder some one was not set up to talk for time; very odd P—— did not speak; however, he is so cursedly rich, he does not care whether he is out or in." "Yes; and Audley Egerton too, just such another: glad, no doubt, to be set free to look after his property; very different tactics if we had men to whom office was as necessary as it is—to me!" said a candid young placeman. Suddenly the silent Leslie felt a friendly grasp on his arm. He turned and saw Levy.

"Did I not tell you?" said the Baron, with an exulting smile.

"You are sure, then, that the Government will be outvoted?"

"I spent the morning in going over the list of members with a parliamentary client of mine, who knows them all as a shepherd does his sheep. Majority for the Opposition at least twenty-five."

"And in that case must the Government resign, sir?" asked the candid young placeman, who had been listening to the smart well-dressed Baron, "his soul planted in his ears."

"Of course, sir," replied the Baron, blandly, and offering his snuff-box, (true Louis Quinze, with a miniature of Madame de Pompadour, set in pearls.) "You are a friend to the present ministers? You could not wish them to be mean enough to stay in?" Randal drew aside the Baron.

"If Audley's affairs are as you state, what can he do?"

"I shall ask him that question to-morrow," answered the Baron, with a look of visible hate. "And I have come here just to see how he bears the prospect before him."

"You will not discover that in his face. And those absurd scruples of his! If he had but gone out in time—to come in again with the New Men!"

"Oh, of course, our Right Honourable is too punctilious for that!" answered the Baron, sneering.

Suddenly the doors opened—in rushed the breathless expectants. "What are the numbers? What is the division?"

"Majority against ministers," said a member of Opposition, peeling an orange, "twenty-nine."

The Baron, too, had a Speaker's order; and he came into the House with Randal, and sate by his side. But, to their disgust, some member was talking about the other motions before the House.

"What! has nothing been said as to the division?" asked the Baron of a young county member, who was talking to some non-parliamentary friend in the bench before Levy. The county member was one of the Baron's pet eldest sons—had dined often with Levy —was under "obligations" to him. The young legislator looked very much ashamed of Levy's friendly pat on his shoulder, and answered, hurriedly, "O yes; H—— asked, 'if, after such an expression of the House, it was the intention of ministers to retain their places, and carry on the business of the Government?'"

"Just like H——! Very inquisitive mind! And what was the answer he got?"

"None," said the county member; and returned in haste to his proper seat in the body of the House.

"There comes Egerton," said the Baron. And, indeed, as most of the members were now leaving the House, to talk over affairs at clubs or in saloons, and spread through town the great tidings, Audley Egerton's tall head was seen towering above the rest. And Levy turned away disappointed. For not only was the minister's handsome face, though pale, serene and cheerful, but there was an obvious courtesy, a marked respect, in the mode in which that assembly—heated though it was—made way for the fallen minister as he passed through the jostling crowd. And the frank urbane nobleman, who afterwards, from the force, not of talent but of character, became the leader in that House, pressed the hand of his old opponent, as they met in the throng near the doors, and said aloud, "I shall not be a proud man if ever I live to have office; but I shall be proud if ever I leave it with as little to be said against me as your bitterest opponents can say against you, Egerton."

"I wonder," exclaimed the Baron aloud, and leaning over the partition that divided him from the throng below, so that his voice reached Egerton—and there was a cry from formal, indignant members, "Order in the strangers' gallery!" "I wonder what Lord L'Estrange will say!"

Audley lifted his dark brows, surveyed the Baron for an instant with flashing eyes, then walked down the narrow defile between the last benches, and vanished from the scene in which, alas! so few of the most admired performers leave more than an actor's short-lived name!

CHAPTER XVI.

BARON LEVY did not execute his threat of calling on Egerton the next morning. Perhaps he shrank from again meeting the flash of those indignant eyes. And indeed Egerton was too busied all the forenoon to see any one not upon public affairs, except Harley, who hastened to console or cheer him. When the House met, it was announced that the ministers had resigned, only holding their offices till their successors were appointed. But already there was some reaction in their favour; and when it became generally known that the new administration was to be formed of men, few indeed of whom had ever before held office, the common superstition in the public mind that government is like a trade, in which a regular apprenticeship must be served, began to prevail; and the talk at the clubs was, that the new men could not stand; that the former ministry, with some modification, would be back in a month. Perhaps that too might be a reason why Baron Levy thought it prudent not prematurely to offer vindictive condolences to Mr. Egerton. Randal spent part of his morning in inquiries, as to what gentlemen in his situation meant to do with regard to their places; he heard with great satisfaction that very few intended to volunteer retirement from their desks. As Randal himself had observed to Egerton, "their country before their party!"

Randal's place was of great moment to him; its duties were easy, its salary amply sufficient for his wants, and defrayed such expenses as were bestowed on the education of Oliver and his sister. For I am bound to do justice to this young man—indifferent as he was towards his species in general, the ties of family were strong with him; and he stinted himself in many temptations most alluring to his age, in the endeavour to raise the dull honest Oliver and the loose-haired pretty Juliet somewhat more to his own level of culture and refinement. Men essentially griping and unscrupulous, often do make the care for their family an apology for their sins against the world. Even Richard III., if the chroniclers are to be trusted, excused the murder of his nephews by his passionate affection for his son. With the loss of that place, Randal lost all means of support, save what Audley could give him; and if Audley were in truth ruined? Moreover, Randal had already established at the office a reputation for ability and industry. It was a career in which, if he abstained from party politics, he might rise to a fair station and to a considerable income. Therefore, much contented with what he learned as to the general determination of his fellow officials, a determination warranted by ordinary precedent in such cases, Randal dined at a club with great relish, and much Christian resignation for the reverse of his patron, and then walked to Grosvenor Square, on the chance of finding Audley within. Learning that he was so, from the porter who opened the door, Randal entered the library. Three gentlemen were seated there with Egerton: one of the three was Lord L'Estrange; the other two were members of the really defunct, though nominally still existing, Government. He was about to withdraw from intruding on this conclave, when Egerton said to him gently, "Come in, Leslie; I was just speaking about yourself."

"About me, sir?"

"Yes; about you and the place you hold. I had asked Sir —— (pointing to a fellow minister) whether I might not, with propriety, request your chief to leave some note of his opinion of your talents, which I know is high, and which might serve you with his successor."

"Oh, sir, at such a time to think of me!" exclaimed Randal, and he was genuinely touched.

"But," resumed Audley, with his usual dryness, "Sir ——, to my surprise, thinks that it would better become you that you should resign. Unless his reasons, which he has not yet stated, are very strong, such would not be my advice."

"My reasons," said Sir ——, with official formality, "are simply these: I have a nephew in a similar situation; he will resign as a matter of course. Every one in the public offices whose relations and near connections hold high appointments in the Government, will do so. I do not think Mr. Leslie will like to feel himself a solitary exception."

"Mr. Leslie is no relation of mine—not even a near connection," answered Egerton.

"But his name is so associated with your own—he has resided so long in your house—is so well known in society, (and don't think I compliment when I add, that we hope so well of him,) that I can't think it worth his while to keep this paltry place, which incapacitates him too from a seat in Parliament."

Sir —— was one of those terribly rich men, to whom all considerations of mere bread and cheese are paltry. But I must add that he supposed Egerton to be still wealthier than himself, and sure to provide handsomely for Randal, whom Sir —— rather liked than not; and for Randal's own sake, Sir —— thought it would lower him in the estimation of Egerton himself, despite that gentleman's advocacy, if he did not follow the example of his avowed and notorious patron.

"You see, Leslie," said Egerton, checking Randal's meditated reply, "that nothing can be said against your honour if you stay where you are; it is a mere question of expediency; I will judge that for you; keep your place."

Unhappily the other member of the Government, who had hitherto been silent, was a literary man. Unhappily, while this talk had proceeded, he had placed his hand upon Randal Leslie's celebrated pamphlet, which lay on the library table; and, turning over the leaves, the whole spirit and matter of that masterly composition in defence of the administration (a composition steeped in all the essence of party) recurred to his too faithful recollection. He, too, liked Randal ; he did more—he admired the author of that striking and effective pamphlet. And therefore, rousing himself from the sublime indifference he had before felt for the fate of a subaltern, he said, with a bland and complimentary smile, "No ; the writer of this most able publication is no ordinary placeman. His opinions here are too vigorously stated ; this fine irony on the very person who in all probability will be the chief in his office, has excited too lively an attention, to allow him the *sedet eternumque sedebit* on an official stool. Ha, ha! this is so good! Read it, L'Estrange. What say you?"

Harley glanced over the page pointed out to him. The original was in one of Burley's broad, coarse, but telling burlesques, strained fine through Randal's more polished satire. It was capital. Harley smiled, and lifted his eyes to Randal. The unlucky plagiarist's face was flushed—the beads stood on his brow. Harley was a good hater ; he loved too warmly not to err on the opposite side ; but he was one of those men who forget hate when its object is distressed and humbled. He put down the pamphlet and said, "I am no politician ; but Egerton is so well known to be fastidious and over-scrupulous in all points of official etiquette, that Mr. Leslie cannot follow a safer counsellor."

"Read that yourself, Egerton," said Sir —— ; and he pushed the pamphlet to Audley.

Now Egerton had a dim recollection that that pamphlet was unlucky ; but he had skimmed over its contents hastily, and at that moment had forgotten all about it. He took up the too famous work with a reluctant hand, but he read attentively the passages pointed out to him, and then said gravely and sadly—

"Mr. Leslie, I retract my advice. I believe Sir —— is right ; that the nobleman here so keenly satirized will be the chief in your office. I doubt whether he will not compel your dismissal ; at all events, he could scarcely be expected to promote your advancement. Under the circumstances, I fear you have no option as a ——" Egerton paused a moment, and, with a sigh that seemed to settle the question, concluded with—"as a gentleman."

Never did Jack Cade, never did Wat Tyler, feel a more deadly hate to that word "gentleman," than the well-born Leslie felt then ; but he bowed his head, and answered with his usual presence of mind—

"You utter my own sentiment."

"You think we are right, Harley?" asked Egerton, with an irresolution that surprised all present.

"I think," answered Harley, with a compassion for Randal that was almost over generous, and yet with an *équivoque* on the words, despite the compassion—"I think whoever has served Audley Egerton, never yet has been a loser by it ; and if Mr. Leslie wrote this pamphlet, he must have well served Audley Egerton. If he undergoes the penalty, we may safely trust to Egerton for the compensation."

"My compensation has long since been made," answered Randal, with grace ; "and that Mr. Egerton could thus have cared for my fortunes, at an hour so occupied, is a thought of pride which—"

"Enough, Leslie! enough!" interrupted Egerton, rising and pressing his *protégé's* hand. "See me before you go to bed."

Then the two other ministers rose also and shook hands with Leslie, and told him he had done the right thing, and that they hoped soon to see him in Parliament ; and hinted, smilingly, that the next administration did not promise to be very long-lived ; and one asked him to dinner, and the other to spend a week at his country seat. And amidst these congratulations at the stroke that left him penniless, the distinguished pamphleteer left the room. How he cursed big John Burley !

CHAPTER XVII.

IT was past midnight when Audley Egerton summoned Randal. The statesman was then alone, seated before his great desk, with its manifold compartments, and engaged on the task of transferring various papers and letters, some to the waste-basket, some to the flames, some to two great iron chests with patent locks, that stood, open-mouthed, at his feet. Strong, stern, and grim, looked those iron chests, silently receiving the relics of power departed ; strong, stern, and grim as the grave. Audley lifted his eyes at Randal's entrance, signed to him to take a chair, continued his task for a few moments, and then turning round, as if by an effort, he plucked himself from his master-passion—Public Life,—he said, with deliberate tones—

"I know not, Randal Leslie, whether you thought me needlessly cautious, or wantonly unkind, when I told you never to expect from me more than such advance to your career as my then position could effect—never to expect from my liberality in life, nor from my testament in death—an addition to your private fortunes. I see by your gesture what would be your reply, and I thank you for it. I now tell you, as yet in confidence, though before long it can be no secret to the world, that my pecuniary affairs have been so neglected by me in my devotion to those of the state, that I am somewhat like the man who portioned out his capital at so much a day, calculating to live just long enough to make it last. Unfortunately he lived too long." Audley smiled—but the smile was cold as a sunbeam upon ice—and went on with the same firm, unfaltering accents ! "The prospects that face me I am prepared for ; they do not take me by surprise. I knew long since how this would end, if I survived the loss of office. I knew it before you came to me, and therefore I spoke to you as I did, judging it manful and right to guard you against hopes which you might otherwise have naturally entertained. On this head, I need say no more. It may excite your surprise, possibly your blame, that I, esteemed methodical and practical enough in the affairs of the state, should be so imprudent as to my own."

"Oh, sir ! you owe no account to me."

"To you, at least, as much as to any one. I am a solitary man ; my few relations need nothing from me. I had a right to spend what I possessed as I pleased ; and if I have spent it recklessly as regards myself, I have not spent it ill in its effect on others. It has been my object for many years to have no *Private Life*—to dispense with its sorrows, joys, affections ; and as to its duties, they did not exist for me.—I have said." Mechanically, as he ended, the minister's hand closed the lid of one of the iron boxes, and on the closed lid he rested his firm foot. "But now," he resumed, "I have failed to advance your career. True, I warned you that you drew into a lottery ; but you had more chance of a prize than a blank. A blank, however, it has turned out, and the question becomes grave—What are you to do ?"

Here, seeing that Egerton came to a full pause, Randal answered readily—

"Still, sir, to go by your advice."

"My advice," said Audley, with a softened look, "would perhaps be rude and unpalatable. I would rather place before you an option. On the one hand, recommence life again. I told you that I would keep your name on your college books. You can return—you can take your degree—after that, you can go to the bar—you have just the talents calculated to succeed in that profession. Success will be slow, it is true ; but, with perseverance it will be sure. And, believe me, Leslie, Ambition is only sweet while it is but the loftier name for Hope. Who would care for a fox's brush if it had not been rendered a prize by the excitement of the chase ?"

"Oxford—again ! It is a long step back in life," said Randal, drearily, and little heeding Egerton's unusual indulgence of illustration. "A long step back—and to what? To a profession in which one never begins to rise till one's hair is gray? Besides, how live in the meanwhile?"

"Do not let that thought disturb you. The modest income that suffices for a student at the bar, I trust, at least, to insure you from the wrecks of my fortune."

"Ah, sir, I would not burthen you farther. What right have I to such kindness, save my name of Leslie?" And in spite of himself, as Randal concluded, a tone of bitterness, that betrayed reproach, broke forth. Egerton was too much the man of the world not to comprehend the reproach, and not to pardon it.

"Certainly," he answered, calmly, "as a Leslie you are entitled to my consideration, and would have been entitled perhaps to more, had I not so explicitly warned you to the contrary. But the bar does not seem to please you?"

"What is the alternative, sir? Let me decide when I hear it," answered Randal, sullenly. He began to lose respect for the man who owned he could do so little for him, and who evidently recommended him to shift for himself.

If one could have pierced into Egerton's gloomy heart as he noted the young man's change of tone, it may be a doubt whether one would have seen there, pain or pleasure—pain, for merely from the force of habit he had begun to like Randal—or pleasure, at the thought that he might have reason to withdraw that liking. So lone and stoical had grown the man, who had made it his object to have no private life! Revealing, however, neither pleasure nor pain, but with the composed calmness of a judge upon the bench, Egerton replied—

"The alternative is, to continue in the course you have begun, and still to rely on me."

"Sir, my dear Mr. Egerton," exclaimed Randal, regaining all his usual tenderness of look and voice, "rely on you! But that is all I ask! Only—"

"Only, you would say, I am going out of power, and you don't see the chance of my return?"

"I did not mean that."

"Permit me to suppose that you did: very true; but the party I belong to is as sure of return as the pendulum of that clock is sure to obey the mechanism that moves it from left to right. Our successors profess to come in upon a popular question. All administrations who do that are necessarily short-lived. Either they do not go far enough to please present supporters, or they go so far as to arm new enemies in the rivals who outbid them with the people. 'Tis the history of all revolutions, and of all reforms. Our own administration in reality is destroyed for having passed what was called a popular measure a year ago, which lost us half our friends, and refusing to propose another popular measure this year, in the which we are outstripped by the men who halloo'd us on to the last. Therefore, whatever our successors do, we shall, by the law of reaction, have another experiment of power afforded to ourselves. It is but a question of time ; you can wait for it ; whether I can is uncertain. But if I die before that day arrives, I have influence enough still left with those who will come in, to obtain a promise of a better provision for you than that which you have lost. The promises of public men are proverbially uncertain. But I shall entrust your cause to a man who never failed a friend, and whose rank will enable him to see that justice is done to you—I speak of Lord L'Estrange."

"Oh, not him ; he is unjust to me ; he dislikes me ; he—"

"May dislike you (he has his whims), but he loves me ; and though for no other human being but you would I ask Harley L'Estrange a favour, yet for *you* I will," said Egerton, betraying, for the first time in that dialogue, a visible emotion—"for you, a Leslie, a kinsman, however remote, to the wife from whom I received my fortune ! And despite all my cautions, it is possible that in wasting that fortune I may have wronged you. Enough : You have now before you the two options, much as you had at first ; but you have at present more experience to aid you in your choice. You are a man, and with more brains than most men ; think over it well, and decide for yourself. Now to bed, and postpone thought till the morrow. Poor Randal, you look pale ! "

Audley, as he said the last words, put his hand on Randal's shoulder, almost with a father's gentleness ; and then suddenly drawing himself up, as the hard inflexible expression, stamped on that face by years, returned, he moved away and resettled to Public Life and the iron box.

CHAPTER XVIII.

EARLY the next day Randal Leslie was in the luxurious business-room of Baron Levy. How unlike the cold Doric simplicity of the statesman's library ! Axminster carpets, three inches thick, *portières à la Française* before the doors ; Parisian bronzes on the chimney-piece ; and all the receptacles that lined the room, and contained title-deeds, and post-obits, and bills, and promises to pay, and lawyer-like japan boxes, with many a noble name written thereon in large white capitals—

"making ruin pompous"—all these sepulchres of departed patrimonies veneered in rosewood that gleamed with French polish, and blazed with ormolu.   There was a coquetry, an air of *petit maître*, so diffused over the whole room, that you could not for the life of you recollect you were with an usurer!   Plutus wore the aspect of his enemy Cupid; and how realize your idea of Harpagon in that Baron, with his easy French "*Mon cher*," and his white, warm hands that pressed yours so genially, and his dress so exquisite, even at the earliest morn?   No man ever yet saw that Baron in a dressing-gown and slippers!   As one fancies some feudal baron of old (not half so terrible) everlastingly clad in mail, so all one's notions of this grand marauder of civilization were inseparably associated with varnished boots and a camellia in the button-hole.

"And this is all that he does for you!" cried the Baron, pressing together the points of his ten taper fingers.   "Had he but let you conclude your career at Oxford, I have heard enough of your scholarship to know that you would have taken high honours—been secure of a fellowship—have betaken yourself with content to a slow and laborious profession, and prepared yourself to die on the woolsack."

"He proposes to me now to return to Oxford," said Randal. "It is not too late!"

"Yes it is," said the Baron.   "Neither individuals nor nations ever go back of their own accord.   There must be an earthquake before a river recedes to its source."

"You speak well," answered Randal, "and I cannot gainsay you.   But now!"

"Ah, the *now* is the grand question in life—the *then* is obsolete, gone by—out of fashion; and *now, mon cher*, you come to ask my advice?"

"No, Baron, I come to ask your explanation."

"Of what?"

"I want to know why you spoke to me of Mr. Egerton's ruin; why you spoke to me of the lands to be sold by Mr. Thornhill; and why you spoke to me of Count Peschiera.   You touched on each of those points within ten minutes—you omitted to indicate what link can connect them?"

"By Jove," said the Baron, rising, and with more admiration in his face than you could have conceived that face, so smiling and so cynical, could exhibit—"by Jove, Randal Leslie, but your shrewdness is wonderful.   You really are the first young man of your day; and I will 'help you,' as I helped Audley Egerton.   Perhaps you will be more grateful."

Randal thought of Egerton's ruin.   The parallel implied by the Baron did not suggest to him the rare enthusiasm of gratitude.

However, he merely said, "Pray, proceed—I listen to you with interest."

"As for politics, then," said the Baron, "we will discuss that topic later. I am waiting myself to see how these new men get on. The first consideration is for your private fortunes. You should buy this ancient Leslie property—Rood and Dulmansberry—only £20,000 down; the rest may remain on mortgage for ever—or at least till I find you a rich wife—as in fact I did for Egerton. Thornhill wants the £20,000 now—wants them very much."

"And where," said Randal, with an iron smile, "are the £20,000 you ascribe to me to come from?"

"Ten thousand shall come to you the day Count Peschiera marries the daughter of his kinsman with your help and aid—the remaining ten thousand I will lend you. No scruple—I shall hazard nothing —the estates will bear that additional burden. What say you— shall it be so?"

"Ten thousand pounds from Count Peschiera!" said Randal, breathing hard. "You cannot be serious? Such a sum—for what? —for a mere piece of information? How otherwise can I aid him? There must be trick and deception intended here."

"My dear fellow," answered Levy, "I will give you a hint. There is such a thing in life as being over-suspicious. If you have a fault, it is that. The information you allude to is, of course, the first assistance you are to give. Perhaps more may be needed— perhaps not. Of that you will judge yourself, since the £10,000 are contingent on the marriage aforesaid."

"Over-suspicious or not," answered Randal, "the amount of the sum is too improbable, and the security too bad, for me to listen to this proposition, even if I could descend to—"

"Stop, *mon cher.* Business first, scruples afterwards. The security too bad—what security?"

"The word of Count di Peschiera."

"He has nothing to do with it—he need know nothing about it. 'Tis my word you doubt. I am your security."

Randal thought of that dry witticism in Gibbon, "Abu Rafe says he will be witness for this fact, but who will be witness for Abu Rafe?" but he remained silent, only fixing on Levy those dark observant eyes, with their contracted, wary pupils.

"The fact is simply this," resumed Levy: "Count di Peschiera has promised to pay his sister a dowry of £20,000, in case he has the money to spare. He can only have it to spare by the marriage we are discussing. On my part, as I manage his affairs in England for him, I have promised that, for the said sum of £20,000, I will guarantee the expenses in the way of that marriage, and settle with

Madame di Negra. Now, though Peschiera is a very liberal, warm-hearted fellow, I don't say that he would have named so large a sum for his sister's dowry, if in strict truth he did not owe it to her. It is the amount of her own fortune, which, by some arrangements with her late husband, not exactly legal, he possessed himself of. If Madame di Negra went to law with him for it, she could get it back. I have explained this to him; and, in short, you now understand why the sum is thus assessed. But I have bought up Madame di Negra's debts. I have bought up young Hazeldean's (for we must make a match between these two a part of our arrangements). I shall present to Peschiera, and to these young persons, an account that will absorb the whole £20,000. That sum will come into my hands. If I settle the claims against them for half the money, which, making myself the sole creditor, I have the right to do, the moiety will remain. And if I choose to give it to you in return for the services which provide Peschiera with a princely fortune—discharge the debts of his sister—and secure her a husband in my promising young client, Mr. Hazeldean, that is my look-out—all parties are satisfied, and no one need ever be the wiser. The sum is large, no doubt; it answers to me to give it to you; does it answer to you to receive it?"

Randal was greatly agitated; but, vile as he was, and systematically as in thought he had brought himself to regard others merely as they could be made subservient to his own interest, still, with all who have not hardened themselves in actual crime, there is a wide distinction between the thought and the act; and though, in the exercise of ingenuity and cunning, he would have had few scruples in that moral swindling which is mildly called "outwitting another," yet thus nakedly and openly to accept a bribe for a deed of treachery towards the poor Italian who had so generously trusted him—he recoiled. He was nerving himself to refuse, when Levy, opening his pocket-book, glanced over the memoranda therein, and said, as to himself, "Rood Manor—Dulmansberry, sold to the Thornhills by Sir Gilbert Leslie, knight of the shire; estimated present net rental £2250 7s. 0d. It is the greatest bargain I ever knew. And with this estate in hand, and your talents, Leslie, I don't see why you should not rise higher than Audley Egerton. He was poorer than you once!"

The old Leslie lands—a positive stake in the country—the restoration of the fallen family; and on the other hand, either long drudgery at the bar,—a scanty allowance on Egerton's bounty—his sister wasting her youth at slovenly, dismal Rood—Oliver debased into a boor!—or a mendicant's dependence on the contemptuous pity of Harley L'Estrange—Harley who had refused his hand to

him—Harley, who perhaps would become the husband of Violante!
Rage seized him as these contrasting pictures rose before his view.
He walked to and fro in disorder, striving to recollect his thoughts,
and reduce himself from the passions of the human heart into the
mere mechanism of calculating intellect. "I cannot conceive,"
said he, abruptly, "why you should tempt me thus—what interest
it is to you!"

Baron Levy smiled, and put up his pocket-book. He saw from
that moment that the victory was gained.

"My dear boy," said he, with the most agreeable *bonhommie*,
"it is very natural that you should think a man would have a personal interest in whatever he does for another. I believe that view of
human nature is called utilitarian philosophy, and is much in fashion
at present. Let me try and explain to you. In this affair I shan't
injure myself. True, you will say, if I settle claims, which amount
to £20,000, for £10,000, I might put the surplus into my own
pocket instead of yours. Agreed. But I shall not get the £20,000,
nor repay myself Madame di Negra's debts, (whatever I may do as
to Hazeldean's;) unless the Count gets this heiress. You can help
in this. I want you; and I don't think I could get you by a less
offer than I make. I shall soon pay myself back the £10,000 if
the Count get hold of the lady and her fortune. Brief—I see my
way here to my own interests. Do you want more reasons—you
shall have them. I am now a very rich man. How have I become
so? Through attaching myself from the first to persons of expectations, whether from fortune or talent. `I have made connections in
society, and society has enriched me. I have still a passion for making
money. *Que voulez vous?* It is my profession, my hobby. It will
be useful to me in a thousand ways, to secure as a friend a young
man who will have influence with other young men, heirs to something better than Rood Hall. You may succeed in public life. A
man in public life may attain to the knowledge of state secrets that
are very profitable to one who dabbles a little in the Funds. We
can perhaps hereafter do business together that may put yourself in
a way of clearing off all mortgages on these estates—on the encumbered possession of which I shall soon congratulate you. You see
I am frank; 'tis the only way of coming to the point with so clever
a fellow as you. And now, since the less we rake up the mud in
a pond from which we have resolved to drink, the better, let us
dismiss all other thoughts but that of securing our end. Will you
tell Peschiera where the young lady is, or shall I? Better do it
yourself; reason enough for it, that he has confided to you his hope,
and asked you to help him; why should not you? Not a word
to him about our little arrangement; he need never know it. You

need never be troubled." Levy rang the bell : "Order my carriage round."

Randal made no objection. He was deathlike pale, but there was a sinister expression of firmness on his thin, bloodless lips.

"The next point," Levy resumed, "is to hasten the match between Frank and the fair widow. How does that stand ?"

"She will not see me, nor receive him."

"Oh, learn why ! And if you find on either side there is a hitch, just let me know ; I will soon remove it."

"Has Hazeldean consented to the post-obit ?"

"Not yet ; I have not pressed it ; I wait the right moment, if necessary."

"It will be necessary."

"Ah, you wish it. It shall be so."

Randal Leslie again paced the room, and after a silent self-commune came up close to the Baron, and said—

"Look you, sir, I am poor and ambitious ; you have tempted me at the right moment, and with the right inducement. I succumb. But what guarantee have I that this money will·be paid—these estates made mine upon the conditions stipulated ?"

"Before anything is settled," replied the Baron, "go and ask my character of any of our young friends, Borrowell, Spendquick— whom you please ; you will hear me abused, of course ; but they will all say this of me, that when I pass my word, I keep it. If I say, '*Mon cher*, you shall have the money,' a man·has it ; if I say, 'I renew your bill for six months,' it is renewed. 'Tis my way of doing business. In all cases my word is my bond. In this case, where no writing can pass between us, my only bond must be my word. Go, then, make your mind clear as to your security, and come here and dine at eight. We will call on Peschiera afterwards."

"Yes," said Randal, "I will at all events take the day to con- sider. Meanwhile, I say this, I do not disguise from myself the nature of the proposed transaction, but what I have once resolved I go through with. My sole vindication to myself is, that if I play here with a false die, it will be for a stake so grand, as once won, the magnitude of the prize will cancel the ignominy of the play. It is not this sum of money for which I sell myself—it is for what that sum will aid me to achieve. And in the marriage of young Hazel- dean with the Italian woman, I have another, and it may be a larger interest. I have slept on it lately—I wake to it now. Insure that marriage, obtain the post-obit from Hazeldean, and whatever the issue of the more direct scheme for which you seek my services, rely on my gratitude, and believe that you will have put me in the way to render gratitude of avail. At eight I will be with you."

Randal left the room.

The Baron sate thoughtful. "It is true," said he to himself, "this young man is the next of kin to the Hazeldean estate, if Frank displease his father sufficiently to lose his inheritance; that must be the clever boy's design.   Well, in the long-run, I should make as much, or more, out of him than out of the spendthrift Frank. Frank's faults are those of youth. He will reform and retrench. But *this* man !   No, I shall have *him* for life.   And should he fail in this project, and have but this encumbered property—a landed proprietor mortgaged up to his ears—why, he is my slave, and I can foreclose when I wish, or if he prove useless ;—no, I risk nothing. And if I did—if I lost ten thousand pounds—what then ?   I can afford it for revenge !—afford it for the luxury of leaving Audley Egerton alone with penury and ruin, deserted, in his hour of need, by the pensioner of his bounty—as he will be by the last friend of his youth—when it so pleases me—me whom he has called 'scoundrel !' and whom he—" Levy's soliloquy halted there, for the servant entered to announce the carriage.   And the Baron hurried his hand over his features, as if to sweep away all trace of the passions that distorted their smiling effrontery.   And so, as he took up his cane and gloves, and glanced at the glass, the face of the fashionable usurer was once more as varnished as his boots.

CHAPTER XIX.

WHEN a clever man resolves on a villainous action, he hastens, by the exercise of his cleverness, to get rid of the sense of his villainy. With more than his usual alert-ness, Randal employed the next hour or two in ascertain-ing how far Baron Levy merited the character he boasted, and how far his word might be his bond. He repaired to young men whom he esteemed better judges on these points than Spendquick and Borrowell—young men who resembled the Merry Monarch, inas-much as

> "They never said a foolish thing,
> And never did a wise one."

There are many such young men about town—sharp and able in all affairs except their own. No one knows the world better, nor judges of character more truly than your half-beggared *roué*. From all these Baron Levy obtained much the same testimonials: he was ridiculed as a would-be dandy, but respected as a very responsible man of business, and rather liked as a friendly accommodating species of the Sir Epicure Mammon, who very often did what were thought handsome liberal things; and, "in short," said one of these experienced referees, "he is the best fellow going—for a money-lender! You may always rely on what he promises, and he is generally very forbearing and indulgent to *us* of good society; perhaps for the same reason that our tailors are;—to send one of us to prison would hurt his custom. His foible is to be thought a gentleman. I believe, much as I suppose he loves money, he would give up half his fortune rather than do anything for which we could cut him. He allows a pension of three-hundred a-year to Lord S——. True; he was his man of business for twenty years, and before then S—— was rather a prudent fellow, and had fifteen thousand a-year. He has helped on, too, many a clever young man;—the best borough-monger you ever knew. He likes having friends in Parliament. In fact, of course, he is a rogue; but if one wants a rogue, one can't find a pleasanter. I should like to see him on the French stage—a prosperous *Macaire;* Le Maître could hit him off to the life."

From information in these more fashionable quarters, gleaned with his usual tact, Randal turned to a source less elevated, but to which he attached more importance. Dick Avenel associated with the Baron—Dick Avenel must be in his clutches. Now Randal did justice to that gentleman's practical shrewdness. Moreover, Avenel was by profession a man of business. He must know more of Levy than these men of pleasure could; and, as he was a plain-spoken person, and evidently honest, in the ordinary acceptation of the word, Randal did not doubt that out of Dick Avenel he should get the truth.

On arriving in Eaton Square, and asking for Mr. Avenel, Randal was at once ushered into the drawing-room. The apartment was not in such good, solid, mercantile taste as had characterized Avenel's more humble bachelor's residence at Screwstown. The taste now was the Honourable Mrs. Avenel's; and, truth to say, no taste could be worse. Furniture of all epochs heterogeneously clumped together, here a sofa *à la renaissance* in *Gobelin*—there a rosewood Console from Gillow—a tall mock-Elizabethan chair in black oak, by the side of a modern Florentine table of mosaic marbles. All kinds of colours in the room, and all at war with each other. Very bad copies of the best-known pictures in the world, in the most gaudy frames, and impudently labelled by the names of their murdered originals—"Raffaele," "Corregio," "Titian," "Sebastian del Piombo." Nevertheless, there had been plenty of money spent, and there was plenty to show for it. Mrs. Avenel was seated on her sofa *à la renaissance,* with one of her children at her feet, who was employed in reading a new Annual in crimson silk binding. Mrs. Avenel was in an attitude as if sitting for her portrait.

Polite society is most capricious in its adoptions or rejections. You see many a very vulgar person firmly established in the *beau monde;* others, with very good pretensions as to birth, fortune, &c., either rigorously excluded, or only permitted a peep over the pales. The Honourable Mrs. Avenel belonged to families unquestionably noble, both by her own descent and by her first marriage; and if poverty had kept her down in her earlier career, she now, at least, did not want wealth to back her pretensions. Nevertheless, all the dispensers of fashion concurred in refusing their support to the Honourable Mrs. Avenel. One might suppose it was solely on account of her plebeian husband; but indeed it was not so. Many a woman of high family can marry a low-born man not so presentable as Avenel, and, by the help of his money, get the fine world at her feet. But Mrs. Avenel had not that art. She was still a very handsome, showy woman; and as for dress, no duchess could be more extravagant. Yet these very circumstances had perhaps gone against her ambition; for your quiet little plain woman, provoking no envy, slips into the *coteries,* when a handsome, flaunting lady— whom, once seen in your drawing-room, can be no more overlooked than a scarlet poppy amidst a violet bed—is pretty sure to be weeded out as ruthlessly as a poppy would be in a similar position.

Mr. Avenel was sitting by the fire, rather moodily, his hands in his pockets, and whistling to himself. To say truth, that active mind of his was very much bored in London, at least during the fore part of the day. He hailed Randal's entrance with a smile of relief, and rising and posting himself before the fire—a coat tail under each arm—he scarcely allowed Randal to shake hands with Mrs. Avenel, and pat the child on the head, murmuring, "Beautiful creature." (Randal was ever civil to children—that sort of wolf in sheep's clothing always is—don't be taken in, O you foolish young mothers!) Dick, I say, scarcely allowed his visitor these preliminary courtesies, before he plunged far beyond depth of wife and child, into the political ocean. "Things now were coming right—a vile oligarchy was to be destroyed. British respectability and British talent were to have fair play." To have heard him you would have thought the day fixed for the millennium! "And what is more," said Avenel, bringing down the fist of his right hand upon the palm of his left, "if there is to be a new parliament, we must have new men—not worn-out old brooms that never sweep clean, but men who understand how to govern the country, sir. I INTEND TO COME IN MYSELF!"

"Yes," said Mrs. Avenel, hooking in a word at last, "I am

sure, Mr. Leslie, you will think I did right. I persuaded Mr. Avenel that, with his talents and property, he ought, for the sake of his country, to make a sacrifice ; and then you know his opinions now are all the fashion, Mr. Leslie ; formerly they would have been called shocking and vulgar !"

Thus saying, she looked with fond pride at Dick's comely face, which at that moment, however, was all scowl and frown. I must do justice to Mrs. Avenel ; she was a weak, silly woman in some things, and a cunning one in others, but she was a good wife, as wives go. Scotch women generally are.

"Bother !" said Dick. "What do women know about politics ? I wish you'd mind the child—it is crumpling up, and playing almighty smash with that flim-flam book, which cost me one pound one."

Mrs. Avenel submissively bowed her head, and removed the Annual from the hands of the young destructive ; the destructive set up a squall, as destructives usually do when they don't have their own way. Dick clapped his hand to his ears. "Whe-e-ew, I can't stand this ; come and take a walk, Leslie : I want stretching !" He stretched himself as he spoke, first half-way up to the ceiling, and then fairly out of the room.

Randal, with his May Fair manner, turned towards Mrs. Avenel as if to apologize for her husband and himself.

"Poor Richard !" said she, "he is in one of his humours—all men have them. Come and see me again soon. When does Almacks open ?"

"Nay, I ought to ask you that question, you who know everything that goes on in our set," said the young serpent. Any tree planted in "our set," if it had been but a crab-tree, would have tempted Mr. Avenel's Eve to jump at its boughs.

"*Are* you coming, there ?" cried Dick from the foot of the stairs.

CHAPTER XX.

"I HAVE just been at our friend Levy's," said Randal, when he and Dick were outside the street door. "He, like you, is full of politics—pleasant man—for the business he is said to do."

"Well," said Dick slowly, "I suppose he *is* pleasant, but make the best of it—and still—"

"Still what, my dear Avenel ?" (Randal here for the first time discarded the formal Mister.)

MR. AVENEL.—"Still the thing itself is not pleasant."

Randal (with his soft hollow laugh).—"You mean borrowing money upon more than five per cent."

"Oh, curse the per centage. I agree with Bentham on the Usury Laws—no shackles in trade for me, whether in money or anything else. That's not it. But when one owes a fellow money even at two per cent., and 'tis not convenient to pay him, why, somehow or other, it makes one feel small ; it takes the British Liberty out of a man ! "

" I should have thought you more likely to lend money than to borrow it."

" Well, I guess you are right there, as a general rule. But I tell you what it is, sir ; there is too great a mania for competition getting up in this rotten old country of ours. I am as liberal as most men. I like competition to a certain extent, but there is too much of it, sir—too much of it."

Randal looked sad and convinced. But if Leonard had heard Dick Avenel, what would have been his amaze? Dick Avenel rail against competition ! Think there could be too much of it ! Of course, "heaven and earth are coming together," said the spider, when the housemaid's broom invaded its cobweb. Dick was all for sweeping away other cobwebs ; but he certainly thought heaven and earth coming together when he saw a great Turk's-head besom poked up at his own.

Mr. Avenel, in his genius for speculation and improvement, had established a factory at Screwstown, the first which had ever eclipsed the church spire with its Titanic chimney. It succeeded well at first. Mr. Avenel transferred to this speculation nearly all his capital. "Nothing," quoth he, "paid such an interest. Manchester was getting worn out—time to show what Screwstown could do. Nothing like competition." But by and by a still greater capitalist than Dick Avenel, finding out that Screwstown was at the mouth of a coal mine, and that Dick's profits were great, erected a still uglier edifice, with a still taller chimney. And having been brought up to the business, and making his residence in the town, while Dick employed a foreman and flourished in London, this infamous competitor so managed, first to share, and then gradually to sequester, the profits which Dick had hitherto monopolized, that no wonder Mr. Avenel thought competition should have its limits. "The tongue touches where the tooth aches," as Dr. Riccabocca would tell us. By little and little our Juvenile Talleyrand (I beg the elder great man's pardon) wormed out from Dick this grievance, and in the grievance discovered the origin of Dick's connection with the money-lender.

"But Levy," said Avenel, candidly, "is a decentish chap in his way—friendly too. Mrs. A. finds him useful; brings some of your young highflyers to her *soirées*. To be sure, they don't dance—stand all in a row at the door, like mutes at a funeral. Not but what they have been uncommon civil to me lately—Spendquick particularly. By the bye, I dine with him to-morrow. The aristocracy are behindhand—not smart, sir—not up to the march; but when a man knows how to take 'em, they beat the New Yorkers in good manners. I'll say that for them, I have no prejudice."

"I never saw a man with less; no prejudice even against Levy."

"No, not a bit of it! Every one says he's a Jew; he says he's not. I don't care a button what he is. His money is English—that's enough for any man of a liberal turn of mind. His charges, too, are moderate. To be sure, he knows I shall pay them; only what I don't like in him is a sort of way he has of *mon-cher*-ing and my-good-fellow-ing one, to do things quite out of the natural way of that sort of business. He knows I have got Parliamentary influence. I could return a couple of members for Screwstown, and one, or perhaps two, for Lansmere, where I have of late been cooking up an interest; and he dictates to—no, not *dictates*—but tries to *humbug* me into putting in his own men. However, in one respect, we are likely to agree. He says you want to come into Parliament. You seem a smart young fellow; but you must throw over that stiff red-tapist of yours, and go with Public Opinion, and—Myself."

"You are very kind, Avenel; perhaps when we come to compare opinions we may find that we agree entirely. Still, in Egerton's present position, delicacy to him—however, we'll not discuss that now. But you really think I might come in for Lansmere—against the L'Estrange interest, too, which must be strong there?"

"It *was* very strong, but I've smashed it, I calculate."

"Would a contest there cost very much?"

"Well, I guess you must come down with the ready. But, as you say, time enough to discuss that when you have squared your account with 'delicacy;' come to me then, and we'll go into it."

Randal, having now squeezed his orange dry, had no desire to waste his time in brushing up the rind with his coat-sleeve, so he unhooked his arm from Avenel's, and, looking at his watch, discovered he should be just in time for an appointment of the most urgent business—hailed a cab, and drove off.

Dick looked hipped and disconsolate at being left alone; he yawned very loud, to the astonishment of three prim old maiden Belgravians who were passing that way; and then his mind began to turn towards his factory at Screwstown, which had led to his connection with the Baron; and he thought over a letter he had received

from his foreman that morning, informing him that it was rumoured at
Screwstown that Mr. Dyce, his rival, was about to have new
machinery on an improved principle ; and that Mr. Dyce had
already gone up to town, it was supposed, with the intention of
concluding a purchase for a patent discovery to be applied to the
new machinery, and which that gentleman had publicly declared in
the corn-market " would shut up Mr. Avenel's factory before the
year was out."   As this menacing epistle recurred to him, Dick felt
his desire to yawn incontinently checked.   His brow grew very
dark ; and he walked, with restless strides, on and on, till he found
himself in the Strand.   He then got into an omnibus, and proceeded to the city, wherein he spent the rest of the day, looking
over machines and foundries, and trying in vain to find out what
diabolical invention the over-competition of Mr. Dyce had got hold
of.   " If," said Dick Avenel to himself, as he returned fretfully
homeward—"if a man like me, who has done so much for British
industry and go-a-head principles, is to be catawampously champed
up by a mercenary selfish cormorant of a capitalist like that inter-
loping blockhead in drab breeches, Tom Dyce, all I can say is, that
the sooner this cursed old country goes to the dogs, the better
pleased I shall be.   I wash my hands of it."

CHAPTER XXI.

RANDAL'S mind was made up.   All he had learned in
regard to Levy had confirmed his resolves or dissipated
his scruples.   He had started from the improbability that
Peschiera would offer, and the still greater improbability
that Peschiera would pay him, ten thousand pounds for such information or aid as he could bestow in furthering the Count's object.
But when Levy took such proposals entirely on himself, the main
question to Randal became this—could it be Levy's interest to make
so considerable a sacrifice?   Had the Baron implied only friendly
sentiments as his motives, Randal would have felt sure he was to be
taken in ; but the usurer's frank assurance that it would answer to
him in the long-run to concede to Randal terms so advantageous,
altered the case, and led our young philosopher to look at the affair
with calm contemplative eyes.   Was it sufficiently obvious that Levy
counted on an adequate return?   Might he calculate on reaping
help by the bushel if he sowed it by the handful?   The result of
Randal's cogitations was, that the Baron might fairly deem himself
no wasteful sower.   In the first place, it was clear that Levy, not

without reasonable ground, believed that he could soon replace, with exceeding good interest, any sum he might advance to Randal, out of the wealth which Randal's prompt information might bestow on Levy's client, the Count ; and, secondly, Randal's self-esteem was immense, and could he but succeed in securing a pecuniary independence on the instant, to free him from the slow drudgery of the bar, or from a precarious reliance on Audley Egerton, as a politician out of power—his convictions of rapid triumph in public life were as strong as if whispered by an angel or promised by a fiend.   On such triumphs, with all the social position they would secure, Levy might well calculate for repayment by a thousand indirect channels. Randal's sagacity detected that, through all the good-natured or liberal actions ascribed to the usurer, Levy had steadily pursued his own interests—he saw that Levy meant to get him into his power, and use his abilities as instruments for digging new mines, in which Baron Levy would claim the right of large royalties.   But at that thought Randal's pale lip curled disdainfully ; he confided too much in his own powers not to think that he could elude the grasp of the usurer, whenever it suited him to do so.   Thus, on a survey, all conscience hushed itself—his mind rushed buoyantly on to anticipations of the future.   He saw the hereditary estates regained—no matter how mortgaged—for the moment still his own—legally his own—yielding for the present what would suffice for competence to one of few wants, and freeing his name from that title of Adventurer, which is so prodigally given in rich old countries to those who have no estates but their brains.   He thought of Violante but as the civilized trader thinks of a trifling coin, of a glass bead, which he exchanges with some barbarian for gold dust ;—he thought of Frank Hazeldean married to the foreign woman of beggared means, and repute that had known the breath of scandal—married, and living on post-obit instalments of the Casino property ;—he thought of the poor Squire's resentment ;—his avarice swept from the lands annexed to Rood on to the broad fields of Hazeldean ;—he thought of Avenel, of Lansmere, of Parliament ;—with one hand he grasped fortune, with the next power.   "And yet I entered on life with no patrimony—(save a ruined Hall and a barren waste)—no patrimony but knowledge.   I have but turned knowledge from books to men ; for books may give fame after death, but men give us power in life." And all the while he thus ruminated, his act was speeding his purpose.   Though it was but in a miserable hack cab that he erected airy scaffoldings round airy castles, still the miserable hack cab was flying fast, to secure the first foot of solid ground whereon to transfer the mental plan of the architect to foundations of positive slime and clay.   The cab stopped at the door of Lord Lansmere's house. Randal had suspected Violante to be there : he resolved to ascertain. Randal descended from his vehicle and rang the bell. The lodge-keeper opened the great wooden gates.

"I have called to see the young lady staying here—the foreign young lady."

Lady Lansmere had been too confident of the security of her roof to condescend to give any orders to her servants with regard to her guest, and the lodge-keeper answered directly—·

"At home, I believe, sir. I rather think she is in the garden with my lady."

"I see," said Randal. And he did see the form of Violante at a distance. "But, since she is walking, I will not disturb her at present. I will call another day."

The lodge-keeper bowed respectfully, Randal jumped into his cab—"To Curzon Street—quick!"

CHAPTER XXII.

ARLEY had made one notable oversight in that appeal to Beatrice's better and gentler nature, which he entrusted to the advocacy of Leonard—a scheme in itself very characteristic of Harley's romantic temper, and either wise or foolish, according as his indulgent theory of human idiosyncrasies in general, and of those peculiar to Beatrice di Negra in especial, was the dream of an enthusiast, or the inductive conclusion of a sound philosopher.

Harley had warned Leonard not to fall in love with the Italian— he had forgotten to warn the Italian not to fall in love with Leonard ; nor had he ever anticipated the probability of that event. This is not to be very much wondered at ; for if there be anything on which the most sensible men are dull-eyed, where those eyes are not lighted by jealousy, it is as to the probabilities of another male creature being beloved. All, the least vain of the whiskered gender, think it prudent to guard themselves against being too irresistible to the fair sex ; and each says of his friend, "Good fellow enough, but the last man for *that* woman to fall in love with!"

But certainly there appeared on the surface more than ordinary cause for Harley's blindness in the special instance of Leonard.

Whatever Beatrice's better qualities, she was generally esteemed worldly and ambitious. She was pinched in circumstances—she was luxuriant and extravagant ; how was it likely that she could distinguish any aspirant of the humble birth and fortunes of the young peasant author? As a coquette, she might try to win his admiration and attract his fancy; but her own heart would surely be guarded in the triple mail of pride, poverty, and the conventional opinions of the world in which she lived. Had Harley thought it possible that Madame di Negra could stoop below her station, and love, not wisely, but too well, he would rather have thought that the object would be some brilliant adventurer of fashion—some one who could turn against herself all the arts of deliberate fascination, and all the experience bestowed by frequent conquest. One so simple as Leonard—so young and so new! Harley L'Estrange would have smiled at himself, if the idea of that image subjugating the ambitious woman to the disinterested love of a village maid, had once crossed his mind. Nevertheless, so it was, and precisely from those causes which would have seemed to Harley to forbid the weakness.

It *was* that fresh, pure heart—it was that simple, earnest sweetness—it was that contrast in look, in tone, in sentiment, and in reasonings, to all that had jaded and disgusted her in the circle of her admirers—it was all this that captivated Beatrice at the first interview with Leonard. Here was what she had confessed to the sceptical Randal she had dreamed and sighed for. Her earliest youth had passed into abhorrent marriage, without the soft, innocent crisis of human life—virgin love. Many a wooer might have touched her vanity, pleased her fancy, excited her ambition—her heart had never been awakened; it woke now. The world, and the years that the world had wasted, seemed to fleet away as a cloud. She was as if restored to the blush and the sigh of youth—the youth of the Italian maid. As in the restoration of our golden age is the spell of poetry with us all, so such was the spell of the poet himself on her.

Oh, how exquisite was that brief episode in the life of the woman palled with the "hack sights and sounds" of worldly life! How strangely happy were those hours, when, lured on by her silent sympathy, the young scholar spoke of his early struggles between circumstance and impulse, musing amidst the flowers, and hearkening to the fountain; or of his wanderings in the desolate, lamp-lit streets, while the vision of Chatterton's glittering eyes shone dread through the friendless shadows. And as he spoke, whether of his hopes or his fears, her looks dwelt fondly on the young face, that varied between pride and sadness—pride ever so gentle, and sadness ever so nobly touching. She was never weary of gazing on that brow, with its quiet power; but her lids dropped before those eyes, with their serene, unfathomable passion. She felt, as they haunted her, what a deep and holy thing love in such souls must be. Leonard never spoke to her of Helen—that reserve every reader can comprehend. To natures like his, first love is a mystery ; to confide it is to profane. But he fulfilled his commission of interesting her in the exile and his daughter. And his description of them brought tears to her eyes. She inly resolved not to aid Peschiera in his designs on Violante. She forgot for the moment that her own fortune was to depend on the success of those designs.—Levy had arranged so that she was not reminded of her poverty by creditors—she knew not how. She knew nothing of business. She gave herself up to the delight of the present hour, and to vague prospects of a future, associated with that young image—with that face of a guardian angel that she saw before her, fairest in the moments of absence ; for in those moments came the life of fairy-land, when we shut our eyes on the world, and see through the haze of golden reverie. Dangerous, indeed, to Leonard would have been the soft society of Beatrice di Negra, had not his heart been wholly devoted to one object, and had not his ideal of woman been from that object one sole and indivisible reflection. But Beatrice guessed not this barrier between herself and him. Amidst the shadows that he conjured up from his past life, she beheld no rival form. She saw him lonely in the world as she was herself. And in his lowly birth, his youth, in the freedom from presumption which characterized him in all things (save that confidence in his intellectual destinies, which is the essential attribute of genius), she but grew the bolder by the belief that, even if he loved her, he would not dare to hazard the avowal.

And thus, one day, yielding, as she had ever been wont to yield, to the impulse of her quick Italian heart—how she never remembered —in what words she could never recall—she spoke—she owned her love—she pleaded, with tears and blushes, for love in return. All that passed was to her as a dream—a dream from which she woke with a fierce sense of agony, of humiliation—woke as the woman "scorned." No matter how gratefully, how tenderly Leonard had replied—the reply was refusal. For the first time she learned she had a rival ; that all he could give of love was long since, from his boyhood, given to another. For the first time in her life, that ardent nature knew jealousy, its torturing stings, its thirst for vengeance, its tempest of loving hate. But, to outward appearance, silent and cold she stood as marble. Words that sought to soothe fell on her ear unheeded : they were drowned by the storm within. Pride was the first feeling which dominated the warring elements that raged in her soul. She tore her hand from that which clasped hers with so loyal a respect. She could have spurned the form that knelt at her feet, not for love, but for pardon. She pointed to the door with the gesture of an insulted queen. She knew no more till she was alone. Then came that rapid flash of conjecture peculiar to the storms of jealousy; that which seems to single from all nature the one object to dread and to destroy; the conjecture so often false; yet received at once by our convictions as the revelation of instinctive truth. He to whom she had humbled herself loved another; whom but Violante?—whom else, young and beautiful, had he named in the record of his life?—None! And he had sought to interest her, Beatrice di Negra, in the object of his love;—hinted at dangers which Beatrice knew too well;—implied trust in Beatrice's will to protect. Blind fool that she had been! This, then, was the reason why he had come, day after day, to Beatrice's house; this was the charm that had drawn him thither; this—she pressed her hands to her burning temples, as if to stop the tortures of thought. Suddenly a voice was heard below, the door opened, and Randal Leslie entered.

CHAPTER XXIII.

PUNCTUALLY at eight o'clock that evening, Baron Levy welcomed the new ally he had secured. The pair dined *en tête à tête*, discussing general matters till the servants left them to their wine. Then said the Baron, rising and stirring the fire—then said the Baron, briefly and significantly—

"Well!"

"As regards the property you spoke of," answered Randal, "I am willing to purchase it on the terms you name. The only point that perplexes me is how to account to Audley Egerton, to my parents, to the world, for the power of purchasing it."

"True," said the Baron, without even a smile at the ingenious and truly Greek manner in which Randal had contrived to denote his meaning, and conceal the ugliness of it—"true, we must think of that. If we could manage to conceal the real name of the purchaser for a year or so—it might be easy—you may be supposed to have speculated in the Funds; or Egerton may die, and people may believe that he had secured to you something handsome from the ruins of his fortune."

"Little chance of Egerton's dying."

"Humph!" said the Baron. "However, this is a mere detail, reserved for consideration. You can now tell us where the young lady is?"

"Certainly. I could not this morning—I can now. I will go

with you to the Count. Meanwhile, I have seen Madame di Negra ; she will accept Frank Hazeldean if he will but offer himself at once."

"Will he not?"

"No! I have been to him. He is overjoyed at my represent- ations, but considers it his duty to ask the consent of his parents. Of course they will not give it ; and if there be delay, she will retract. She is under the influence of passions, on the duration of which there is no reliance."

"What passions? Love?"

"Love ; but not for Hazeldean. The passions that bring her to accept his hand are pique and jealousy. She believes, in a word, that one, who seems to have gained the mastery over her affections with a strange suddenness, is but blind to her charms, because dazzled by Violante's. She is prepared to aid in all that can give her rival to Peschiera ; and yet, such is the inconsistency of woman, (added the young philosopher, with a shrug of the shoulders,) that she is also prepared to lose all chance of securing him she loves, by bestowing herself on another!"

"Woman, indeed, all over!" said the Baron, tapping his snuff- box (Louis Quinze), and regaling his nostrils with a scornful pinch. "But who is the man whom the fair Beatrice has thus honoured? Superb creature! I had some idea of her myself when I bought up her debts ; but it might have embarrassed me, in more general plans, as regards the Count. All for the best. Who's the man? Not Lord L'Estrange?"

"I do not think it is he ; but I have not yet ascertained. I have told you all I know. I found her in a state so excited, so unlike herself, that I had no little difficulty in soothing her into confidence so far. I could not venture more."

"And she will accept Frank?"

"Had he offered to-day she would have accepted him!"

"It may be a great help to your fortunes, *mon cher*, if Frank Hazeldean married this lady without his father's consent. Perhaps he may be disinherited. You are next of kin."

"How do you know that?" asked Randal, sullenly.

"It is my business to know all about the chances and connections of any one with whom I do money matters. I do money matters with young Mr. Hazeldean ; so I know that the Hazeldean property is not entailed ; and, as the Squire's half-brother has no Hazeldean blood in him, you have excellent expectations."

"Did Frank tell you I was next of kin?"

"I rather think so ; but I am sure *you* did."

"I—when?"

"When you told me how important it was to you that Frank

should marry Madame di Negra. *Peste! mon cher*, do you think I am a blockhead?"

"Well, Baron, Frank is of age, and can marry to please himself. You implied to me that you could help him in this."

"I will try. See that he call at Madame di Negra's to-morrow, at two precisely."

"I would rather keep clear of all apparent interference in this matter. Will you not arrange that he call on her? And do not forget to entangle him in a *post-obit*."

"Leave it to me. Any more wine? No;—then let us go to the Count's."

CHAPTER XXIV.

THE next morning Frank Hazeldean was sitting over his solitary breakfast-table. It was long past noon. The young man had risen early, it is true, to attend his military duties, but he had contracted the habit of breakfasting late. One's appetite does not come early when one lives in London, and never goes to bed before daybreak.

There was nothing very luxurious or effeminate about Frank's rooms, though they were in a very dear street, and he paid a monstrous high price for them. Still, to a practised eye, they betrayed an inmate who can get through his money, and make very little show for it. The walls were covered with coloured prints of racers and steeple-chases, interspersed with the portraits of opera-dancers—all smirk and caper. Then there was a semi-circular recess covered with red cloth, and fitted up for smoking, as you might perceive by sundry stands full of Turkish pipes in cherry-stick and jessamine, with amber mouth-pieces ; while a great serpent hookah, from which Frank could no more have smoked than he could have smoked out of the head of a boa-constrictor, coiled itself up on the floor ; over the chimney-piece was a collection of Moorish arms. What use on earth, ataghan and scimitar, and damasquined pistols, that would not carry straight three yards, could be to an officer in His Majesty's Guards is more than I can conjecture, or even Frank satisfactorily explain. I have strong suspicions that this valuable arsenal passed to Frank in part payment of a bill to be discounted. At all events, if so, it was an improvement on the bear that he had sold to the hair-dresser. No books were to be seen anywhere, except a Court Guide, a Racing Calendar, an Army List, the Sporting Magazine complete, (whole bound in scarlet morocco, at about a guinea per volume,) and a small book, as small as an Elzevir, on the chimney-piece, by the side of a cigar-case. That small book had cost Frank more than all the rest put together; it was his Own Book, his book *par excellence;* book made up by himself—his BETTING BOOK!

On a centre table were deposited Frank's well-brushed hat—a satin-wood box, containing kid-gloves, of various delicate tints, from primrose to lilac—a tray full of cards and three-cornered notes—an opera-glass, and an ivory subscription ticket to his opera stall.

In one corner was an ingenious receptacle for canes, sticks, and whips—I should not like, in these bad times, to have paid the bill for them ; and mounting guard by that receptacle, stood a pair of boots as bright as Baron Levy's—"the force of brightness could no further go." Frank was in his dressing-gown—very good taste— quite Oriental—guaranteed to be true India cashmere, and charged as such. Nothing could be more neat, though perfectly simple, than the appurtenances of his breakfast-table :—silver tea-pot, ewer and basin—all fitting into his dressing-box—(for the which may Storr and Mortimer be now praised, and some day paid !) Frank looked very handsome—rather tired, and exceedingly bored. He had been trying to read the *Morning Post*, but the effort had proved too much for him.

" Poor dear Frank Hazeldean !—true type of many a poor dear fellow who has long since gone to the dogs. And if, in this road to ruin, there had been the least thing to do the traveller any credit by the way ! One feels a respect for the ruin of a man like Audley Egerton. He is ruined *en roi !* From the wrecks of his fortune he can look down and see stately monuments built from the stones of that dismantled edifice. In every institution which attests the humanity of England, was a record of the princely bounty of the public man. In those objects of party, for which the proverbial sinews of war are necessary—in those rewards for service, which private liberality can confer—the hand of Egerton had been opened as with the heart of a king. Many a rising member of Parliament, in those days when talent was brought forward through the aid of wealth and rank, owed his career to the seat which Audley Egerton's large subscription had secured to him ; many an obscure supporter in letters and the press looked back to the day when he had been freed from the gaol by the gratitude of the patron. The city he represented was embellished at his cost ; through the shire that held his mortgaged lands, which he had rarely ever visited, his gold had flowed as a Pactolus ; all that could animate its public spirit, or increase its civilization, claimed kindred with his munificence, and never had a claim disallowed. Even in his grand, careless household, with its large retinue and superb hospitality, there was some-thing worthy of a representative of that time-honoured portion of our true nobility—the untitled gentlemen of the land. The Great Commoner had, indeed, "something to show" for the money he had disdained and squandered. But for Frank Hazeldean's mode of getting rid of the dross, when gone, what would be left to tell the tale? Paltry prints in a bachelor's lodging; a collection of canes and cherry-sticks; half-a-dozen letters in ill-spelt French from a *figurante;* some long-legged horses, fit for nothing but to lose a race; that damnable Betting-Book; and—*sic transit gloria* —down sweeps some hawk of a Levy, on the wings of an I O U, and not a feather is left of the pigeon!

Yet Frank Hazeldean has stuff in him—a good heart, and strict honour. Fool though he seem, there is sound sterling sense in some odd corner of his brains, if one could but get at it. All he wants to save him from perdition is, to do what he has never yet done—viz., pause and think. But, to be sure, that same operation of thinking is not so easy for folks unaccustomed to it, as people who think—think!

"I can't bear this," said Frank, suddenly, and springing to his feet. "This woman, I cannot get her out of my head. I ought to go down to the governor's; but then if he gets into a passion, and refuses his consent, where am I? And he will, too, I fear. I wish I could make out what Randal advises. He seems to recommend that I should marry Beatrice at once, and trust to my mother's influence to make all right afterwards. But when I ask, '*Is* that your advice?' he backs out of it. Well, I suppose he is right there. I can understand that he is unwilling, good fellow, to recommend anything that my father would disapprove. But still—"

Here Frank stopped in his soliloquy, and did make his first desperate effort to—think!

Now, O dear reader, I assume, of course, that thou art one of the class to which thought is familiar; and, perhaps, thou hast smiled in disdain or incredulity at that remark on the difficulty of thinking which preceded Frank Hazeldean's discourse to himself. But art thou quite sure that when thou hast tried to *think* thou hast always succeeded? Hast thou not often been duped by that pale visionary simulacrum of thought which goes by the name of *reverie?* Honest old Montaigne confessed that he did not understand that pro-cess of sitting down to think, on which some folks express themselves so glibly. He could not think unless he had a pen in his hand, and a sheet of paper before him; and so, by a manual operation, seized and connected the links of ratiocination. Very often has it happened to myself, when I have said to Thought peremptorily,

"Bestir thyself—a serious matter is before thee—ponder it well—think of it," that that same thought has behaved in the most refractory, rebellious manner conceivable—and, instead of concentrating its rays into a single stream of light, has broken into all the desultory tints of the rainbow, colouring senseless clouds, and running off into the seventh heaven—so that after sitting a good hour by the clock, with brows as knit as if I was intent on squaring the circle, I have suddenly discovered that I might as well have gone comfortably to sleep—I have been doing nothing but dream—and the most nonsensical dreams ! So when Frank Hazeldean, as he stopped at that meditative "But still "—and leaning his arm on the chimney-piece, and resting his face on his hand, felt himself at the grave crisis of life, and fancied he was going "to think on it," there only rose before him a succession of shadowy pictures. Randal Leslie, with an unsatisfactory countenance, from which he could extract nothing ;—the Squire, looking as black as thunder in his study at Hazeldean ;—his mother trying to plead for him, and getting herself properly scolded for her pains ;—and then off went that Will-o'-the-wisp which pretended to call itself Thought, and began playing round the pale charming face of Beatrice di Negra, in the drawing-room at Curzon Street, and repeating, with small elfin voice, Randal Leslie's assurance of the preceding day, "as to her affection for you, Frank, there is no doubt of *that ;* she only begins to think you are trifling with her." And then there was a rapturous vision of a young gentleman on his knee, and the fair pale face bathed in blushes, and a clergyman standing by the altar, and a carriage-and-four with white favours at the church-door ; and of a honeymoon, which would have astonished as to honey all the bees of Hymettus. And in the midst of these phantasmagoria, which composed what Frank fondly styled "making up his mind," there came a single man's elegant rat-tat-tat at the street door.

"One never *has* a moment for *thinking*," cried Frank, and he called out to his valet, "Not at home."

But it was too late. Lord Spendquick was in the hall, and presently within the room. How d'ye do's were exchanged and hands shaken.

Lord Spendquick.—"I have a note for you, Hazeldean."

Frank (lazily).—"From whom ?"

Lord Spendquick.—"Levy. Just come from him—never saw him in such a fidget. He was going into the city—I suppose to see X. Y. Dashed off this note for you—and would have sent it by a servant, but I said I would bring it."

Frank (looking fearfully at the note).—"I hope he does not want his money yet. '*Private and confidential*'—that looks bad."

SPENDQUICK.—"Devilish bad, indeed."

Frank opens the note and reads, half aloud, "Dear Hazeldean."

SPENDQUICK (interrupting).—"Good sign! He always 'Spend-quicks' me when he lends me money; and 'tis 'My dear Lord' when he wants it back. Capital sign!"

Frank reads on, but to himself, and with a changing coun-tenance—

"DEAR HAZELDEAN,—I am very sorry to tell you that, in con-sequence of the sudden failure of a house at Paris with which I had large dealings, I am pressed on a sudden for all the ready money I can get. I don't want to inconvenience you, but do try and see if you can take up those bills of yours which I hold, and which, as you know, have been due some little time. I had hit on a way of arranging your affairs; but when I hinted at it, you seemed to dis-like the idea; and Leslie has since told me that you have strong objections to giving any security on your prospective property. So no more of that, my dear fellow. I am called out in haste to try what I can do for a very charming client of mine, who is in great pecuniary distress, though she has for a brother a foreign Count, as rich as a Crœsus. There is an execution in her house. I am going down to the tradesman who put it in, but have no hope of softening him; and I fear there will be others before the day is out. Another reason for wanting money, if you can help me, *mon cher!*—An execution in the house of one of the most brilliant women in London —an execution in Curzon Street, May Fair! It will be all over the town, if I can't stop it.—Yours in haste, LEVY.

"*P.S.*—Don't let what I have said vex you too much. I should not trouble you if Spendquick and Borrowell would pay me some-thing. Perhaps you can get them to do so."

Struck by Frank's silence and paleness, Lord Spendquick here, in the kindest way possible, laid his hand on the young Guardsman's shoulder, and looked over the note with that freedom which gentle-men in difficulties take with each other's private and confidential correspondence. His eye fell on the postscript. "Oh, damn it," cried Spendquick, "but that's too bad—employing you to get me to pay him! Such horrid treachery. Make yourself easy, my dear Frank; I could never suspect you of anything so unhandsome. I could as soon suspect myself of—paying him—"

"Curzon Street! Count!" muttered Frank, as if waking from a dream. "It must be so." To thrust on his boots—change his dressing-robe for a frock-coat—snatch at his hat, gloves, and cane —break from Spendquick—descend the stairs—a flight at a leap— gain the street—throw himself into a cabriolet ; all this was done before his astounded visitor could even recover breath enough to ask "What's the matter?"

Left thus alone, Lord Spendquick shook his head—shook it twice, as if fully to convince himself that there was nothing in it ; and then re-arranging his hat before the looking-glass, and drawing on his gloves deliberately, he walked down-stairs, and strolled into White's, but with a bewildered and absent air. Standing at the celebrated bow-window for some moments in musing silence, Lord Spendquick at last thus addressed an exceedingly cynical, sceptical, old *roué*—

"Pray, do you think there is any truth in the stories about people in former times selling themselves to the devil?"

"Ugh," answered the *roué*, much too wise ever to be surprised. "Have you any personal interest in the question?"

"I!—no ; but a friend of mine has just received a letter from Levy, and he flew out of the room in the most ex-tra-or-di-na-ry manner—just as people did in those days when their time was up ! And Levy, you know, is—"

"Not quite as great a fool as the other dark gentleman to whom you would compare him : for Levy never made such bad bargains for himself. Time up ! No doubt it is. I should not like to be in your friend's shoes."

"Shoes !" said Spendquick, with a sort of shudder ; "you never saw a neater fellow, nor one, to do him justice, who takes more time in dressing than he does in general. And talking of shoes— he rushed out with the right boot on the left foot, and the left boot on the right. Very mysterious." And a third time Lord Spend-quick shook his head—and a third time that head seemed to him wondrous empty.

END OF VOL. II.